Legends from China
THREE KINGDOMS

Vol.
04

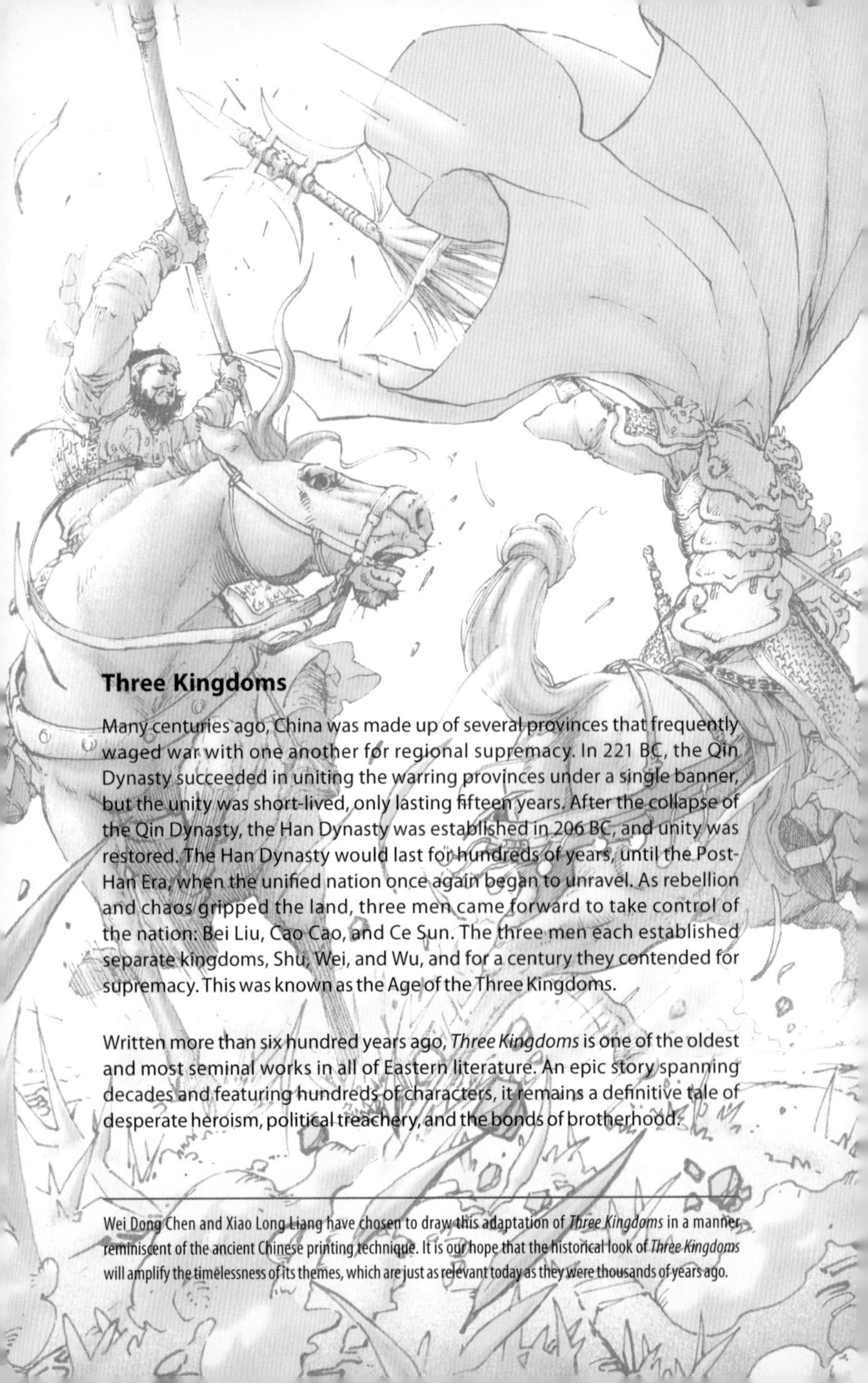

Three Kingdoms

Many centuries ago, China was made up of several provinces that frequently waged war with one another for regional supremacy. In 221 BC, the Qin Dynasty succeeded in uniting the warring provinces under a single banner, but the unity was short-lived, only lasting fifteen years. After the collapse of the Qin Dynasty, the Han Dynasty was established in 206 BC, and unity was restored. The Han Dynasty would last for hundreds of years, until the Post-Han Era, when the unified nation once again began to unravel. As rebellion and chaos gripped the land, three men came forward to take control of the nation: Bei Liu, Cao Cao, and Ce Sun. The three men each established separate kingdoms, Shu, Wei, and Wu, and for a century they contended for supremacy. This was known as the Age of the Three Kingdoms.

Written more than six hundred years ago, *Three Kingdoms* is one of the oldest and most seminal works in all of Eastern literature. An epic story spanning decades and featuring hundreds of characters, it remains a definitive tale of desperate heroism, political treachery, and the bonds of brotherhood.

Wei Dong Chen and Xiao Long Liang have chosen to draw this adaptation of *Three Kingdoms* in a manner reminiscent of the ancient Chinese printing technique. It is our hope that the historical look of *Three Kingdoms* will amplify the timelessness of its themes, which are just as relevant today as they were thousands of years ago.

THREE KINGDOMS
Vol. 04
Revenge and Betrayal

Created by *WEI DONG CHEN*

Wei Dong Chen, a highly acclaimed and beloved artist, and an influential leader in the "New Chinese Cartoon" trend, is the founder of Creator World in Tianjin, the largest comics studio in China. Recently the Chinese government entrusted him with the role of general manager of the Beijing Book Fair, and his reputation as a pillar of Chinese comics has brought him many students. He has published more than three hundred cartoons, which have been recognized for their strong literary value not only in Korea, but in Europe and Japan, as well. Free spirited and energetic, Wei Dong Chen's positivist philosophy is reflected in the wisdom of his work. He is published serially in numerous publications while continuing to conceive projects that explore new dimensions of the form.

Illustrated by *XIAO LONG LIANG*

XiaoLong Liang is considered one of Wei Dong Chen's greatest students. One of the most highly regarded cartoonists in China today, XiaoLong's fantastic technique and expression of Chinese culture have won him the acclaim of cartoon lovers throughout China. His other works include "Outlaws of the Marsh" and "A Story on the Motorbike".

Original Story
"The Romance of the Three Kingdoms" by Luo, GuanZhong

Editing & Designing
Design Hongs, Jonathan Evans, KH Lee, YK Kim,
HJ Lee, JS Kim, Lampin, Qing Shao, Xiao Nan Li, Ke Hu

CE SUN

Ce Sun is the son of Jian Sun, the legendary military commander killed in 192 AD. Ce Sun inherited his father's possessions, including a royal seal stolen during the attack of LuoYang. He also pledged allegiance to Shu Yuan, and lived in his shadow for years. When the time comes for him to assert himself, he entrusts the royal seal to Shu Yuan and sets out to reclaim the eastern lands that once belonged to his father.

SHU YUAN

When Shu Yuan takes possession of the royal seal from Ce Sun, he ceases to deal with the reality that Ce Sun is a powerful leader and potential adversary. Instead, Shu Yuan remains fixated on the royal seal, even coming to think of himself as the emperor and orders his subjects to build him a royal palace. When he does make a play for Xu Province, it is through a marriage proposal between his son and Bu Lu's daughter. When the proposal is rejected, Shu Yuan attacks Bu Lu, but Cao Cao and Bei Liu come to Bu Lu's aid, and Shu Yuan is dealt a devastating defeat.

SHOU JU AND FENG TIAN

Shou Jin and Feng Tian are advisors to Shao Yuan (Shu Yuan's brother). When Cao Cao manipulates Shao Yuan by offering him a meaningless royal appointment, Shou Jin and Feng Tian know their master is being tricked, and are flabbergasted by Shao Yuan's eagerness in accepting Cao Cao's offer.

BEI LIU AND HIS SWORN BROTHERS

Having handed over Xu Province to Bu Lu, Bei Liu and his
sworn brothers are allowed by Bu Lu to dwell in the barren
region of Xu called XiaoPei. Bu Lu leads an attack on XiaoPei,
supposedly because Fei Zhang stole some of his horses. But
the theft is just an excuse, as Bu Lu has been advised to drive
Bei Liu out of Xu and rid himself of a likely future adversary.
The three sworn brothers barely survive a daring nighttime
escape to the lands governed by Cao Cao. Bei Liu pledges
fidelity to Cao Cao, offering him the chance to take control of
Xu and defeat Bu Lu. Before that can happen, Cao Cao must
pacify Bu Lu by recognizing him as the head of Xu Province.
Cao Cao then sends Bei Liu and Bu Lu to defeat Shu Yuan's
forces, which have invaded Xu following a refused marriage
proposal. Following the destruction of Shu Yuan's forces, Cao
Cao goes after Bu Lu, and the resulting chaos and violence
eats at Bei Liu's conscience, since he once pledged to bring
peace to his nation and protect the people from the same
kind of violence he now commits.

GUI CHEN

Gui Chen is a wealthy merchant in the Xu Province whose
financial support of Bu Lu affords him the chance to offer
his counsel in person. When Gui Chen learns that Shu
Yuan wants his son to marry Bu Lu's daughter, Gui Chen
senses immediately that it is a trap. He advises Bu Lu against
accepting the proposal, and is so convincing that Bu Lu calls
off the engagement.

BU LU

Bu Lu is a legendary and greatly feared military commander who long served as Zhuo Dong's most powerful enforcer. After killing Zhuo Dong, Bu Lu wandered the land in search of a home. After many battles and fragile alliances, Bu Lu took control of Xu Province from Bei Liu, but allowed him and his people to remain in a remote area of the province. A short time later Bu Lu decides Bei Liu is too much of a potential threat and drives him from the land. Bei Liu escapes, after which Bu Lu entertains a marriage proposal between his daughter and the son of Shu Yuan. Gong Chen, Bu Lu's chief advisor, advocates for the marriage, but Bu Lu is persuaded by Gui Chen to veto the proposal. Shu Yuan retaliates by attacking Bu Lu, though his army is destroyed when Cao Cao and Bei Liu come to Bu Lu's aid. However, Cao Cao may have other reasons for helping Bu Lu, and rejecting Shu Yuan's proposal could prove to be a fatal mistake.

GONG CHEN

Gong Chen is Bu Lu's highest advisor, and has provided wise counsel since the time when Bu Lu had no place to call home. Unfortunately, Bu Lu also has a tendency to ignore Gong Chen's counsel and let his pride determine his course of action.

CAO CAO

Cao Cao is a cunning and ambitious man who has allied himself with the emperor so that he may act with royal authority. When Bei Liu and his sworn brothers seek sanctuary, Cao Cao's advisors counsel against accepting them. However, Cao Cao thinks it is better to be seen as benevolent as well as ruthless, and decides to help Bei Liu, who is beloved by the people. He also sees Bei Liu as a necessary ally against Shu Yuan and Bu Lu, consequently enlisting the fugitive lord in an extended military campaign to expand his rule.

YU XUN AND JIA GUO

Yu Xun and Jia Guo are Cao Cao's chief strategists. They give conflicting counsel on the matter of whether to welcome Bei Liu and his brothers into their territory. In the end, Jia Guo's counsel persuades Cao Cao to ally himself with Bei Liu.

DUN XIAHOU

He is Cao Cao's officer who leads the attack against Bu Lu. The battle will cost him dearly, though he will go to grotesque lengths to keep what's his.

Chapter 1

Ce Sun Comes of Age ^{AD 196}

Summary

When Jian Sun was killed in battle in 192 AD, his son Ce took possession of the Emperor's Hereditary Seal, a powerful token of the Han Dynasty that Jian Sun had stolen off a corpse during the battle of LuoYang. Though in possession of the seal, Ce Sun chose to be humble, allowing himself to be taken under Shu Yuan's wing.

Several years later, Ce Sun learns that his uncle is being persecuted by Governor Yao Liu in YangZhou. Ce Sun decides to help his uncle, entrusting Shu Yuan with the royal seal before departing. But Ce Sun isn't only interested in helping family; he seeks to emerge from Shu Yuan's shadow by conquering an eastern region once controlled by his father. He sets out with 3,000 men and 500 of Shu Yuan's horses and soon conquers the cities of YangZhou and KuaiJi, which he intends to make the foundation of his empire.

Shu Yuan, meanwhile, is so preoccupied with the emperor's seal that he ignores the counsel of his advisors, who want him to subdue Ce Sun before his ambition gets out of control. But Shu Yuan will not be persuaded, and instead of ordering his men into battle, he orders a palace be built for him.

Zhuo
XiLiang
ChangShan
BeiHai
PuYang
XiaoPei
HuLuo
GuanDu
XiaPi
LuoYang
ChangAn
XuChang
XuZhou
HanZhong
NanYang
ShouChun
A
HeFei
XiangYang
Wu
B
ChengDu
NanJun
KuaiJi
ChaiSang
Red Cliffs
BoYang
YuZhang
ChangSha

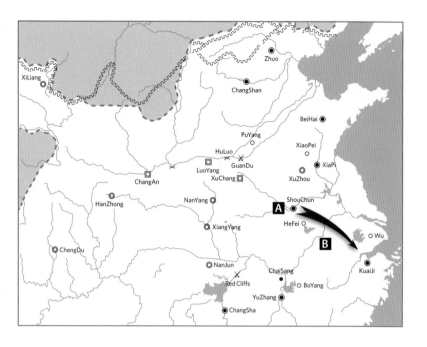

A Ce Sun entrusts the royal seal to Shu Yuan and, along with 3,000 men and 500 horses, sets out for YangZhou to help his uncle.

B After conquering YangZhou, Ce Sun turns his eyes toward Wu and KuaiJi, which he then conquers by attacking their supply base. Ce Sun is named governor of KuaiJi, which will become the foundation of his attempt at the throne.

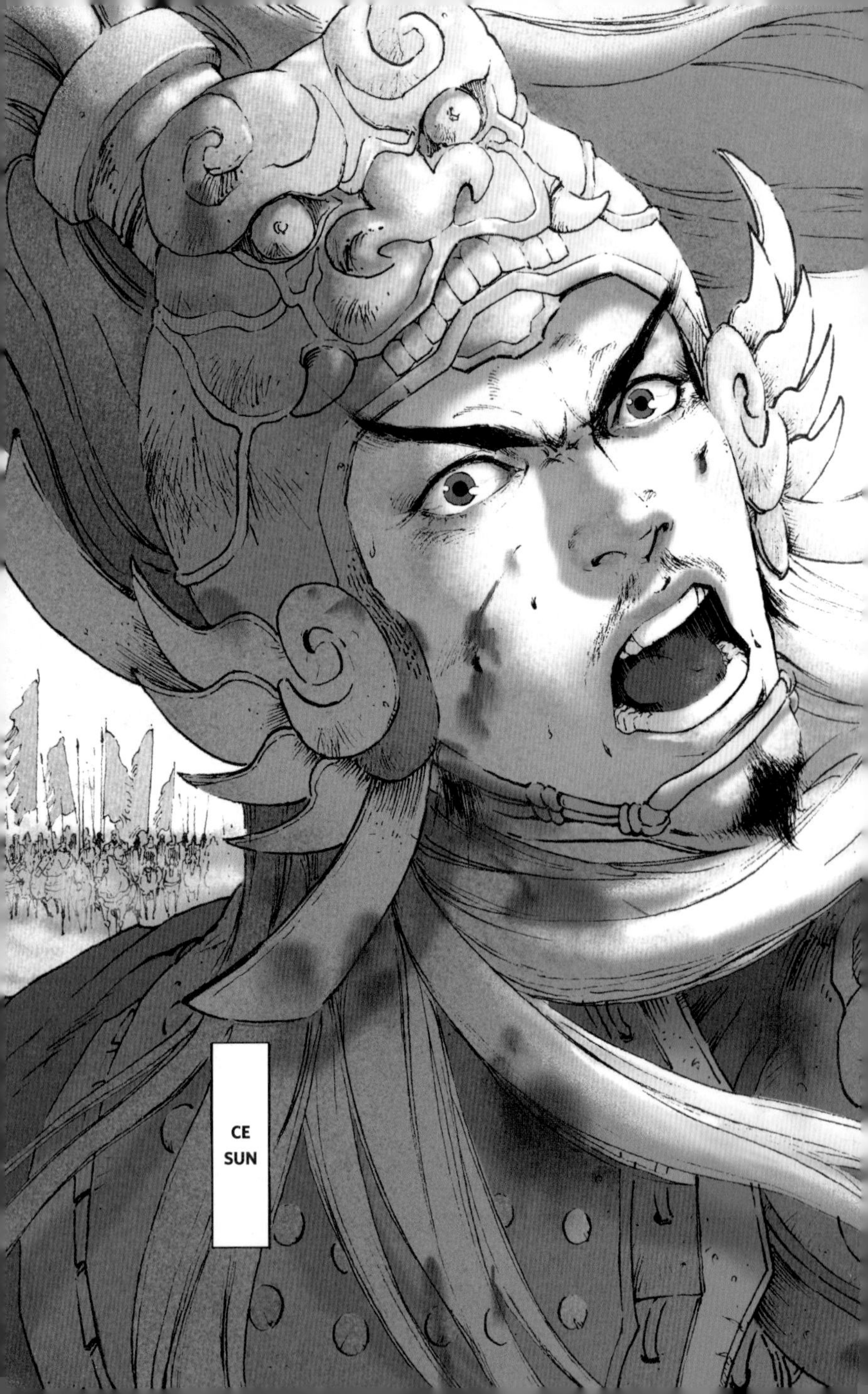
CE
SUN

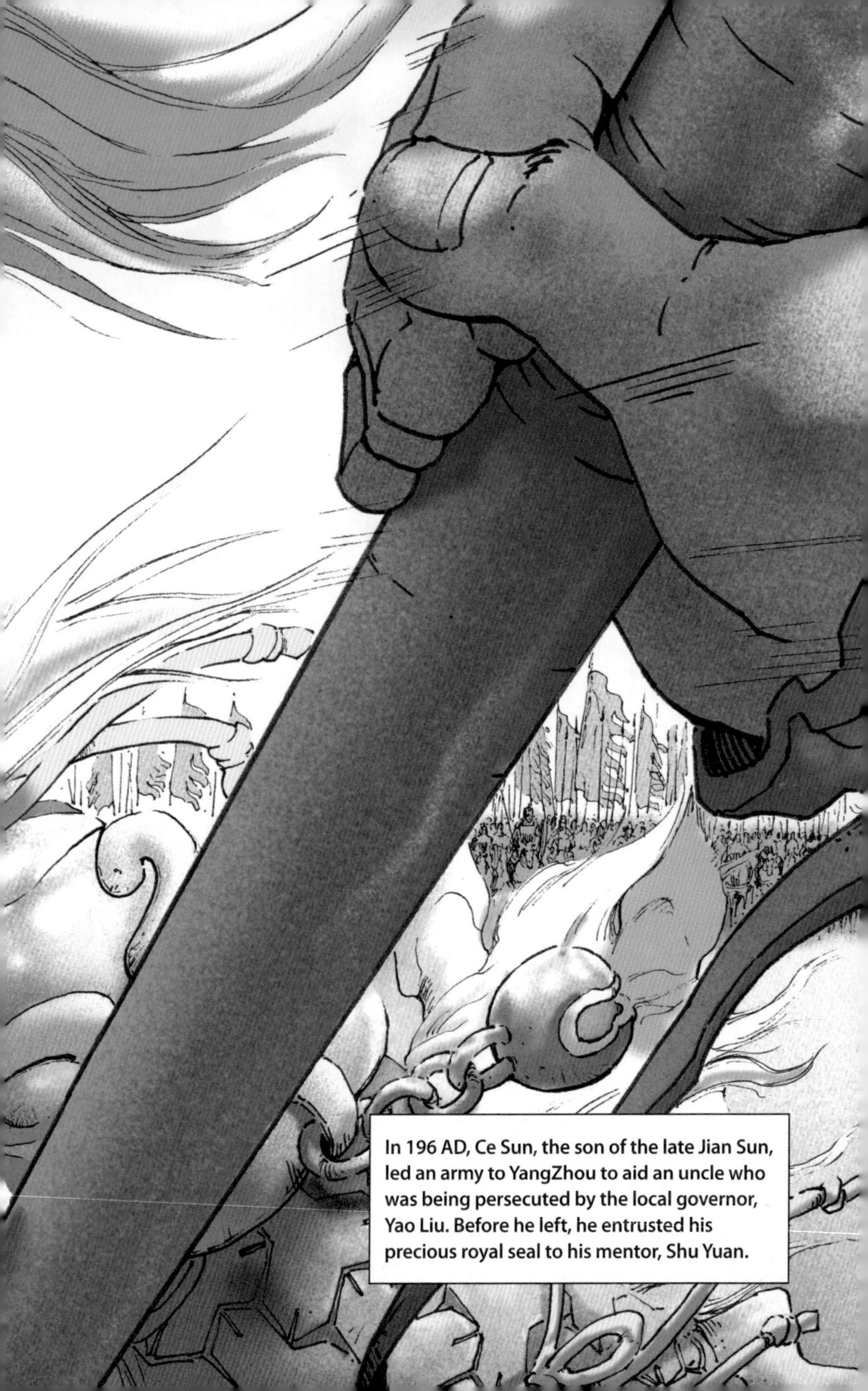
In 196 AD, Ce Sun, the son of the late Jian Sun, led an army to YangZhou to aid an uncle who was being persecuted by the local governor, Yao Liu. Before he left, he entrusted his precious royal seal to his mentor, Shu Yuan.

Ce Sun's temperament in battle was much like his father's.

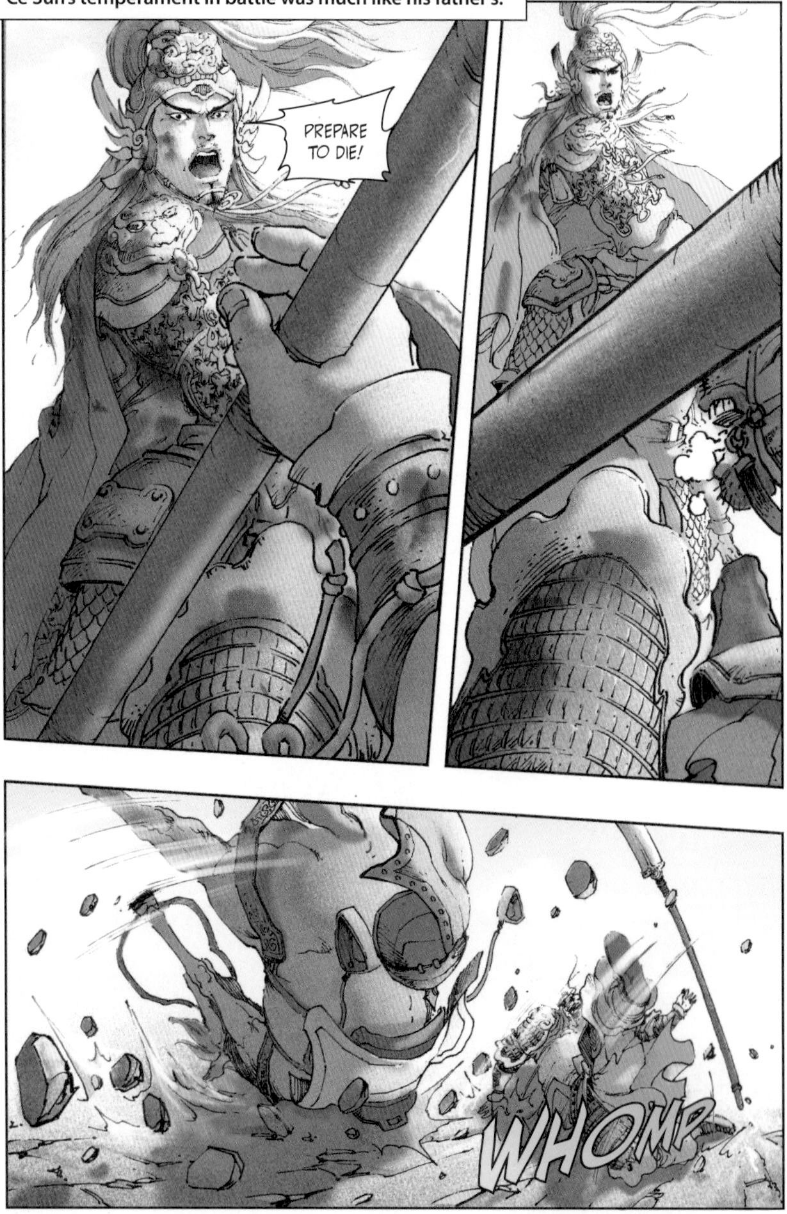
PREPARE TO DIE!
WHOMP

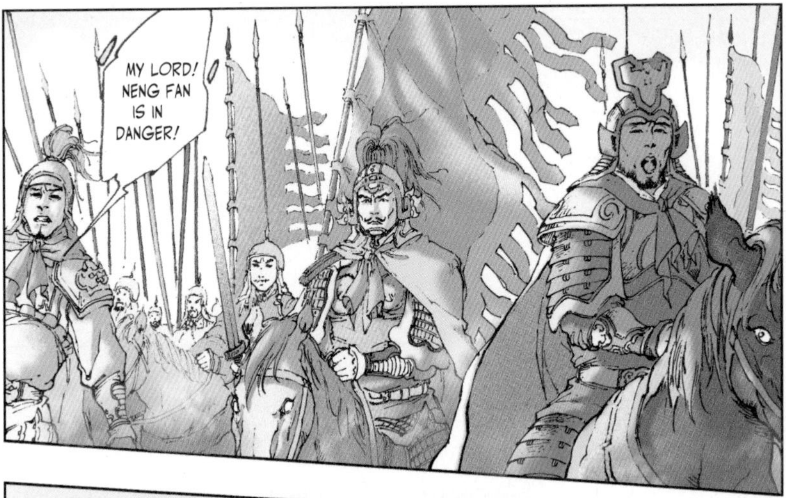
MY LORD! NENG FAN IS IN DANGER!

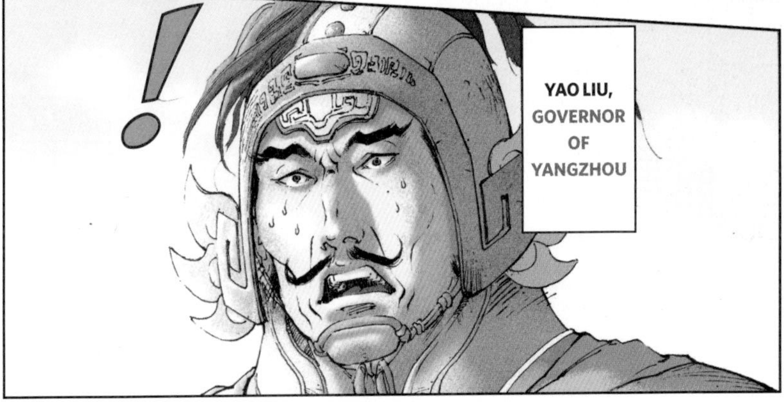
!
YAO LIU, GOVERNOR OF YANGZHOU

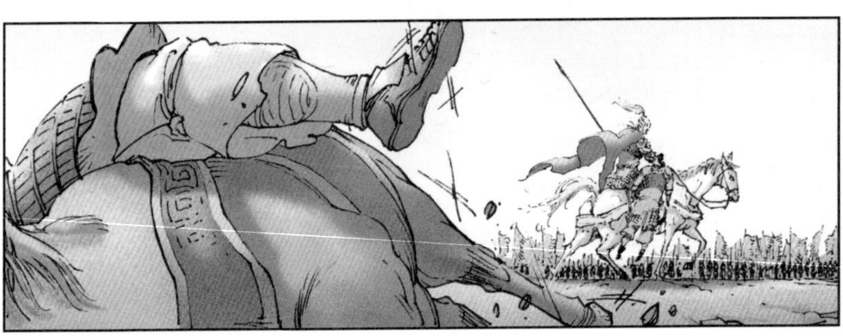

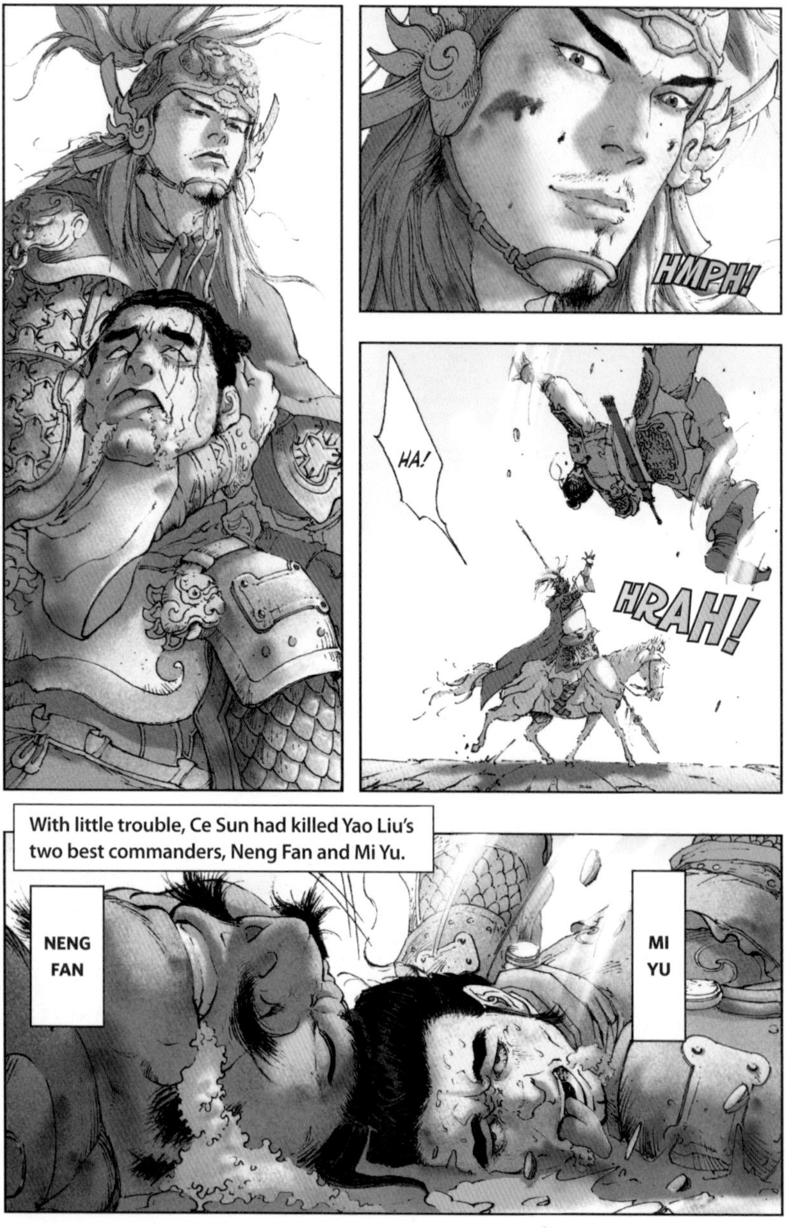
HMPH!
HA!
HRAH!
With little trouble, Ce Sun had killed Yao Liu's two best commanders, Neng Fan and Mi Yu.
NENG FAN
MI YU

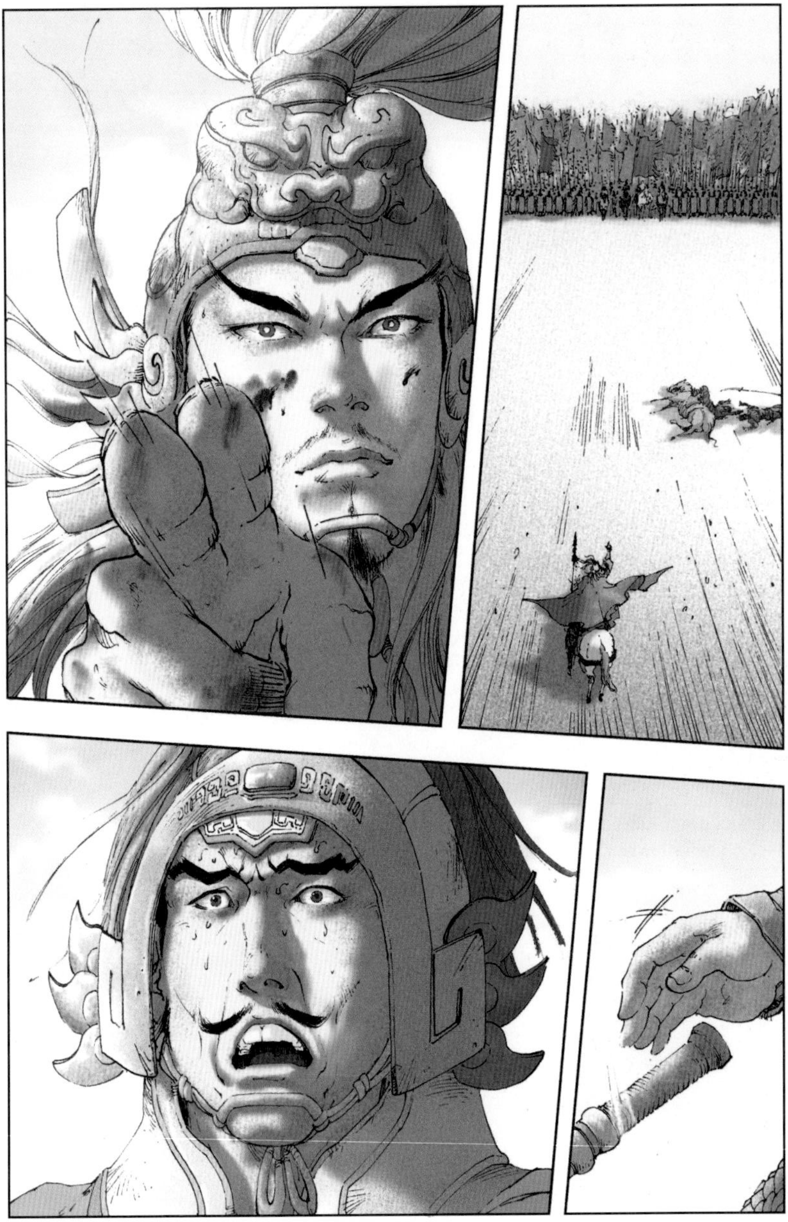

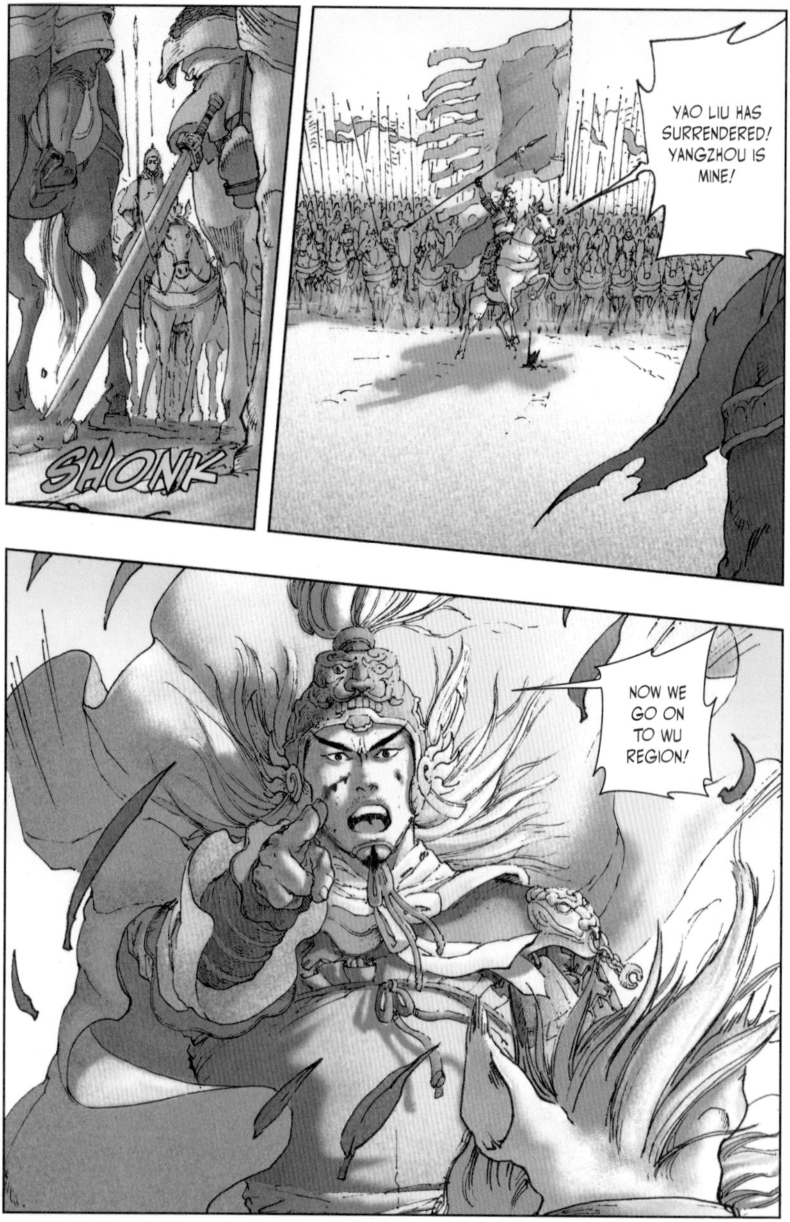
SHONK
YAO LIU HAS SURRENDERED! YANGZHOU IS MINE!
NOW WE GO ON TO WU REGION!

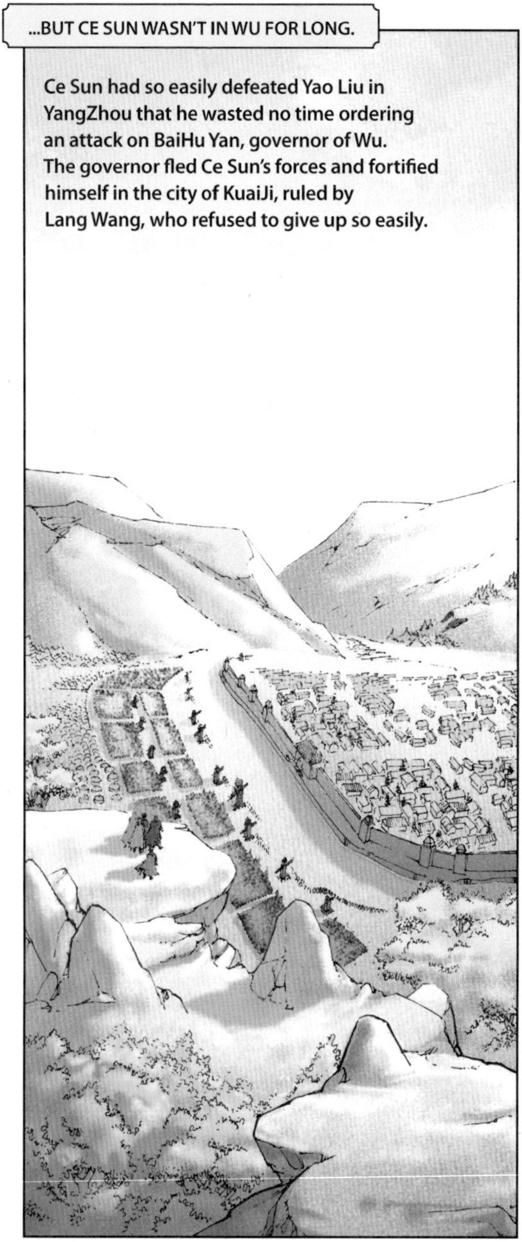
...BUT CE SUN WASN'T IN WU FOR LONG.
Ce Sun had so easily defeated Yao Liu in YangZhou that he wasted no time ordering an attack on BaiHu Yan, governor of Wu. The governor fled Ce Sun's forces and fortified himself in the city of KuaiJi, ruled by Lang Wang, who refused to give up so easily.

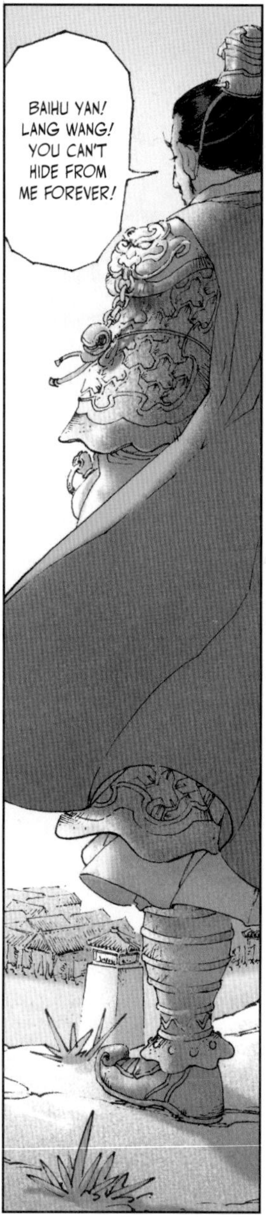
BAIHU YAN! LANG WANG! YOU CAN'T HIDE FROM ME FOREVER!

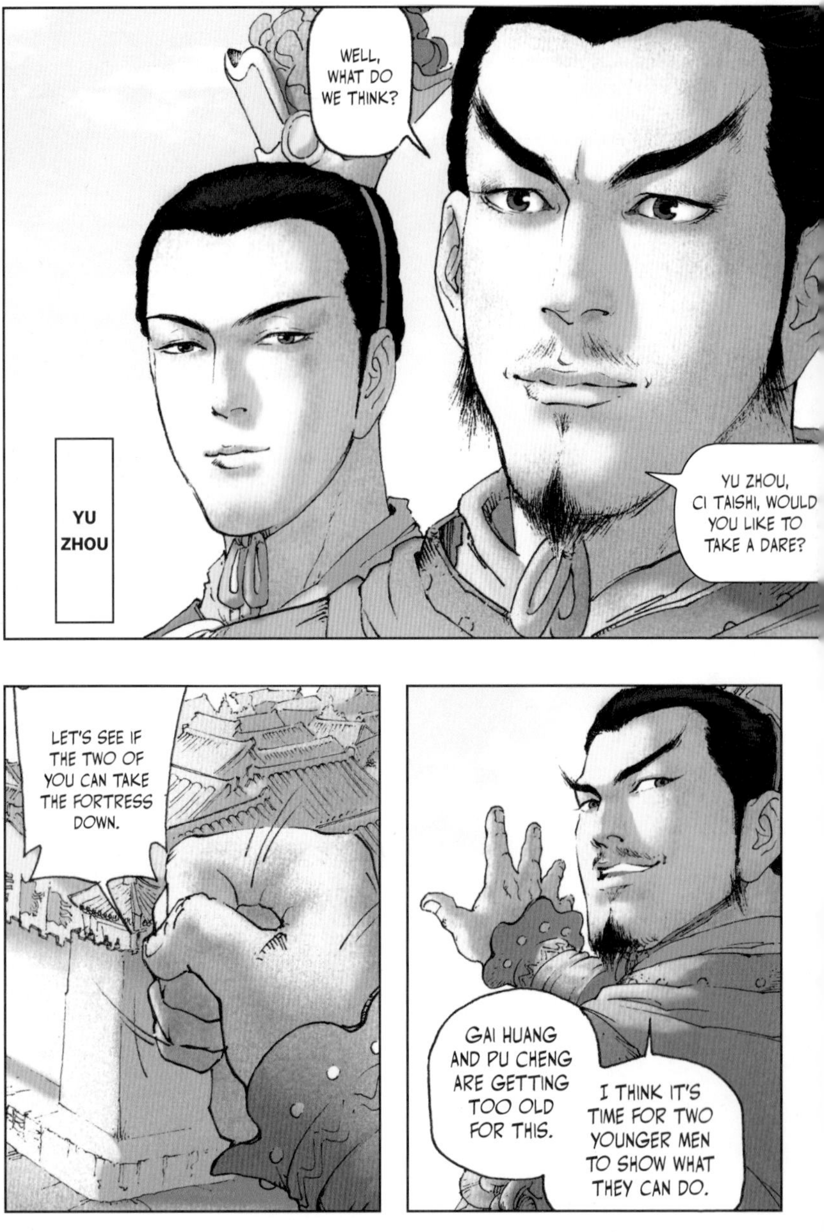
WELL, WHAT DO WE THINK?
YU ZHOU
YU ZHOU, CI TAISHI, WOULD YOU LIKE TO TAKE A DARE?
LET'S SEE IF THE TWO OF YOU CAN TAKE THE FORTRESS DOWN.
GAI HUANG AND PU CHENG ARE GETTING TOO OLD FOR THIS.
I THINK IT'S TIME FOR TWO YOUNGER MEN TO SHOW WHAT THEY CAN DO.

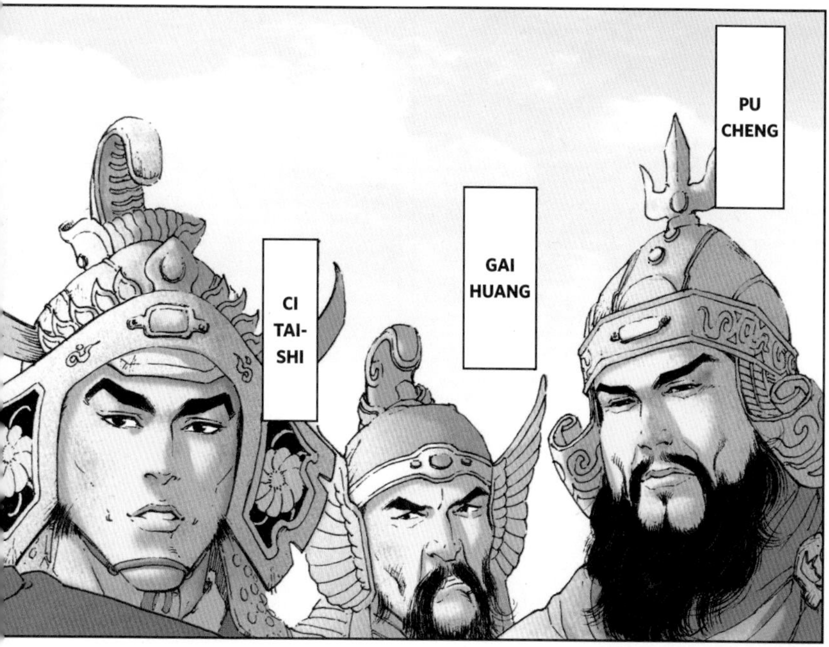
PU CHENG
GAI HUANG
CI TAI-SHI

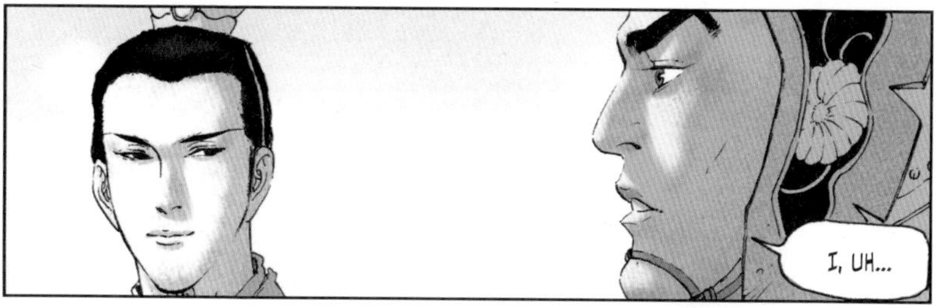
I, UH...

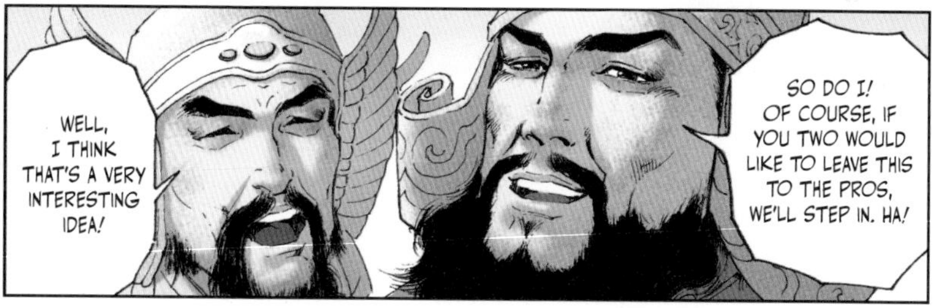
SO DO I! OF COURSE, IF YOU TWO WOULD LIKE TO LEAVE THIS TO THE PROS, WE'LL STEP IN. HA!
WELL, I THINK THAT'S A VERY INTERESTING IDEA!

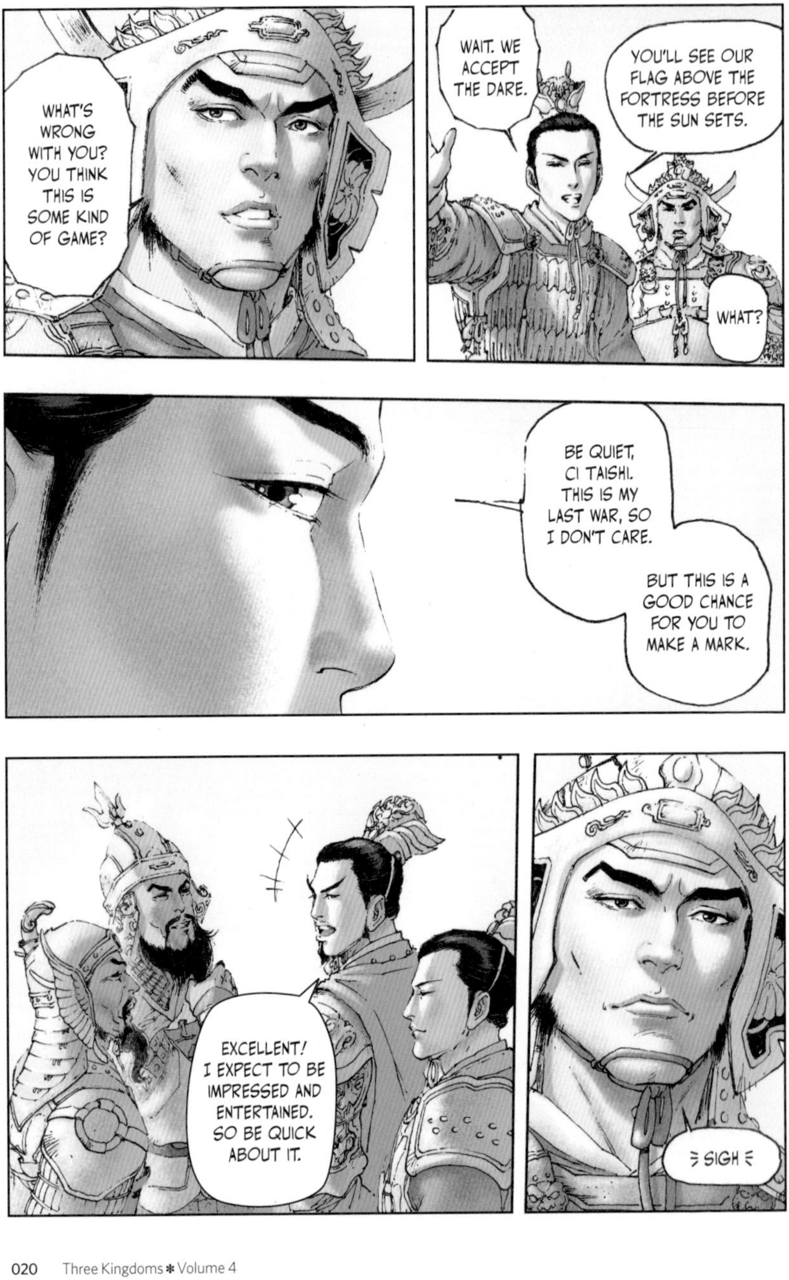
WHAT'S WRONG WITH YOU? YOU THINK THIS IS SOME KIND OF GAME?
WAIT. WE ACCEPT THE DARE.
YOU'LL SEE OUR FLAG ABOVE THE FORTRESS BEFORE THE SUN SETS.
WHAT?
BE QUIET, CI TAISHI. THIS IS MY LAST WAR, SO I DON'T CARE.
BUT THIS IS A GOOD CHANCE FOR YOU TO MAKE A MARK.
EXCELLENT! I EXPECT TO BE IMPRESSED AND ENTERTAINED. SO BE QUICK ABOUT IT.
SIGH

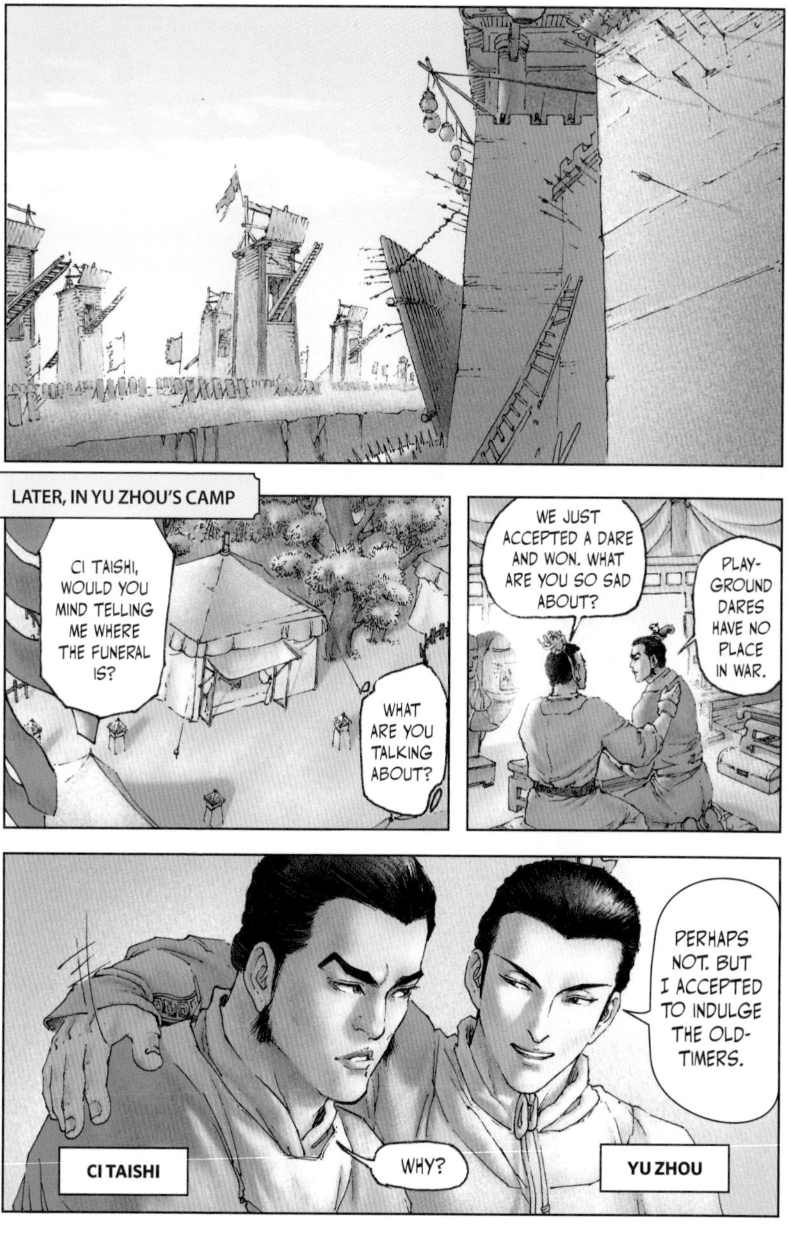
LATER, IN YU ZHOU'S CAMP
CI TAISHI, WOULD YOU MIND TELLING ME WHERE THE FUNERAL IS?
WHAT ARE YOU TALKING ABOUT?
WE JUST ACCEPTED A DARE AND WON. WHAT ARE YOU SO SAD ABOUT?
PLAY-GROUND DARES HAVE NO PLACE IN WAR.
PERHAPS NOT. BUT I ACCEPTED TO INDULGE THE OLD-TIMERS.
WHY?
CI TAISHI
YU ZHOU

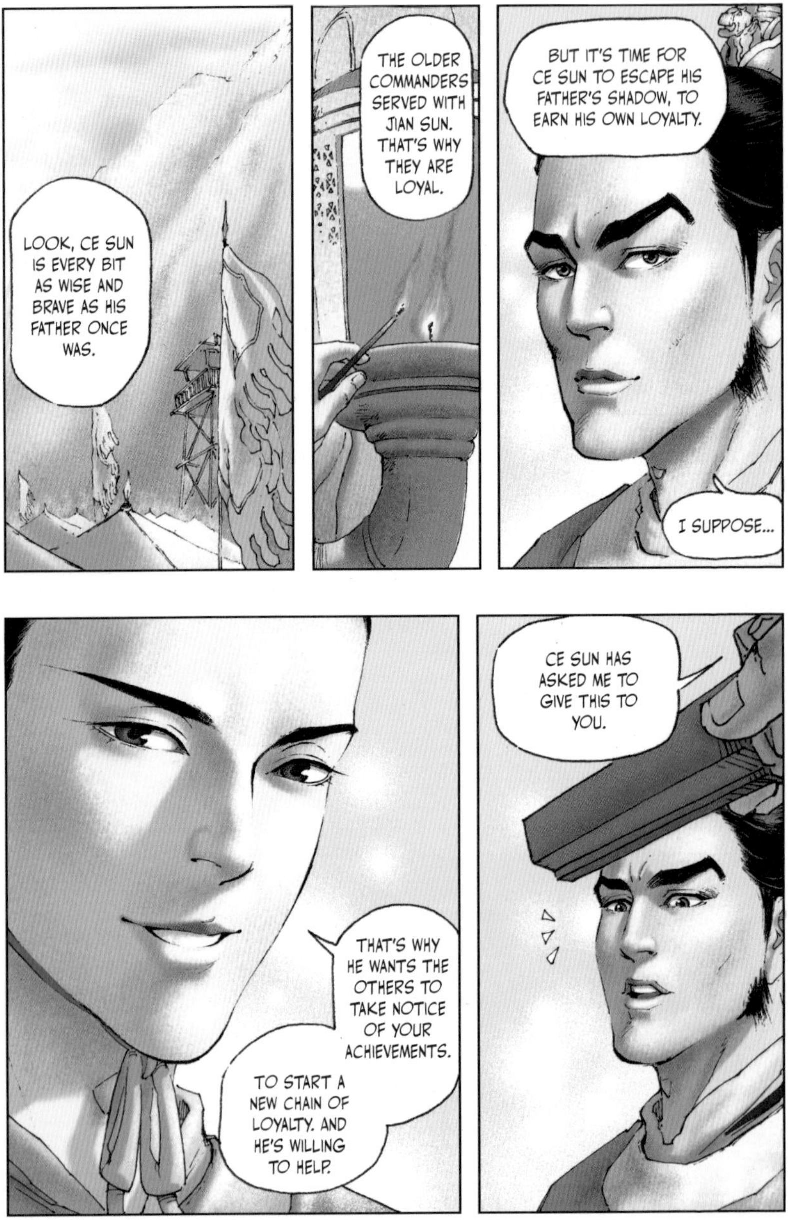
LOOK, CE SUN IS EVERY BIT AS WISE AND BRAVE AS HIS FATHER ONCE WAS.
THE OLDER COMMANDERS SERVED WITH JIAN SUN. THAT'S WHY THEY ARE LOYAL.
BUT IT'S TIME FOR CE SUN TO ESCAPE HIS FATHER'S SHADOW, TO EARN HIS OWN LOYALTY.
I SUPPOSE...
THAT'S WHY HE WANTS THE OTHERS TO TAKE NOTICE OF YOUR ACHIEVEMENTS.
TO START A NEW CHAIN OF LOYALTY. AND HE'S WILLING TO HELP.
CE SUN HAS ASKED ME TO GIVE THIS TO YOU.

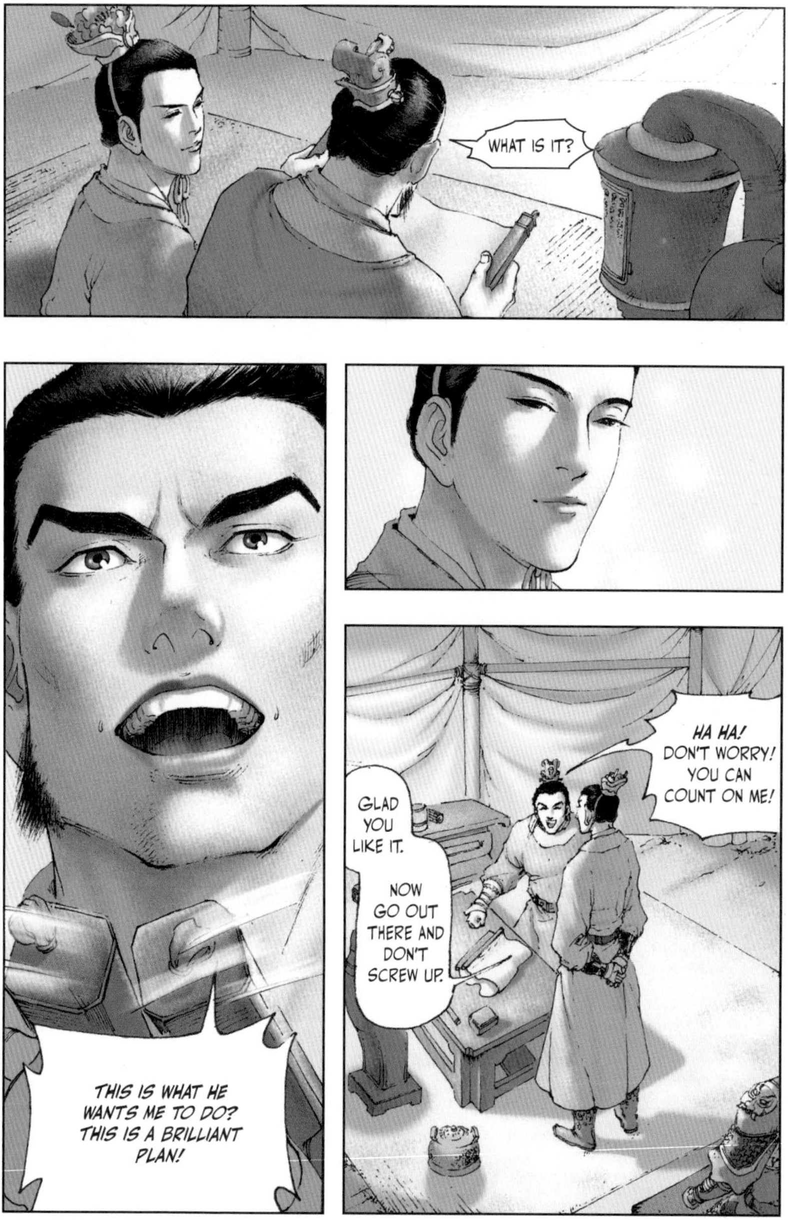
WHAT IS IT?
THIS IS WHAT HE WANTS ME TO DO? THIS IS A BRILLIANT PLAN!
HA HA! DON'T WORRY! YOU CAN COUNT ON ME!
GLAD YOU LIKE IT.
NOW GO OUT THERE AND DON'T SCREW UP.

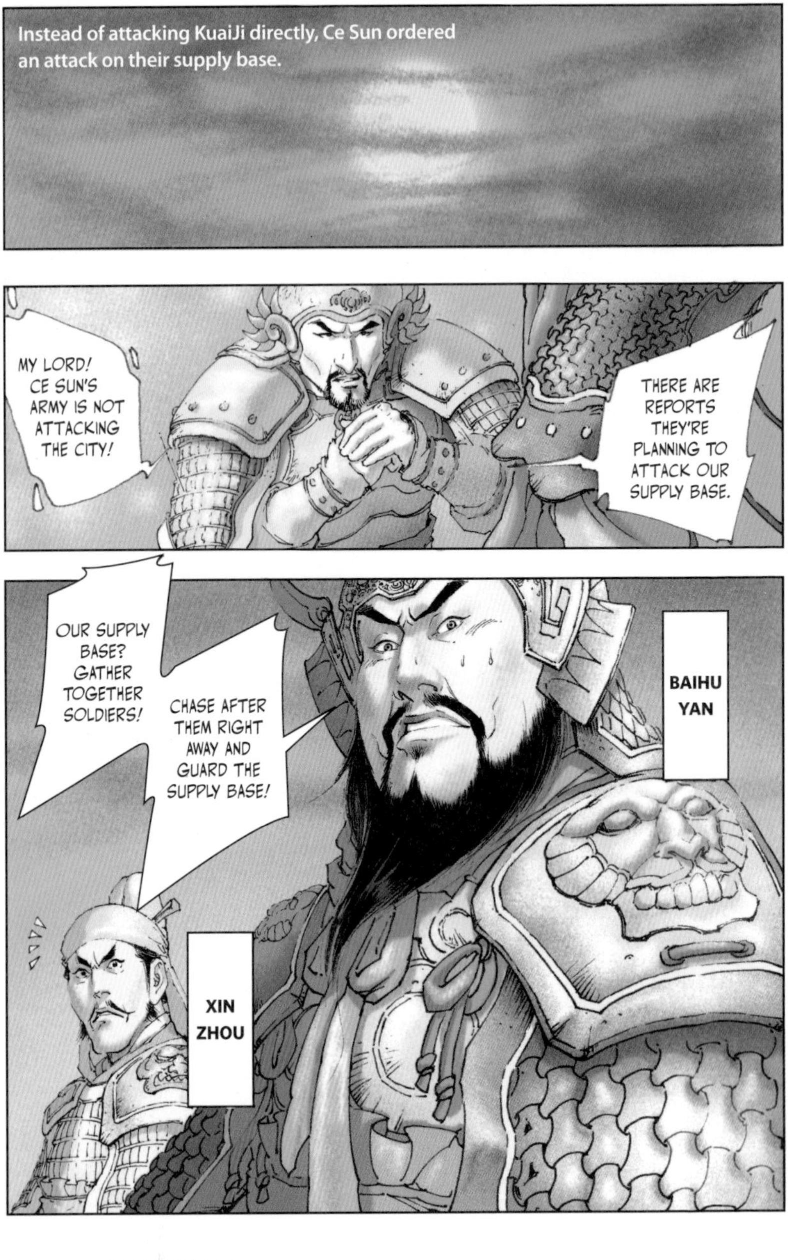
Instead of attacking KuaiJi directly, Ce Sun ordered an attack on their supply base.
MY LORD! CE SUN'S ARMY IS NOT ATTACKING THE CITY!
THERE ARE REPORTS THEY'RE PLANNING TO ATTACK OUR SUPPLY BASE.
BAIHU YAN
OUR SUPPLY BASE? GATHER TOGETHER SOLDIERS!
CHASE AFTER THEM RIGHT AWAY AND GUARD THE SUPPLY BASE!
XIN ZHOU

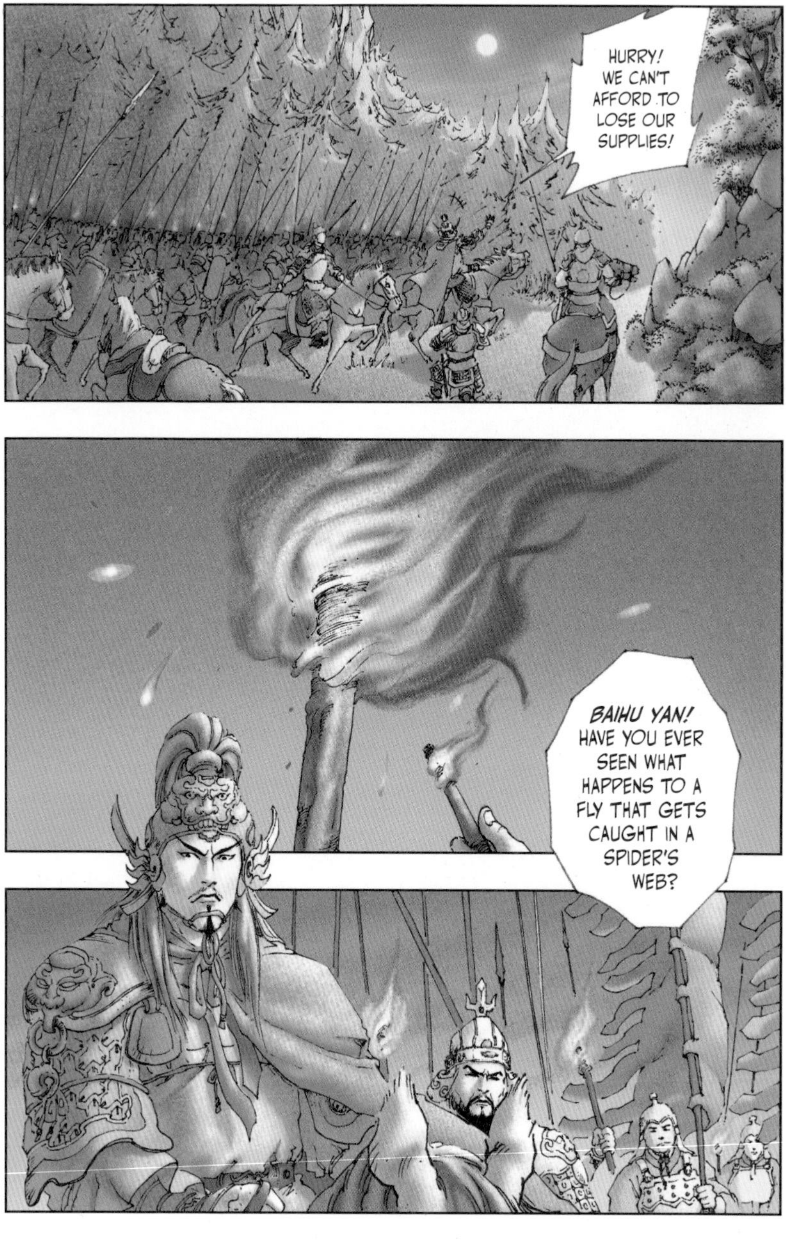
HURRY! WE CAN'T AFFORD TO LOSE OUR SUPPLIES!
BAIHU YAN! HAVE YOU EVER SEEN WHAT HAPPENS TO A FLY THAT GETS CAUGHT IN A SPIDER'S WEB?

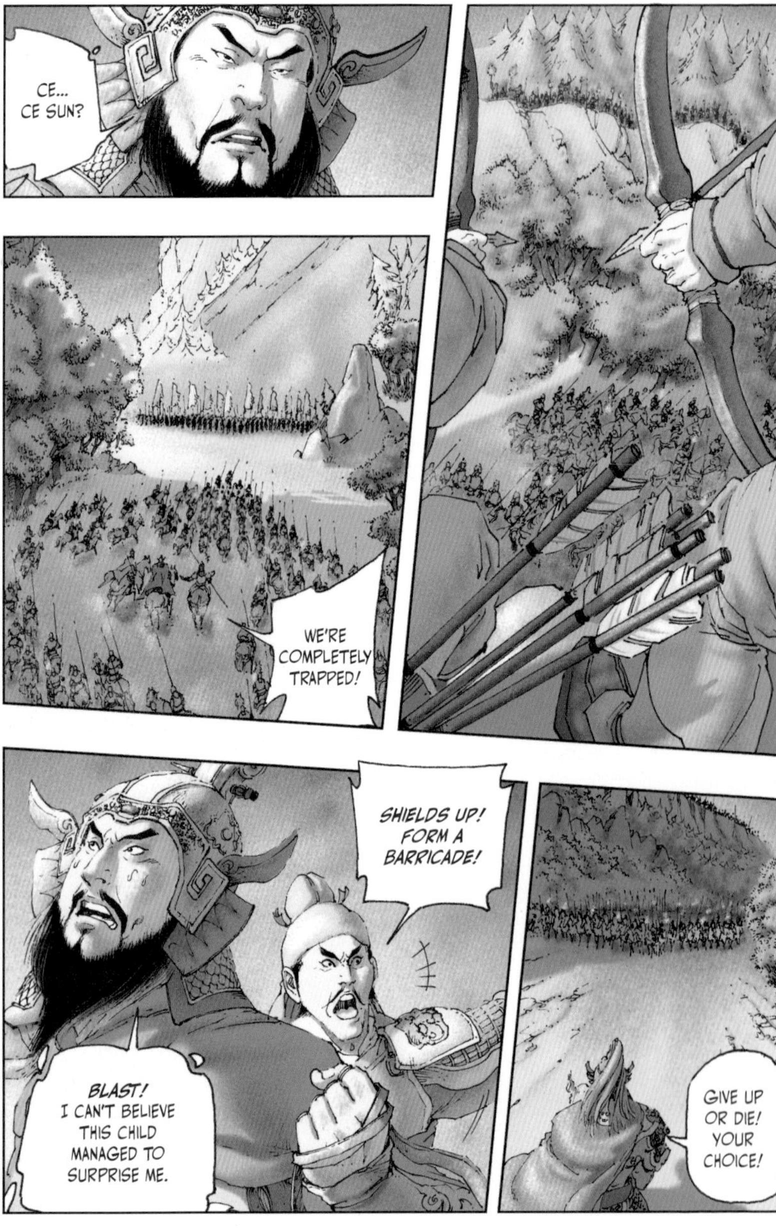
CE... CE SUN?
WE'RE COMPLETELY TRAPPED!
SHIELDS UP! FORM A BARRICADE!
BLAST! I CAN'T BELIEVE THIS CHILD MANAGED TO SURPRISE ME.
GIVE UP OR DIE! YOUR CHOICE!

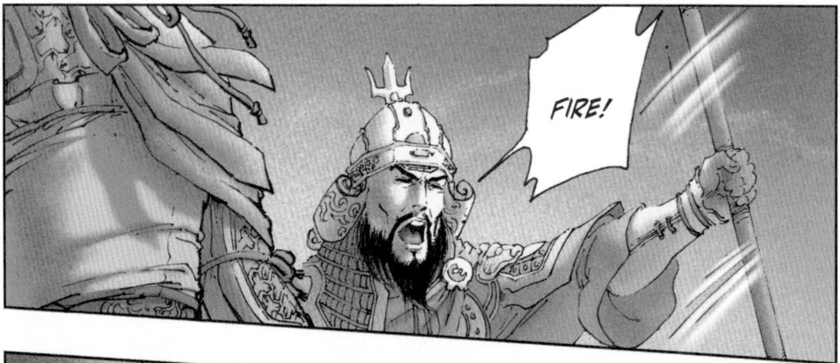
FIRE!

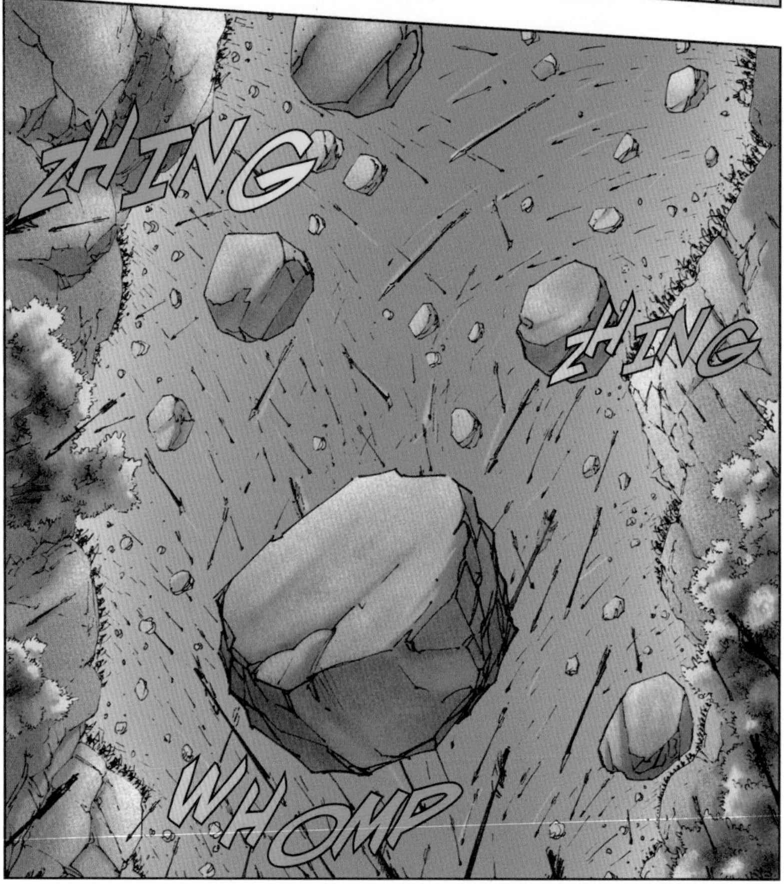
ZHING
ZHING
WHOMP

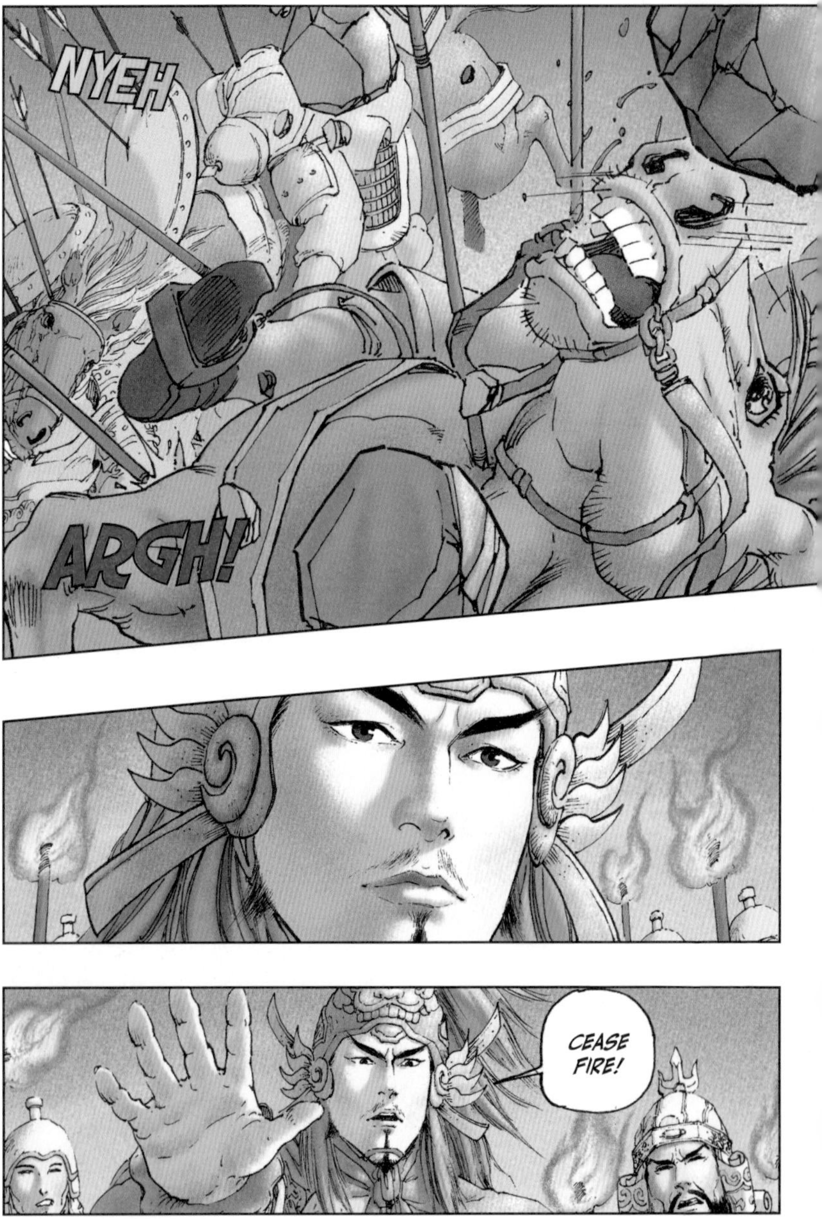
NYEH
ARGH!
CEASE FIRE!

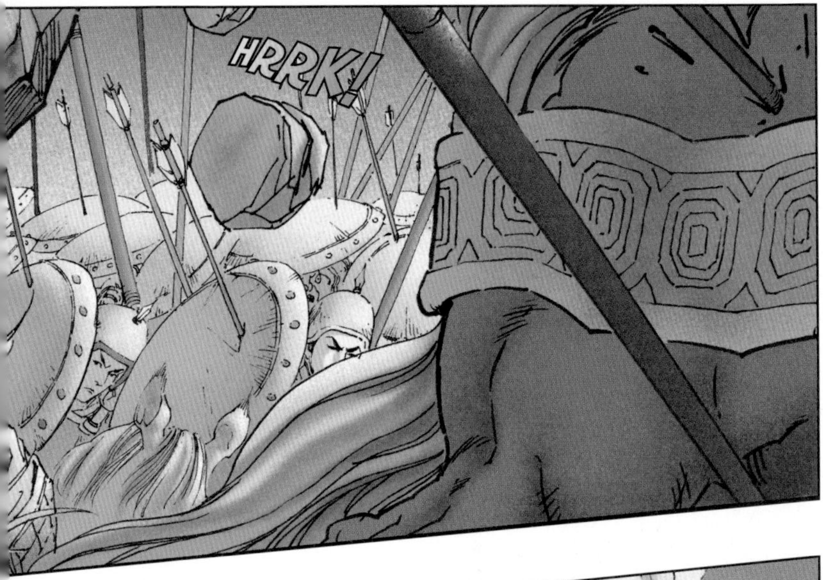
HRRK!

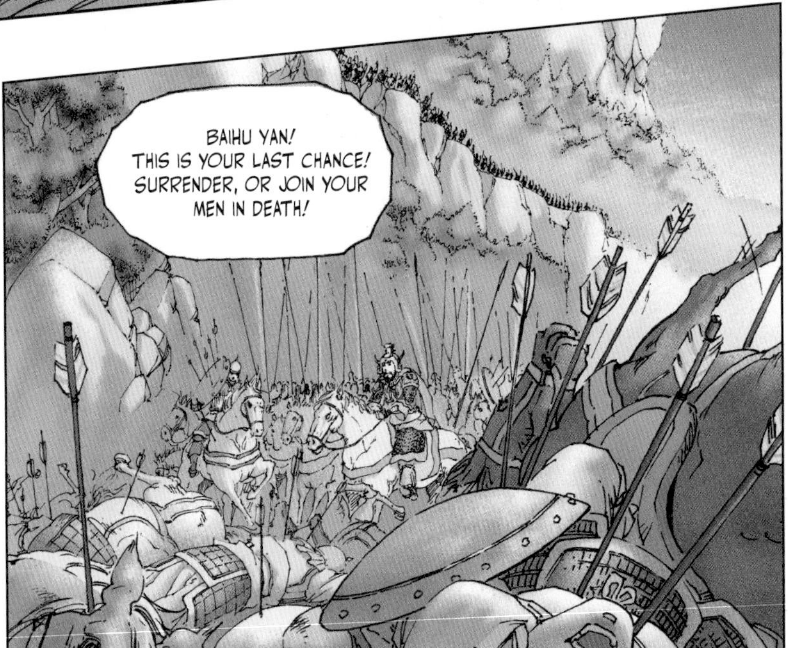
BAIHU YAN! THIS IS YOUR LAST CHANCE! SURRENDER, OR JOIN YOUR MEN IN DEATH!

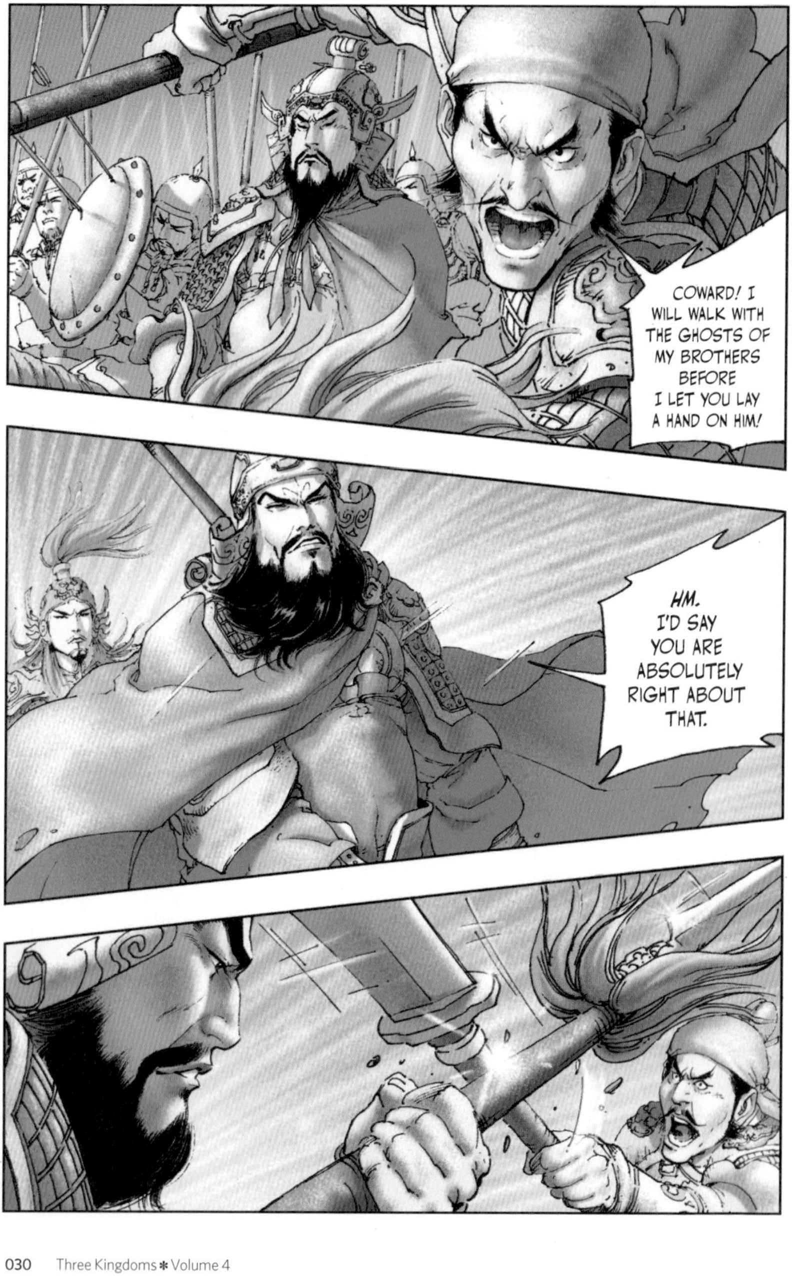
COWARD! I WILL WALK WITH THE GHOSTS OF MY BROTHERS BEFORE I LET YOU LAY A HAND ON HIM!
HM. I'D SAY YOU ARE ABSOLUTELY RIGHT ABOUT THAT.

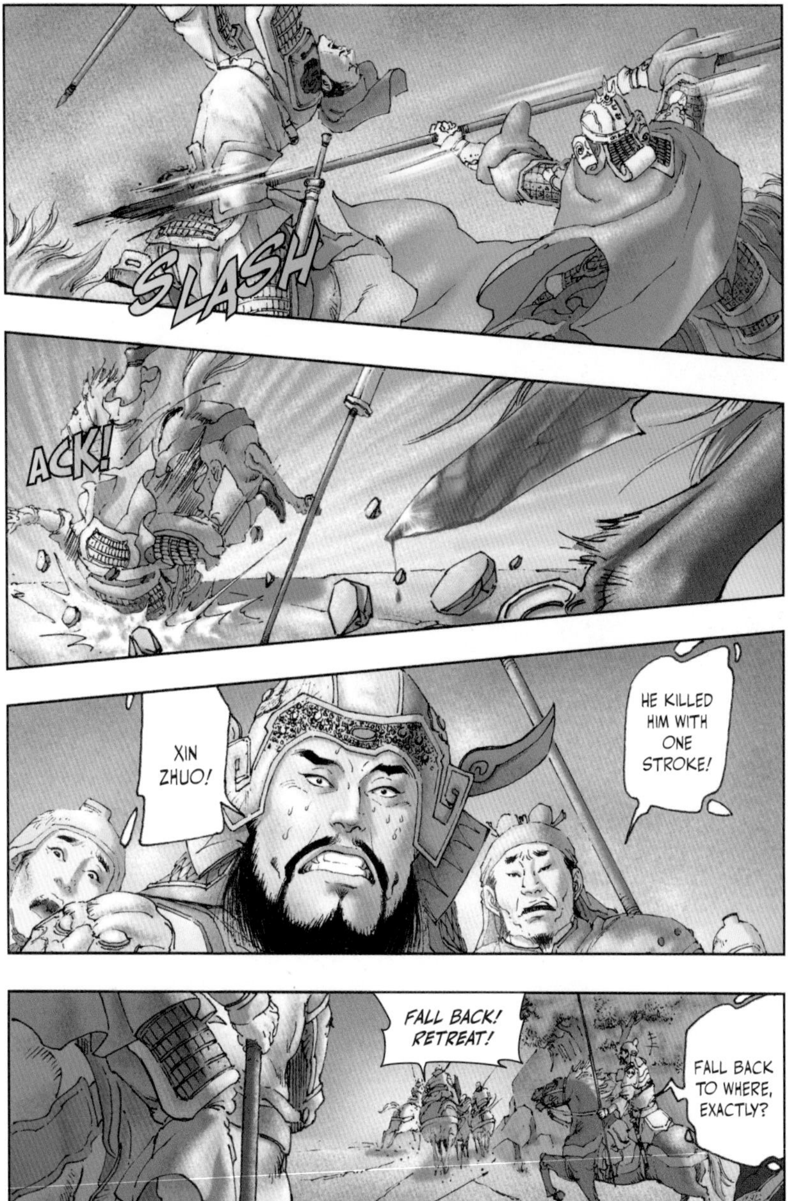
SLASH
ACK!
XIN ZHUO!
HE KILLED HIM WITH ONE STROKE!
FALL BACK! RETREAT!
FALL BACK TO WHERE, EXACTLY?

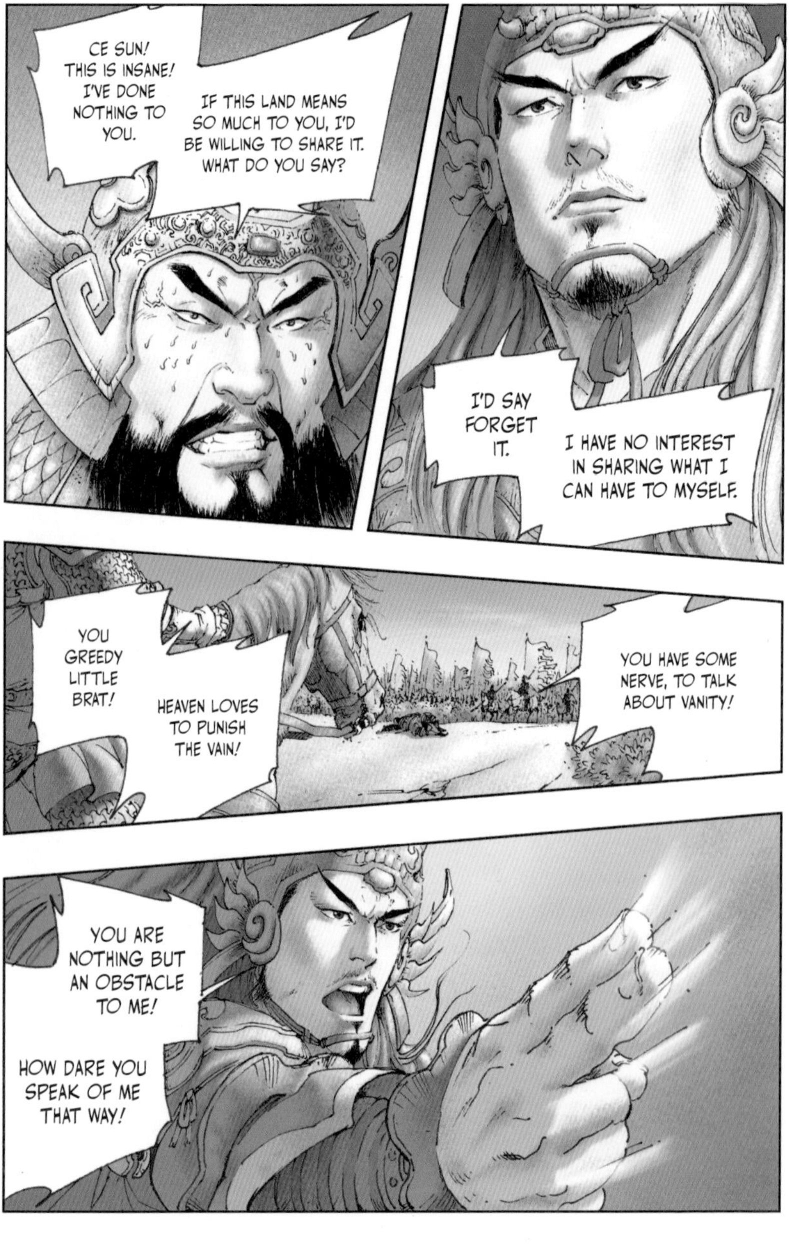
CE SUN! THIS IS INSANE! I'VE DONE NOTHING TO YOU.
IF THIS LAND MEANS SO MUCH TO YOU, I'D BE WILLING TO SHARE IT. WHAT DO YOU SAY?
I'D SAY FORGET IT.
I HAVE NO INTEREST IN SHARING WHAT I CAN HAVE TO MYSELF.
YOU GREEDY LITTLE BRAT!
HEAVEN LOVES TO PUNISH THE VAIN!
YOU HAVE SOME NERVE, TO TALK ABOUT VANITY!
YOU ARE NOTHING BUT AN OBSTACLE TO ME!
HOW DARE YOU SPEAK OF ME THAT WAY!

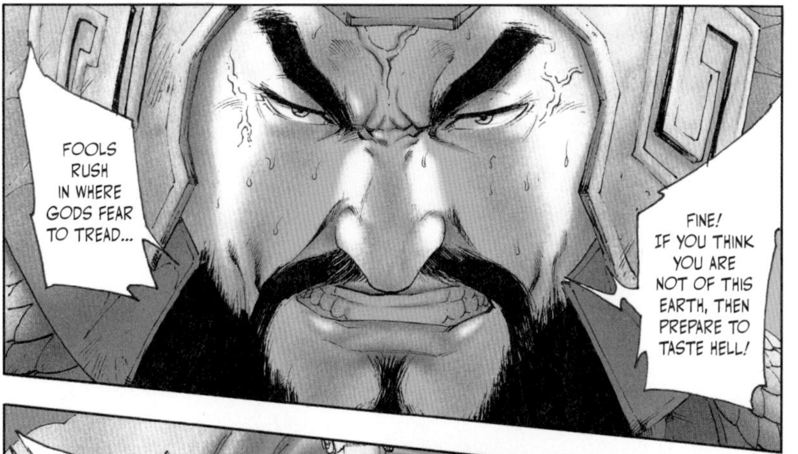
FOOLS RUSH IN WHERE GODS FEAR TO TREAD...
FINE! IF YOU THINK YOU ARE NOT OF THIS EARTH, THEN PREPARE TO TASTE HELL!

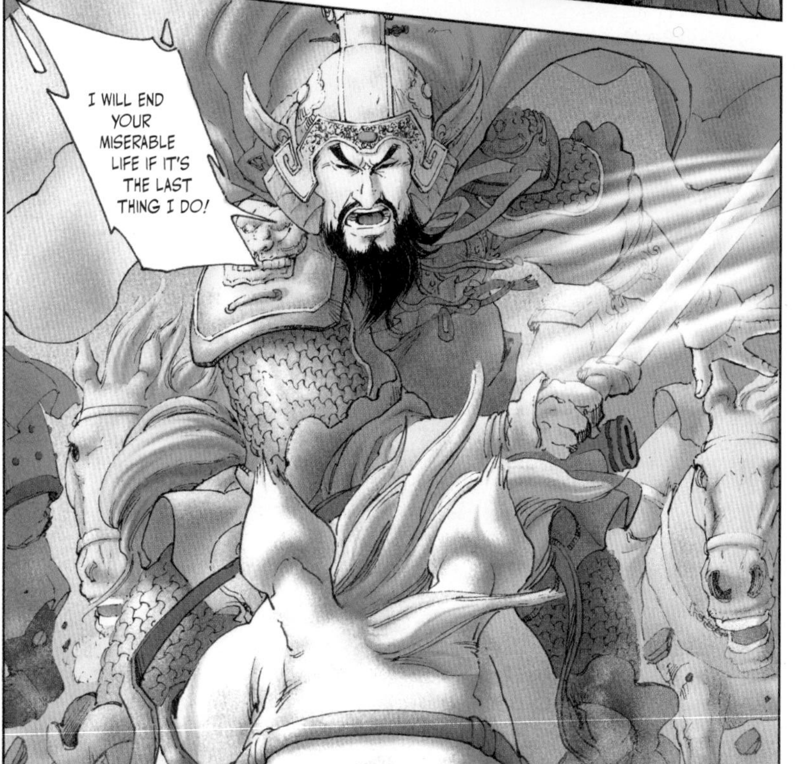
I WILL END YOUR MISERABLE LIFE IF IT'S THE LAST THING I DO!

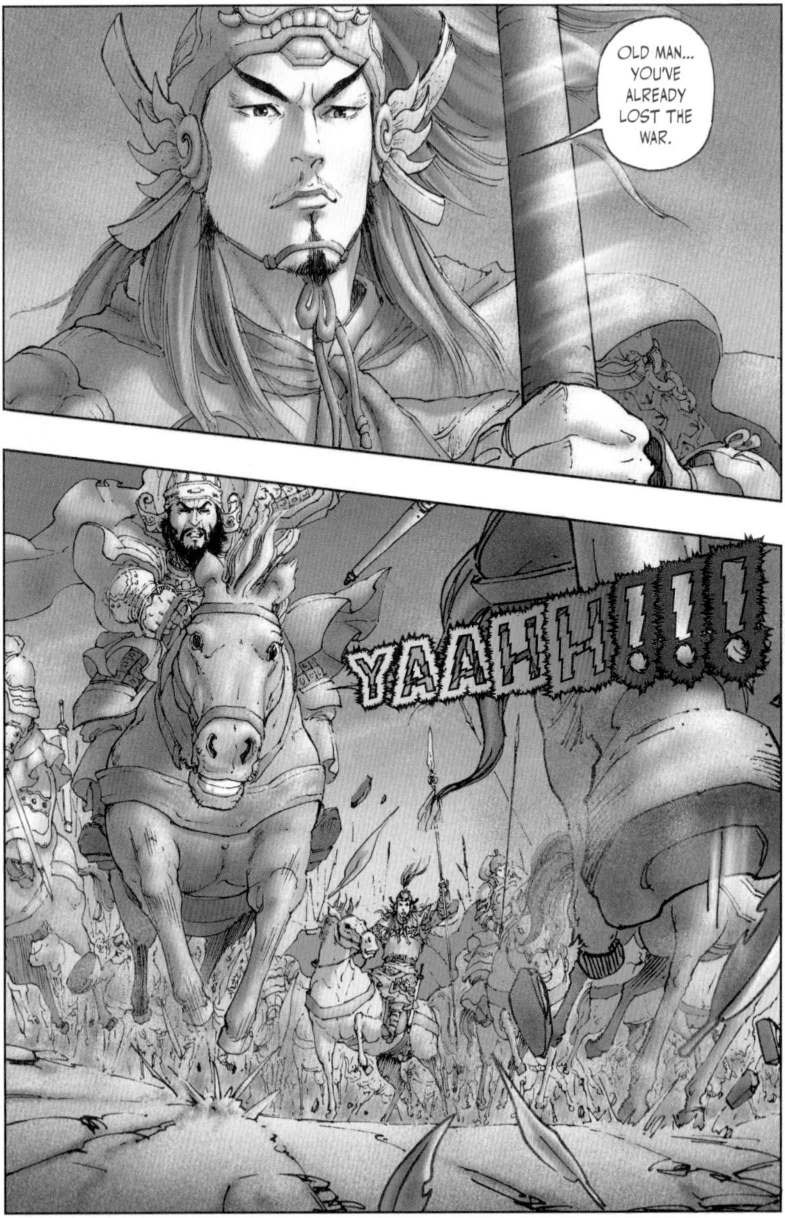
OLD MAN... YOU'VE ALREADY LOST THE WAR.
YAAHH!!!

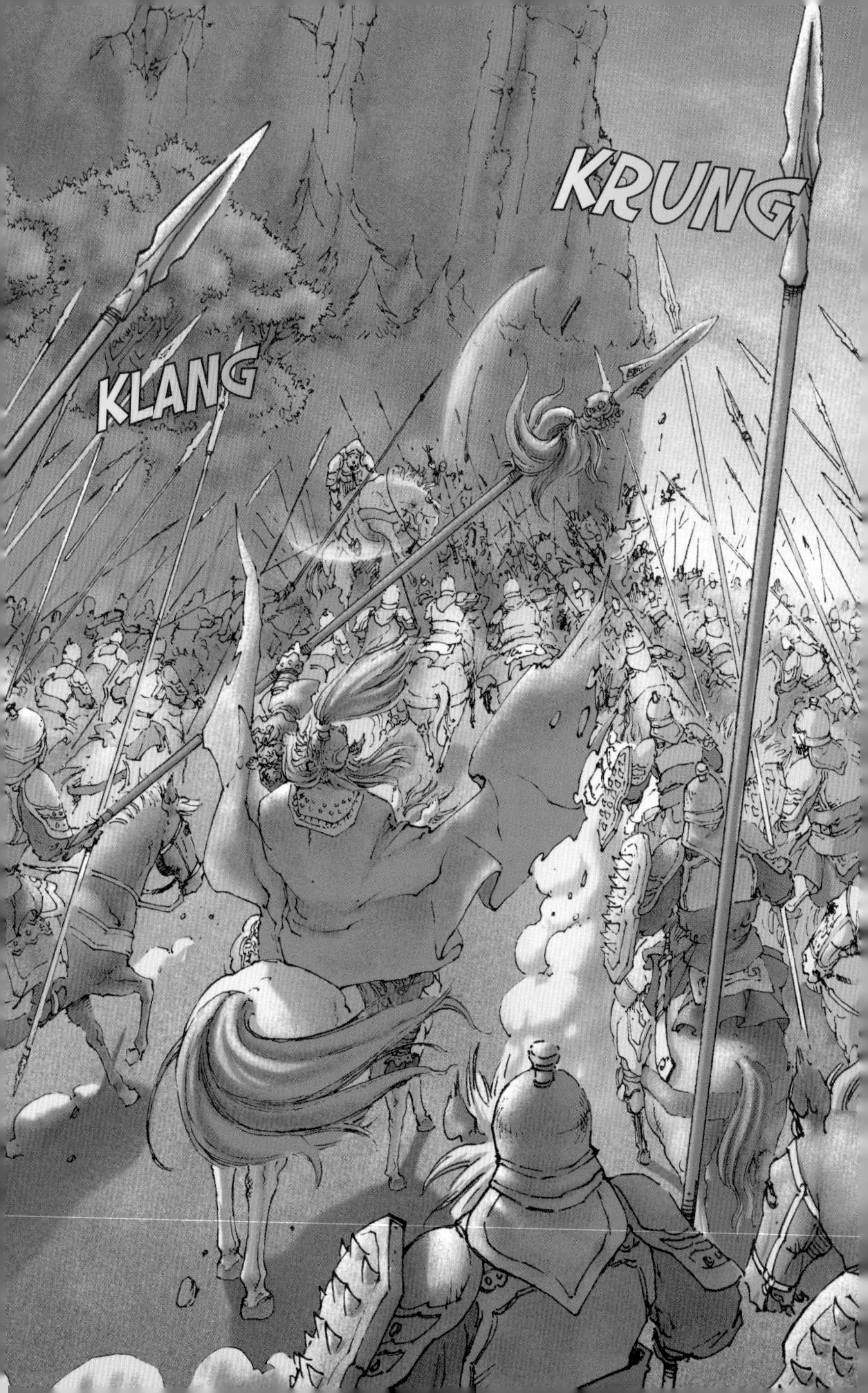
KRUNG
KLANG

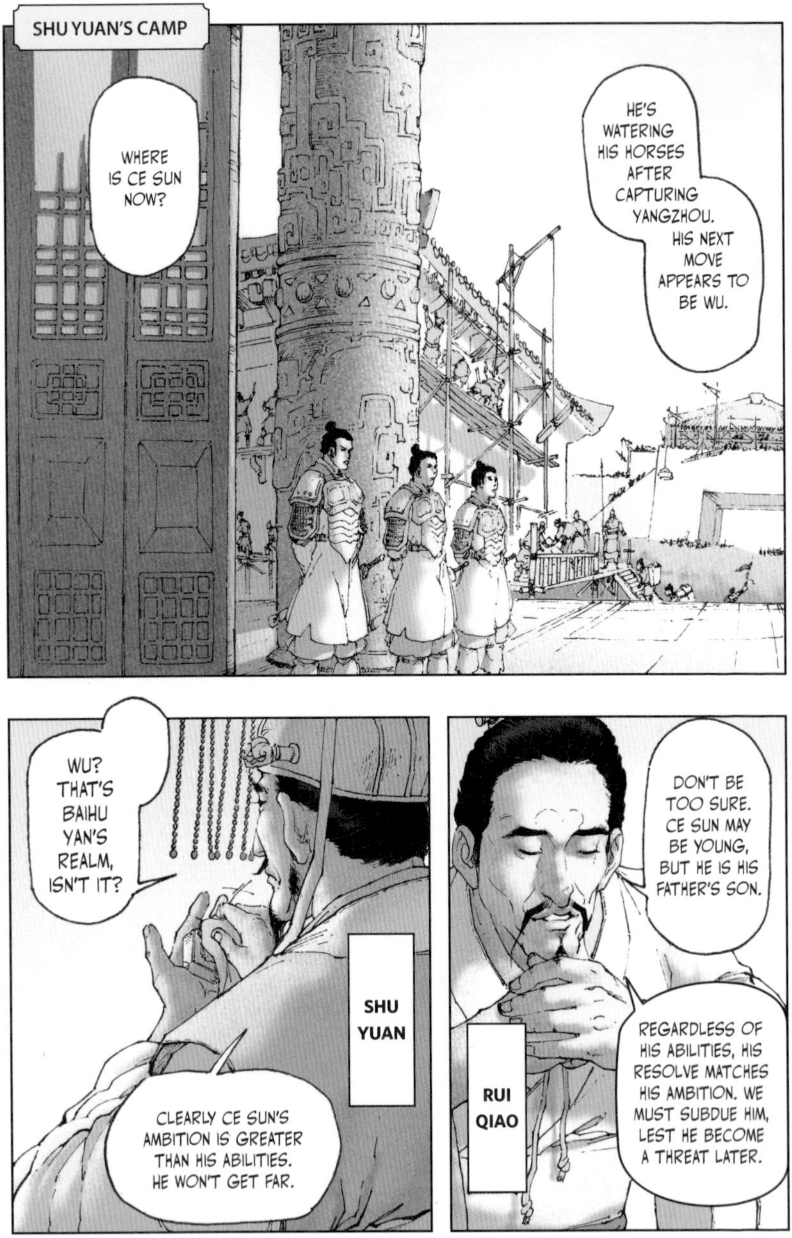
SHU YUAN'S CAMP
WHERE IS CE SUN NOW?
HE'S WATERING HIS HORSES AFTER CAPTURING YANGZHOU. HIS NEXT MOVE APPEARS TO BE WU.
WU? THAT'S BAIHU YAN'S REALM, ISN'T IT?
SHU YUAN
CLEARLY CE SUN'S AMBITION IS GREATER THAN HIS ABILITIES. HE WON'T GET FAR.
DON'T BE TOO SURE. CE SUN MAY BE YOUNG, BUT HE IS HIS FATHER'S SON.
RUI QIAO
REGARDLESS OF HIS ABILITIES, HIS RESOLVE MATCHES HIS AMBITION. WE MUST SUBDUE HIM, LEST HE BECOME A THREAT LATER.

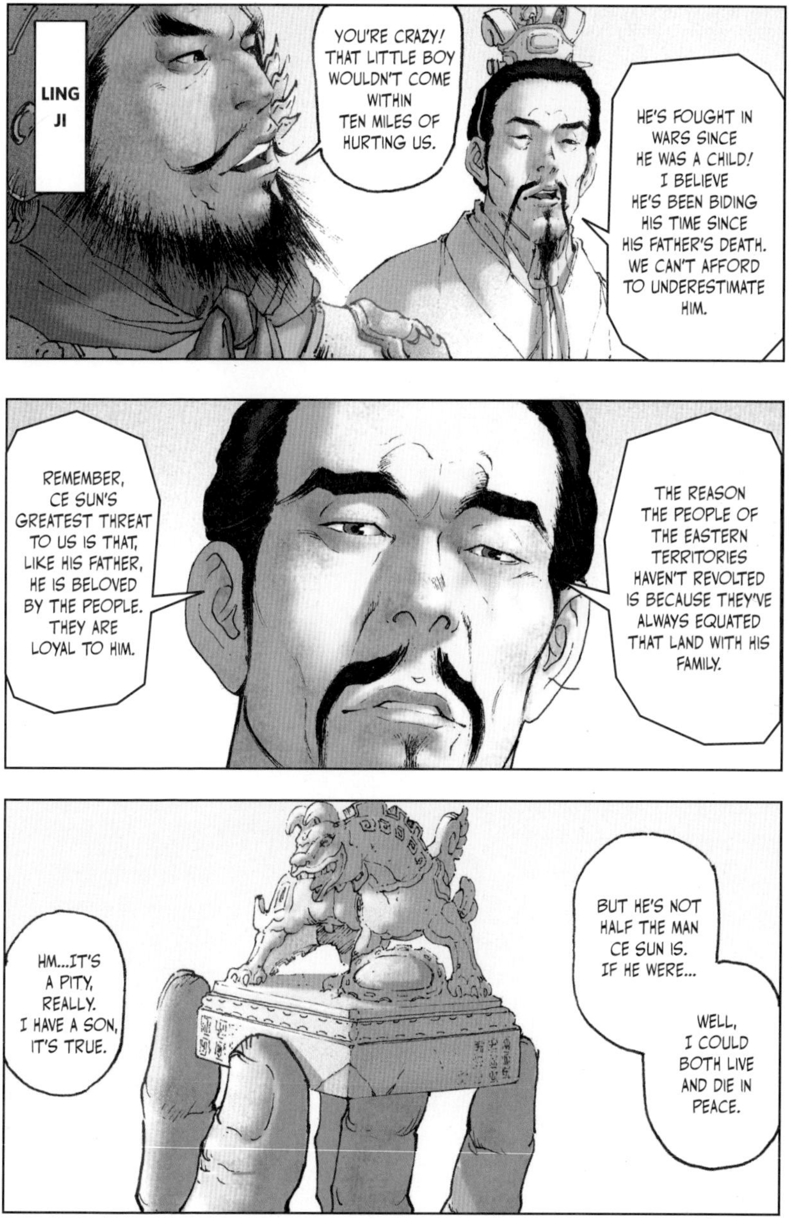
LING JI
YOU'RE CRAZY! THAT LITTLE BOY WOULDN'T COME WITHIN TEN MILES OF HURTING US.
HE'S FOUGHT IN WARS SINCE HE WAS A CHILD! I BELIEVE HE'S BEEN BIDING HIS TIME SINCE HIS FATHER'S DEATH. WE CAN'T AFFORD TO UNDERESTIMATE HIM.
THE REASON THE PEOPLE OF THE EASTERN TERRITORIES HAVEN'T REVOLTED IS BECAUSE THEY'VE ALWAYS EQUATED THAT LAND WITH HIS FAMILY.
REMEMBER, CE SUN'S GREATEST THREAT TO US IS THAT, LIKE HIS FATHER, HE IS BELOVED BY THE PEOPLE. THEY ARE LOYAL TO HIM.
BUT HE'S NOT HALF THE MAN CE SUN IS. IF HE WERE...
WELL, I COULD BOTH LIVE AND DIE IN PEACE.
HM...IT'S A PITY, REALLY. I HAVE A SON, IT'S TRUE.

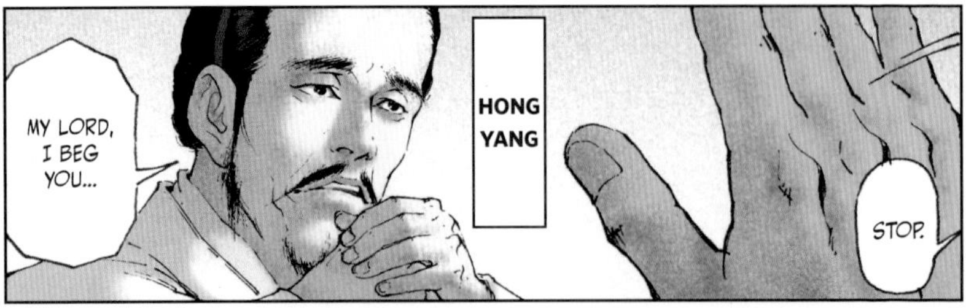
MY LORD, I BEG YOU...
HONG YANG
STOP.

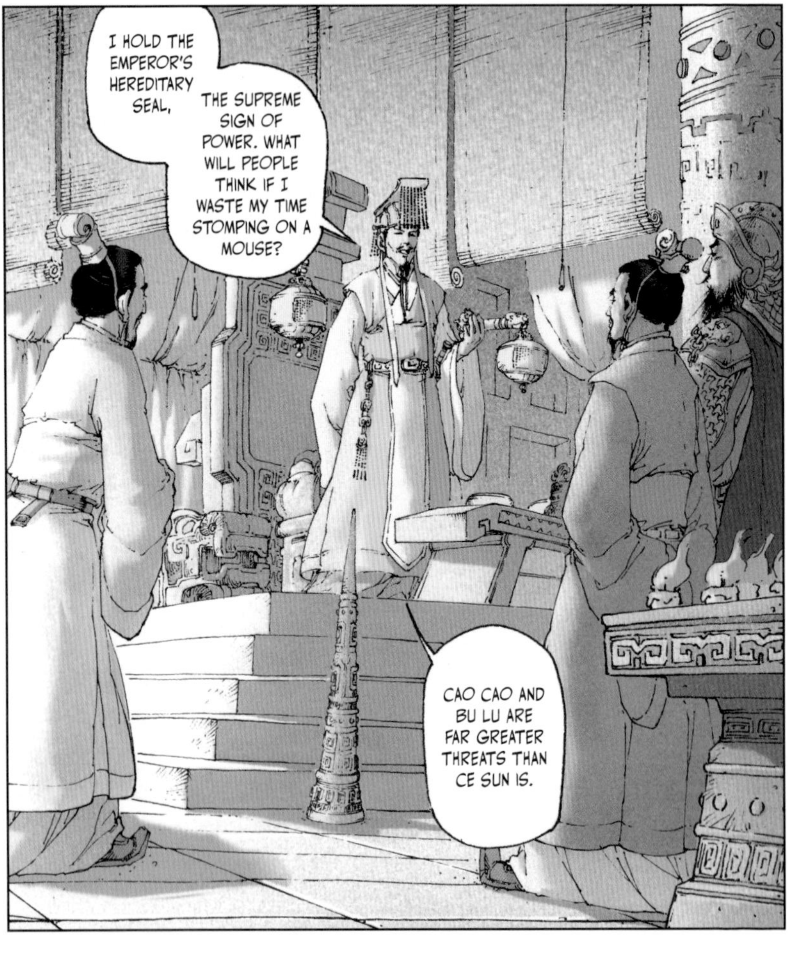
I HOLD THE EMPEROR'S HEREDITARY SEAL,
THE SUPREME SIGN OF POWER. WHAT WILL PEOPLE THINK IF I WASTE MY TIME STOMPING ON A MOUSE?
CAO CAO AND BU LU ARE FAR GREATER THREATS THAN CE SUN IS.

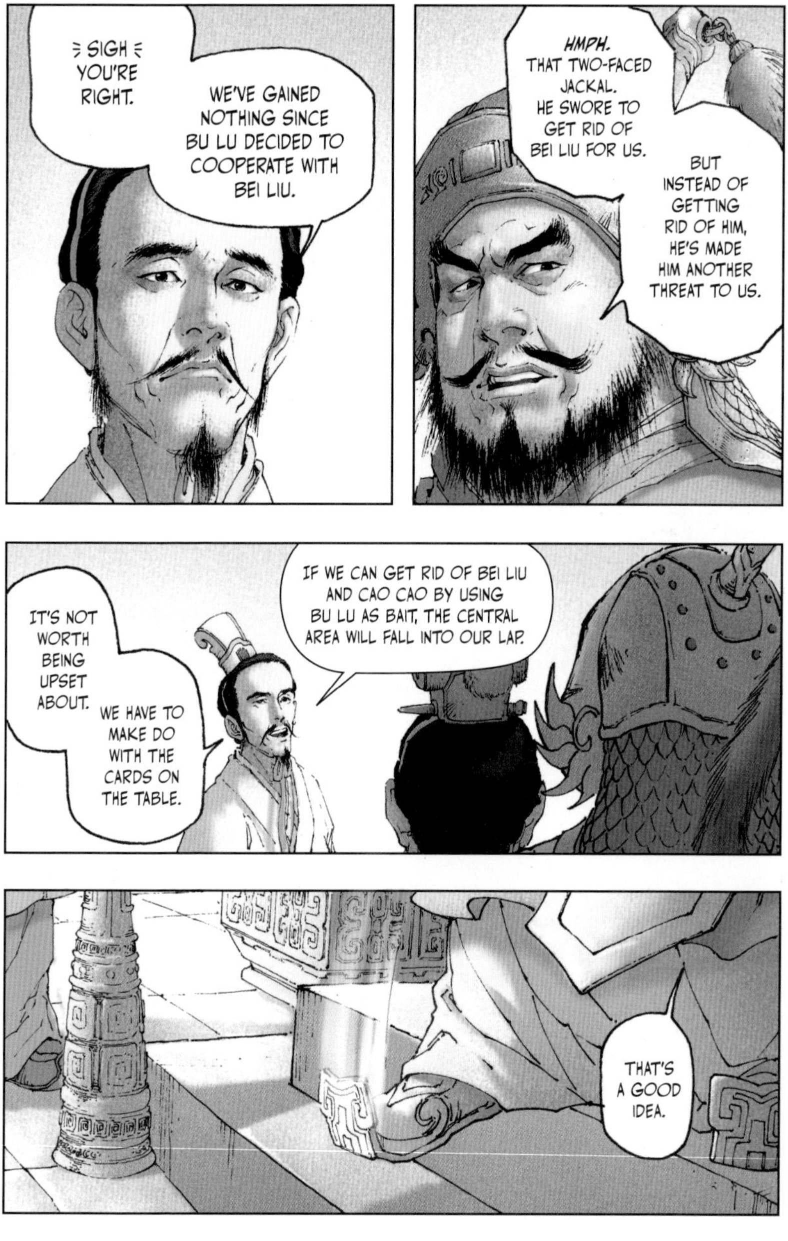
≶ SIGH ≶ YOU'RE RIGHT.
WE'VE GAINED NOTHING SINCE BU LU DECIDED TO COOPERATE WITH BEI LIU.
HMPH. THAT TWO-FACED JACKAL. HE SWORE TO GET RID OF BEI LIU FOR US.
BUT INSTEAD OF GETTING RID OF HIM, HE'S MADE HIM ANOTHER THREAT TO US.
IT'S NOT WORTH BEING UPSET ABOUT.
WE HAVE TO MAKE DO WITH THE CARDS ON THE TABLE.
IF WE CAN GET RID OF BEI LIU AND CAO CAO BY USING BU LU AS BAIT, THE CENTRAL AREA WILL FALL INTO OUR LAP.
THAT'S A GOOD IDEA.

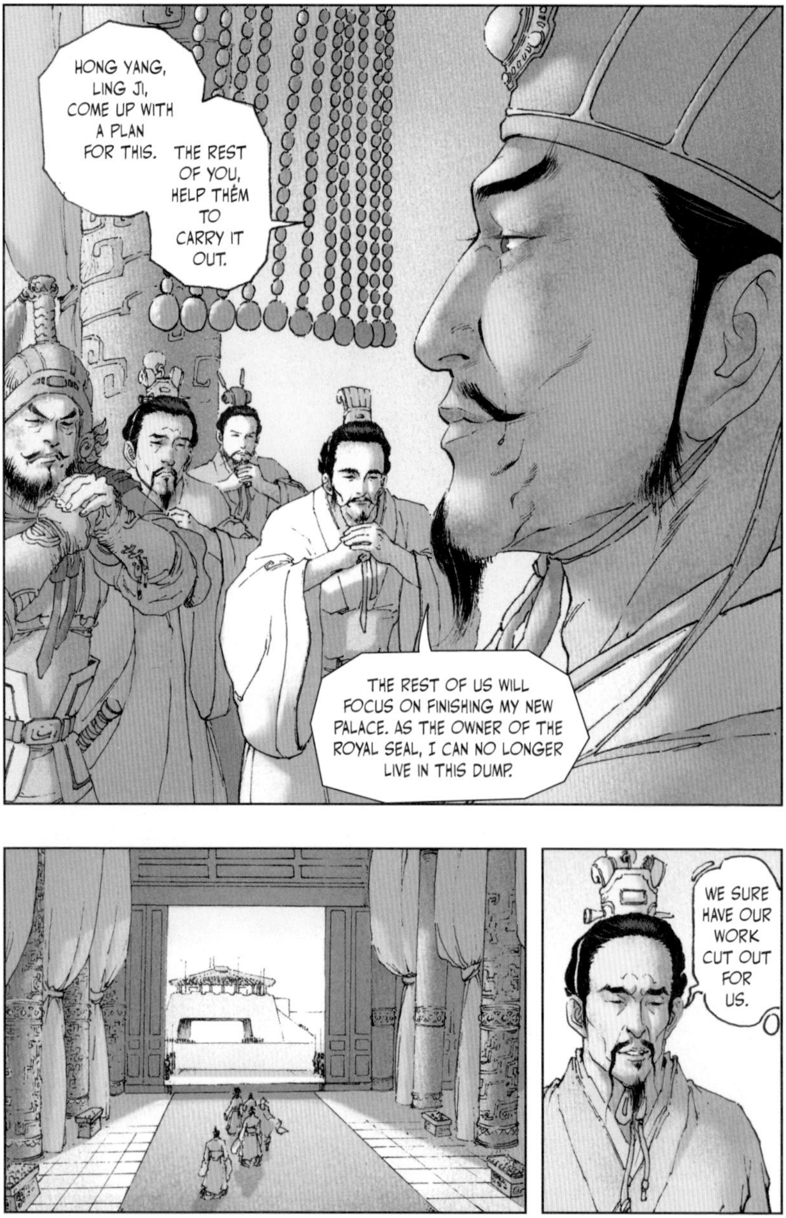
HONG YANG, LING JI, COME UP WITH A PLAN FOR THIS.
THE REST OF YOU, HELP THEM TO CARRY IT OUT.
THE REST OF US WILL FOCUS ON FINISHING MY NEW PALACE. AS THE OWNER OF THE ROYAL SEAL, I CAN NO LONGER LIVE IN THIS DUMP.
WE SURE HAVE OUR WORK CUT OUT FOR US.

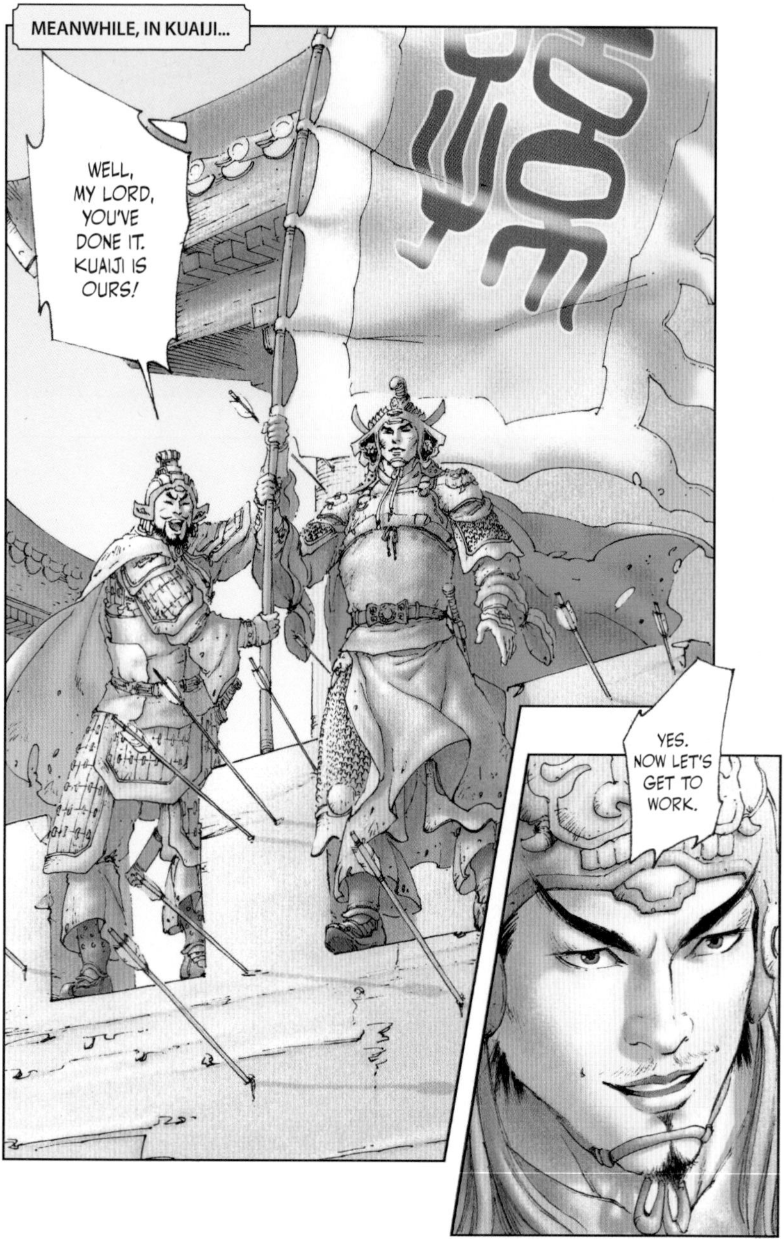
MEANWHILE, IN KUAIJI...
WELL, MY LORD, YOU'VE DONE IT. KUAIJI IS OURS!
YES. NOW LET'S GET TO WORK.

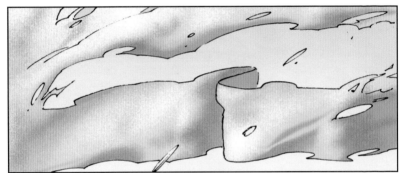

TAI ZHOU

CI TAISHI

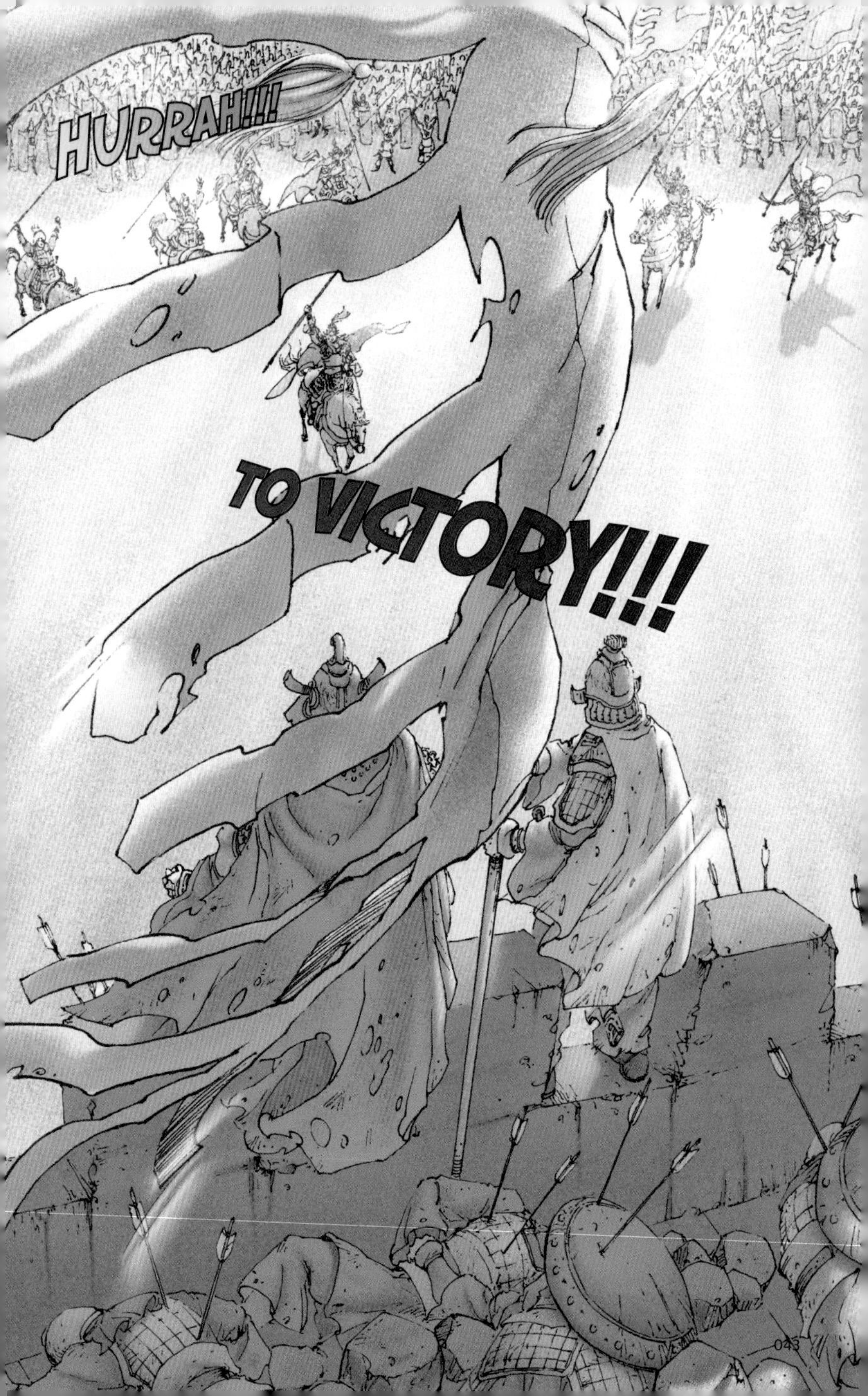
HURRAH!!!
TO VICTORY!!!

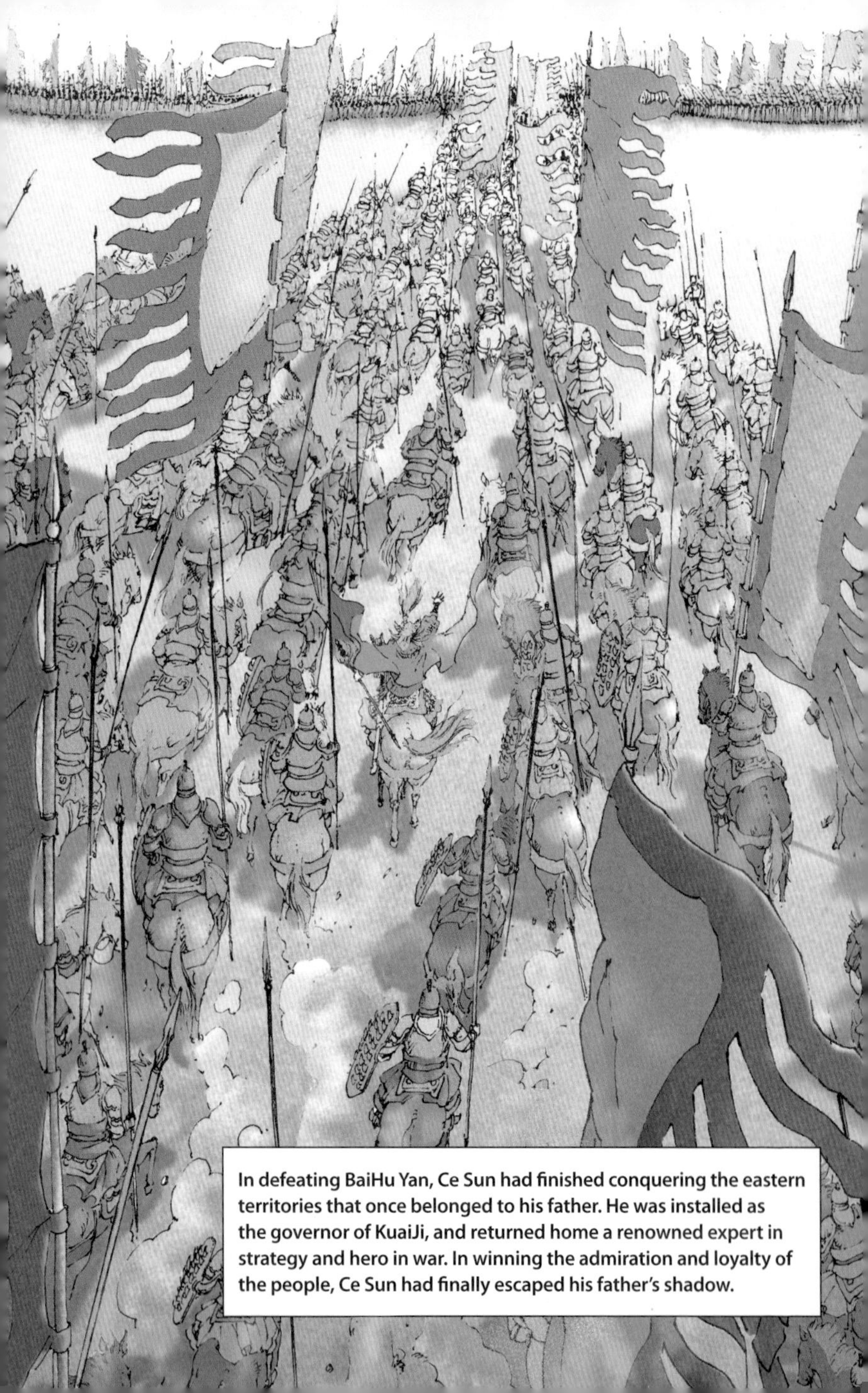
In defeating BaiHu Yan, Ce Sun had finished conquering the eastern territories that once belonged to his father. He was installed as the governor of KuaiJi, and returned home a renowned expert in strategy and hero in war. In winning the admiration and loyalty of the people, Ce Sun had finally escaped his father's shadow.

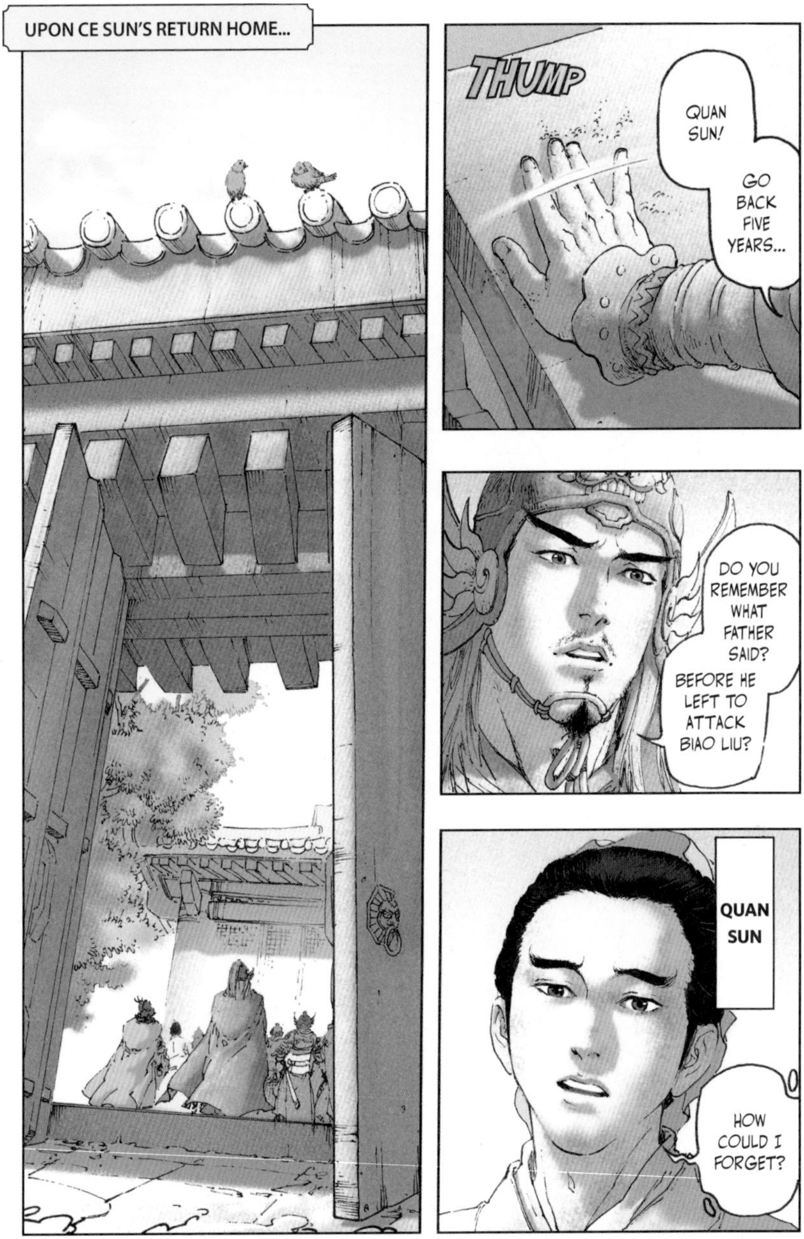
UPON CE SUN'S RETURN HOME...
THUMP
QUAN SUN!
GO BACK FIVE YEARS...
DO YOU REMEMBER WHAT FATHER SAID?
BEFORE HE LEFT TO ATTACK BIAO LIU?
QUAN SUN
HOW COULD I FORGET?

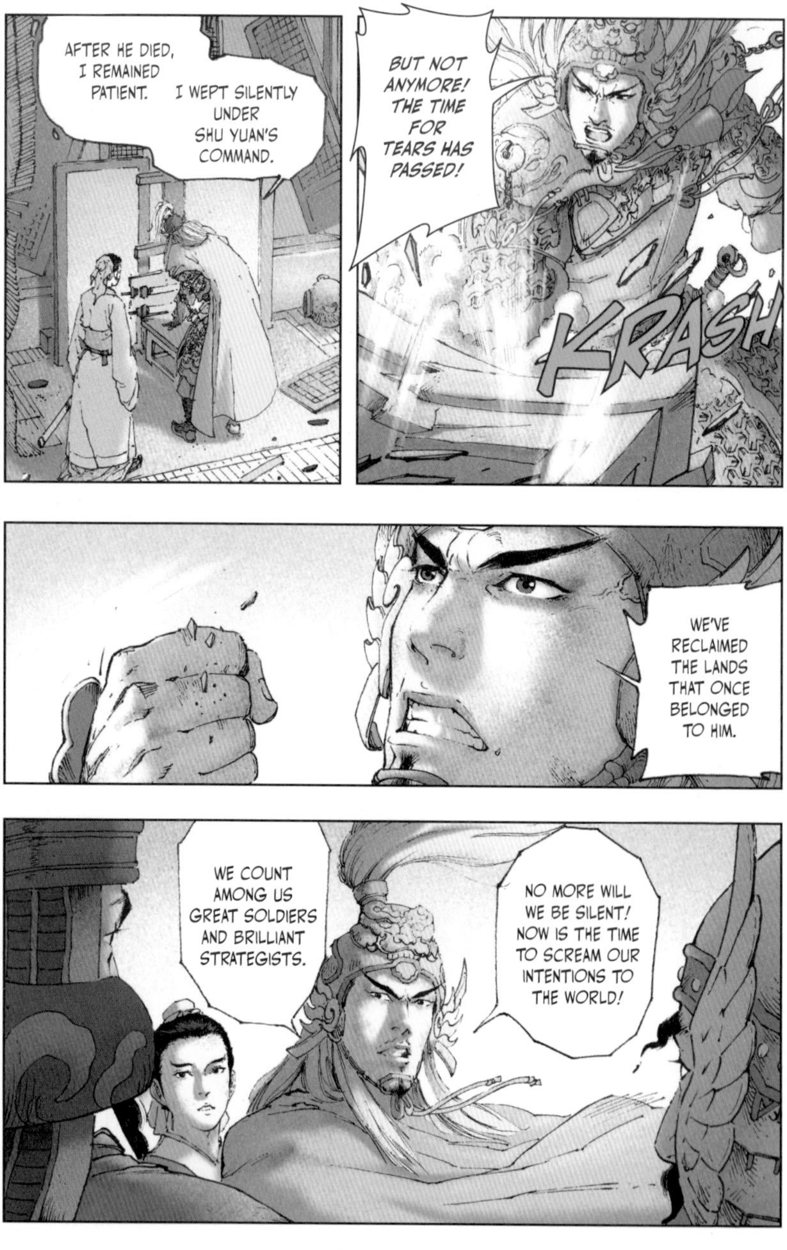
AFTER HE DIED, I REMAINED PATIENT.
I WEPT SILENTLY UNDER SHU YUAN'S COMMAND.
BUT NOT ANYMORE! THE TIME FOR TEARS HAS PASSED!
KRASH
WE'VE RECLAIMED THE LANDS THAT ONCE BELONGED TO HIM.
WE COUNT AMONG US GREAT SOLDIERS AND BRILLIANT STRATEGISTS.
NO MORE WILL WE BE SILENT! NOW IS THE TIME TO SCREAM OUR INTENTIONS TO THE WORLD!

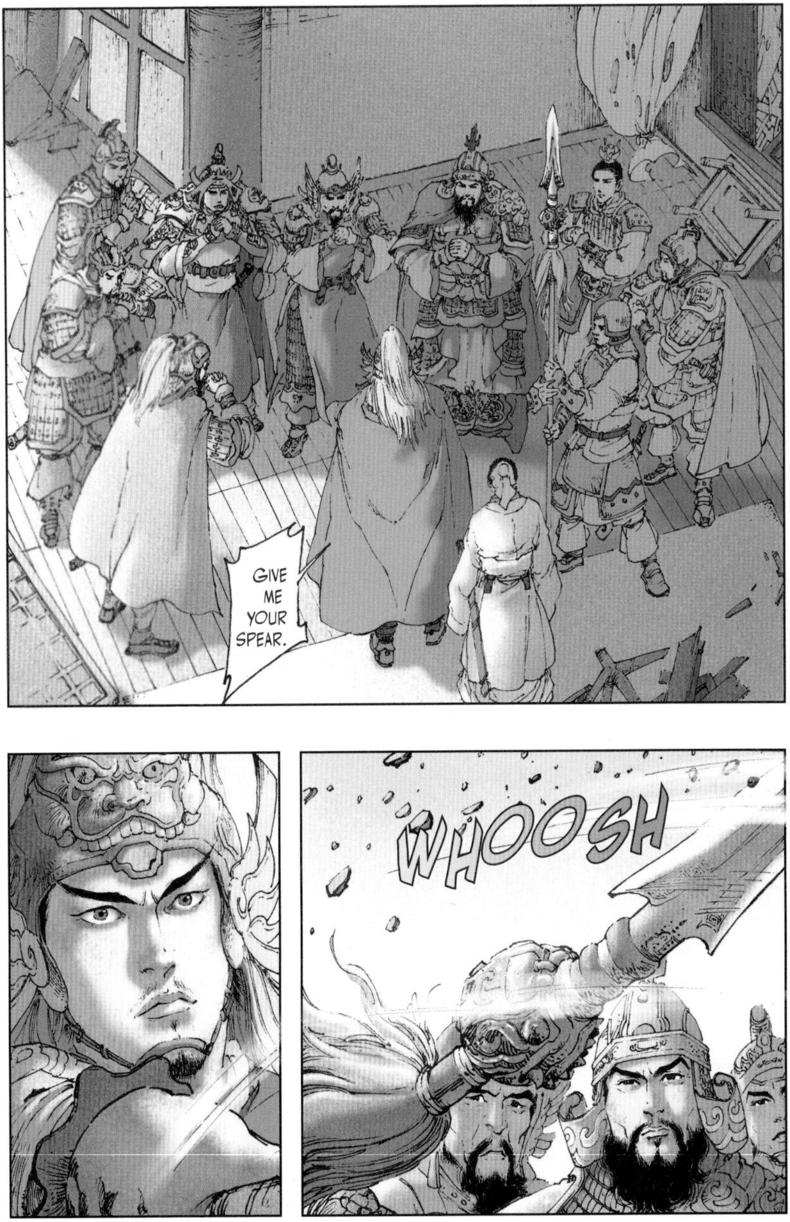
GIVE ME YOUR SPEAR.
WHOOSH

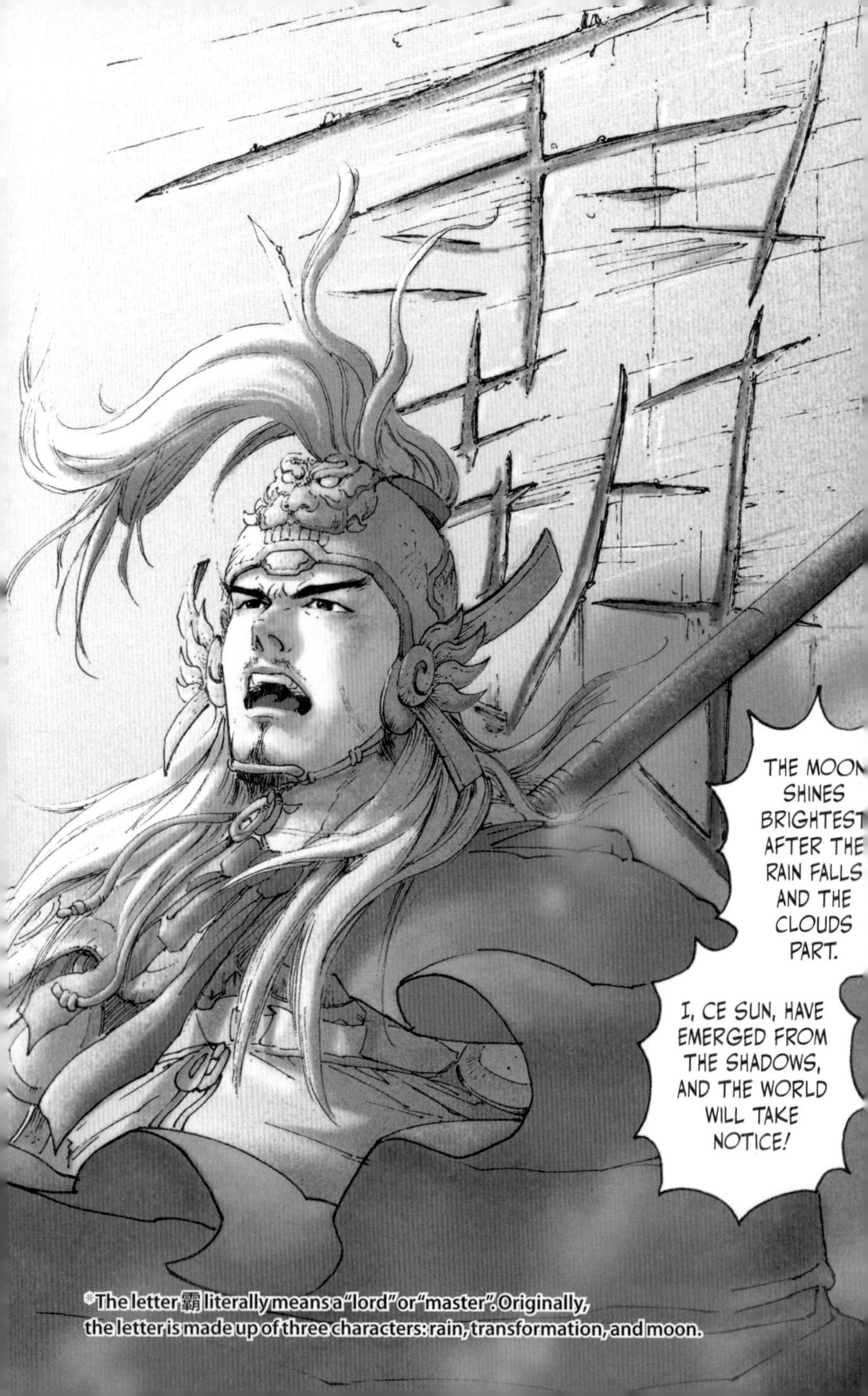
THE MOON SHINES BRIGHTEST AFTER THE RAIN FALLS AND THE CLOUDS PART.
I, CE SUN, HAVE EMERGED FROM THE SHADOWS, AND THE WORLD WILL TAKE NOTICE!

*The letter 覇 literally means a "lord" or "master". Originally, the letter is made up of three characters: rain, transformation, and moon.

CE SUN

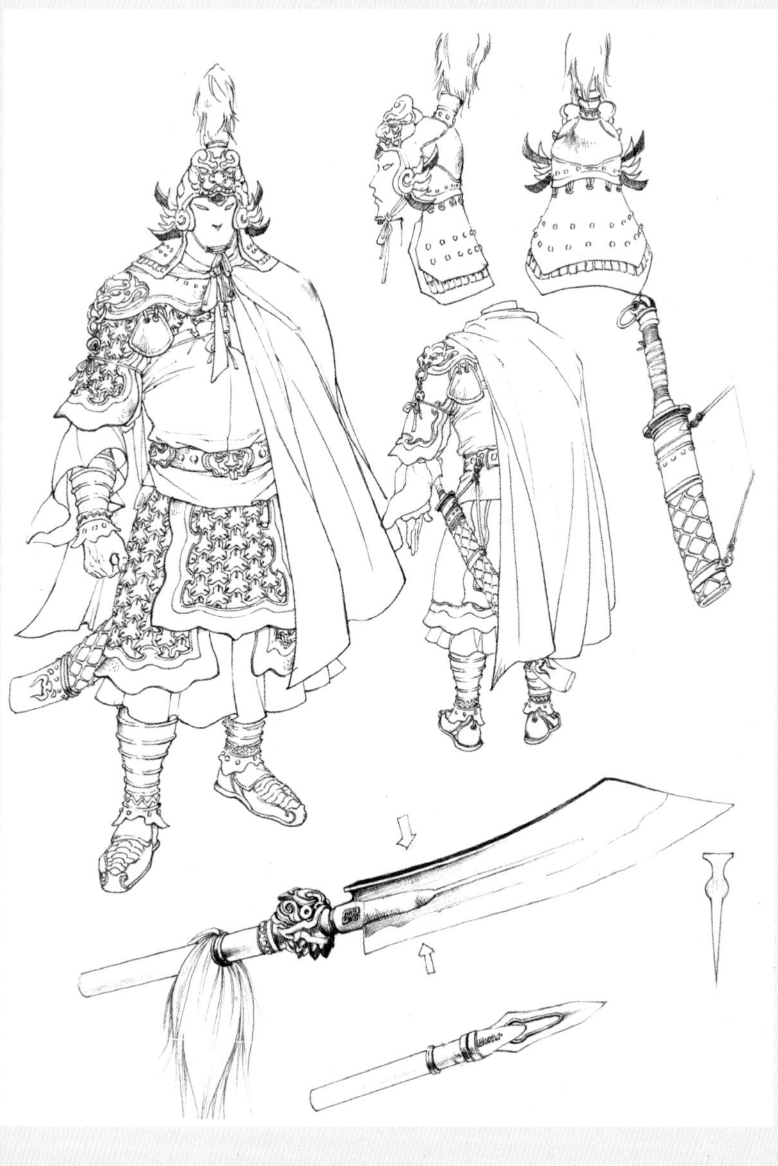

Chapter 2

Bu Lu Drives Bei Liu out of Xu Province ^{AD 196}

Summary

After conceding Xu Province to Bu Lu, Bei Liu takes up residence in XiaoPei with his brothers and advisors to take stock of their situation. The shortage of food and supplies convinces everyone that they would not withstand an attack from Cao Cao. While they are talking, Bu Lu arrives in XiaoPei and surrounds Bei Liu's fortress with his entire army. It turns out Fei Zhang has stolen several horses, but this is not the true reason for Bu Lu's attack. The true reason is that Bu Lu wants to be rid of Bei Liu, whom he sees as a threat. Bei Liu exits the palace and attempts to reason with Bu Lu's forces, but his efforts are in vain and a fight ensues.

Bei Liu is driven back into the palace, and Bu Lu's chief counselor, Gong Chen, advises an immediate attack to eliminate Bei Liu. But Bu Lu instead orders an attack for the following morning, allowing Bei Liu precious time to escape under cover of darkness. Bei Liu escapes along with his brothers and his men, and heads to the lands ruled by Cao Cao in the hopes of forming a new alliance.

ChangShan
BeiHai
PuYang
HuLuo
B
XiaoPei
GuanDu
A
LuoYang
XuZhou
ChangAn
XuChang
NanYang
ShouChun
HeFei
XiangYang

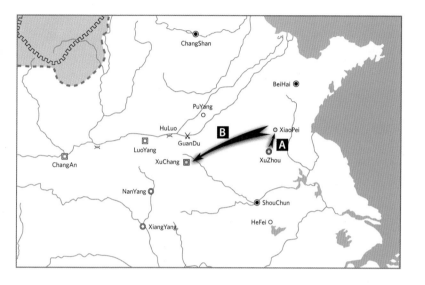

A Bu Lu determines that Bei Liu might join forces with Cao Cao, thus becoming a threat, so he leads his army to XiaoPei to attack Bei Liu.

B Bei Liu escapes under cover of darkness and makes his way toward XuChang, where he plans to ask Cao Cao for help.

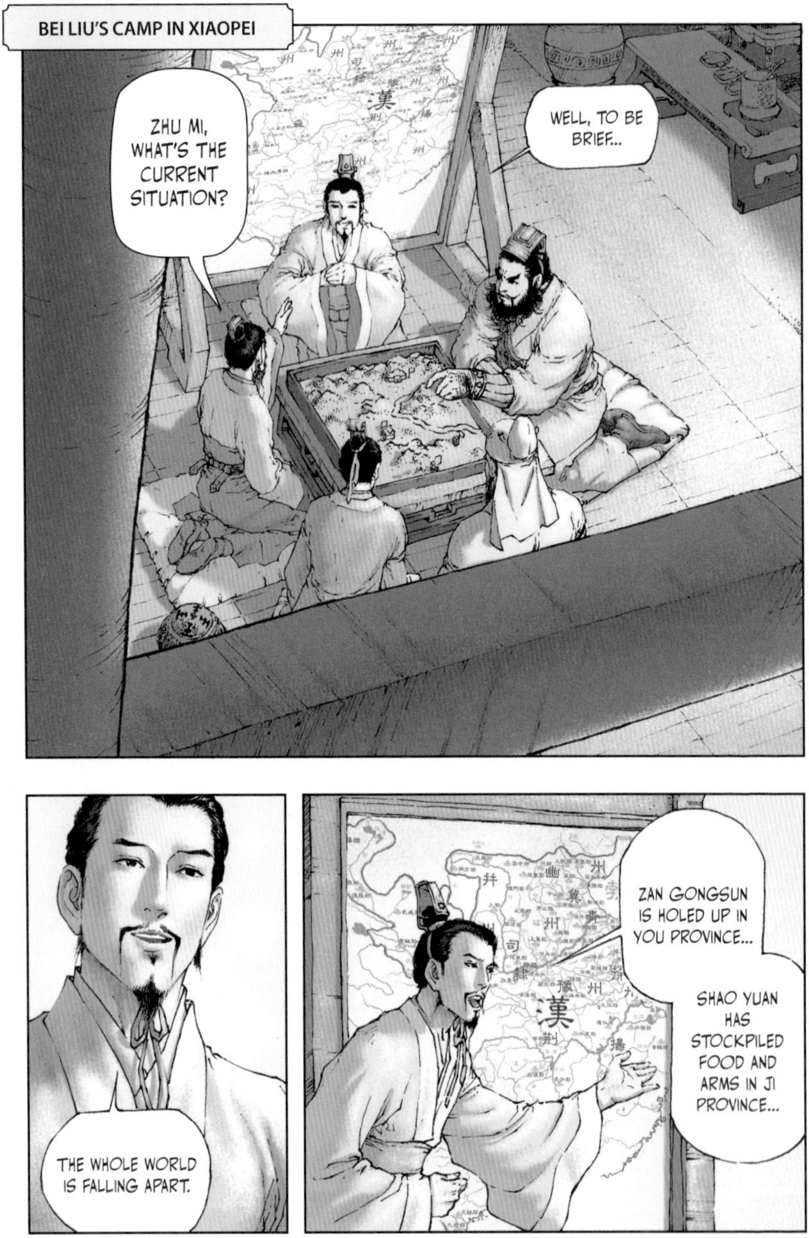
BEI LIU'S CAMP IN XIAOPEI
ZHU MI, WHAT'S THE CURRENT SITUATION?
WELL, TO BE BRIEF...
THE WHOLE WORLD IS FALLING APART.
ZAN GONGSUN IS HOLED UP IN YOU PROVINCE...
SHAO YUAN HAS STOCKPILED FOOD AND ARMS IN JI PROVINCE...

CAO CAO HAS INCREASED HIS POWER AND NOW CONTROLS THE CENTRAL PROVINCES...

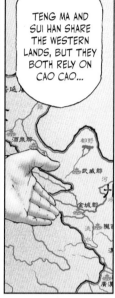

TENG MA AND SUI HAN SHARE THE WESTERN LANDS, BUT THEY BOTH RELY ON CAO CAO...

ZHANG LIU IS COMING INTO HIS OWN IN YI PROVINCE...

AND LU ZHANG OCCUPIES HANZHONG.

AH, AND DON'T FORGET BIAO LIU. HE HOLDS JING PROVINCE...

AND IT LOOKS LIKE SHU YUAN IS BUILDING A NEW PALACE IN YANG PROVINCE, SO HE'S LIKELY TO STAY PUT.

SPEAKING OF SHU YUAN, CE SUN HAS EMERGED FROM HIS MENTOR'S SHADOW AND TAKEN TERRITORIES IN THE EAST.

I PREDICT IT WON'T BE LONG BEFORE HE GATHERS EVEN MORE FORCES TO MAKE A MOVE ON HIS WESTERN NEIGHBORS.

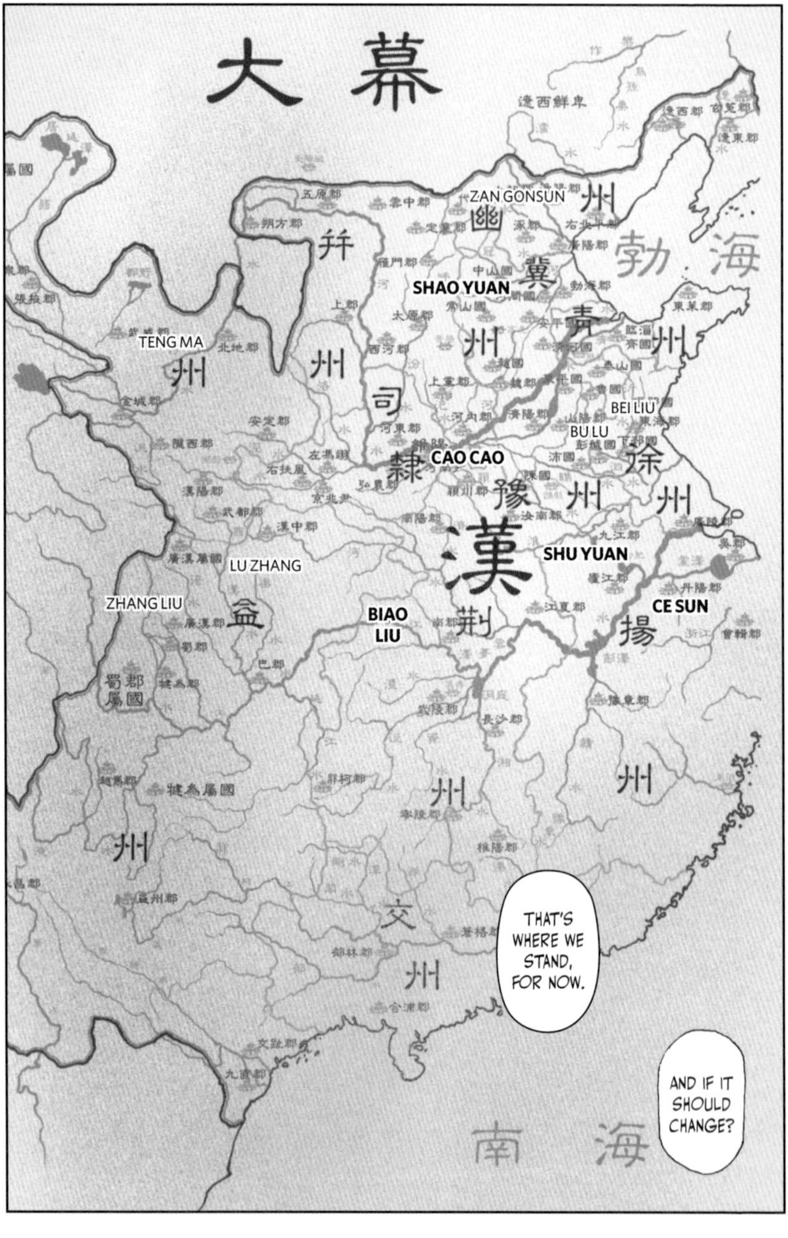

大幕
ZAN GONSUN
SHAO YUAN
TENG MA
BEI LIU
BU LU
CAO CAO
SHU YUAN
LU ZHANG
ZHANG LIU
BIAO
LIU
CE SUN
漢
南 海
THAT'S WHERE WE STAND, FOR NOW.
AND IF IT SHOULD CHANGE?

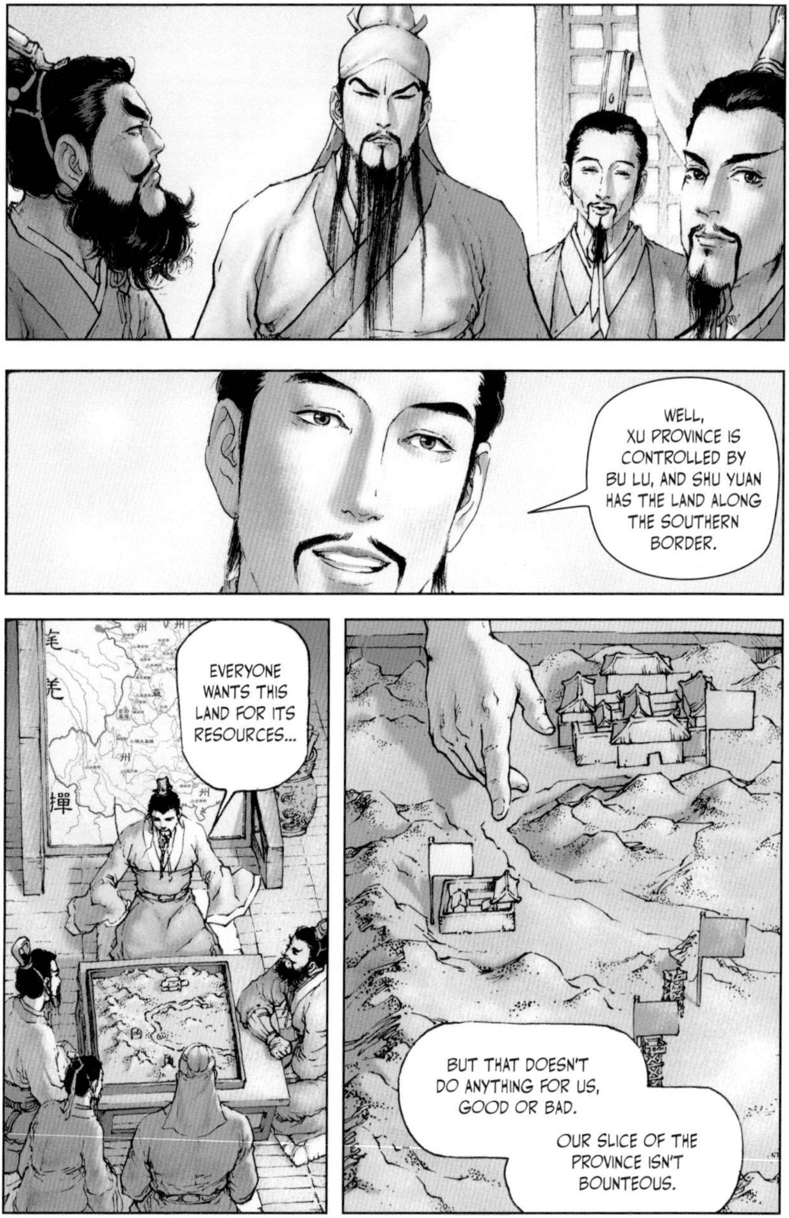
WELL, XU PROVINCE IS CONTROLLED BY BU LU, AND SHU YUAN HAS THE LAND ALONG THE SOUTHERN BORDER.
EVERYONE WANTS THIS LAND FOR ITS RESOURCES...
BUT THAT DOESN'T DO ANYTHING FOR US, GOOD OR BAD.
OUR SLICE OF THE PROVINCE ISN'T BOUNTEOUS.

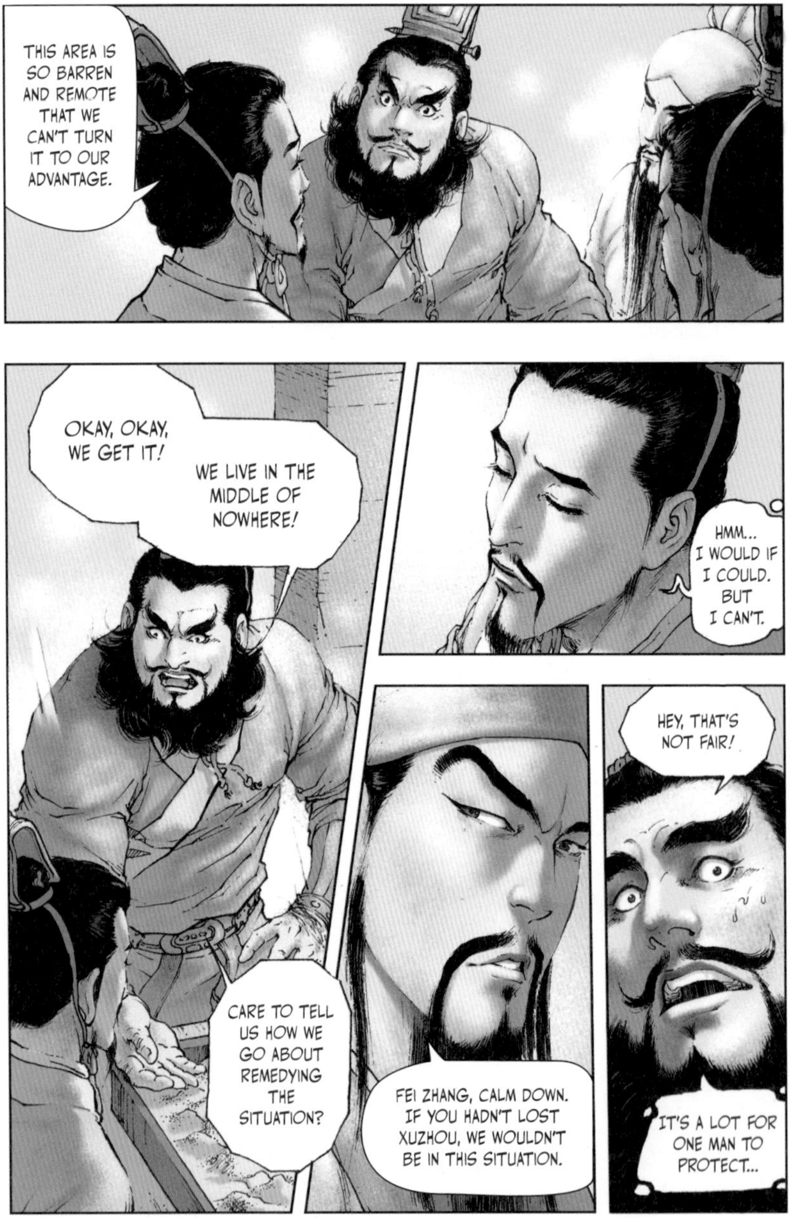
THIS AREA IS SO BARREN AND REMOTE THAT WE CAN'T TURN IT TO OUR ADVANTAGE.
OKAY, OKAY, WE GET IT!
WE LIVE IN THE MIDDLE OF NOWHERE!
CARE TO TELL US HOW WE GO ABOUT REMEDYING THE SITUATION?
HMM... I WOULD IF I COULD. BUT I CAN'T.
FEI ZHANG, CALM DOWN. IF YOU HADN'T LOST XUZHOU, WE WOULDN'T BE IN THIS SITUATION.
HEY, THAT'S NOT FAIR!
IT'S A LOT FOR ONE MAN TO PROTECT...

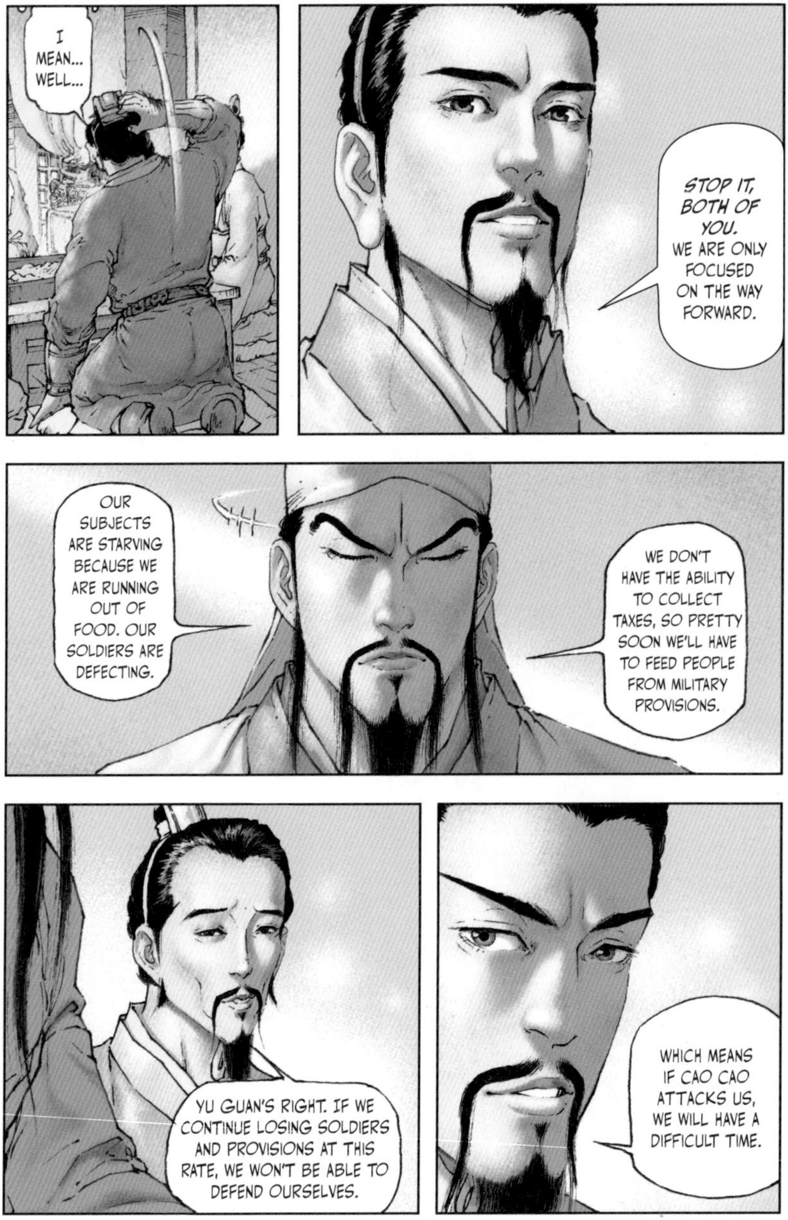
I MEAN... WELL...
STOP IT, BOTH OF YOU. WE ARE ONLY FOCUSED ON THE WAY FORWARD.
OUR SUBJECTS ARE STARVING BECAUSE WE ARE RUNNING OUT OF FOOD. OUR SOLDIERS ARE DEFECTING.
WE DON'T HAVE THE ABILITY TO COLLECT TAXES, SO PRETTY SOON WE'LL HAVE TO FEED PEOPLE FROM MILITARY PROVISIONS.
YU GUAN'S RIGHT. IF WE CONTINUE LOSING SOLDIERS AND PROVISIONS AT THIS RATE, WE WON'T BE ABLE TO DEFEND OURSELVES.
WHICH MEANS IF CAO CAO ATTACKS US, WE WILL HAVE A DIFFICULT TIME.

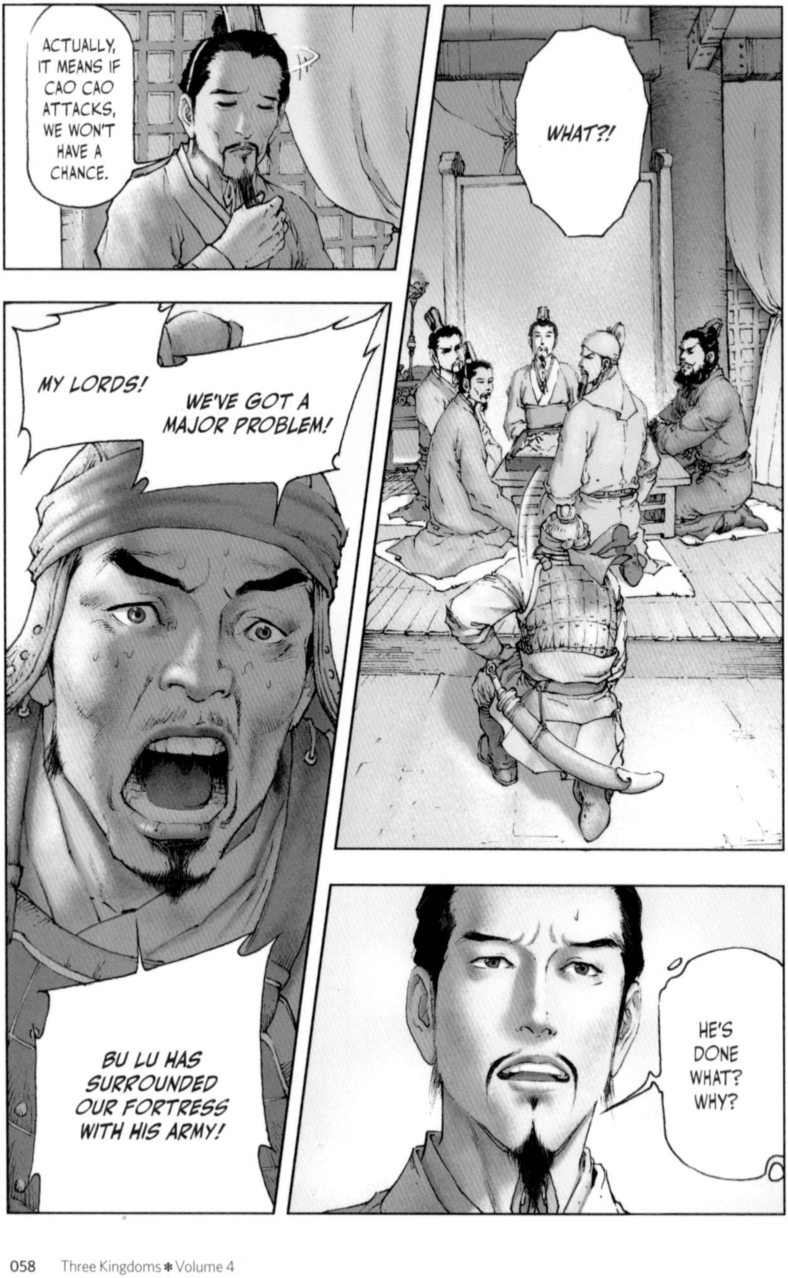

ACTUALLY, IT MEANS IF CAO CAO ATTACKS, WE WON'T HAVE A CHANCE.
WHAT?!
MY LORDS!
WE'VE GOT A MAJOR PROBLEM!
BU LU HAS SURROUNDED OUR FORTRESS WITH HIS ARMY!
HE'S DONE WHAT? WHY?

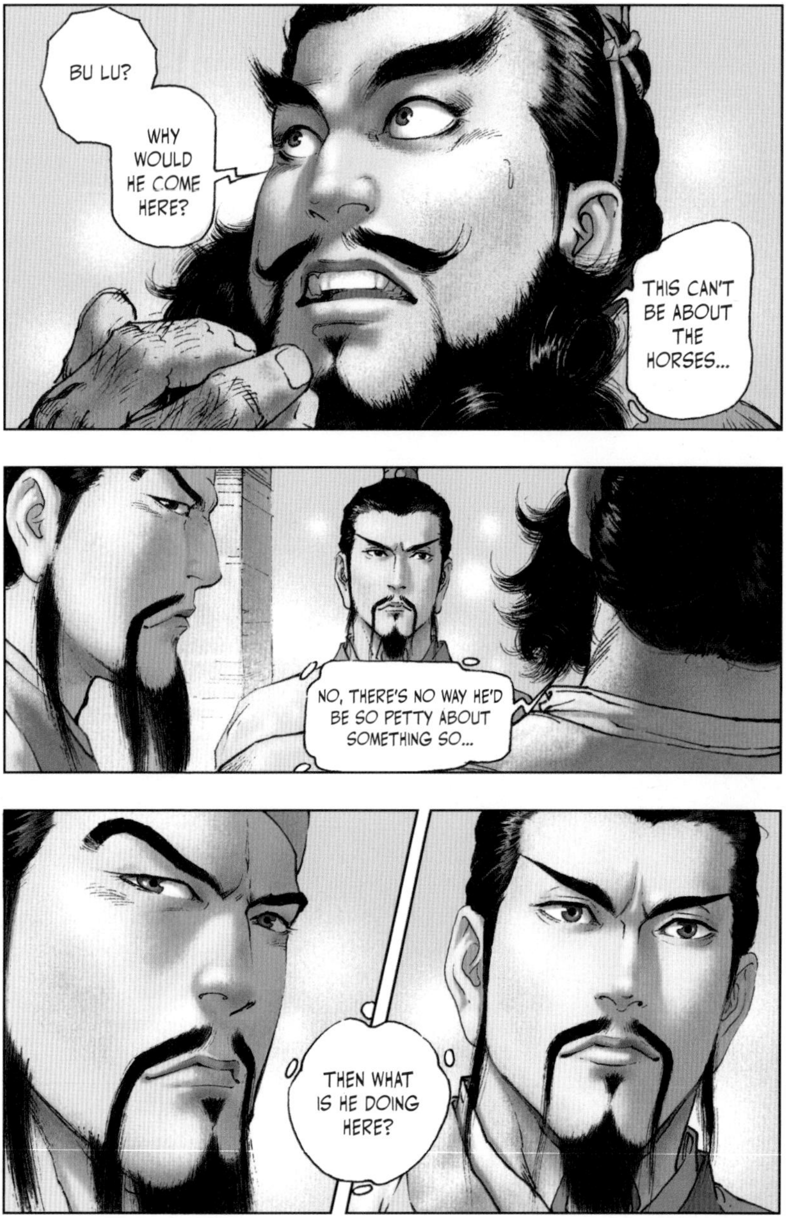
BU LU?
WHY WOULD HE COME HERE?
THIS CAN'T BE ABOUT THE HORSES...
NO, THERE'S NO WAY HE'D BE SO PETTY ABOUT SOMETHING SO...
THEN WHAT IS HE DOING HERE?

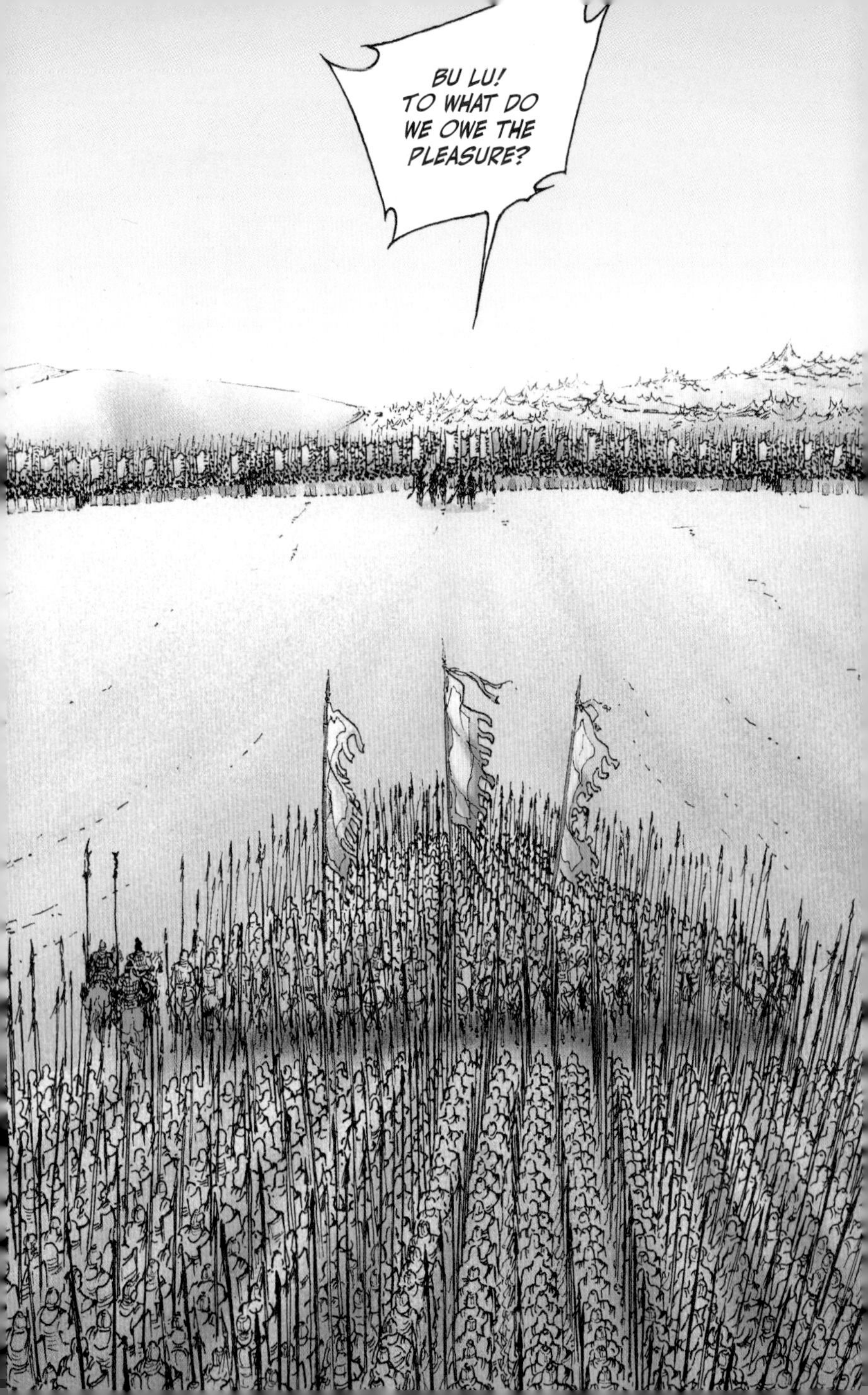
BU LU! TO WHAT DO WE OWE THE PLEASURE?

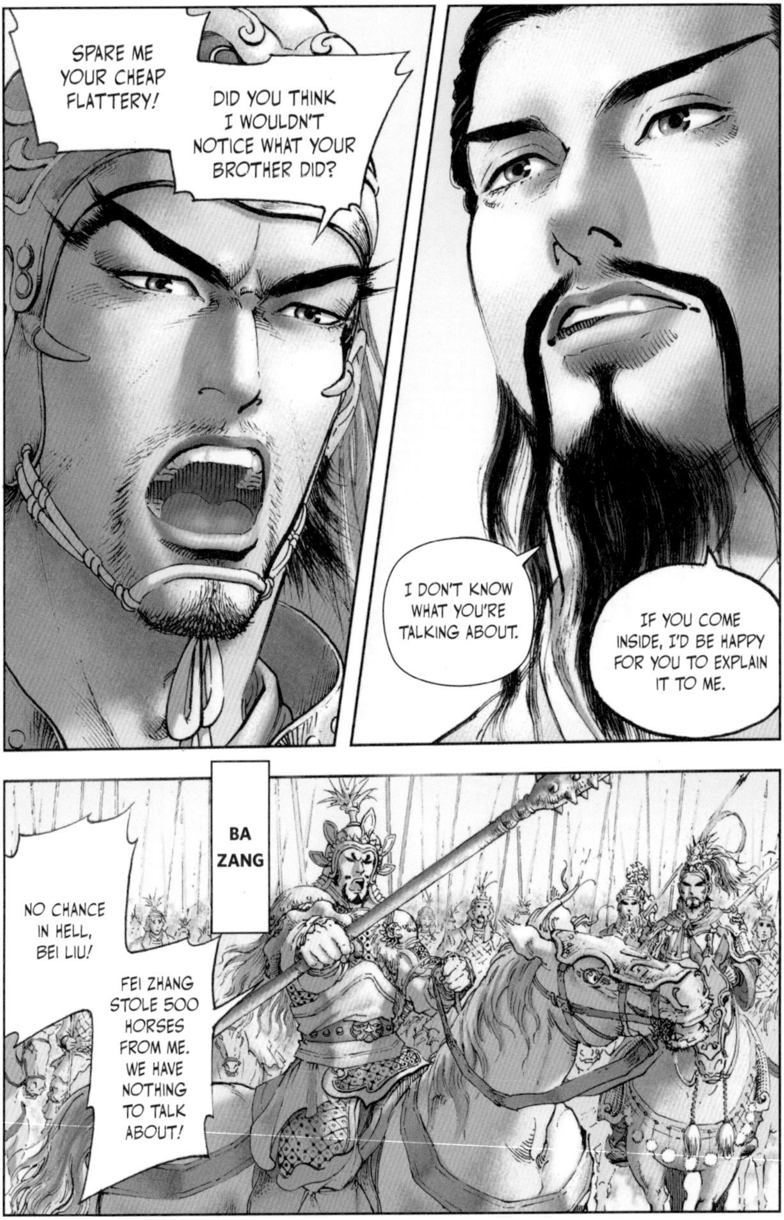
SPARE ME YOUR CHEAP FLATTERY!
DID YOU THINK I WOULDN'T NOTICE WHAT YOUR BROTHER DID?
I DON'T KNOW WHAT YOU'RE TALKING ABOUT.
IF YOU COME INSIDE, I'D BE HAPPY FOR YOU TO EXPLAIN IT TO ME.
BA ZANG
NO CHANCE IN HELL, BEI LIU!
FEI ZHANG STOLE 500 HORSES FROM ME. WE HAVE NOTHING TO TALK ABOUT!

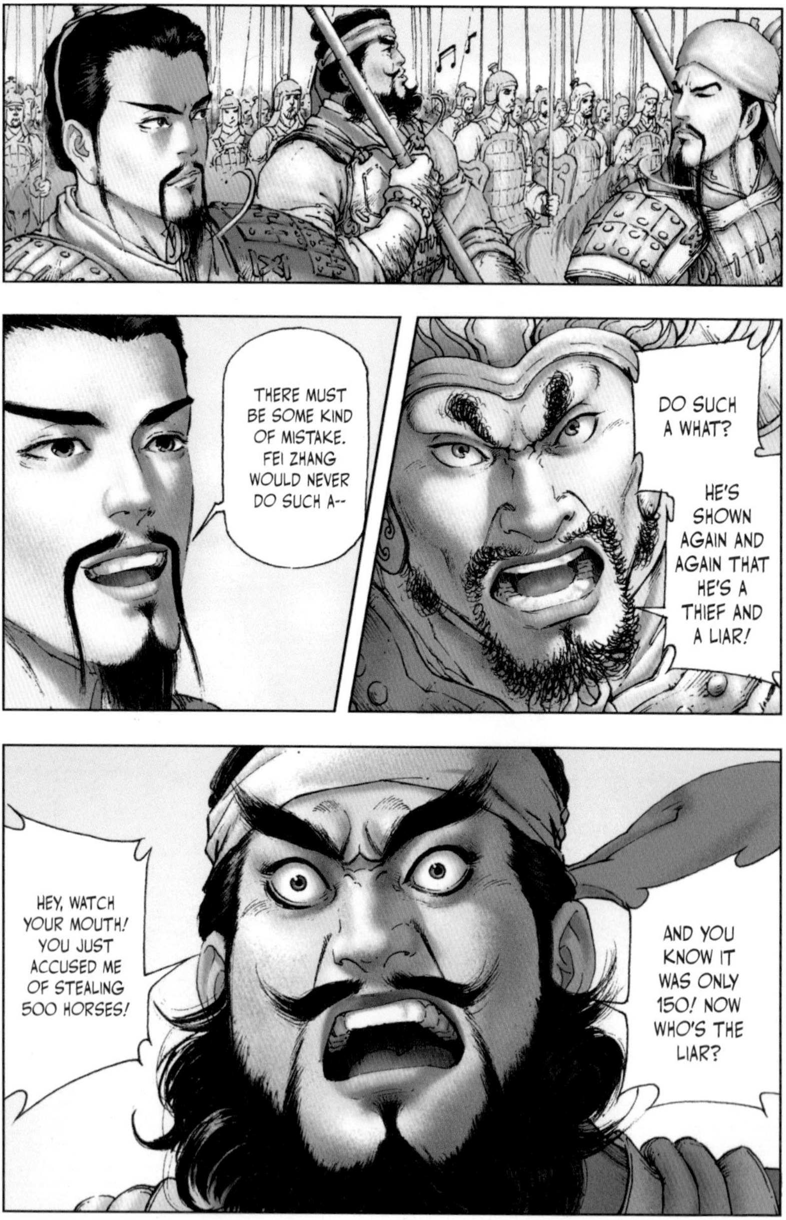
THERE MUST BE SOME KIND OF MISTAKE. FEI ZHANG WOULD NEVER DO SUCH A--
DO SUCH A WHAT?
HE'S SHOWN AGAIN AND AGAIN THAT HE'S A THIEF AND A LIAR!
HEY, WATCH YOUR MOUTH! YOU JUST ACCUSED ME OF STEALING 500 HORSES!
AND YOU KNOW IT WAS ONLY 150! NOW WHO'S THE LIAR?

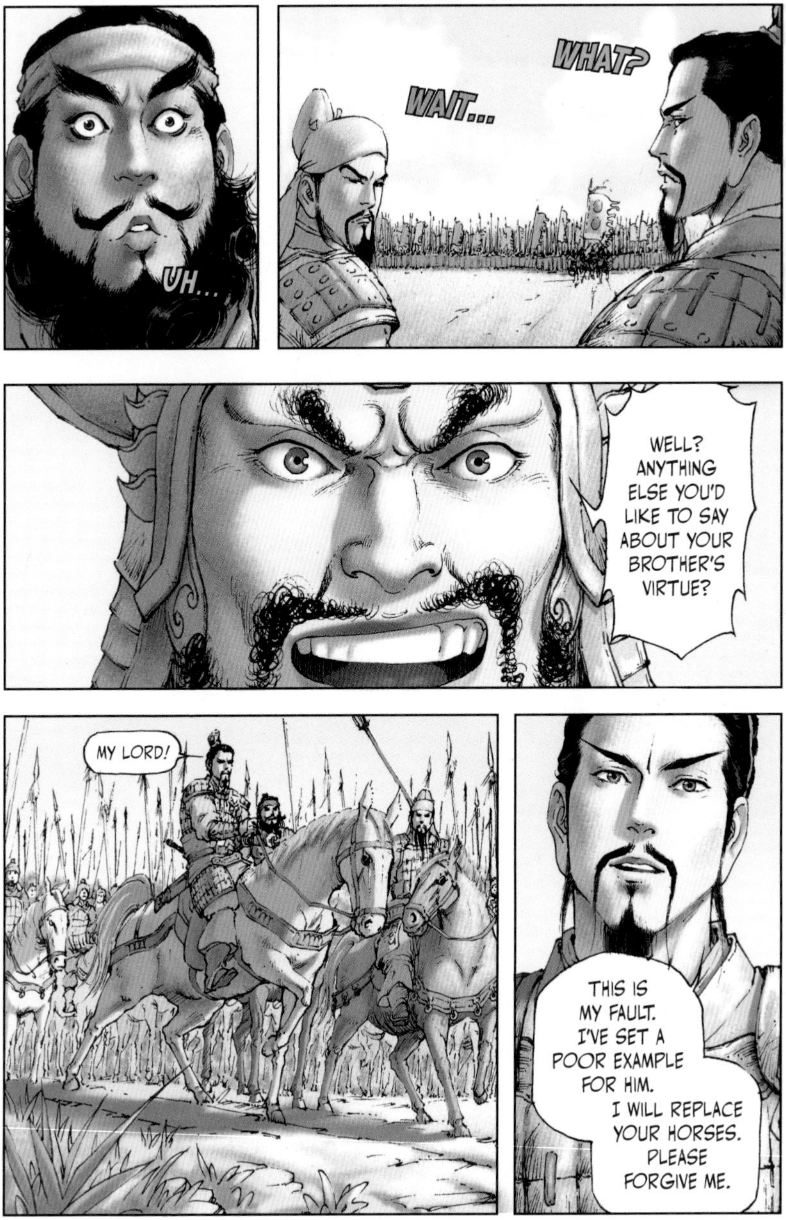
UH...
WAIT...
WHAT?
WELL? ANYTHING ELSE YOU'D LIKE TO SAY ABOUT YOUR BROTHER'S VIRTUE?
MY LORD!
THIS IS MY FAULT. I'VE SET A POOR EXAMPLE FOR HIM.
I WILL REPLACE YOUR HORSES. PLEASE FORGIVE ME.

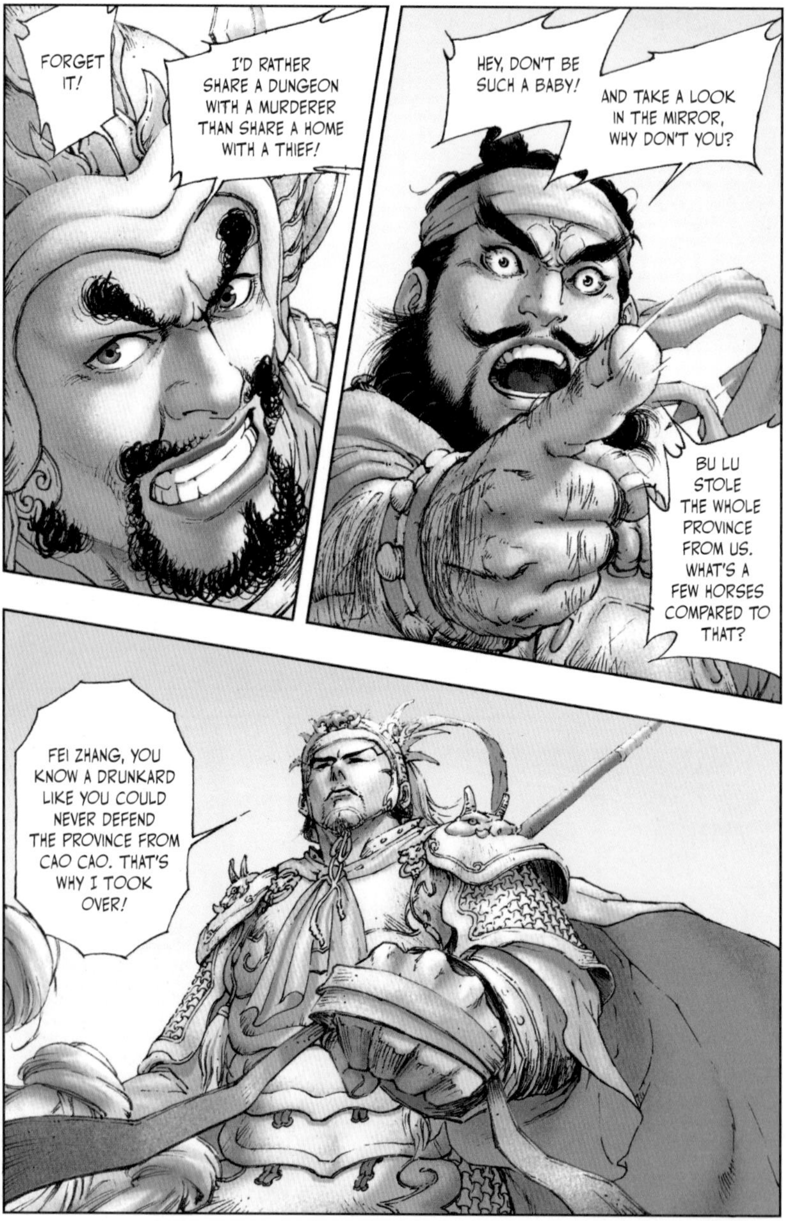
FORGET IT!
I'D RATHER SHARE A DUNGEON WITH A MURDERER THAN SHARE A HOME WITH A THIEF!
HEY, DON'T BE SUCH A BABY!
AND TAKE A LOOK IN THE MIRROR, WHY DON'T YOU?
BU LU STOLE THE WHOLE PROVINCE FROM US. WHAT'S A FEW HORSES COMPARED TO THAT?
FEI ZHANG, YOU KNOW A DRUNKARD LIKE YOU COULD NEVER DEFEND THE PROVINCE FROM CAO CAO. THAT'S WHY I TOOK OVER!

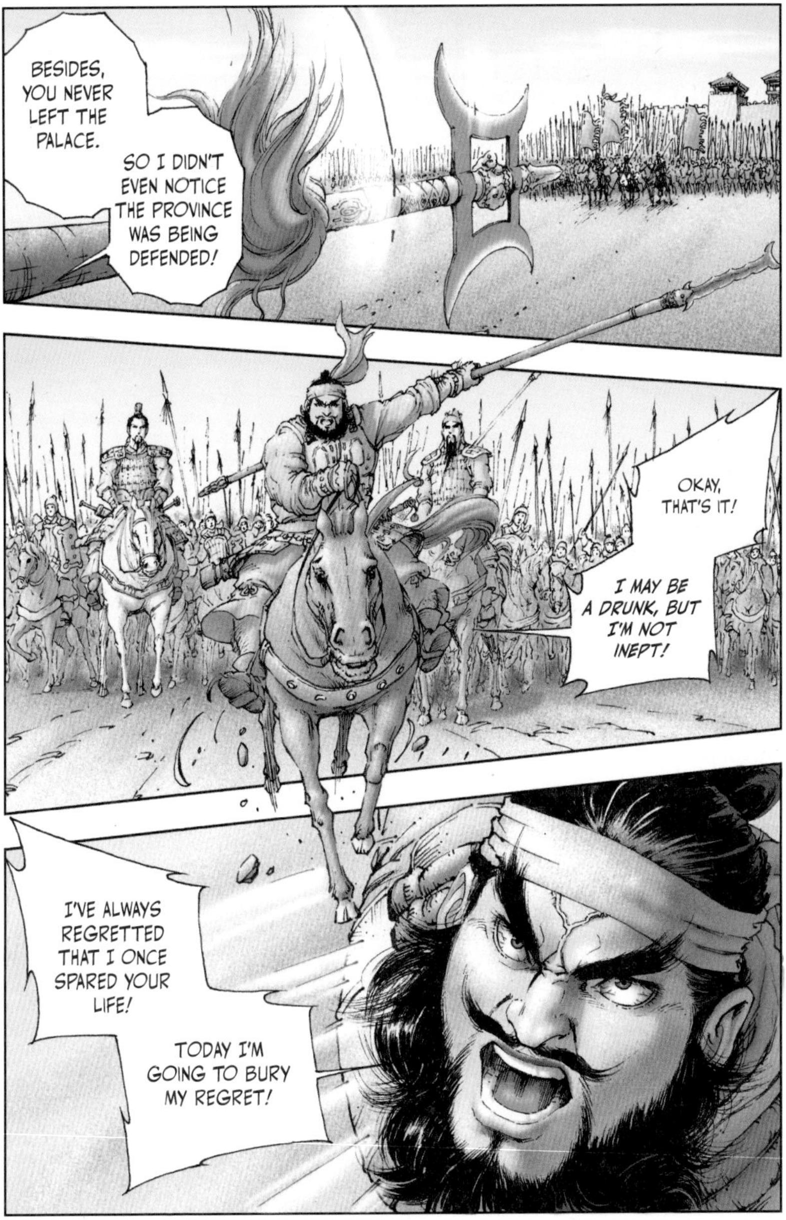
BESIDES, YOU NEVER LEFT THE PALACE.
SO I DIDN'T EVEN NOTICE THE PROVINCE WAS BEING DEFENDED!
OKAY, THAT'S IT!
I MAY BE A DRUNK, BUT I'M NOT INEPT!
I'VE ALWAYS REGRETTED THAT I ONCE SPARED YOUR LIFE!
TODAY I'M GOING TO BURY MY REGRET!

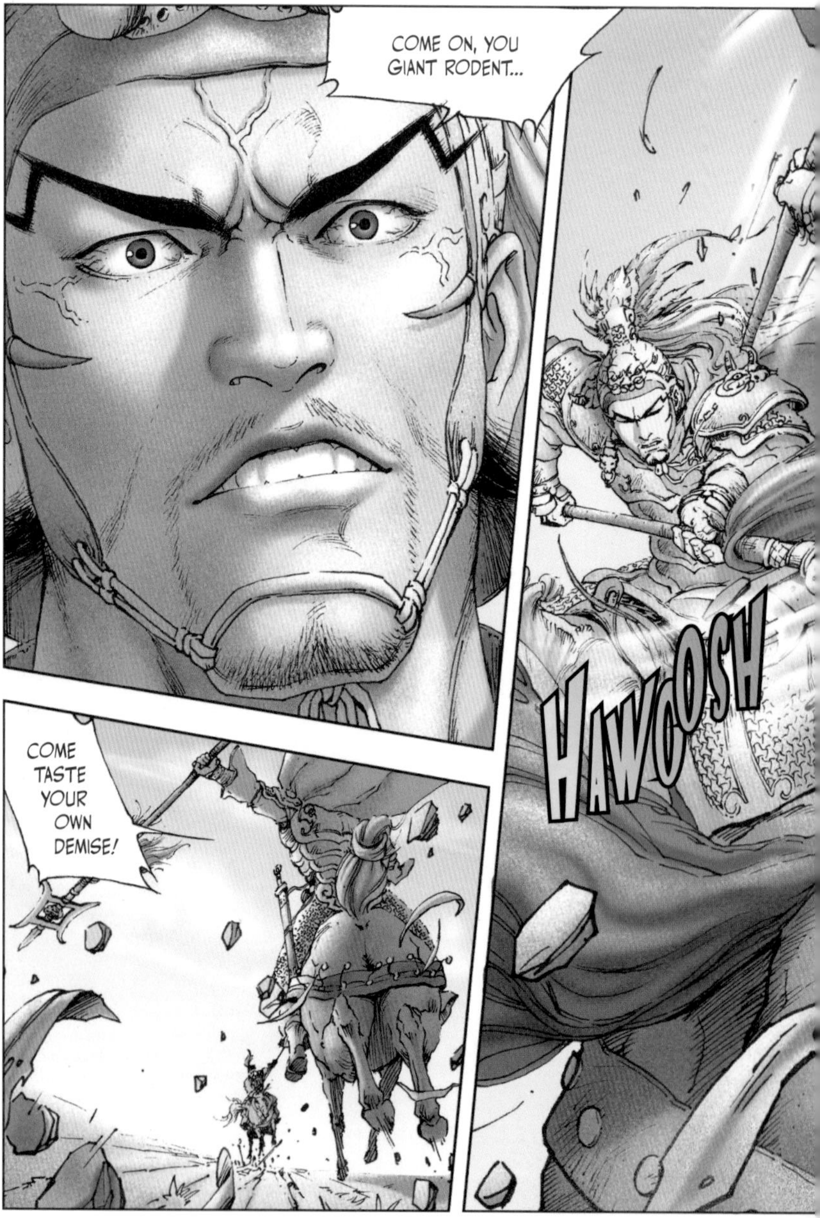
COME ON, YOU GIANT RODENT...
HAWOOSH
COME TASTE YOUR OWN DEMISE!

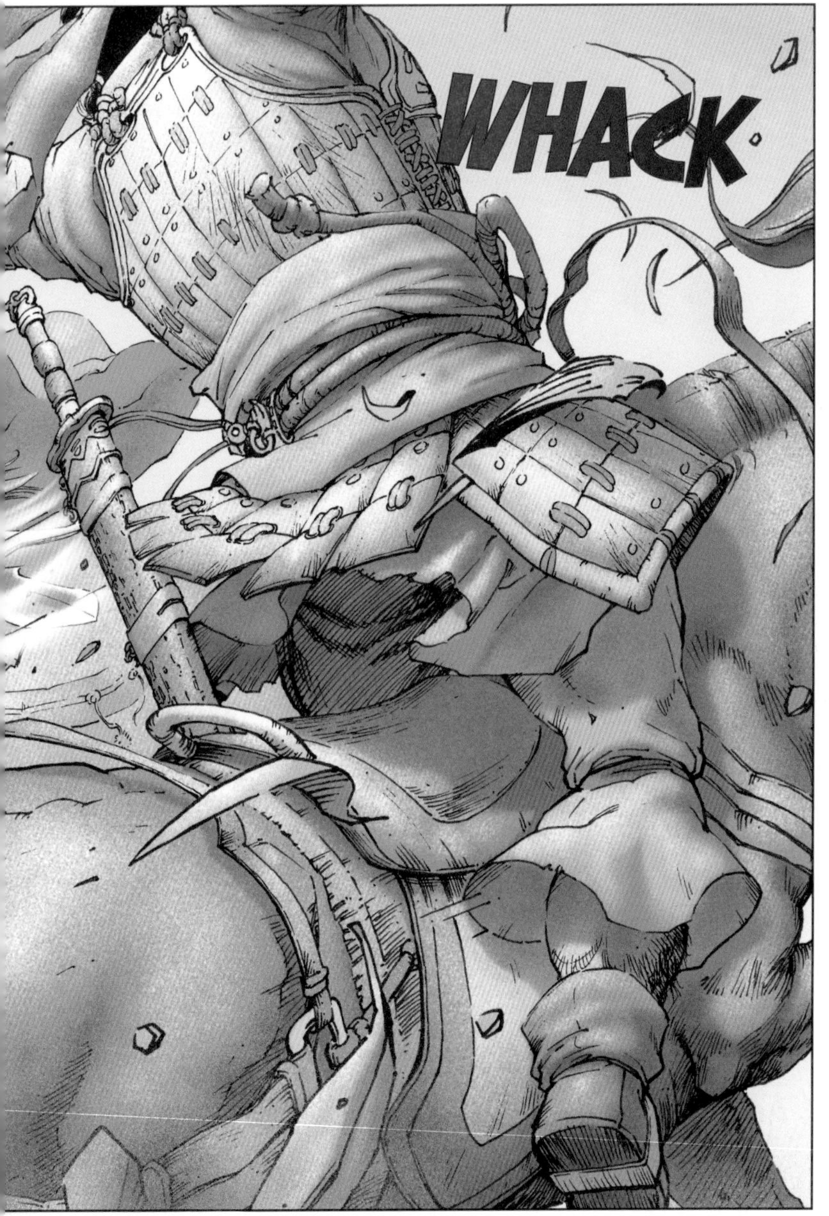
WHACK

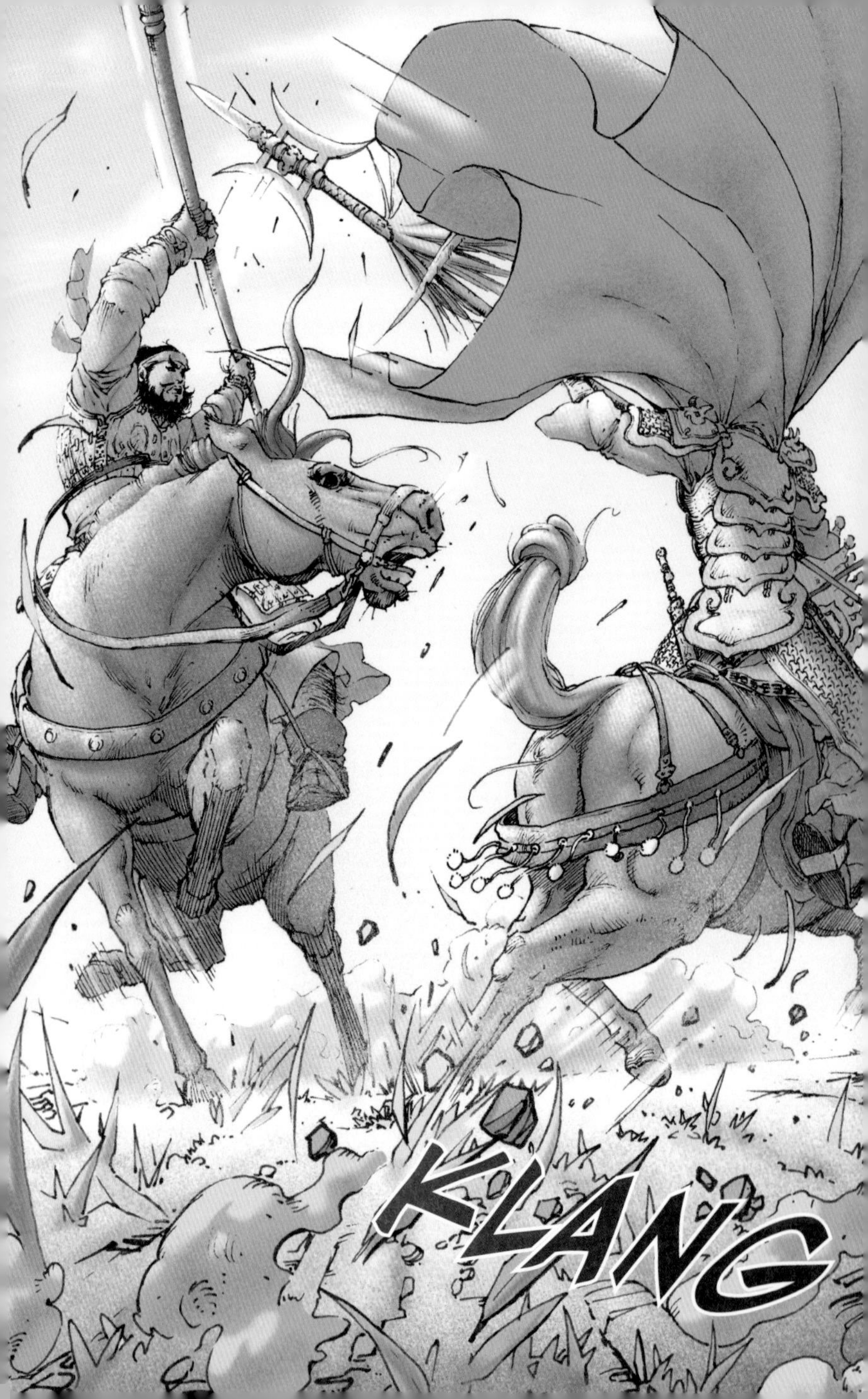
KLANG

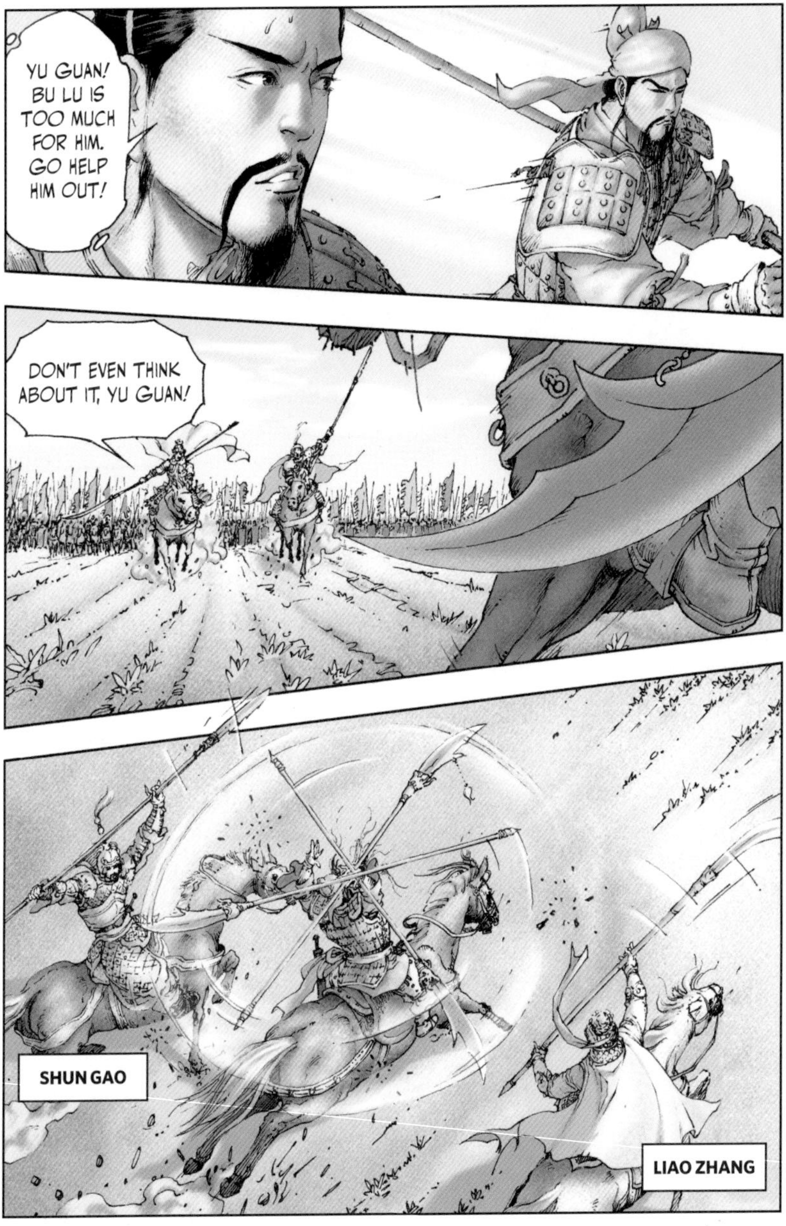
YU GUAN! BU LU IS TOO MUCH FOR HIM. GO HELP HIM OUT!
DON'T EVEN THINK ABOUT IT, YU GUAN!
SHUN GAO
LIAO ZHANG

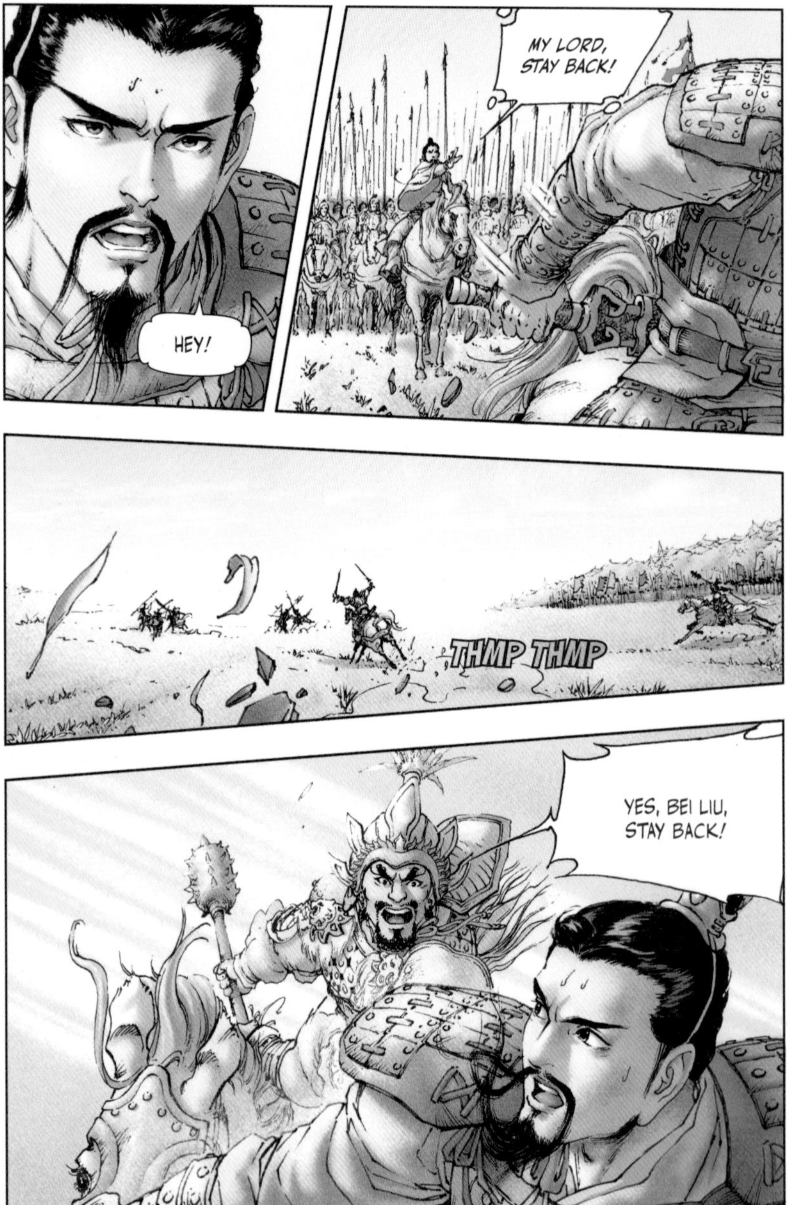
HEY!
MY LORD, STAY BACK!
THMP THMP
YES, BEI LIU, STAY BACK!

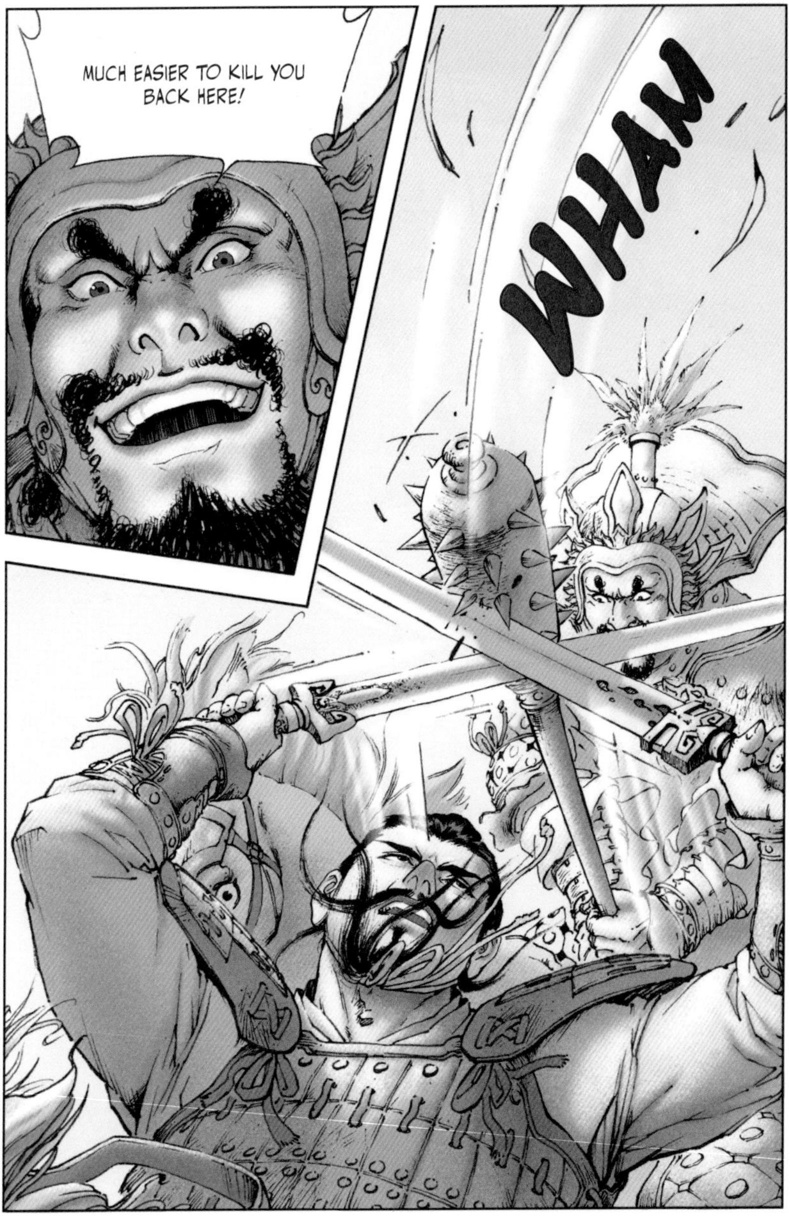
MUCH EASIER TO KILL YOU BACK HERE!
WHAM

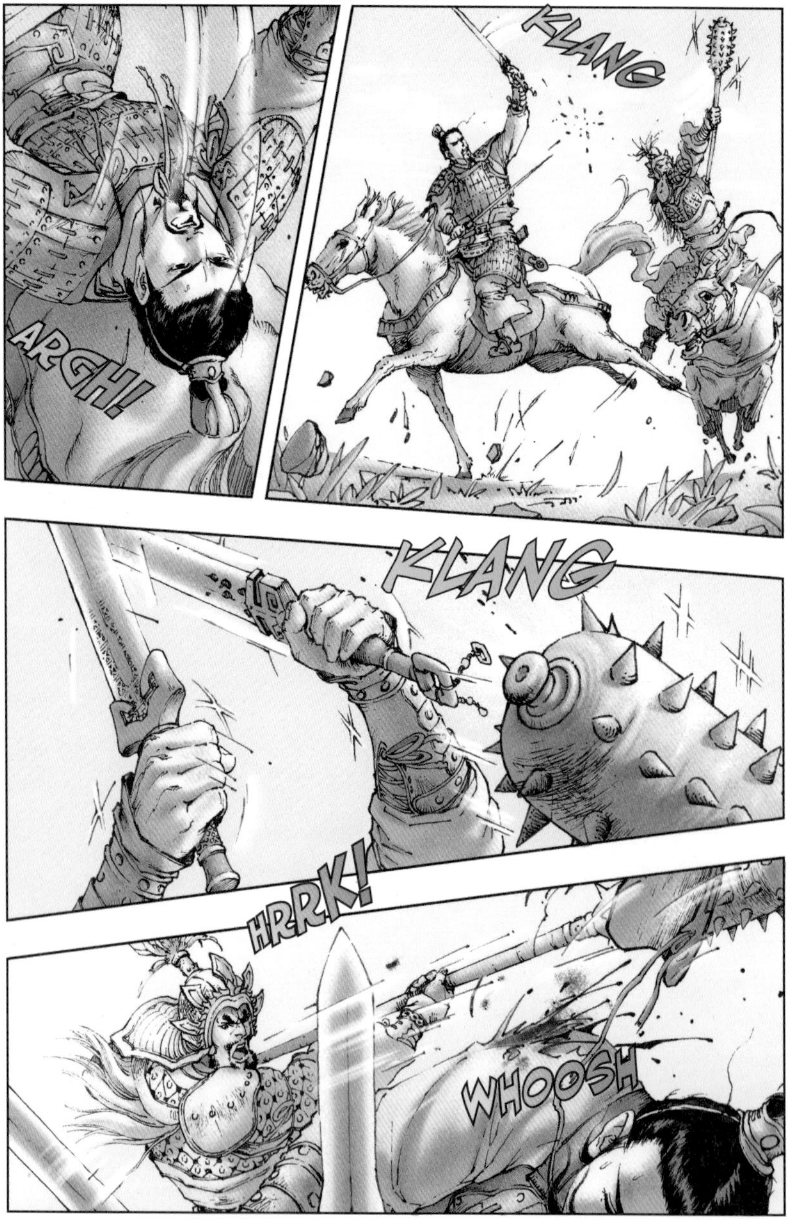
ARGH!
KLANG
KLANG
HRRK!
WHOOSH

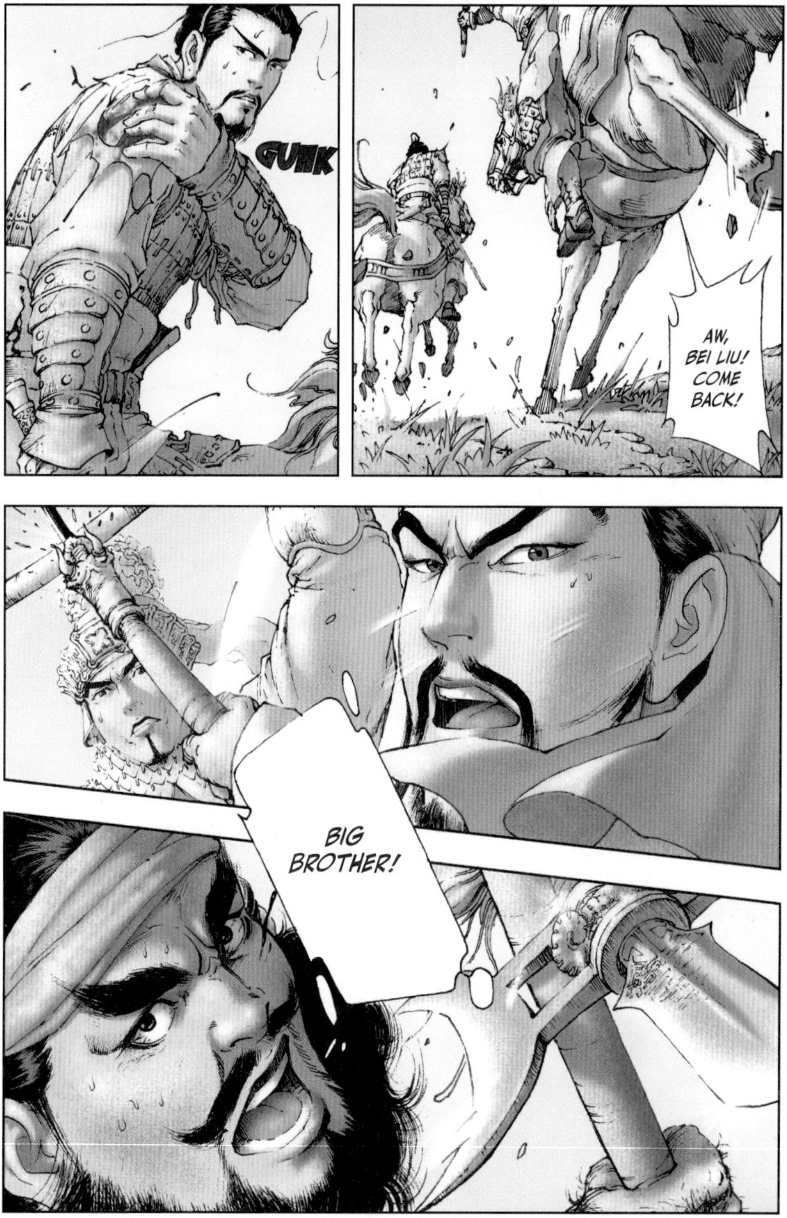
GUNK
AW, BEI LIU! COME BACK!
BIG BROTHER!

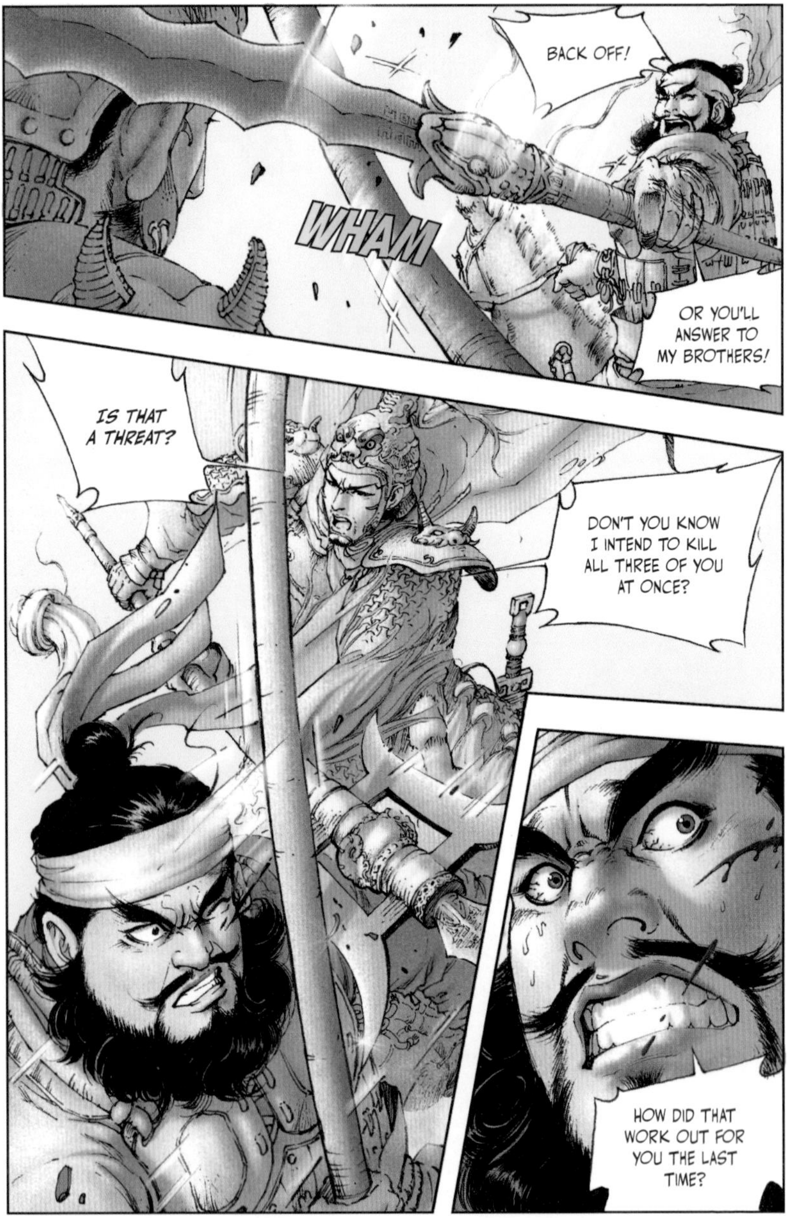
BACK OFF!
WHAM
OR YOU'LL ANSWER TO MY BROTHERS!
IS THAT A THREAT?
DON'T YOU KNOW I INTEND TO KILL ALL THREE OF YOU AT ONCE?
HOW DID THAT WORK OUT FOR YOU THE LAST TIME?

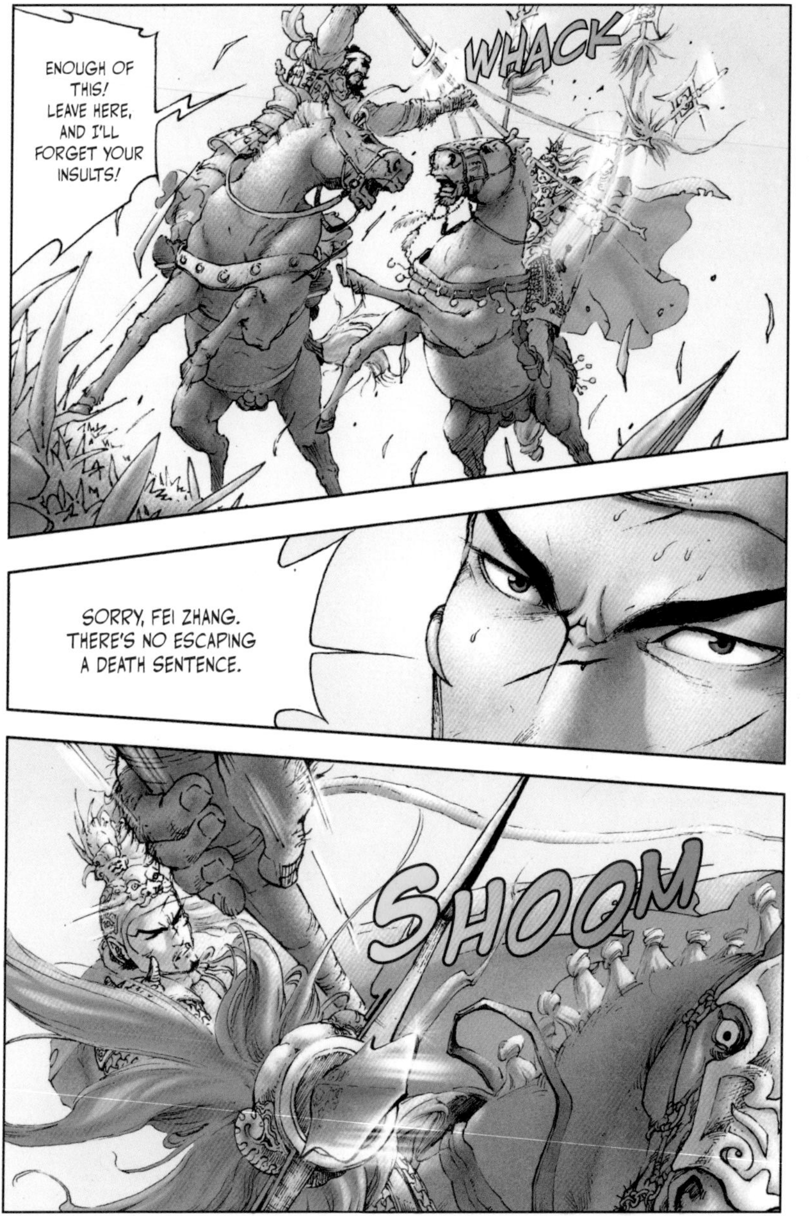
ENOUGH OF THIS! LEAVE HERE, AND I'LL FORGET YOUR INSULTS!
WHACK
SORRY, FEI ZHANG. THERE'S NO ESCAPING A DEATH SENTENCE.
SHOOM

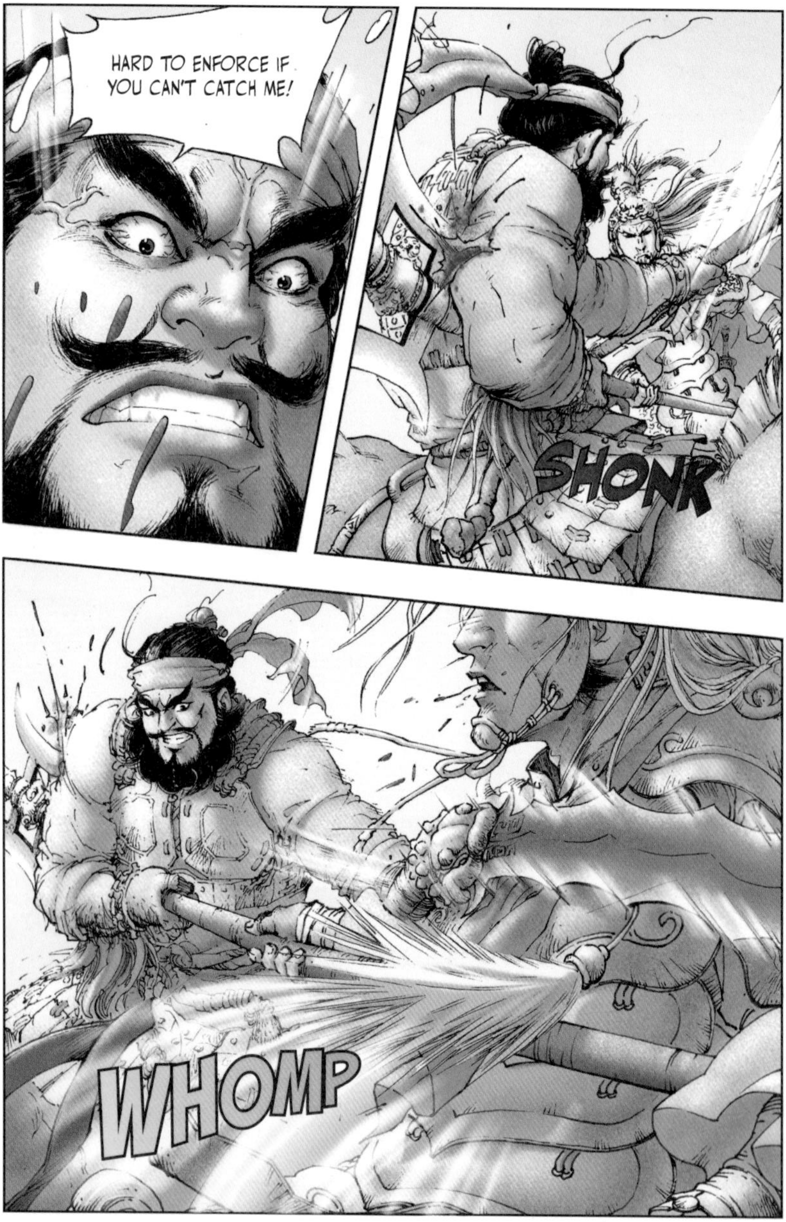
HARD TO ENFORCE IF YOU CAN'T CATCH ME!
SHONK
WHOMP

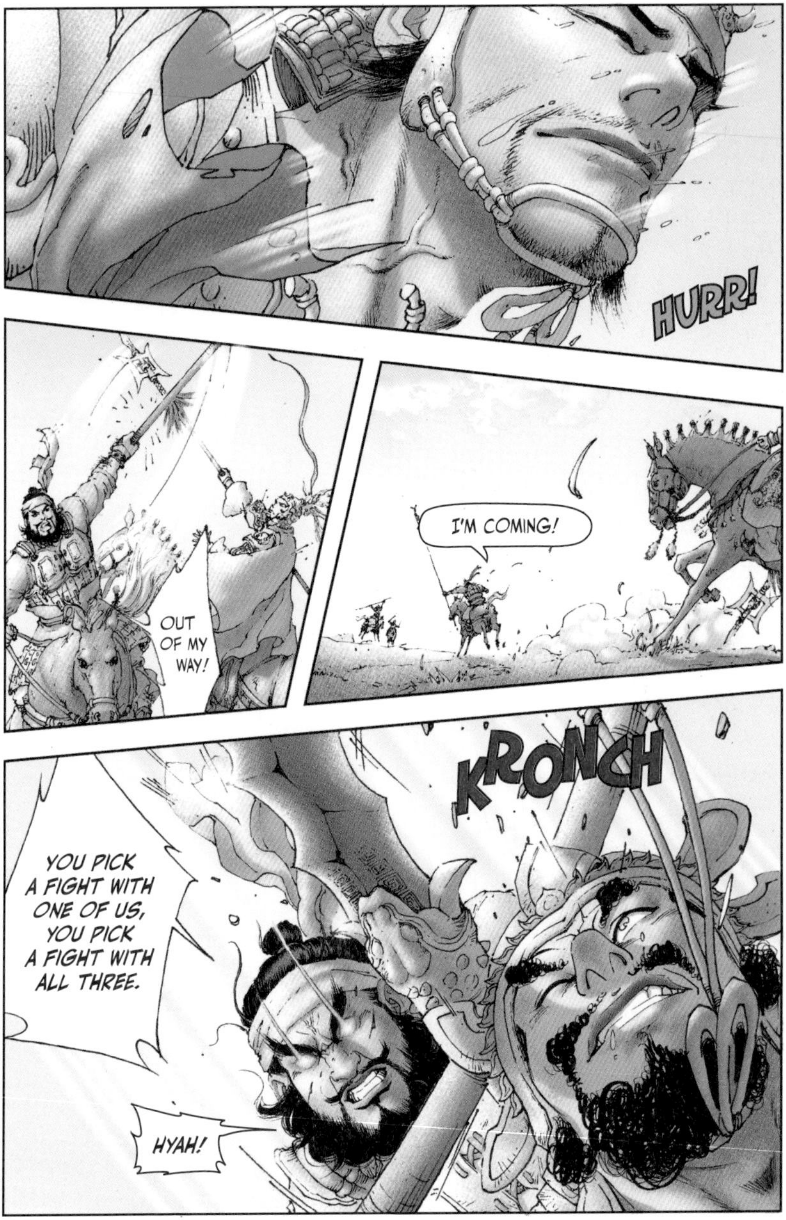
HURR!
OUT OF MY WAY!
I'M COMING!
KRONCH
YOU PICK A FIGHT WITH ONE OF US, YOU PICK A FIGHT WITH ALL THREE.
HYAH!

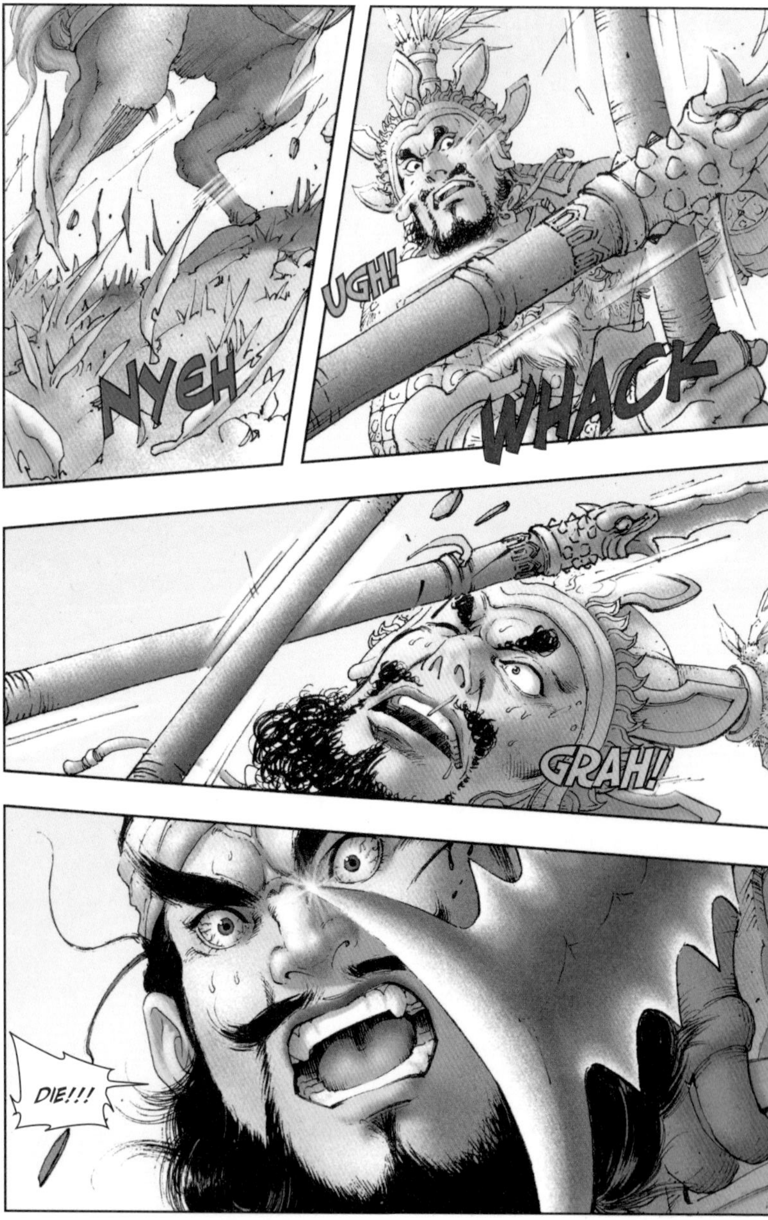
NYEH
UGH!
WHACK
GRAH!
DIE!!!

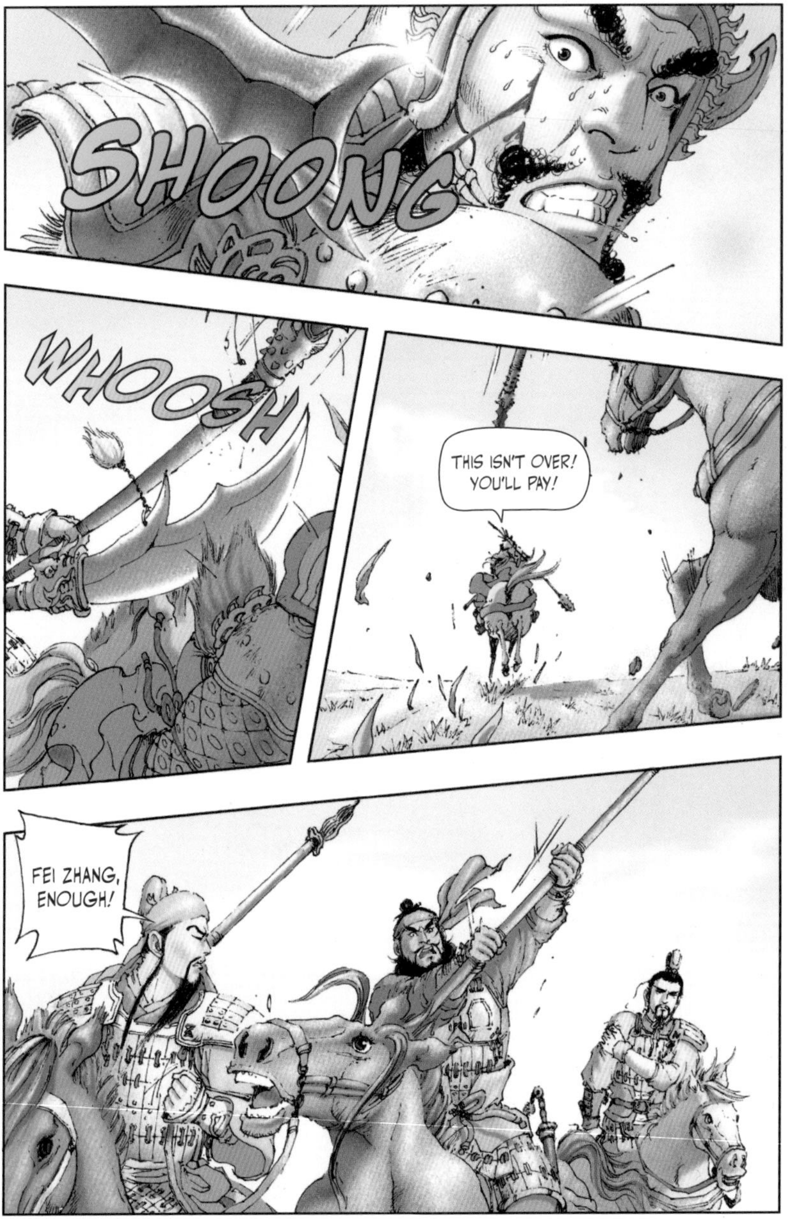
SHOONG
WHOOSH
THIS ISN'T OVER! YOU'LL PAY!
FEI ZHANG, ENOUGH!

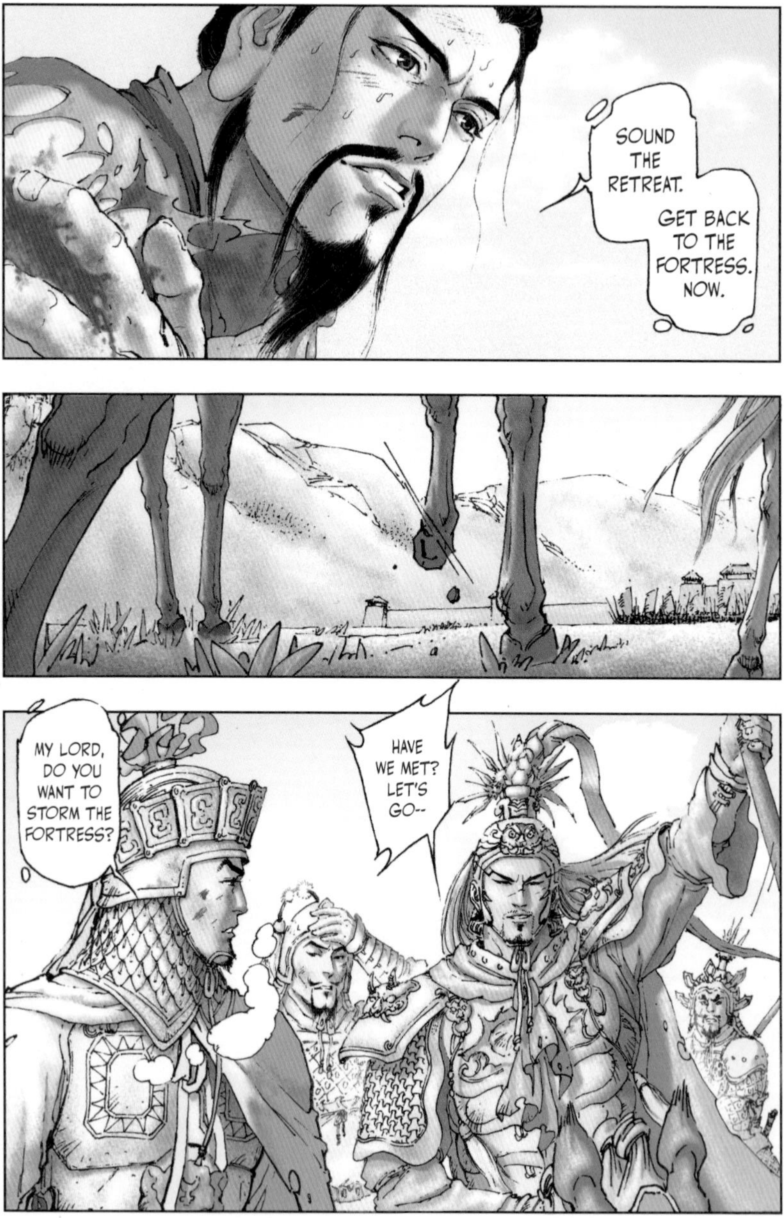
SOUND THE RETREAT.
GET BACK TO THE FORTRESS. NOW.
MY LORD, DO YOU WANT TO STORM THE FORTRESS?
HAVE WE MET? LET'S GO--

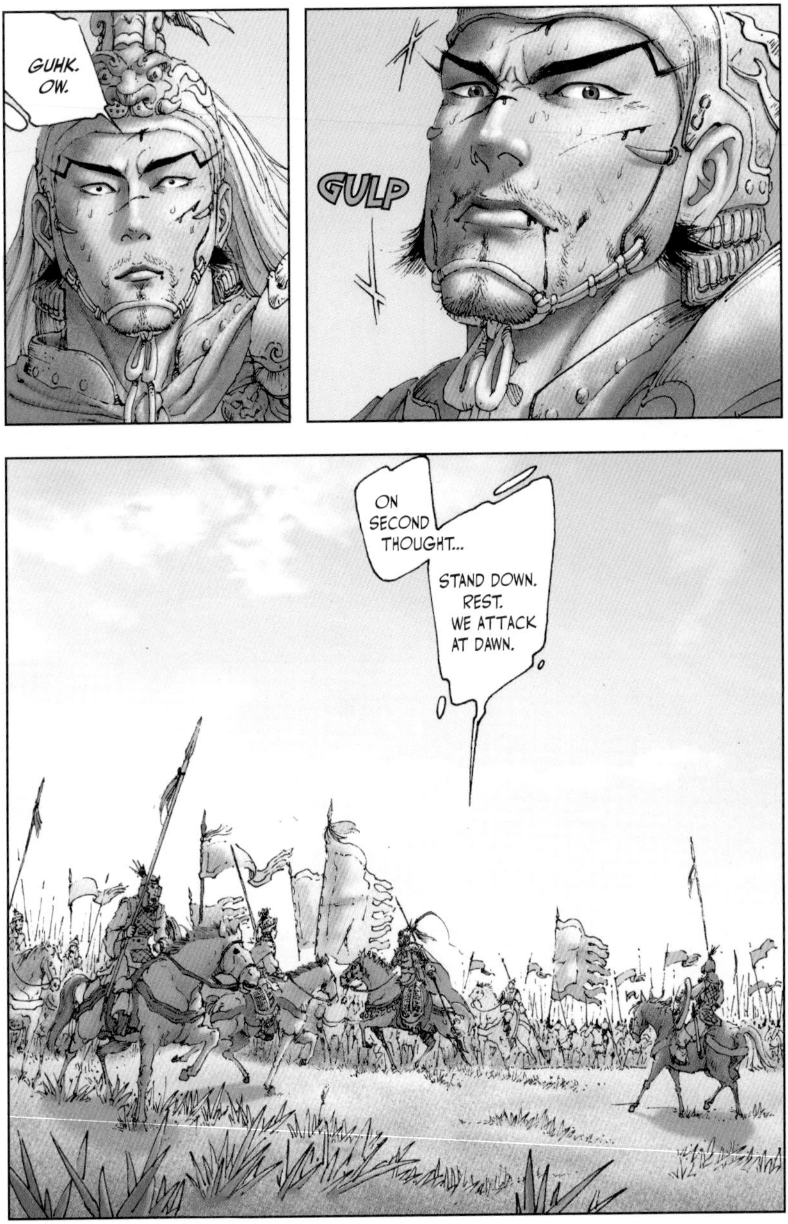
GUHK. OW.
GULP
ON SECOND THOUGHT...
STAND DOWN. REST. WE ATTACK AT DAWN.

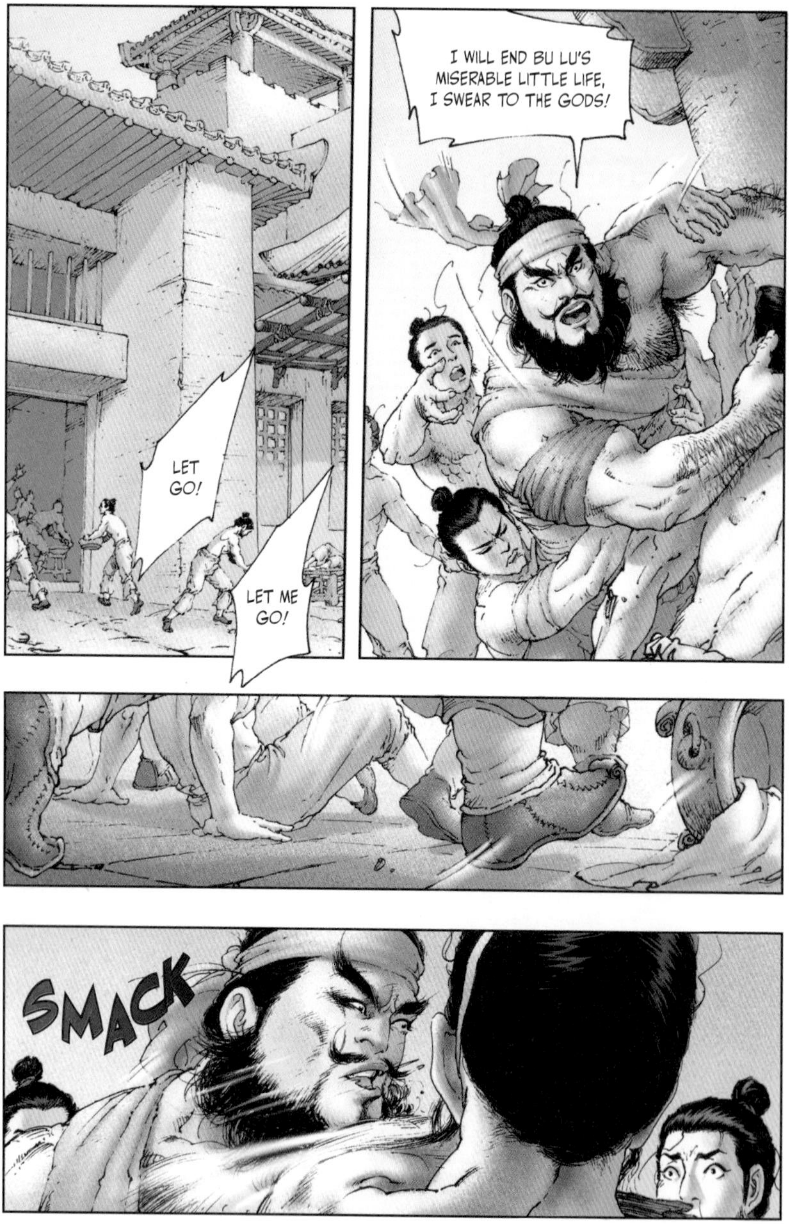
I WILL END BU LU'S MISERABLE LITTLE LIFE, I SWEAR TO THE GODS!
LET GO!
LET ME GO!
SMACK

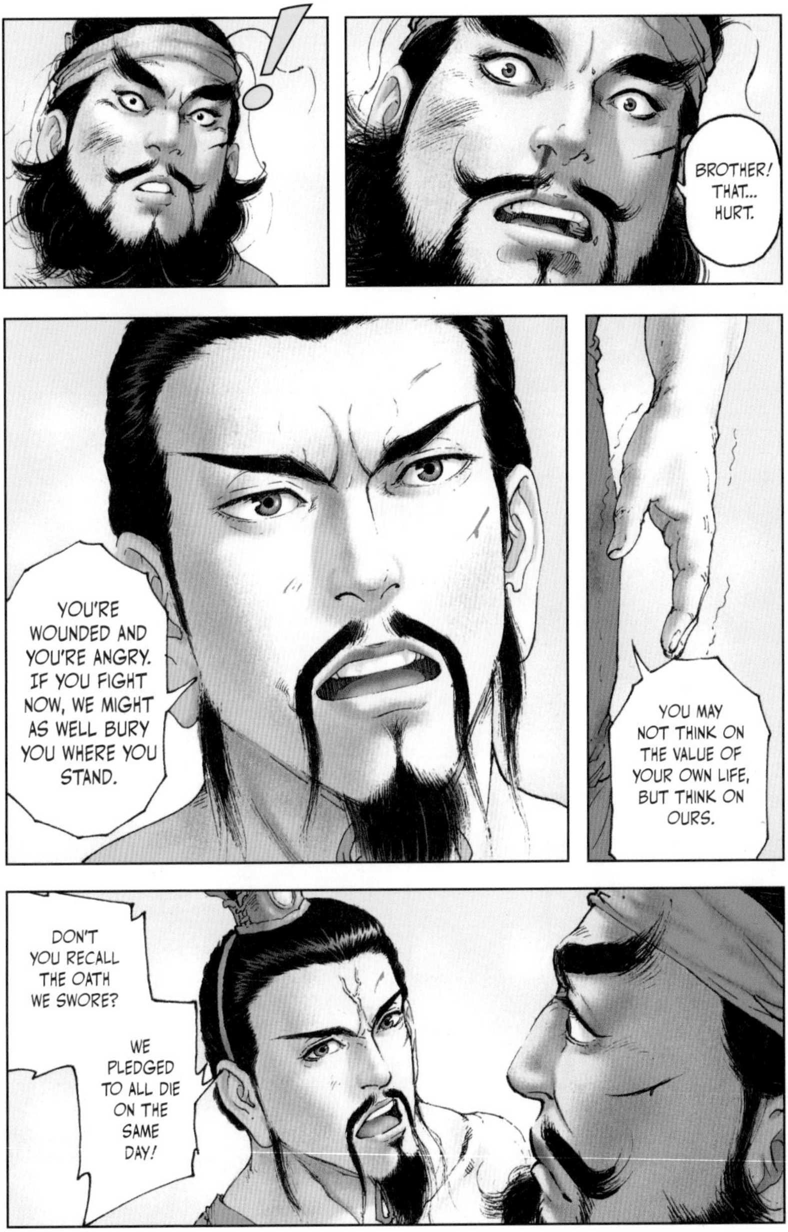
!
BROTHER! THAT... HURT.
YOU'RE WOUNDED AND YOU'RE ANGRY. IF YOU FIGHT NOW, WE MIGHT AS WELL BURY YOU WHERE YOU STAND.
YOU MAY NOT THINK ON THE VALUE OF YOUR OWN LIFE, BUT THINK ON OURS.
DON'T YOU RECALL THE OATH WE SWORE?
WE PLEDGED TO ALL DIE ON THE SAME DAY!

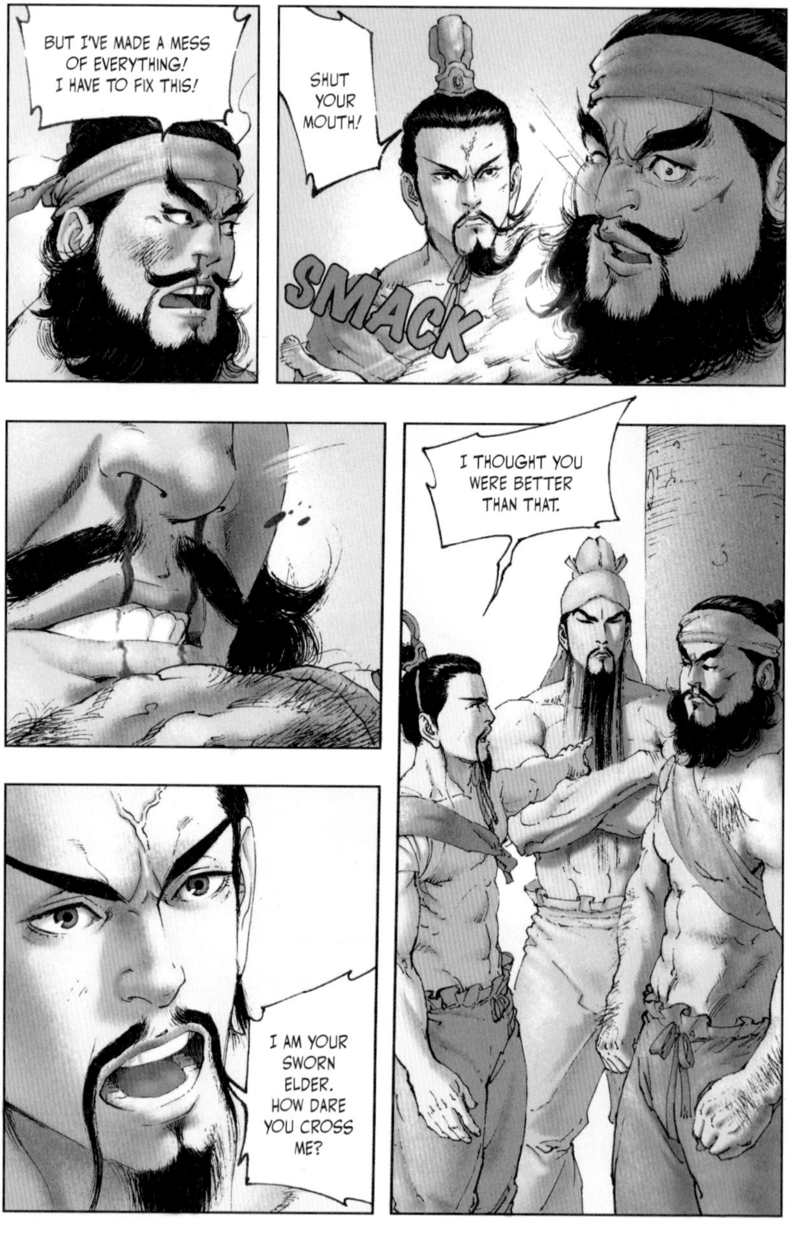
BUT I'VE MADE A MESS OF EVERYTHING! I HAVE TO FIX THIS!
SHUT YOUR MOUTH!
SMACK
I THOUGHT YOU WERE BETTER THAN THAT.
I AM YOUR SWORN ELDER. HOW DARE YOU CROSS ME?

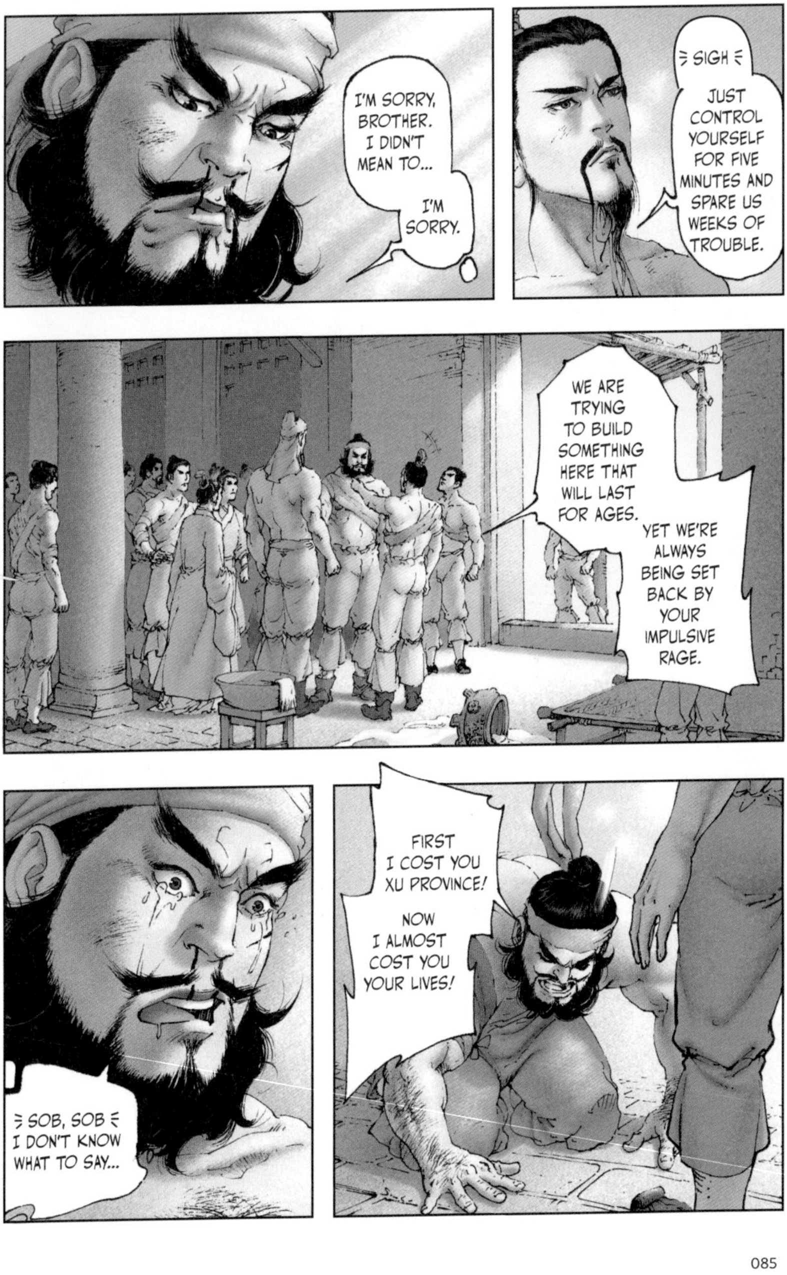
I'M SORRY, BROTHER. I DIDN'T MEAN TO...
I'M SORRY.
≶ SIGH ≶
JUST CONTROL YOURSELF FOR FIVE MINUTES AND SPARE US WEEKS OF TROUBLE.
WE ARE TRYING TO BUILD SOMETHING HERE THAT WILL LAST FOR AGES.
YET WE'RE ALWAYS BEING SET BACK BY YOUR IMPULSIVE RAGE.
≶ SOB, SOB ≶ I DON'T KNOW WHAT TO SAY...
FIRST I COST YOU XU PROVINCE!
NOW I ALMOST COST YOU YOUR LIVES!

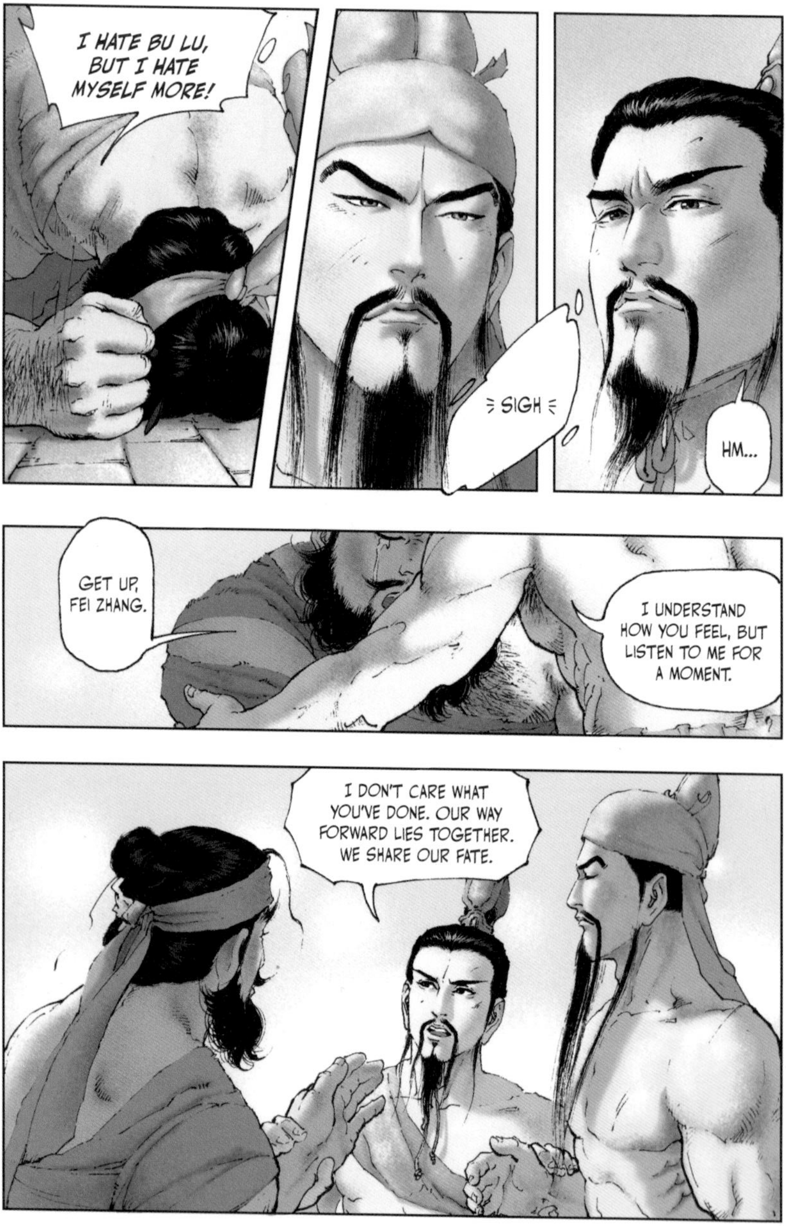
I HATE BU LU, BUT I HATE MYSELF MORE!
SIGH
HM...
GET UP, FEI ZHANG.
I UNDERSTAND HOW YOU FEEL, BUT LISTEN TO ME FOR A MOMENT.
I DON'T CARE WHAT YOU'VE DONE. OUR WAY FORWARD LIES TOGETHER. WE SHARE OUR FATE.

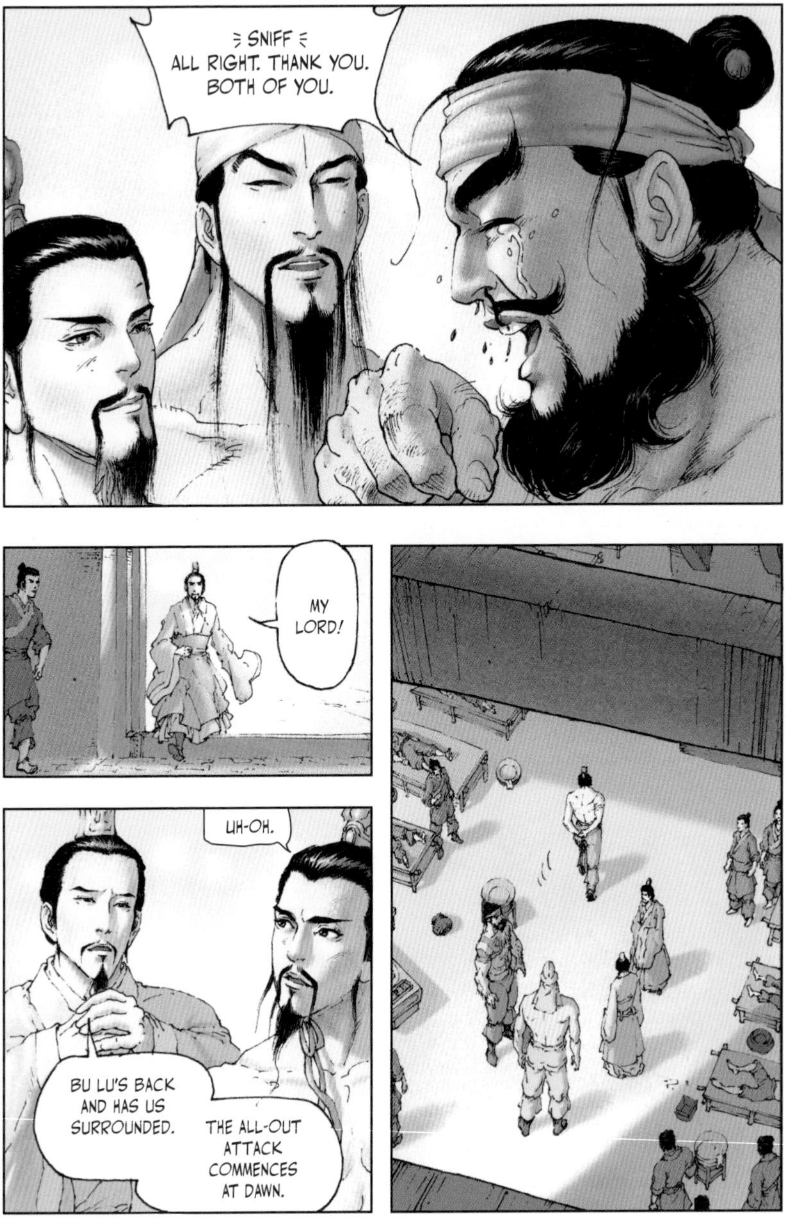
≡ SNIFF ≡
ALL RIGHT. THANK YOU. BOTH OF YOU.
MY LORD!
UH-OH.
BU LU'S BACK AND HAS US SURROUNDED.
THE ALL-OUT ATTACK COMMENCES AT DAWN.

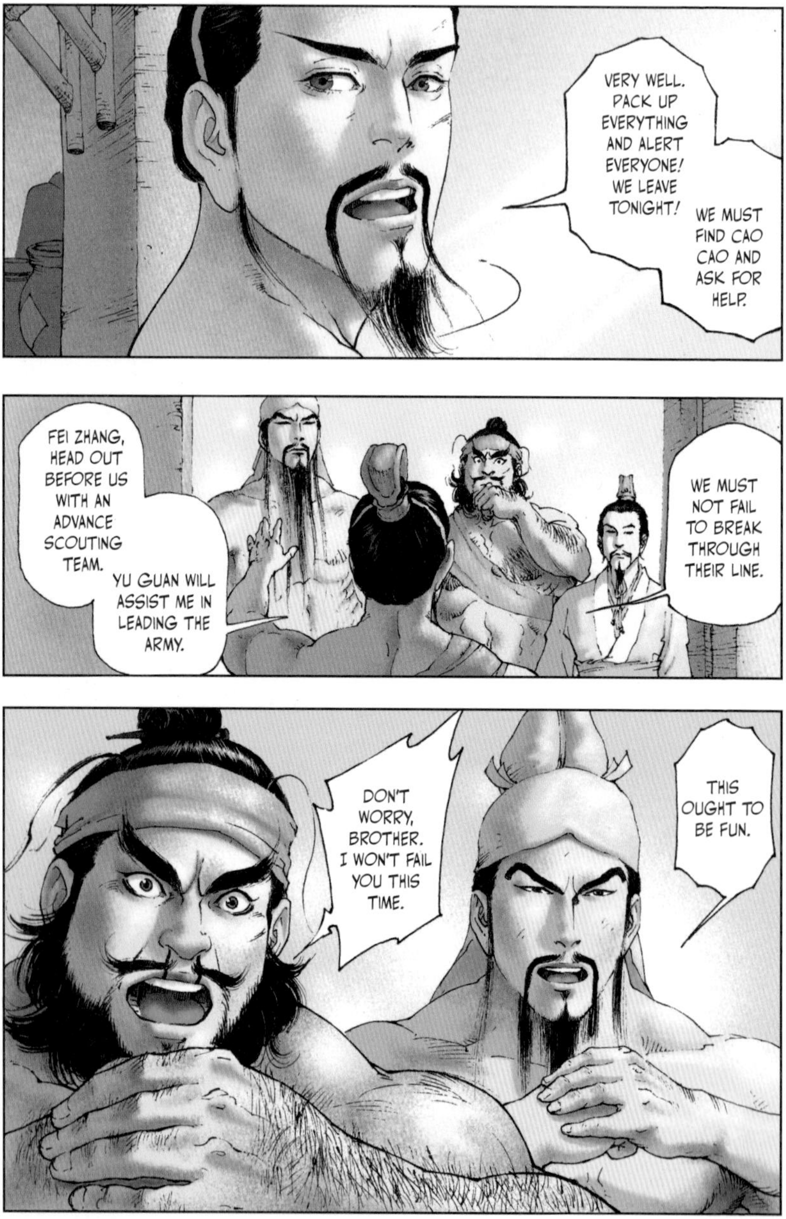
VERY WELL. PACK UP EVERYTHING AND ALERT EVERYONE! WE LEAVE TONIGHT!
WE MUST FIND CAO CAO AND ASK FOR HELP.
FEI ZHANG, HEAD OUT BEFORE US WITH AN ADVANCE SCOUTING TEAM.
YU GUAN WILL ASSIST ME IN LEADING THE ARMY.
WE MUST NOT FAIL TO BREAK THROUGH THEIR LINE.
DON'T WORRY, BROTHER. I WON'T FAIL YOU THIS TIME.
THIS OUGHT TO BE FUN.

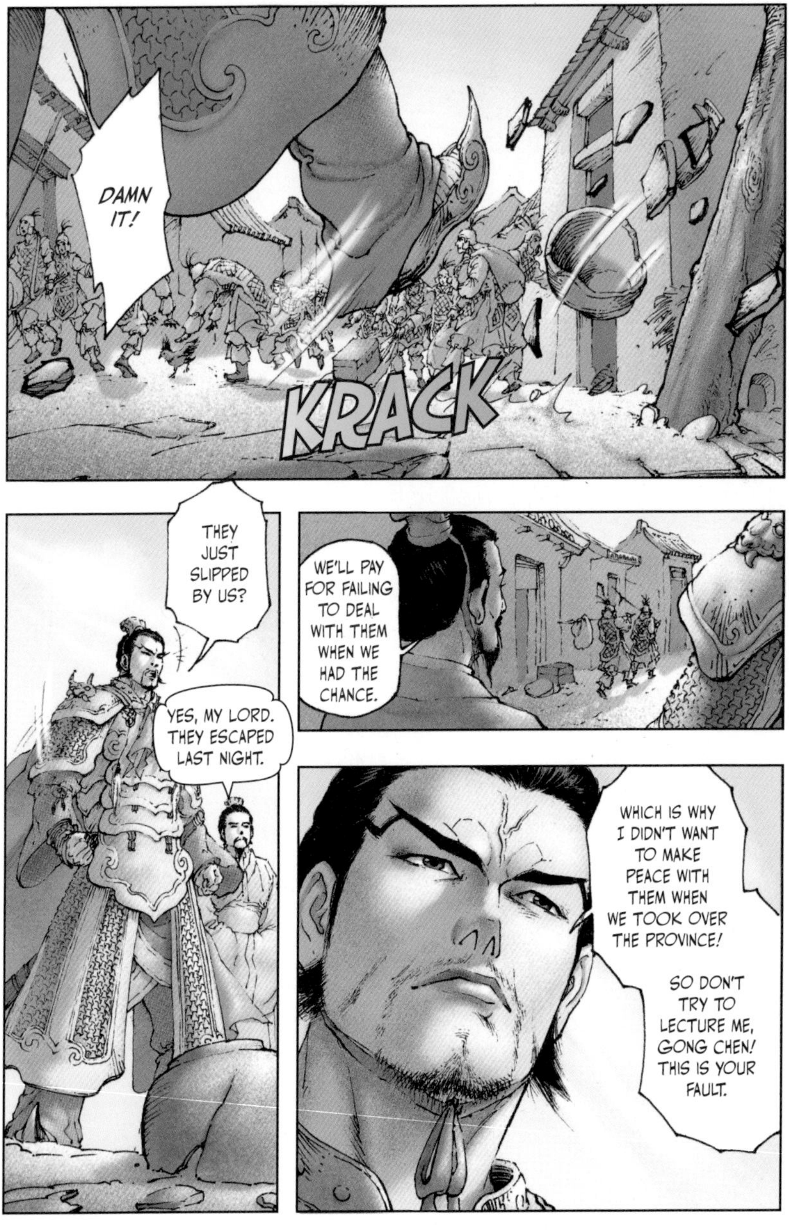
DAMN IT!
KRACK
THEY JUST SLIPPED BY US?
YES, MY LORD. THEY ESCAPED LAST NIGHT.
WE'LL PAY FOR FAILING TO DEAL WITH THEM WHEN WE HAD THE CHANCE.
WHICH IS WHY I DIDN'T WANT TO MAKE PEACE WITH THEM WHEN WE TOOK OVER THE PROVINCE!
SO DON'T TRY TO LECTURE ME, GONG CHEN! THIS IS YOUR FAULT.

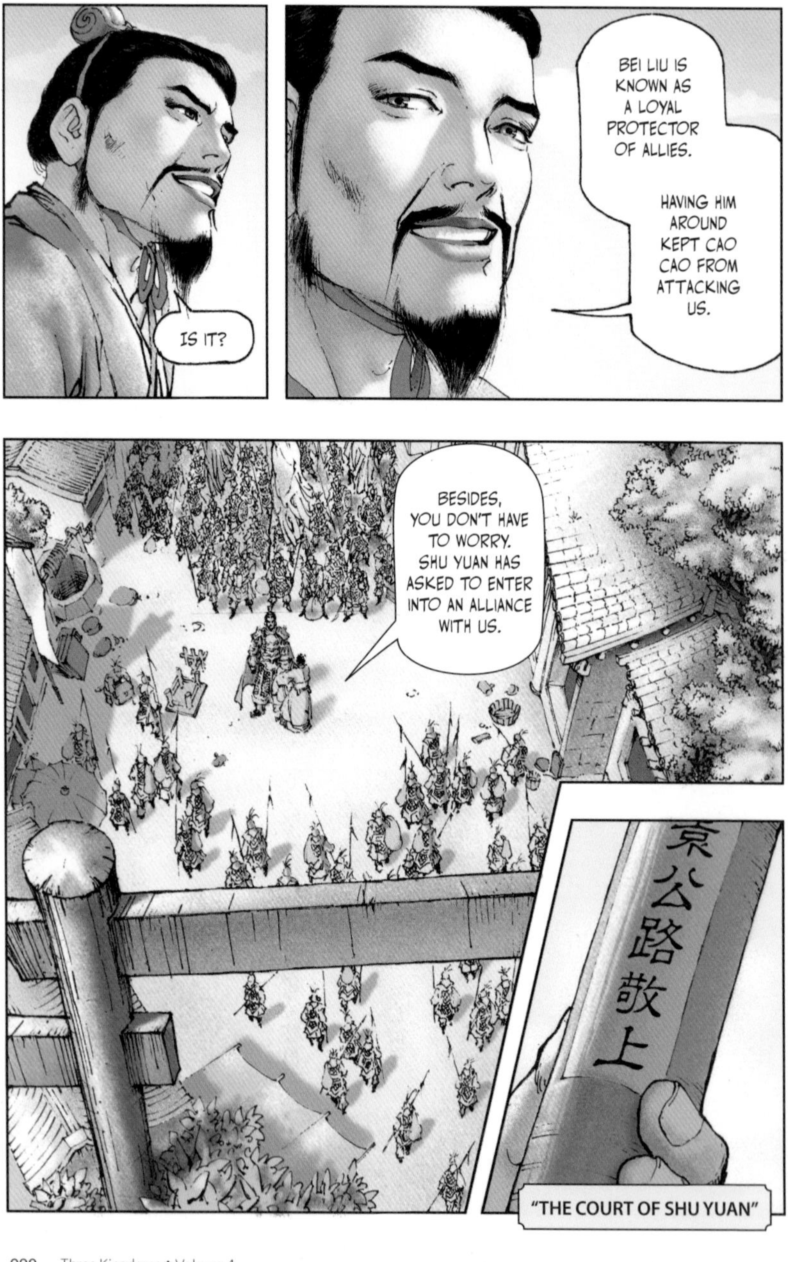
IS IT?
BEI LIU IS KNOWN AS A LOYAL PROTECTOR OF ALLIES.
HAVING HIM AROUND KEPT CAO CAO FROM ATTACKING US.
BESIDES, YOU DON'T HAVE TO WORRY. SHU YUAN HAS ASKED TO ENTER INTO AN ALLIANCE WITH US.
"THE COURT OF SHU YUAN"

Fei Zhang

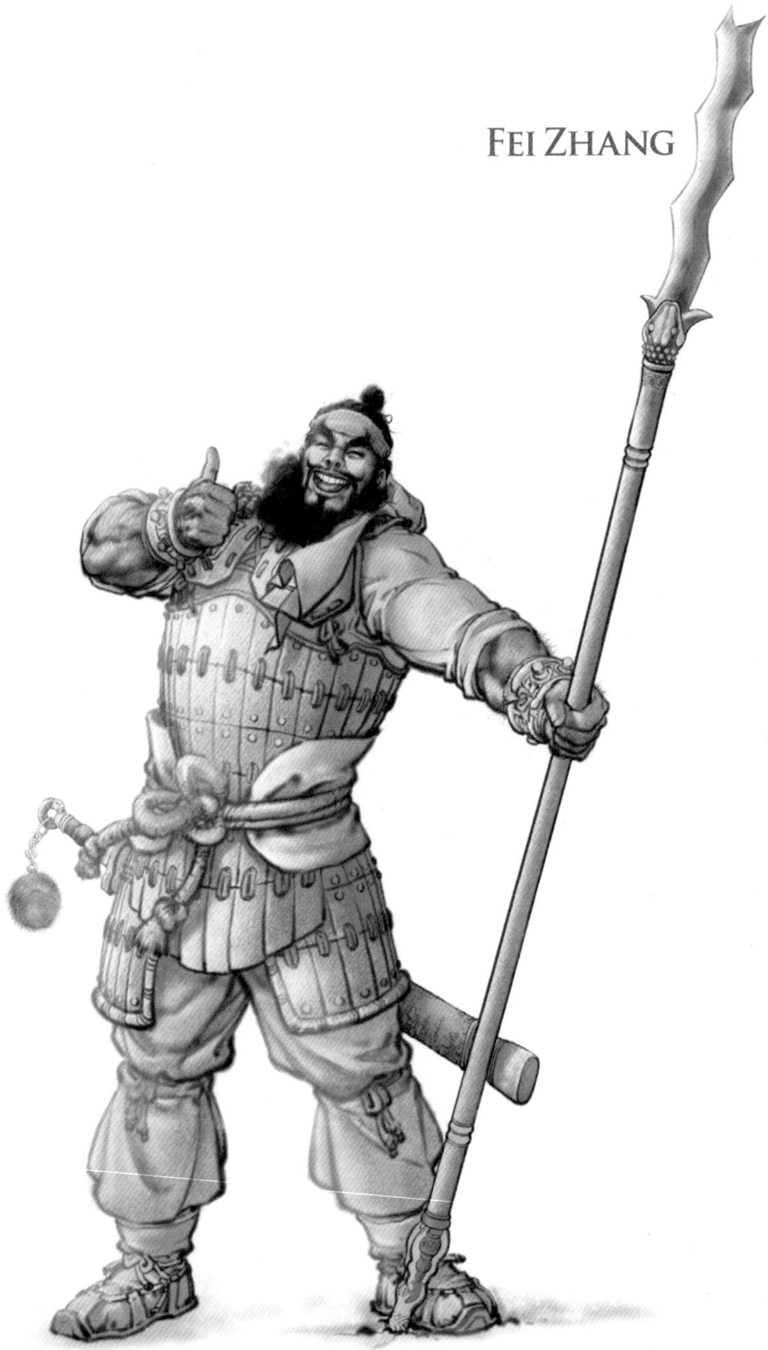

Chapter 3

Bei Liu Takes Shelter AD 196–97

Summary

Bei Liu and his brother escape Xu Province and make for the lands ruled by Cao Cao, who does not view Bei Liu as a threat and allows him to live in the province. Meanwhile, Cao Cao's counselors advise him to move against Xiu Zhang. To do this, Cao Cao must get the approval of Shao Yuan, whom he sways with flattery by offering a meaningless position with a fancy title ("High Commander of the Lower Guard"). Against the counsel of his advisors, Shao Yuan accepts the position and follows Cao Cao's instructions to defend the northern lands. It seems clear, though, that this is just a plot to get Shao Yuan out of the way.

Meanwhile, Bu Lu, who still controls Xu Province, is approached by Shu Yuan, who asks to marry his daughter. Later, the merchant Gui Chen visits Bu Lu and advises him against accepting the marriage proposal, since it is clear that Shu Yuan only wants Bu Lu as a marital relation so that he may send the famous soldier into battle, thus neutralizing a potential threat. Bu Lu accepts Gui Chen's counsel and refuses the marriage proposal. In retaliation, Shu Yuan leads an army of 200,000 soldiers into Xu Province to attack Bu Lu. But Cao Cao and Bei Liu's armies come to Bu Lu's aid, and Shu Yuan's forces are devastated and their leader is forced to retreat.

XiLiang
Zhuo
ChangShan
BeiHai
PuYang
XiaoPei
HuLuo
B
XuZhou
XiaPi
LuoYang
GuanDu
XuChang
ChangAn
A
HanZhong
NanYang
ShouChun
River Huai
HeFei
XiangYang
ChengDu
NanJun
ChaiSang
KuaiJi
Red Cliffs
BoYang
YuZhang
ChangSha

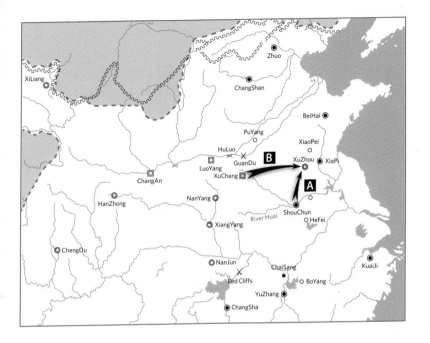

A Shu Yuan asks to marry Bu Lu's daughter so the two men may form an alliance. Bu Lu refuses the offer, and Shu Yuan attacks him with an army of 200,000 soldiers.

B Cao Cao and Bei Liu send their armies to aid Bu Lu. They succeed in destroying Shu Yuan's army and driving him out of the province.

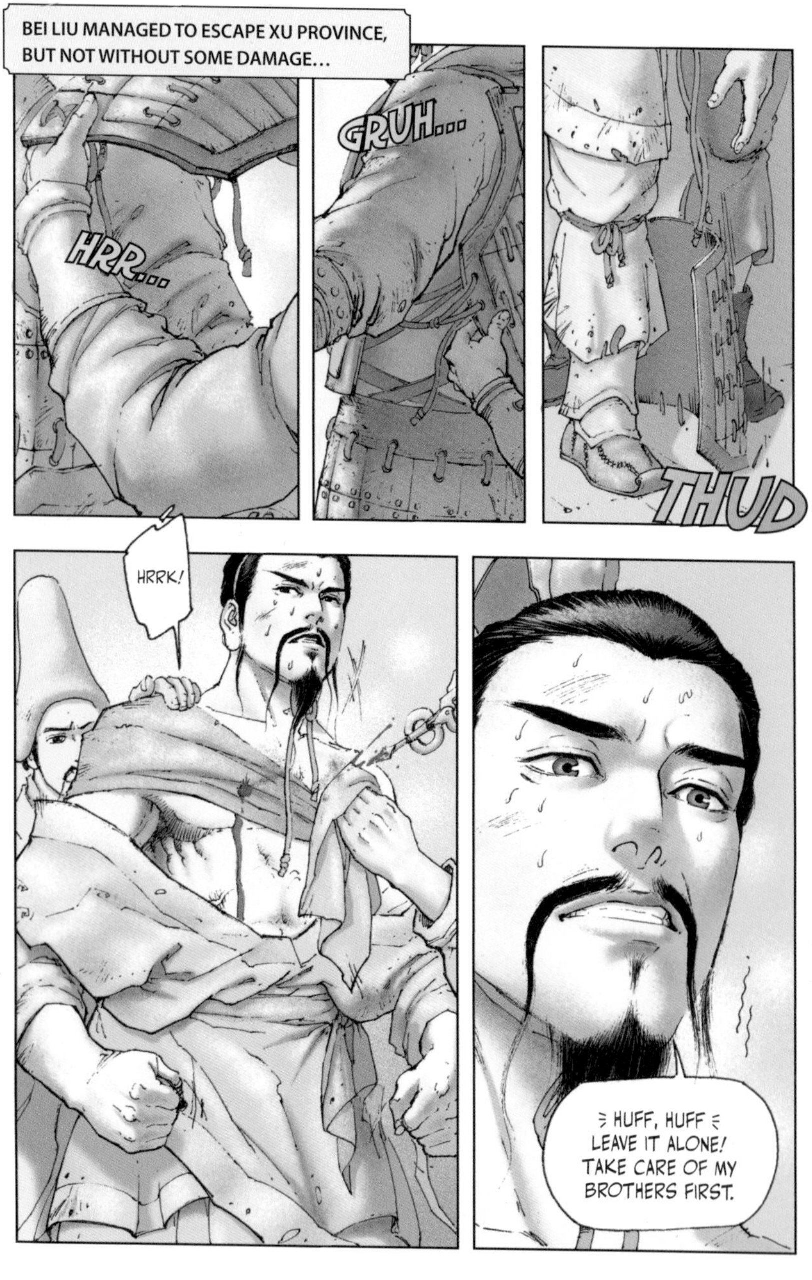
BEI LIU MANAGED TO ESCAPE XU PROVINCE, BUT NOT WITHOUT SOME DAMAGE...
HRR...
GRUH...
THUD
HRRK!
≡ HUFF, HUFF ≡ LEAVE IT ALONE! TAKE CARE OF MY BROTHERS FIRST.

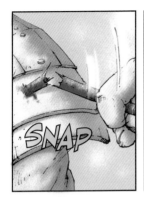

SNAP

I'LL BE FINE. JUST A FLESH WOUND.

TEND TO FEI ZHANG, HE GOT THE WORST OF IT.

HOW ARE YOU HOLDING UP, BRO-THER?

MY LORD! THERE ARE SO MANY WOUNDS, SO MUCH BLOOD!

ZHU MI

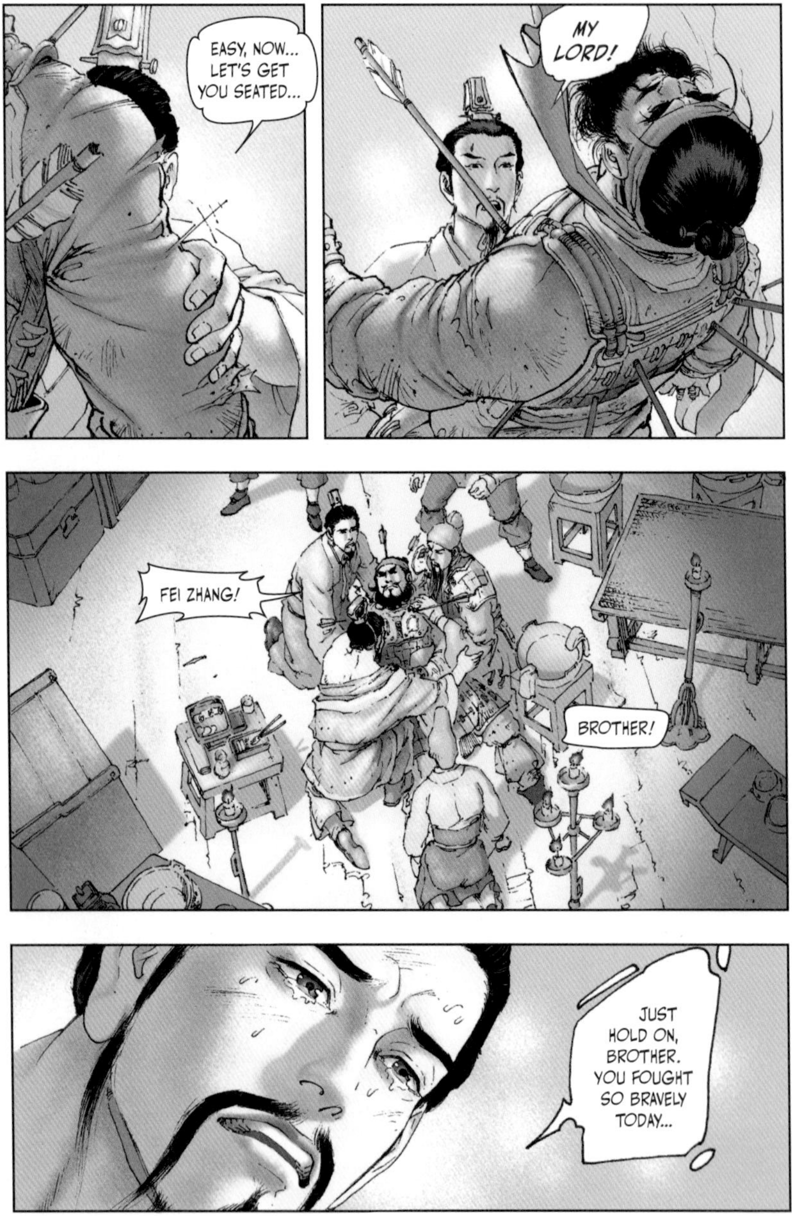
EASY, NOW... LET'S GET YOU SEATED...
MY LORD!
FEI ZHANG!
BROTHER!
JUST HOLD ON, BROTHER. YOU FOUGHT SO BRAVELY TODAY...

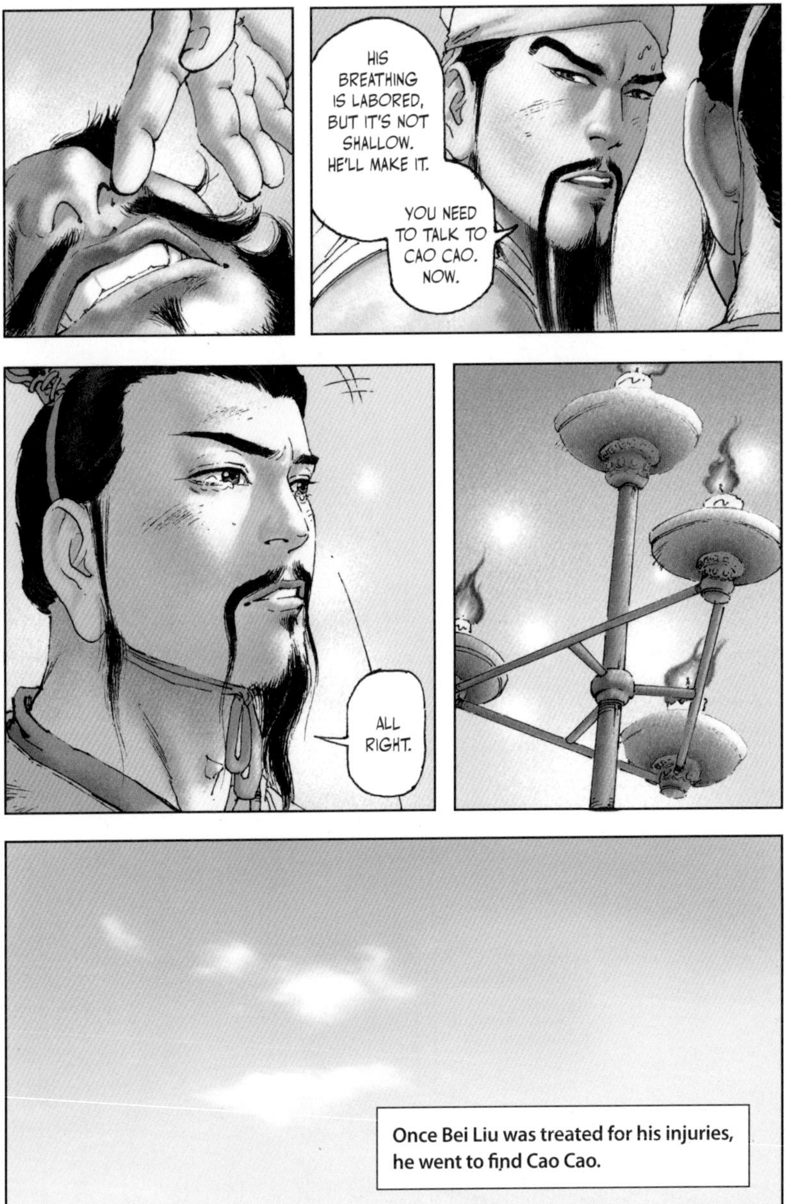
HIS BREATHING IS LABORED, BUT IT'S NOT SHALLOW. HE'LL MAKE IT.
YOU NEED TO TALK TO CAO CAO. NOW.
ALL RIGHT.
Once Bei Liu was treated for his injuries, he went to find Cao Cao.

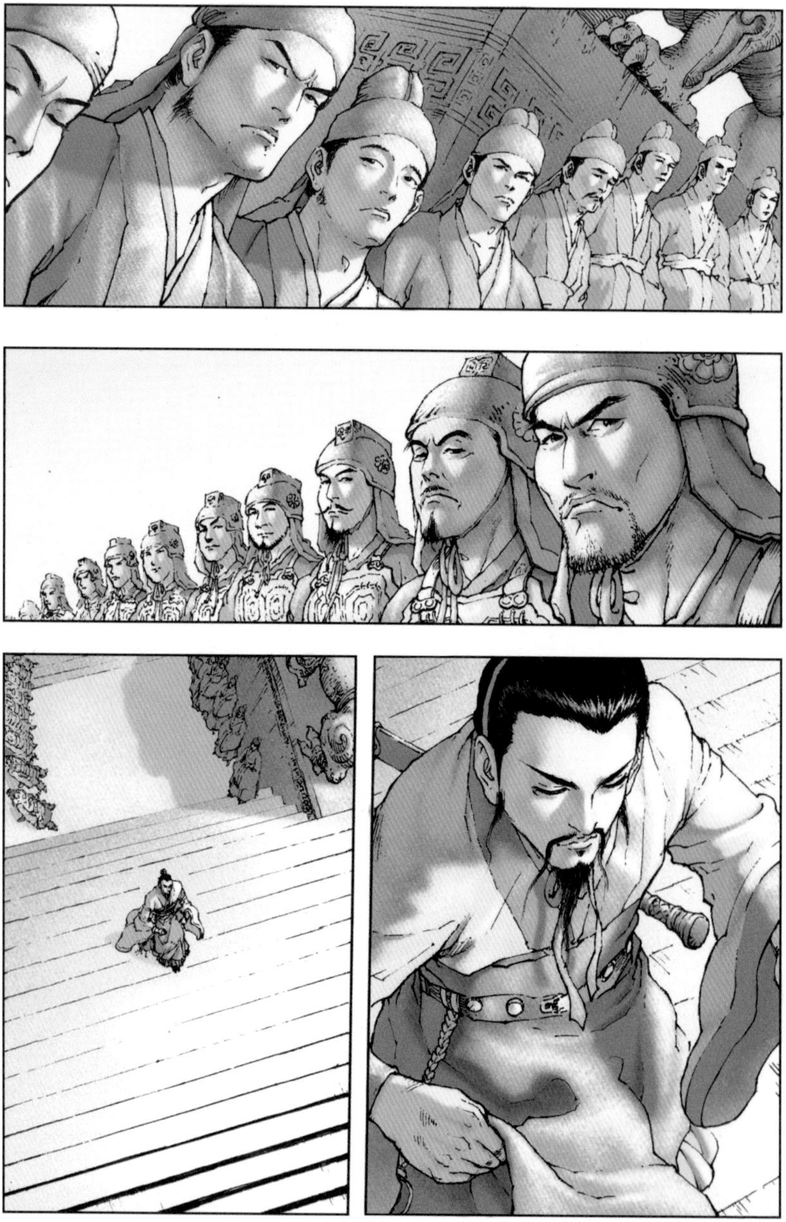

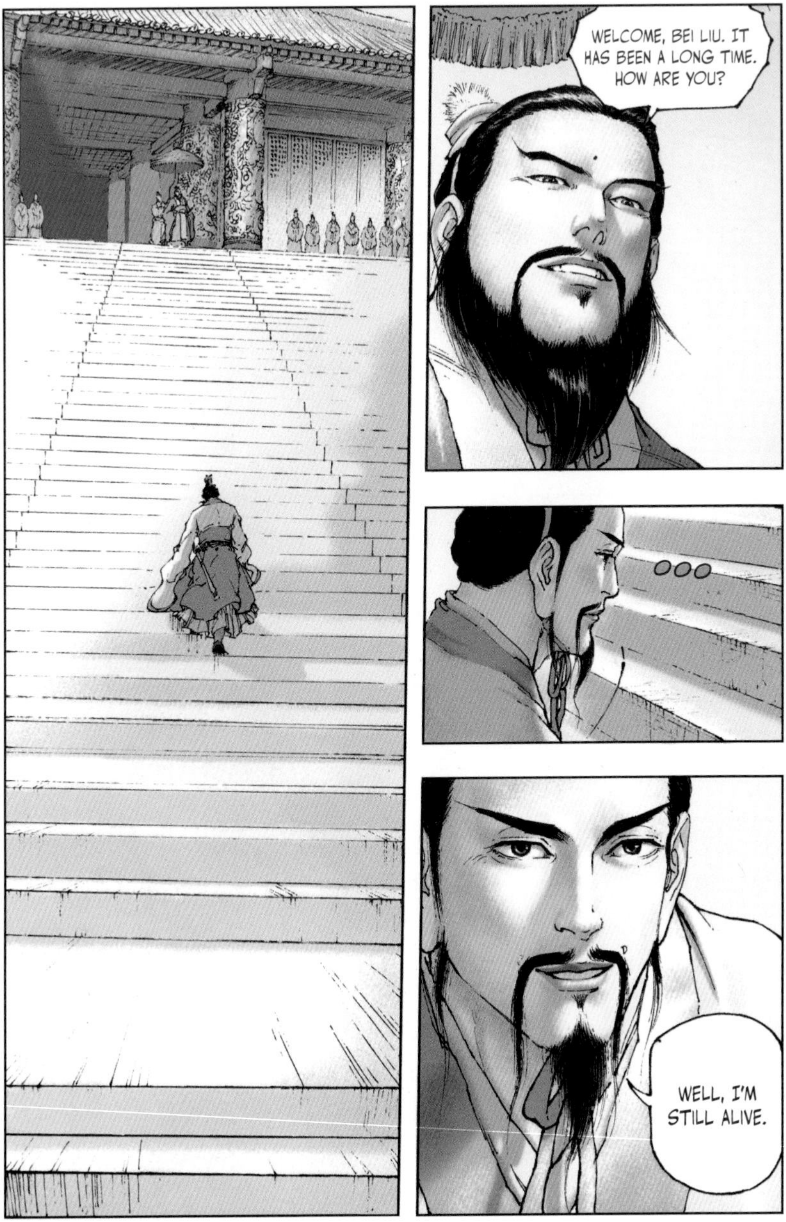
WELCOME, BEI LIU. IT HAS BEEN A LONG TIME. HOW ARE YOU?
WELL, I'M STILL ALIVE.

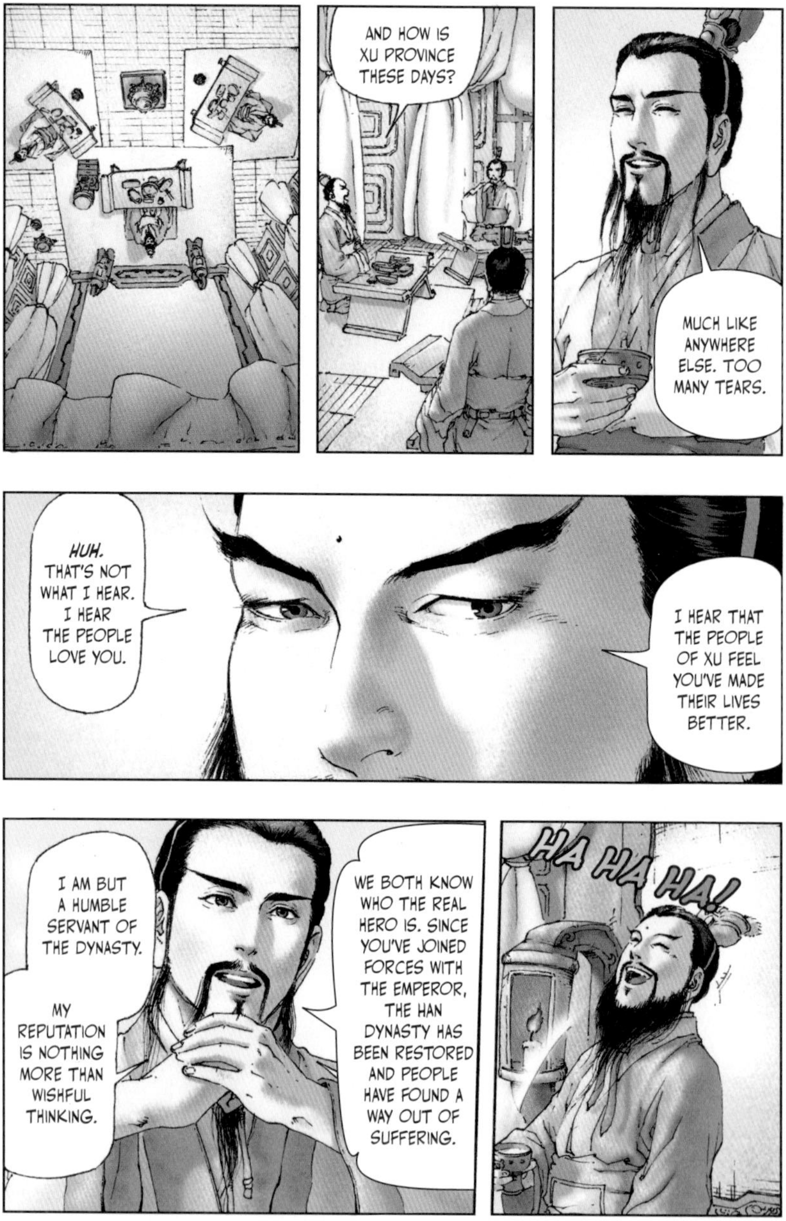
AND HOW IS XU PROVINCE THESE DAYS?
MUCH LIKE ANYWHERE ELSE. TOO MANY TEARS.
HUH. THAT'S NOT WHAT I HEAR. I HEAR THE PEOPLE LOVE YOU.
I HEAR THAT THE PEOPLE OF XU FEEL YOU'VE MADE THEIR LIVES BETTER.
I AM BUT A HUMBLE SERVANT OF THE DYNASTY.
MY REPUTATION IS NOTHING MORE THAN WISHFUL THINKING.
WE BOTH KNOW WHO THE REAL HERO IS. SINCE YOU'VE JOINED FORCES WITH THE EMPEROR, THE HAN DYNASTY HAS BEEN RESTORED AND PEOPLE HAVE FOUND A WAY OUT OF SUFFERING.
HA HA HA!

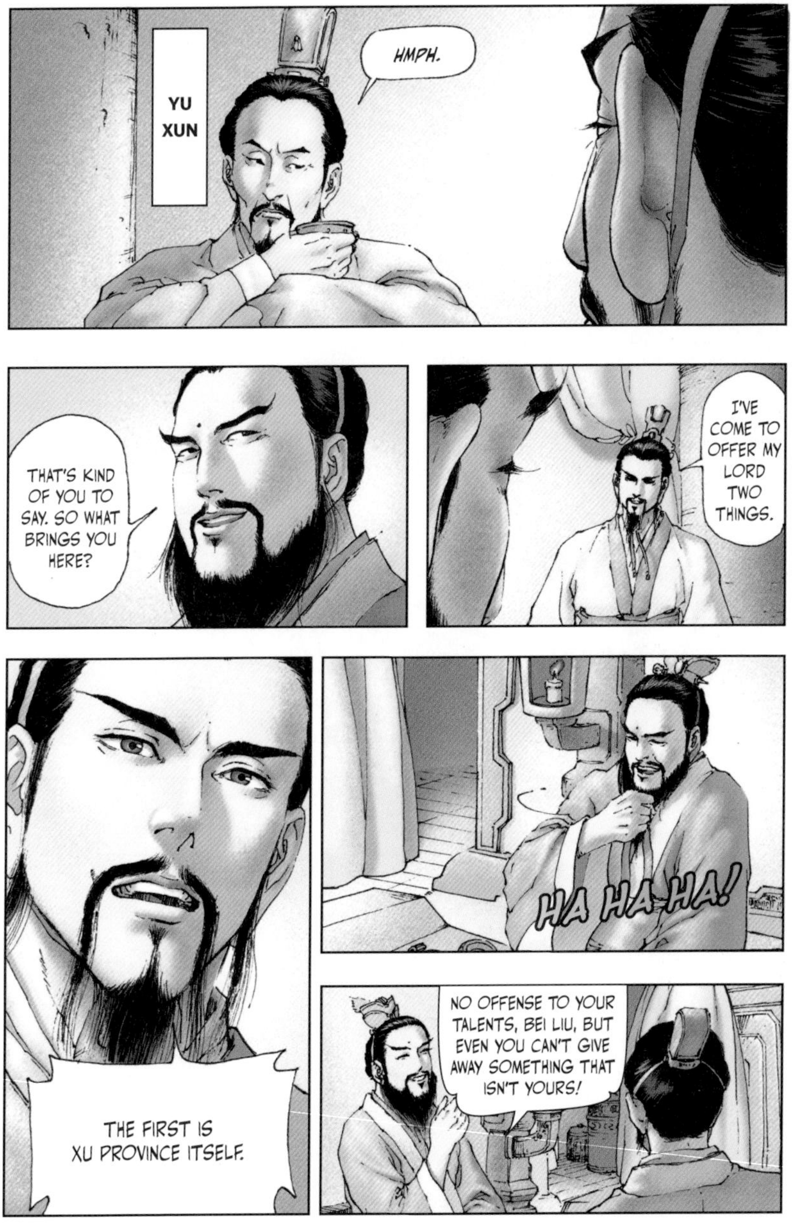
YU XUN
HMPH.
THAT'S KIND OF YOU TO SAY. SO WHAT BRINGS YOU HERE?
I'VE COME TO OFFER MY LORD TWO THINGS.
THE FIRST IS XU PROVINCE ITSELF.
HA HA HA!
NO OFFENSE TO YOUR TALENTS, BEI LIU, BUT EVEN YOU CAN'T GIVE AWAY SOMETHING THAT ISN'T YOURS!

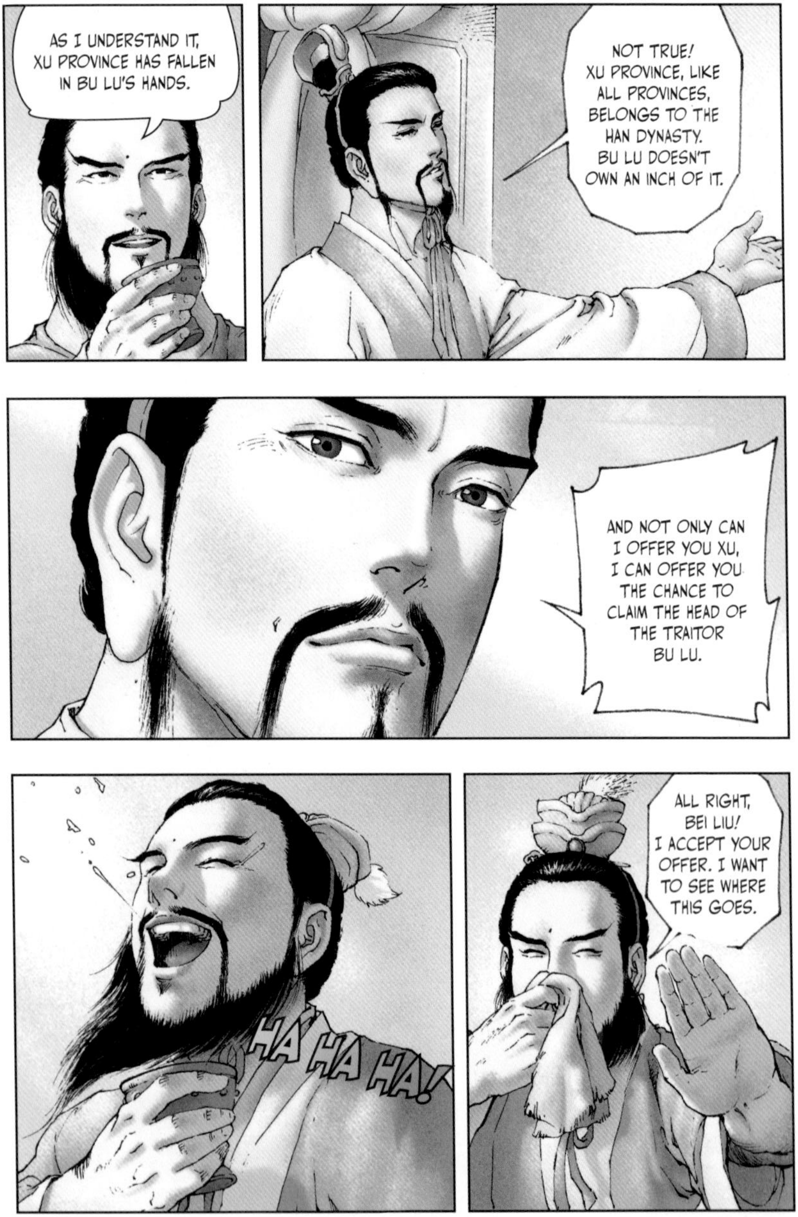
AS I UNDERSTAND IT, XU PROVINCE HAS FALLEN IN BU LU'S HANDS.
NOT TRUE! XU PROVINCE, LIKE ALL PROVINCES, BELONGS TO THE HAN DYNASTY. BU LU DOESN'T OWN AN INCH OF IT.
AND NOT ONLY CAN I OFFER YOU XU, I CAN OFFER YOU THE CHANCE TO CLAIM THE HEAD OF THE TRAITOR BU LU.
HA HA HA!
ALL RIGHT, BEI LIU! I ACCEPT YOUR OFFER. I WANT TO SEE WHERE THIS GOES.

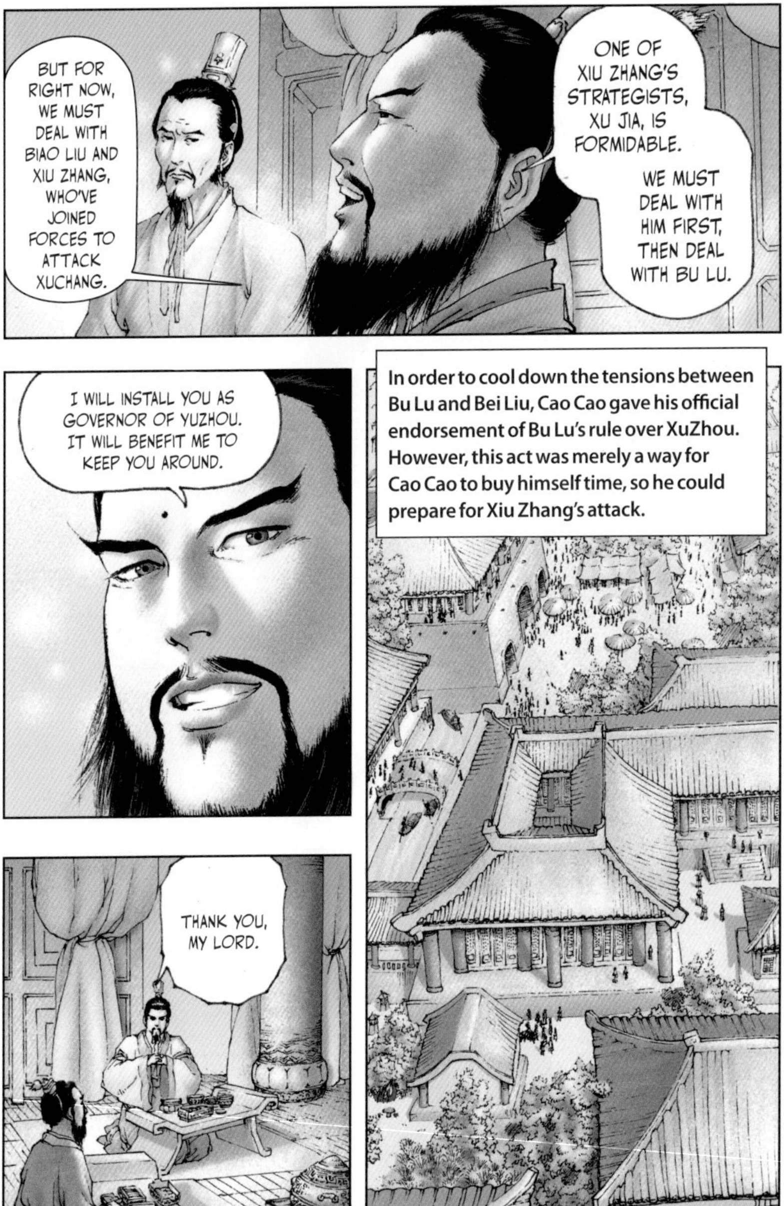

BUT FOR RIGHT NOW, WE MUST DEAL WITH BIAO LIU AND XIU ZHANG, WHO'VE JOINED FORCES TO ATTACK XUCHANG.
ONE OF XIU ZHANG'S STRATEGISTS, XU JIA, IS FORMIDABLE.
WE MUST DEAL WITH HIM FIRST, THEN DEAL WITH BU LU.
I WILL INSTALL YOU AS GOVERNOR OF YUZHOU. IT WILL BENEFIT ME TO KEEP YOU AROUND.
THANK YOU, MY LORD.
In order to cool down the tensions between Bu Lu and Bei Liu, Cao Cao gave his official endorsement of Bu Lu's rule over XuZhou. However, this act was merely a way for Cao Cao to buy himself time, so he could prepare for Xiu Zhang's attack.

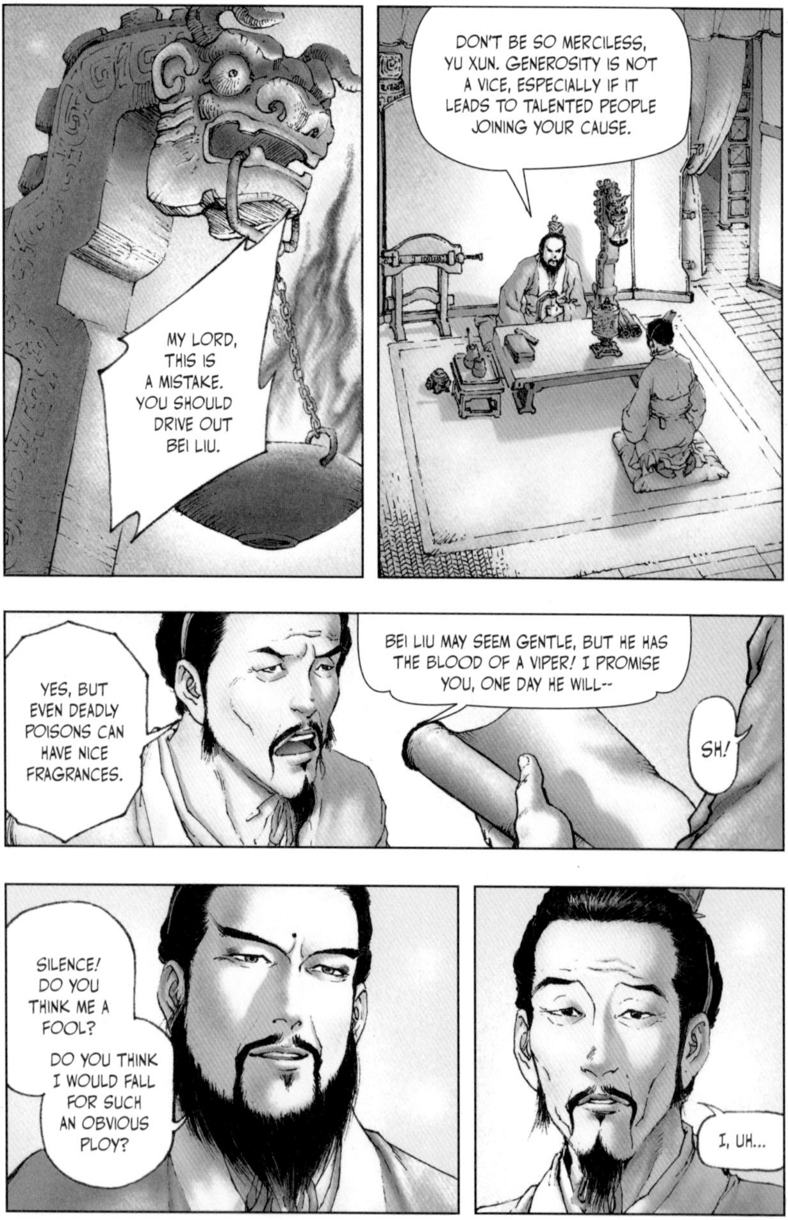
MY LORD, THIS IS A MISTAKE. YOU SHOULD DRIVE OUT BEI LIU.
DON'T BE SO MERCILESS, YU XUN. GENEROSITY IS NOT A VICE, ESPECIALLY IF IT LEADS TO TALENTED PEOPLE JOINING YOUR CAUSE.
YES, BUT EVEN DEADLY POISONS CAN HAVE NICE FRAGRANCES.
BEI LIU MAY SEEM GENTLE, BUT HE HAS THE BLOOD OF A VIPER! I PROMISE YOU, ONE DAY HE WILL--
SH!
SILENCE! DO YOU THINK ME A FOOL?
DO YOU THINK I WOULD FALL FOR SUCH AN OBVIOUS PLOY?
I, UH...

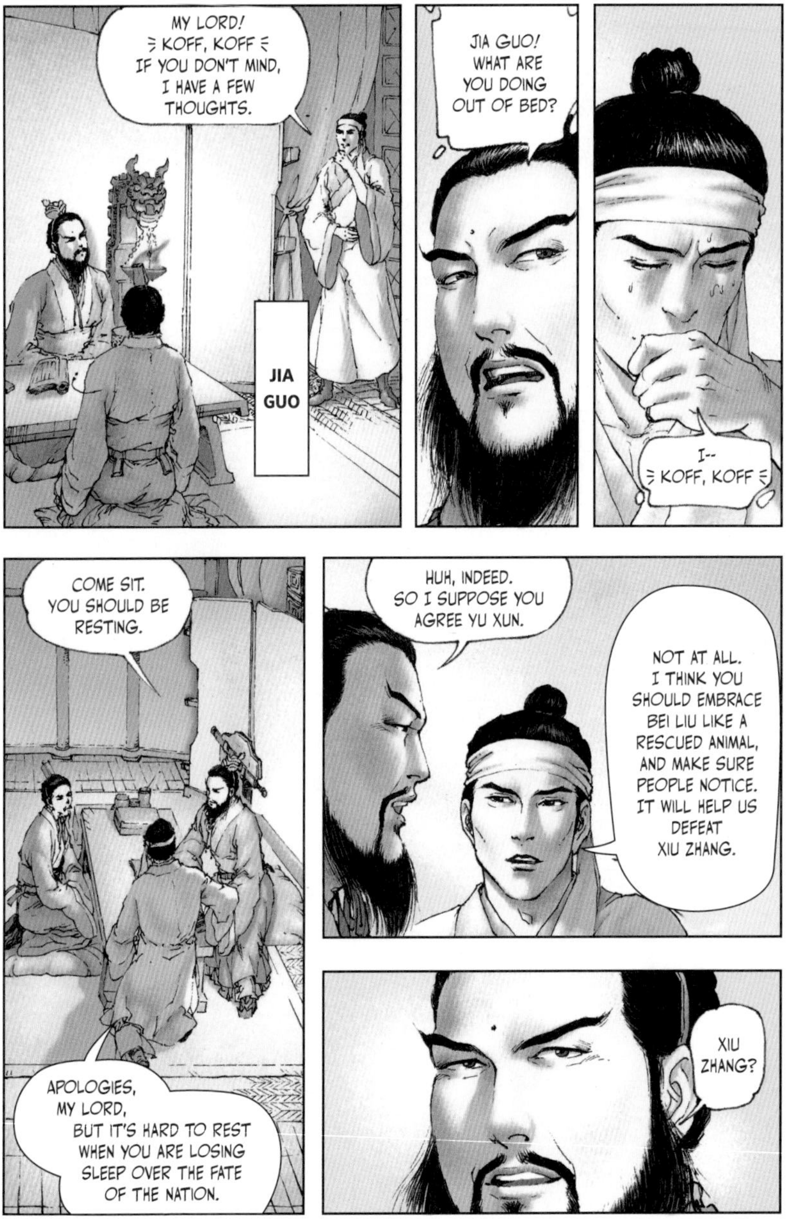
MY LORD! ≡ KOFF, KOFF ≡ IF YOU DON'T MIND, I HAVE A FEW THOUGHTS.
JIA GUO
JIA GUO! WHAT ARE YOU DOING OUT OF BED?
I-- ≡ KOFF, KOFF ≡
COME SIT. YOU SHOULD BE RESTING.
APOLOGIES, MY LORD, BUT IT'S HARD TO REST WHEN YOU ARE LOSING SLEEP OVER THE FATE OF THE NATION.
HUH, INDEED. SO I SUPPOSE YOU AGREE YU XUN.
NOT AT ALL. I THINK YOU SHOULD EMBRACE BEI LIU LIKE A RESCUED ANIMAL, AND MAKE SURE PEOPLE NOTICE. IT WILL HELP US DEFEAT XIU ZHANG.
XIU ZHANG?

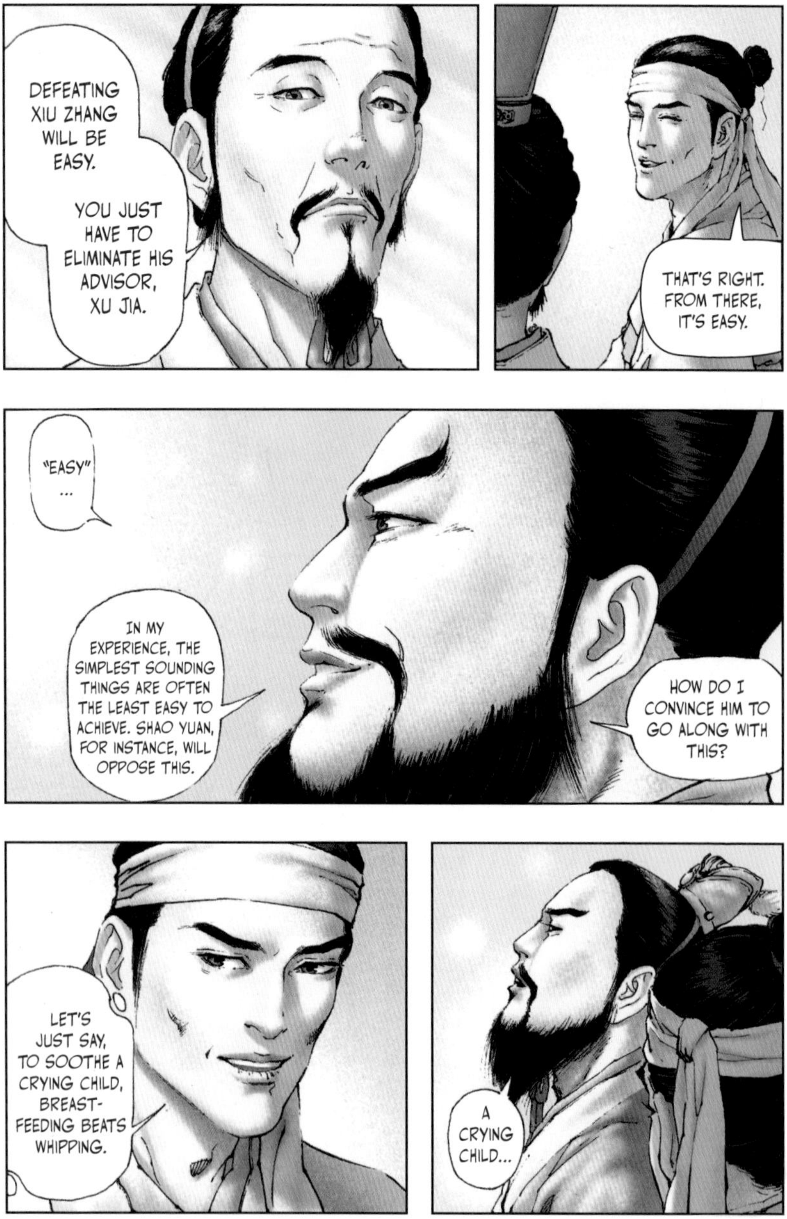
DEFEATING XIU ZHANG WILL BE EASY.
YOU JUST HAVE TO ELIMINATE HIS ADVISOR, XU JIA.
THAT'S RIGHT. FROM THERE, IT'S EASY.
"EASY" ...
IN MY EXPERIENCE, THE SIMPLEST SOUNDING THINGS ARE OFTEN THE LEAST EASY TO ACHIEVE. SHAO YUAN, FOR INSTANCE, WILL OPPOSE THIS.
HOW DO I CONVINCE HIM TO GO ALONG WITH THIS?
LET'S JUST SAY, TO SOOTHE A CRYING CHILD, BREAST-FEEDING BEATS WHIPPING.
A CRYING CHILD...

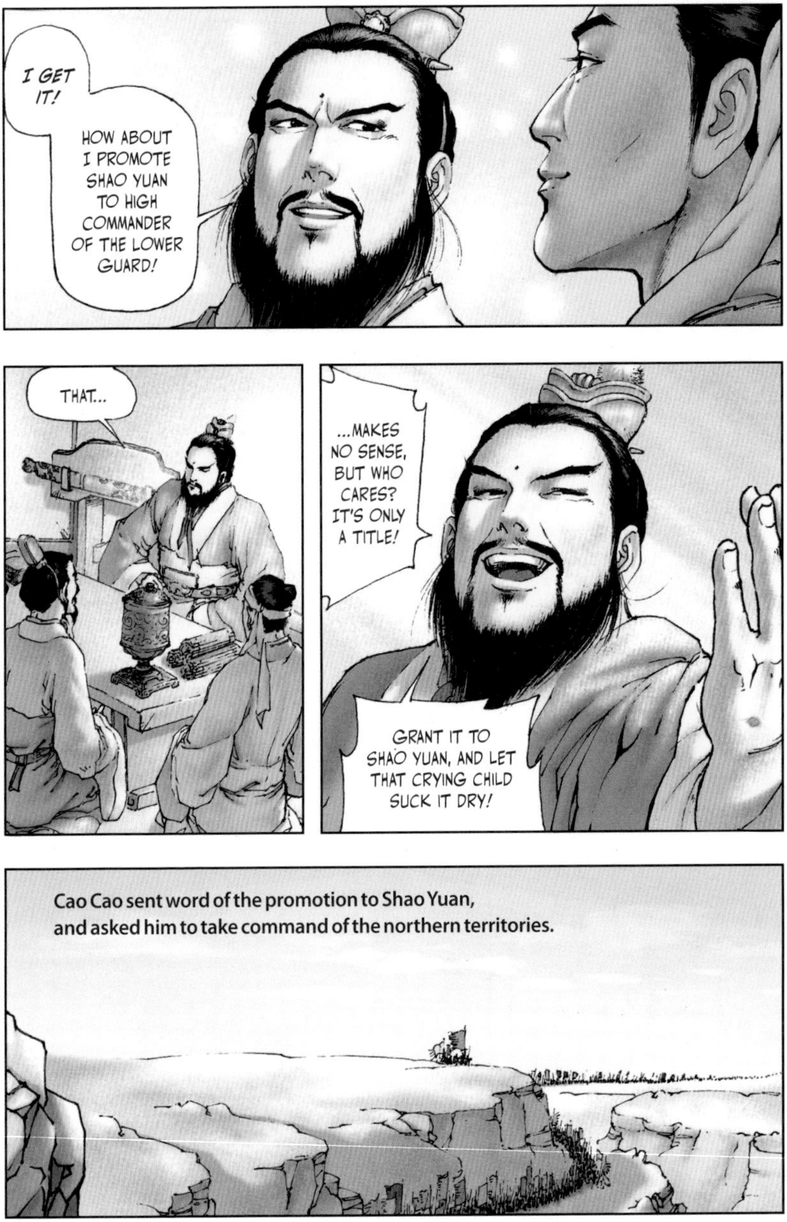
I GET IT!
HOW ABOUT I PROMOTE SHAO YUAN TO HIGH COMMANDER OF THE LOWER GUARD!
THAT...
...MAKES NO SENSE, BUT WHO CARES? IT'S ONLY A TITLE!
GRANT IT TO SHAO YUAN, AND LET THAT CRYING CHILD SUCK IT DRY!
Cao Cao sent word of the promotion to Shao Yuan, and asked him to take command of the northern territories.

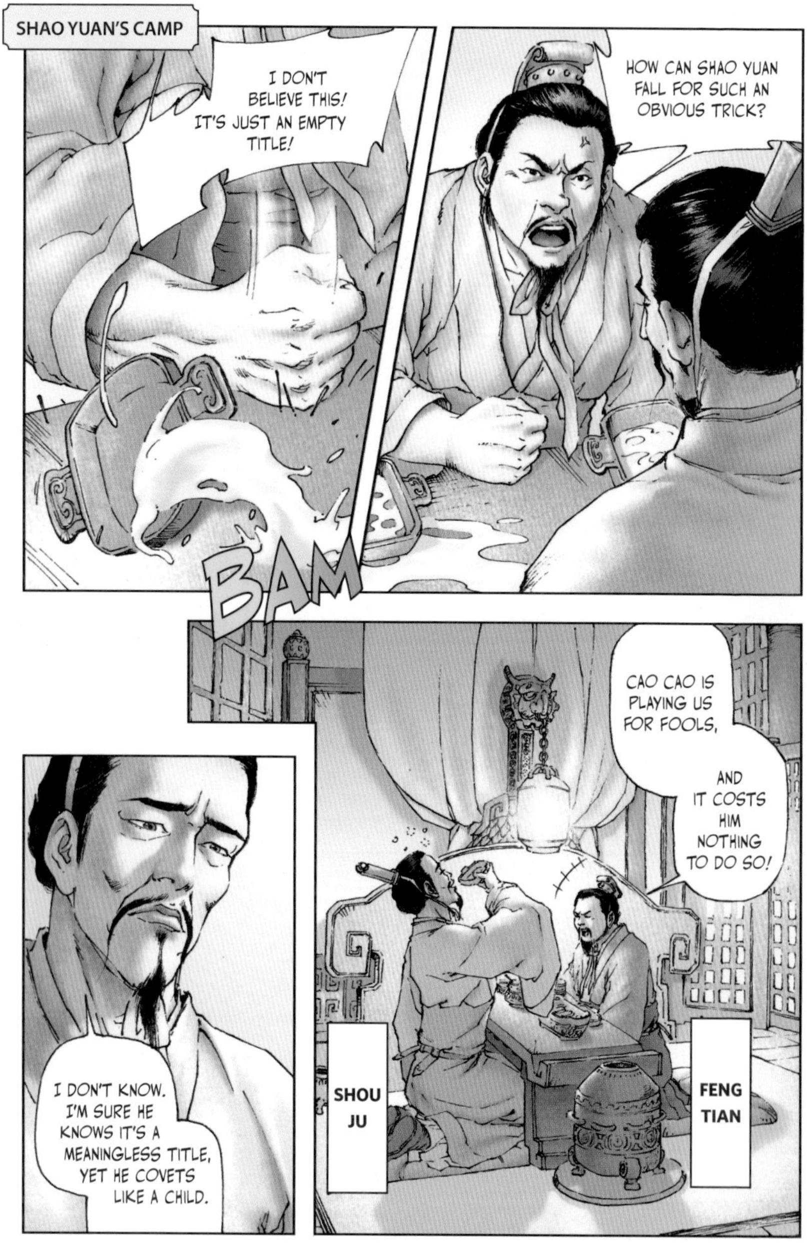
SHAO YUAN'S CAMP
I DON'T BELIEVE THIS! IT'S JUST AN EMPTY TITLE!
HOW CAN SHAO YUAN FALL FOR SUCH AN OBVIOUS TRICK?
BAM
CAO CAO IS PLAYING US FOR FOOLS,
AND IT COSTS HIM NOTHING TO DO SO!
SHOU JU
FENG TIAN
I DON'T KNOW. I'M SURE HE KNOWS IT'S A MEANINGLESS TITLE, YET HE COVETS LIKE A CHILD.

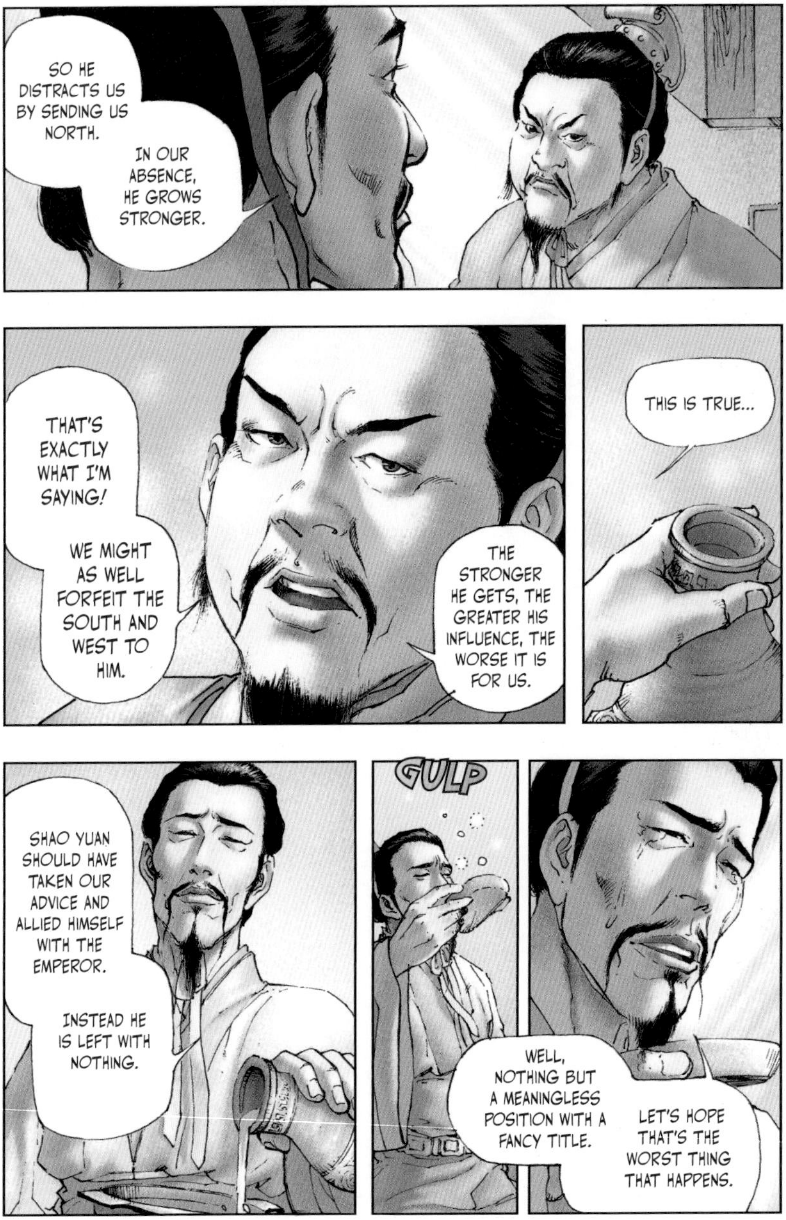
SO HE DISTRACTS US BY SENDING US NORTH.
IN OUR ABSENCE, HE GROWS STRONGER.
THAT'S EXACTLY WHAT I'M SAYING!
WE MIGHT AS WELL FORFEIT THE SOUTH AND WEST TO HIM.
THE STRONGER HE GETS, THE GREATER HIS INFLUENCE, THE WORSE IT IS FOR US.
THIS IS TRUE...
SHAO YUAN SHOULD HAVE TAKEN OUR ADVICE AND ALLIED HIMSELF WITH THE EMPEROR.
INSTEAD HE IS LEFT WITH NOTHING.
GULP
WELL, NOTHING BUT A MEANINGLESS POSITION WITH A FANCY TITLE.
LET'S HOPE THAT'S THE WORST THING THAT HAPPENS.

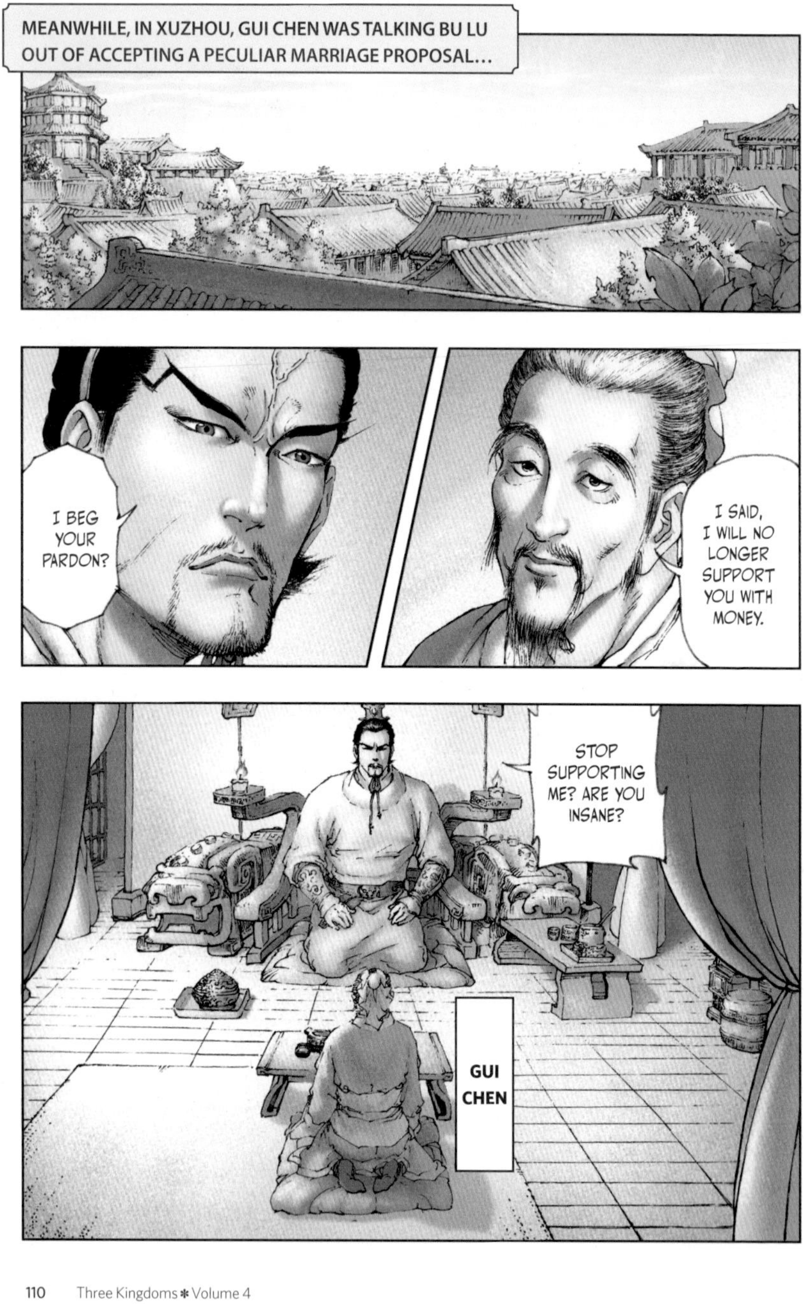
MEANWHILE, IN XUZHOU, GUI CHEN WAS TALKING BU LU OUT OF ACCEPTING A PECULIAR MARRIAGE PROPOSAL…
I BEG YOUR PARDON?
I SAID, I WILL NO LONGER SUPPORT YOU WITH MONEY.
STOP SUPPORTING ME? ARE YOU INSANE?
GUI CHEN

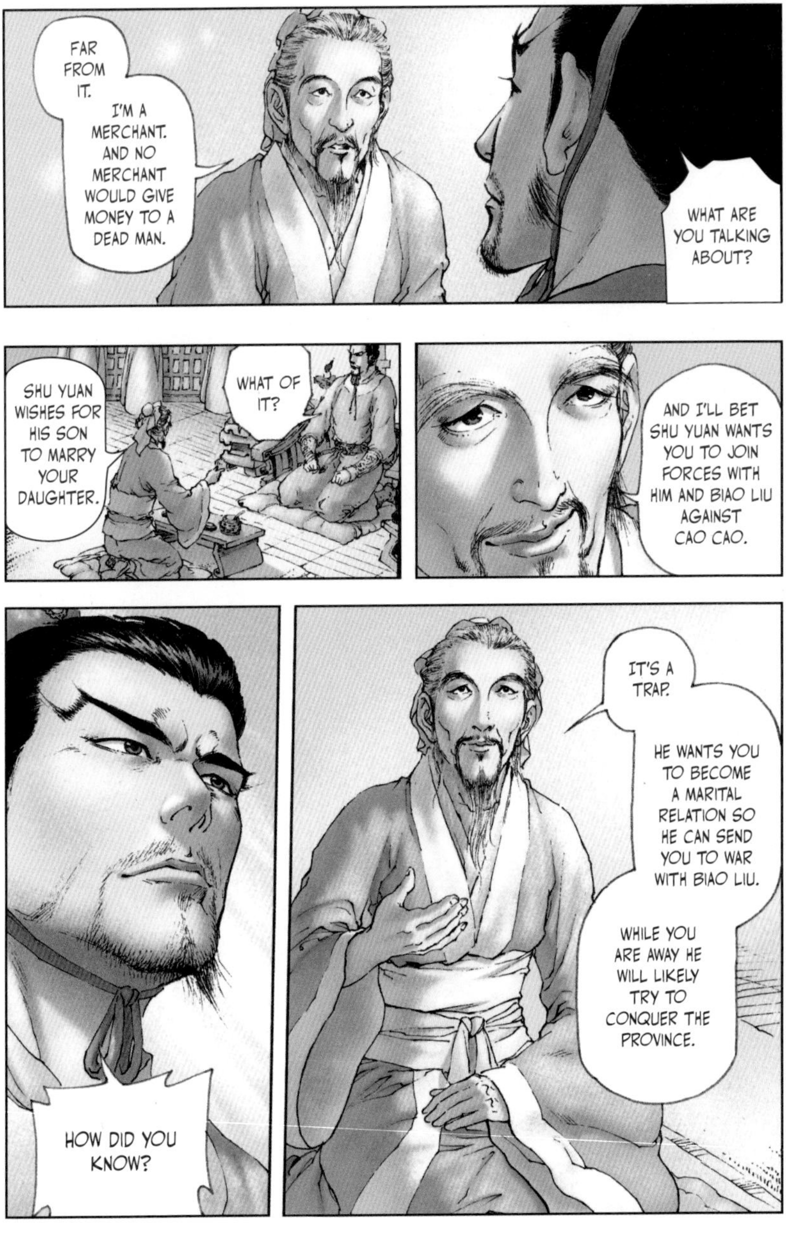
FAR FROM IT.
I'M A MERCHANT. AND NO MERCHANT WOULD GIVE MONEY TO A DEAD MAN.
WHAT ARE YOU TALKING ABOUT?
SHU YUAN WISHES FOR HIS SON TO MARRY YOUR DAUGHTER.
WHAT OF IT?
AND I'LL BET SHU YUAN WANTS YOU TO JOIN FORCES WITH HIM AND BIAO LIU AGAINST CAO CAO.
HOW DID YOU KNOW?
IT'S A TRAP.
HE WANTS YOU TO BECOME A MARITAL RELATION SO HE CAN SEND YOU TO WAR WITH BIAO LIU.
WHILE YOU ARE AWAY HE WILL LIKELY TRY TO CONQUER THE PROVINCE.

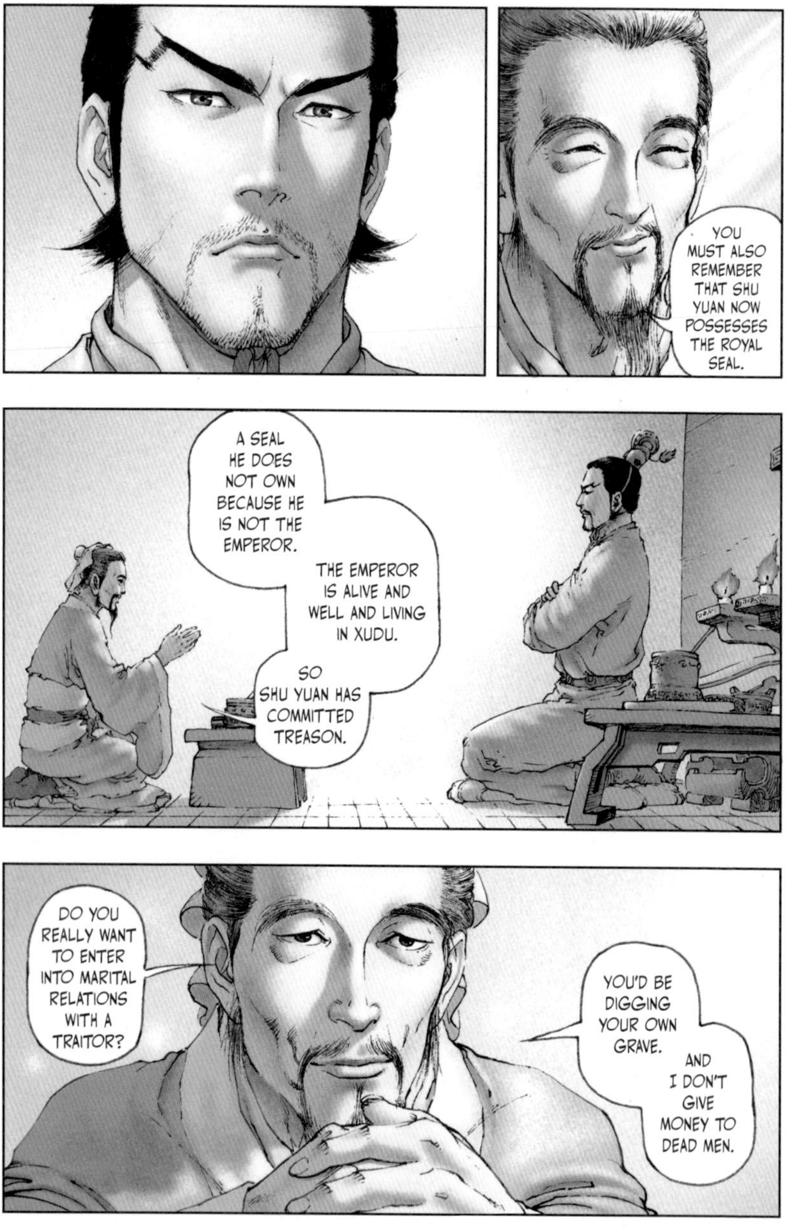
YOU MUST ALSO REMEMBER THAT SHU YUAN NOW POSSESSES THE ROYAL SEAL.
A SEAL HE DOES NOT OWN BECAUSE HE IS NOT THE EMPEROR.
THE EMPEROR IS ALIVE AND WELL AND LIVING IN XUDU.
SO SHU YUAN HAS COMMITTED TREASON.
DO YOU REALLY WANT TO ENTER INTO MARITAL RELATIONS WITH A TRAITOR?
YOU'D BE DIGGING YOUR OWN GRAVE.
AND I DON'T GIVE MONEY TO DEAD MEN.

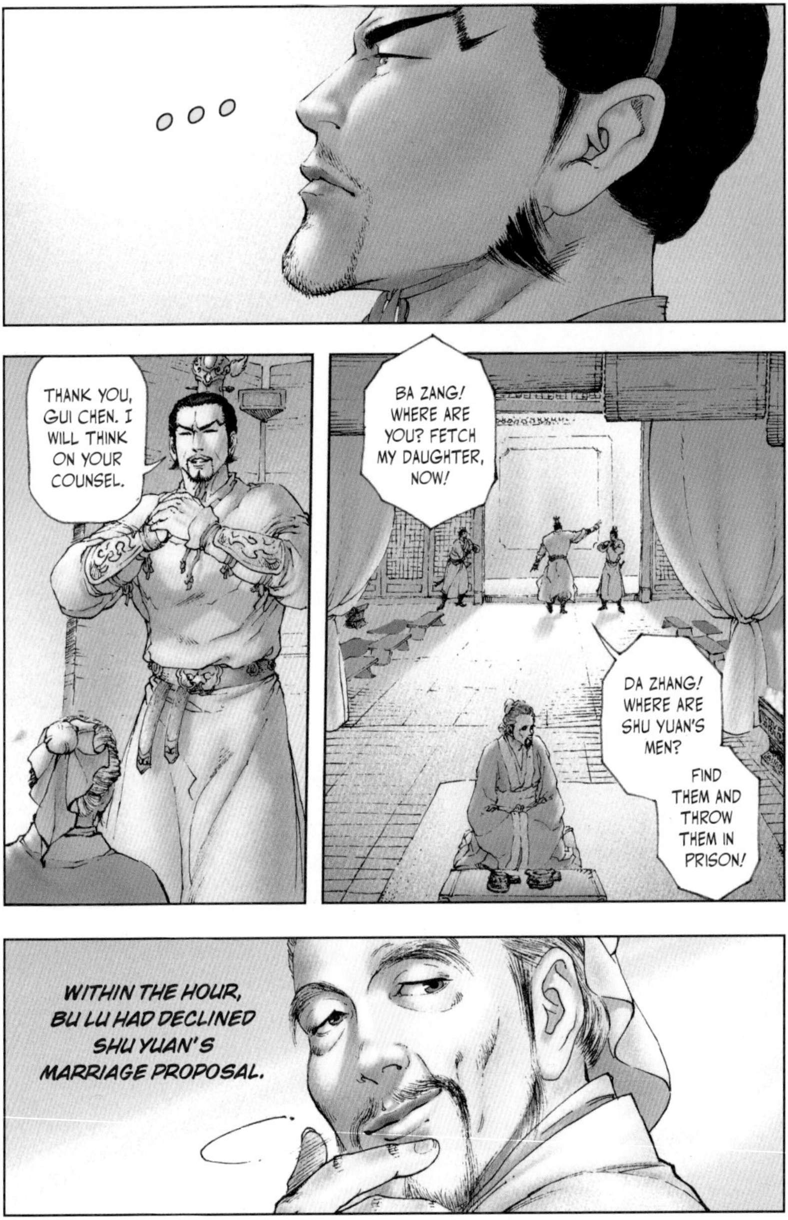

THANK YOU, GUI CHEN. I WILL THINK ON YOUR COUNSEL.
BA ZANG! WHERE ARE YOU? FETCH MY DAUGHTER, NOW!
DA ZHANG! WHERE ARE SHU YUAN'S MEN?
FIND THEM AND THROW THEM IN PRISON!
WITHIN THE HOUR, BU LU HAD DECLINED SHU YUAN'S MARRIAGE PROPOSAL.

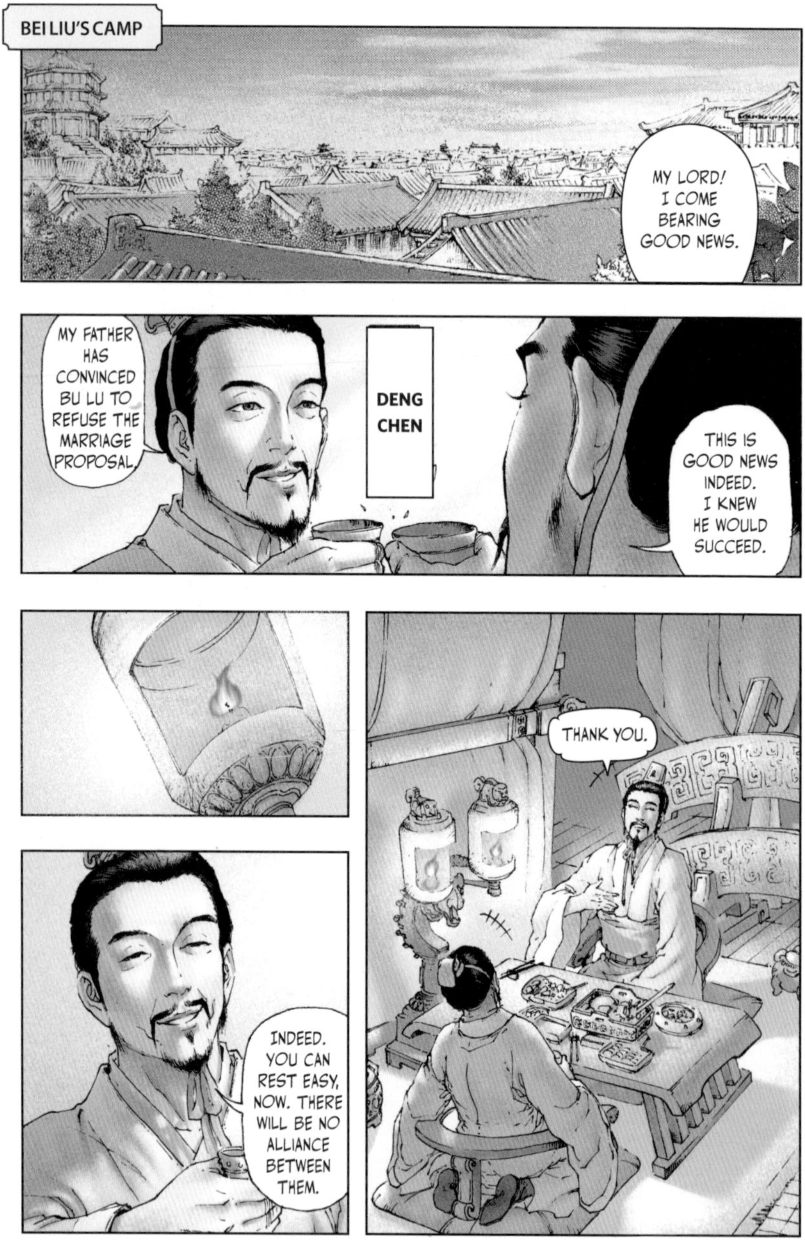
BEI LIU'S CAMP
MY LORD! I COME BEARING GOOD NEWS.
MY FATHER HAS CONVINCED BU LU TO REFUSE THE MARRIAGE PROPOSAL.
DENG CHEN
THIS IS GOOD NEWS INDEED. I KNEW HE WOULD SUCCEED.
THANK YOU.
INDEED. YOU CAN REST EASY, NOW. THERE WILL BE NO ALLIANCE BETWEEN THEM.

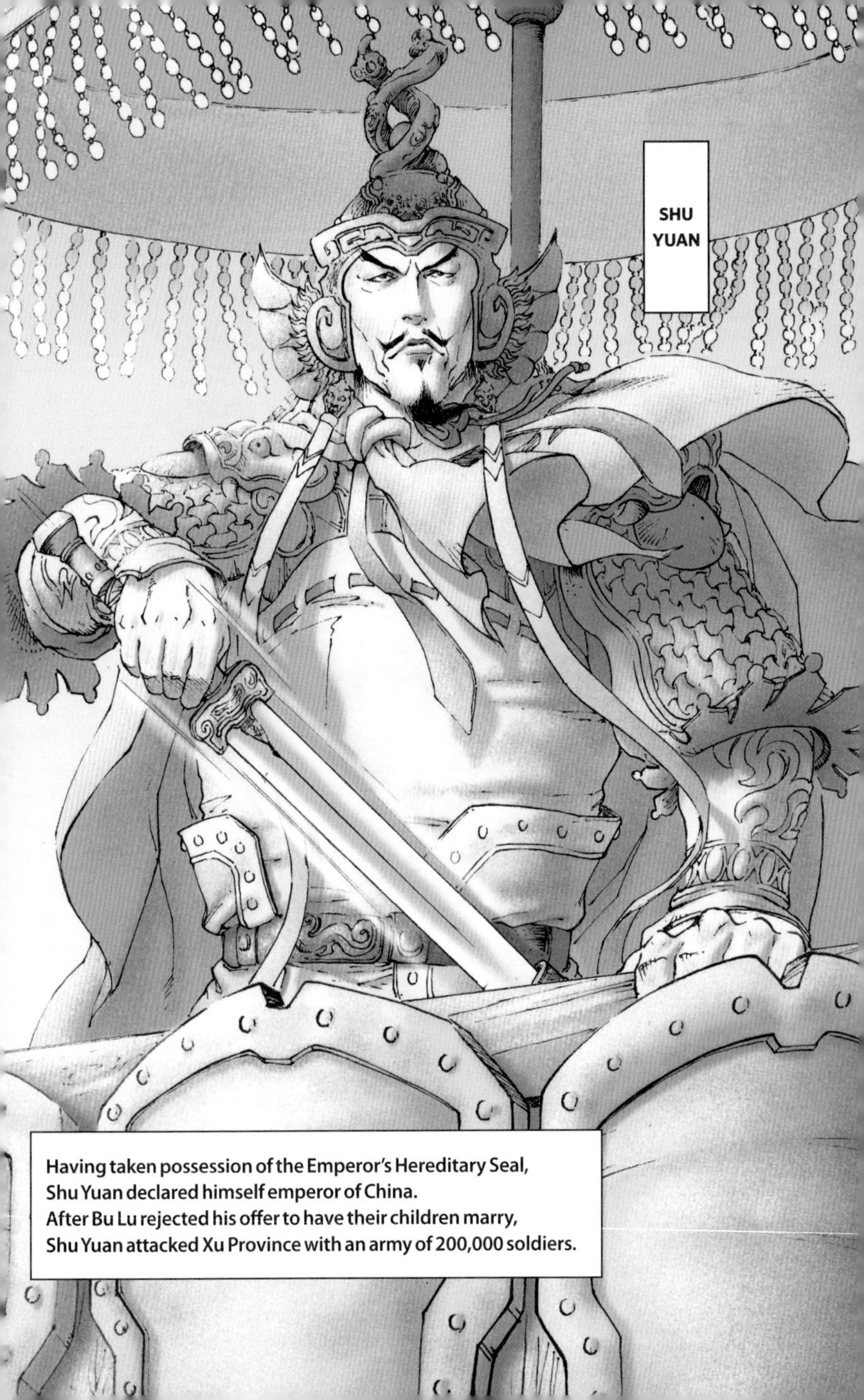
SHU YUAN
Having taken possession of the Emperor's Hereditary Seal,
Shu Yuan declared himself emperor of China.
After Bu Lu rejected his offer to have their children marry,
Shu Yuan attacked Xu Province with an army of 200,000 soldiers.

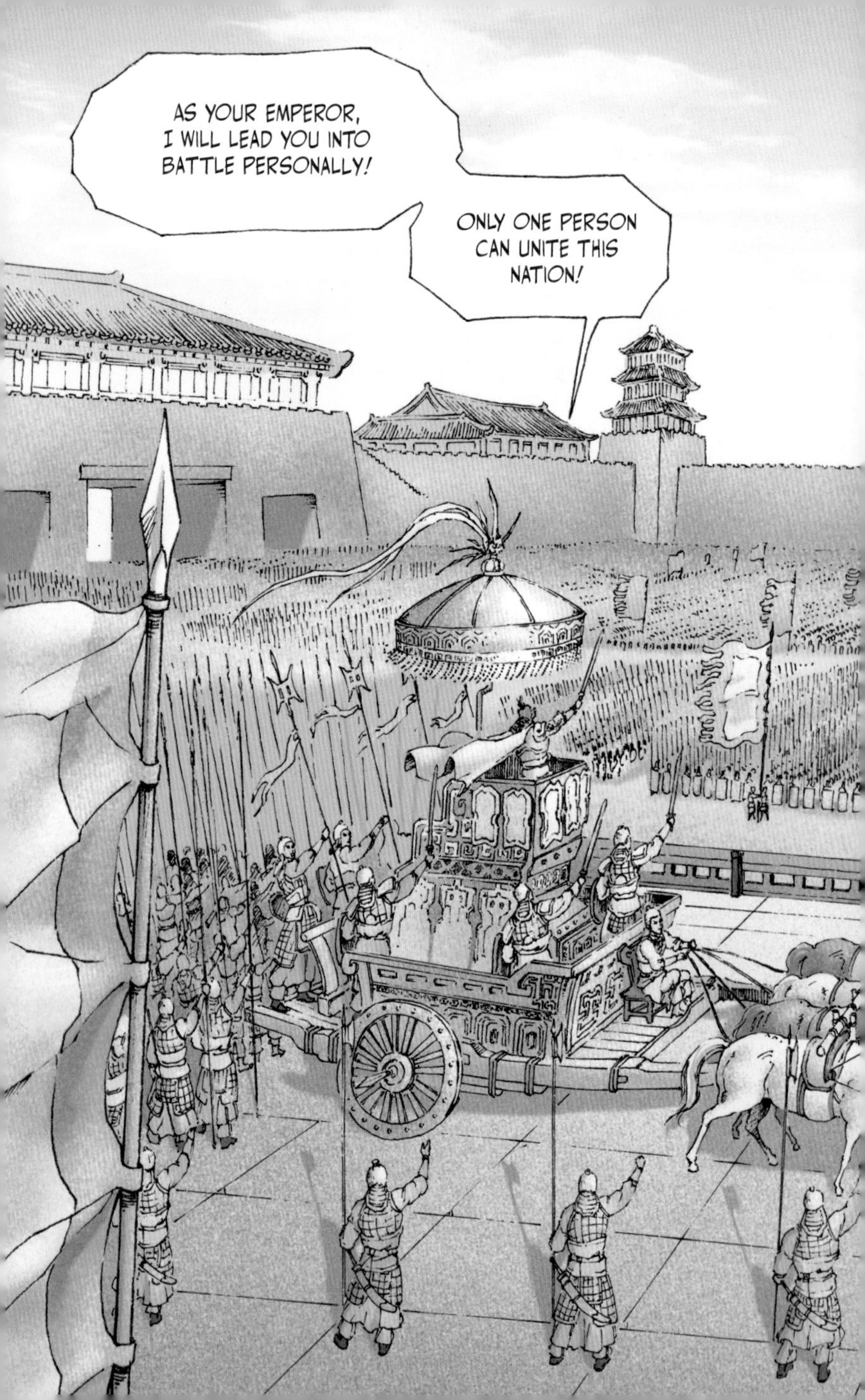
AS YOUR EMPEROR, I WILL LEAD YOU INTO BATTLE PERSONALLY!
ONLY ONE PERSON CAN UNITE THIS NATION!

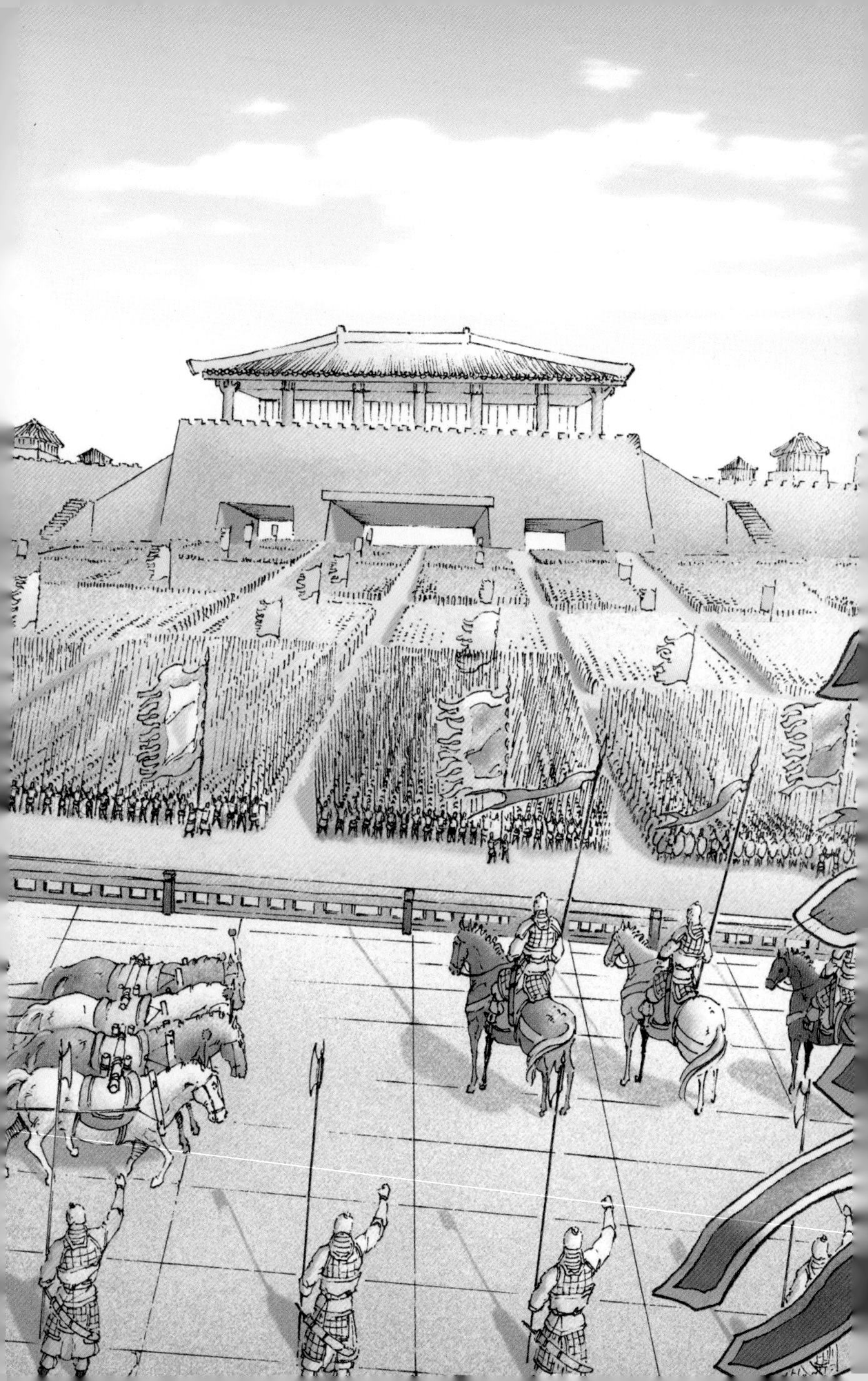

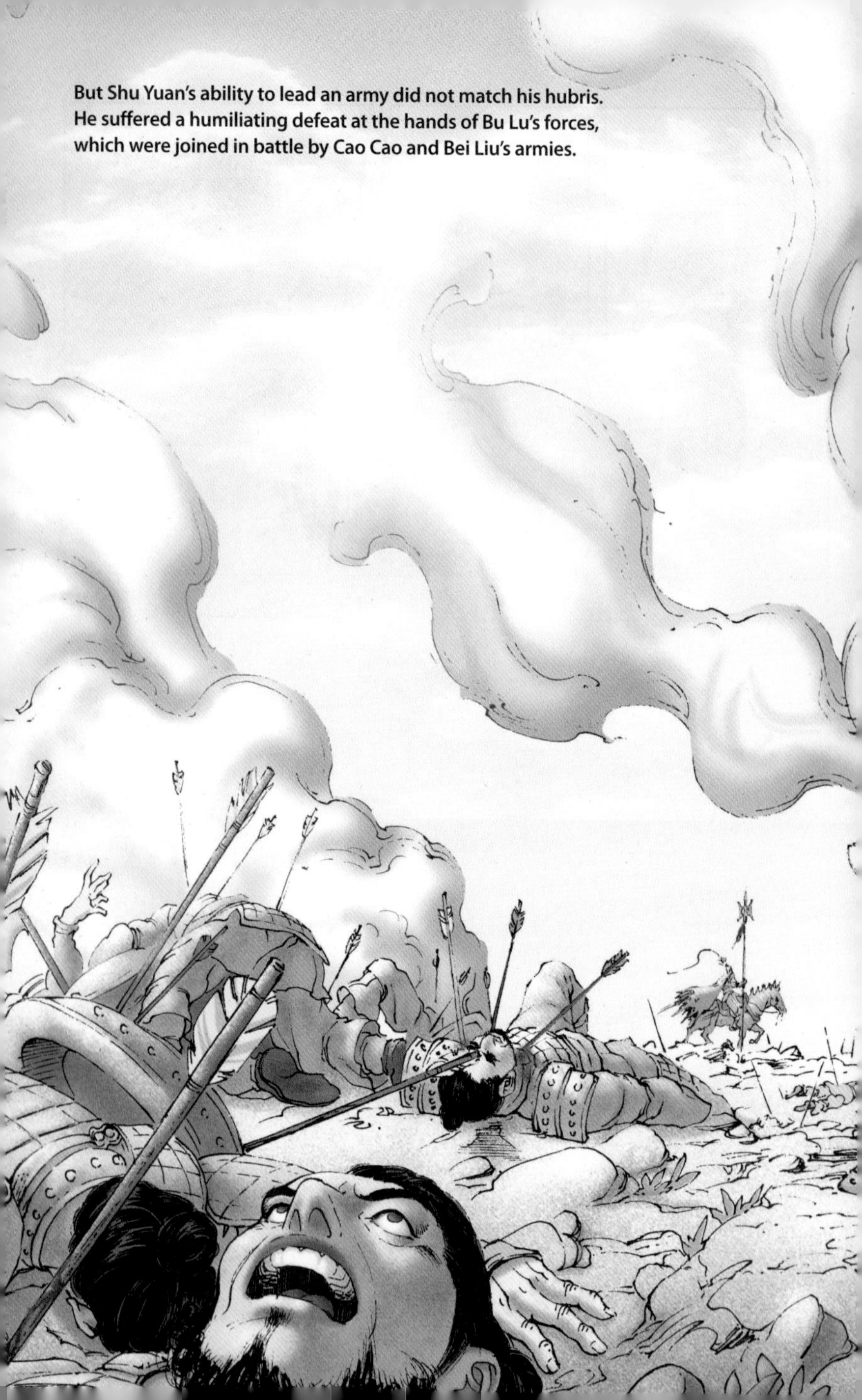
But Shu Yuan's ability to lead an army did not match his hubris. He suffered a humiliating defeat at the hands of Bu Lu's forces, which were joined in battle by Cao Cao and Bei Liu's armies.

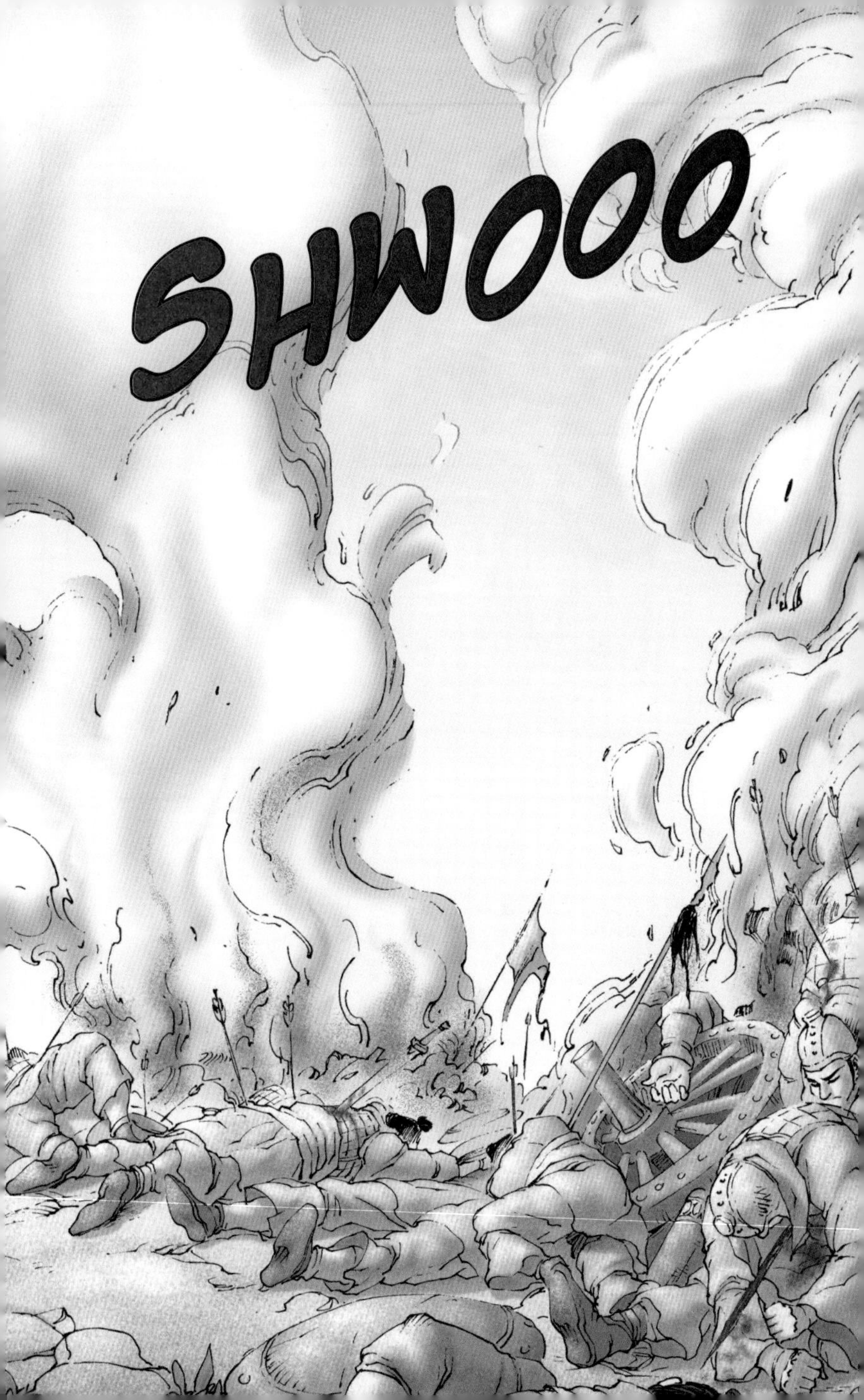
SHWOOO

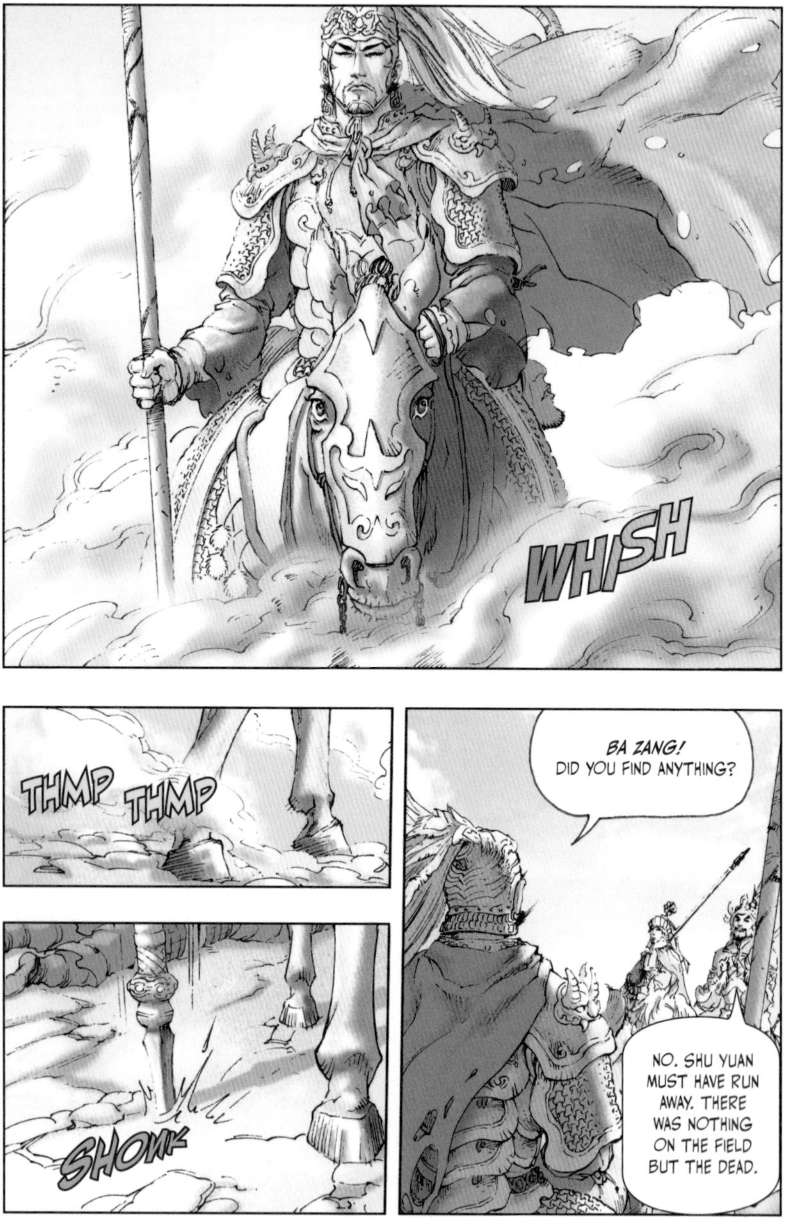
WHISH
THMP THMP
SHONK
BA ZANG!
DID YOU FIND ANYTHING?
NO. SHU YUAN MUST HAVE RUN AWAY. THERE WAS NOTHING ON THE FIELD BUT THE DEAD.

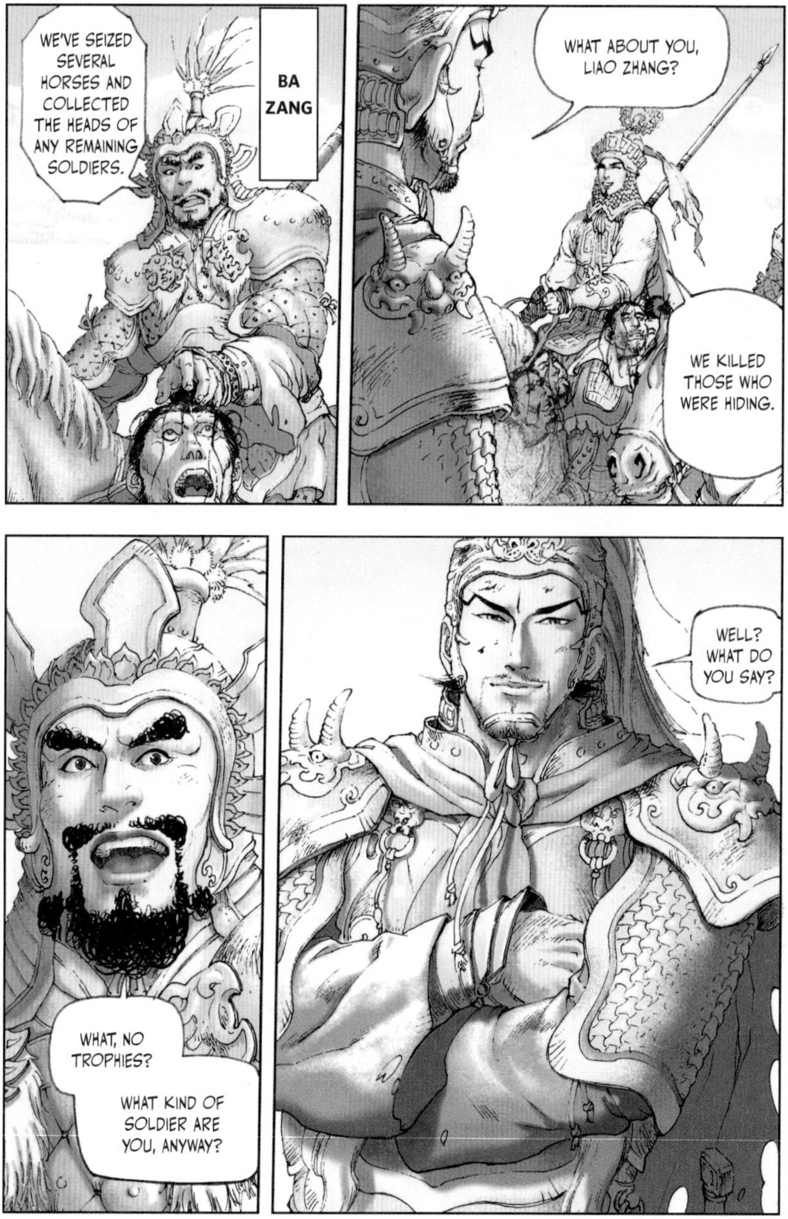
WE'VE SEIZED SEVERAL HORSES AND COLLECTED THE HEADS OF ANY REMAINING SOLDIERS.
BA ZANG
WHAT ABOUT YOU, LIAO ZHANG?
WE KILLED THOSE WHO WERE HIDING.
WELL? WHAT DO YOU SAY?
WHAT, NO TROPHIES?
WHAT KIND OF SOLDIER ARE YOU, ANYWAY?

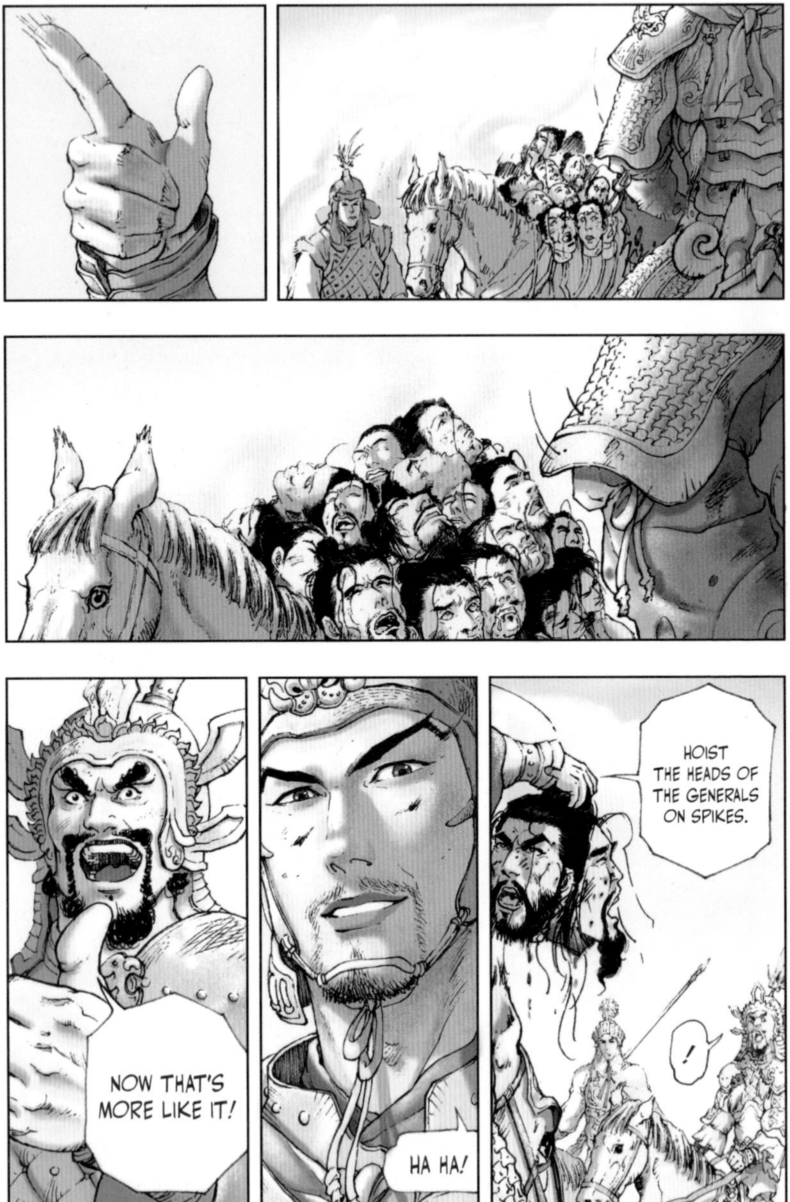
NOW THAT'S MORE LIKE IT!
HA HA!
HOIST THE HEADS OF THE GENERALS ON SPIKES.
!

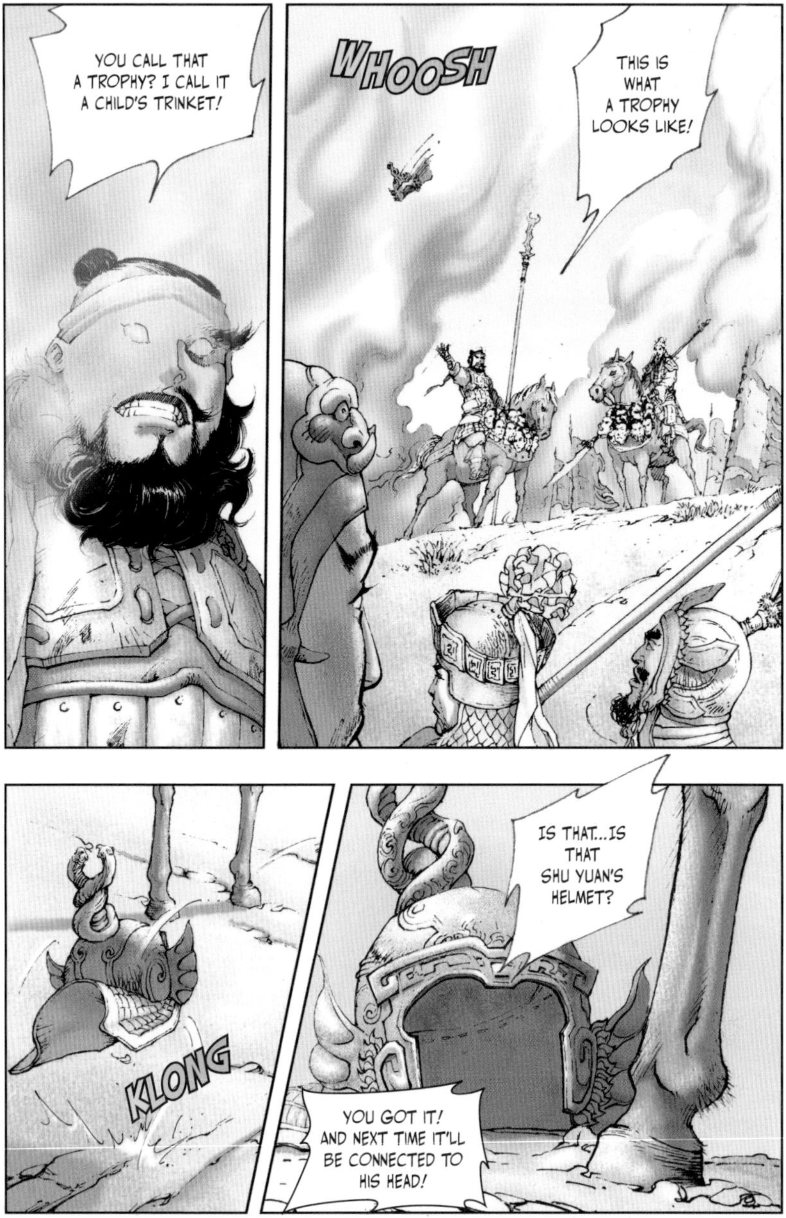
YOU CALL THAT A TROPHY? I CALL IT A CHILD'S TRINKET!
WHOOSH
THIS IS WHAT A TROPHY LOOKS LIKE!
KLONG
IS THAT...IS THAT SHU YUAN'S HELMET?
YOU GOT IT! AND NEXT TIME IT'LL BE CONNECTED TO HIS HEAD!

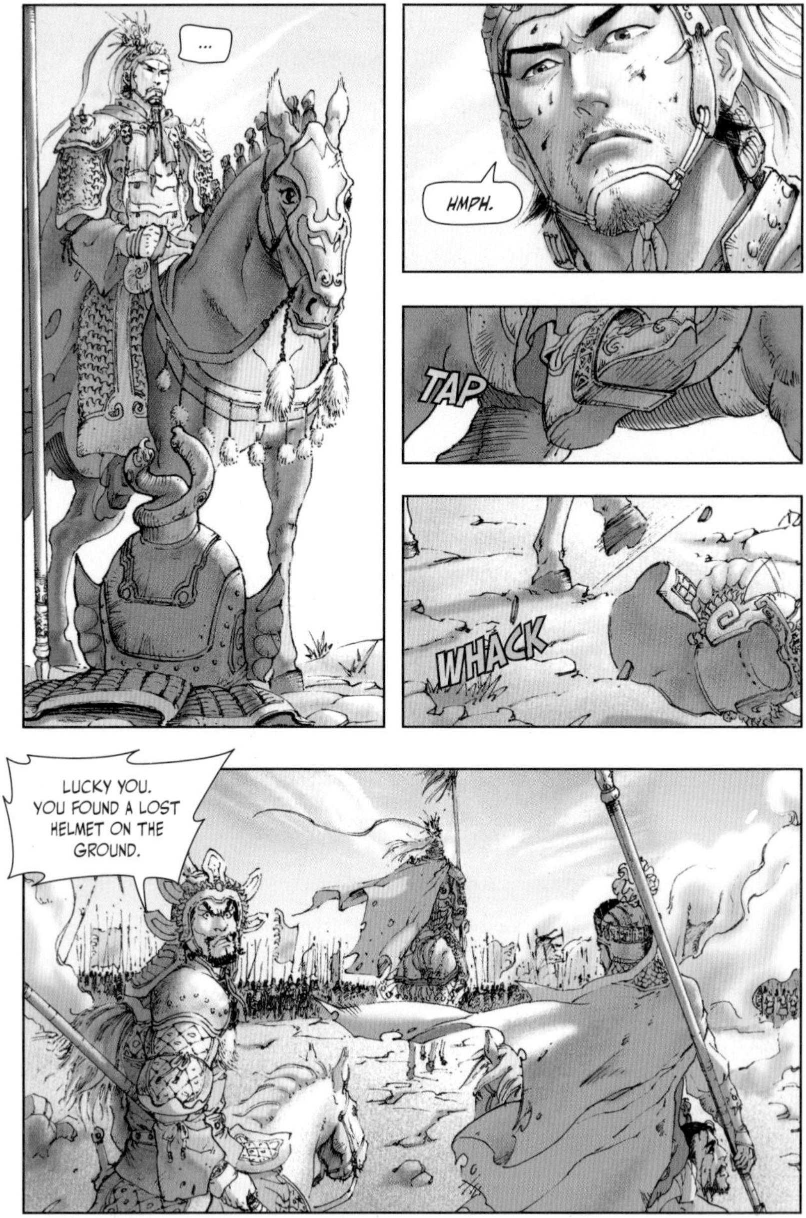
...
HMPH.
TAP
WHACK
LUCKY YOU. YOU FOUND A LOST HELMET ON THE GROUND.

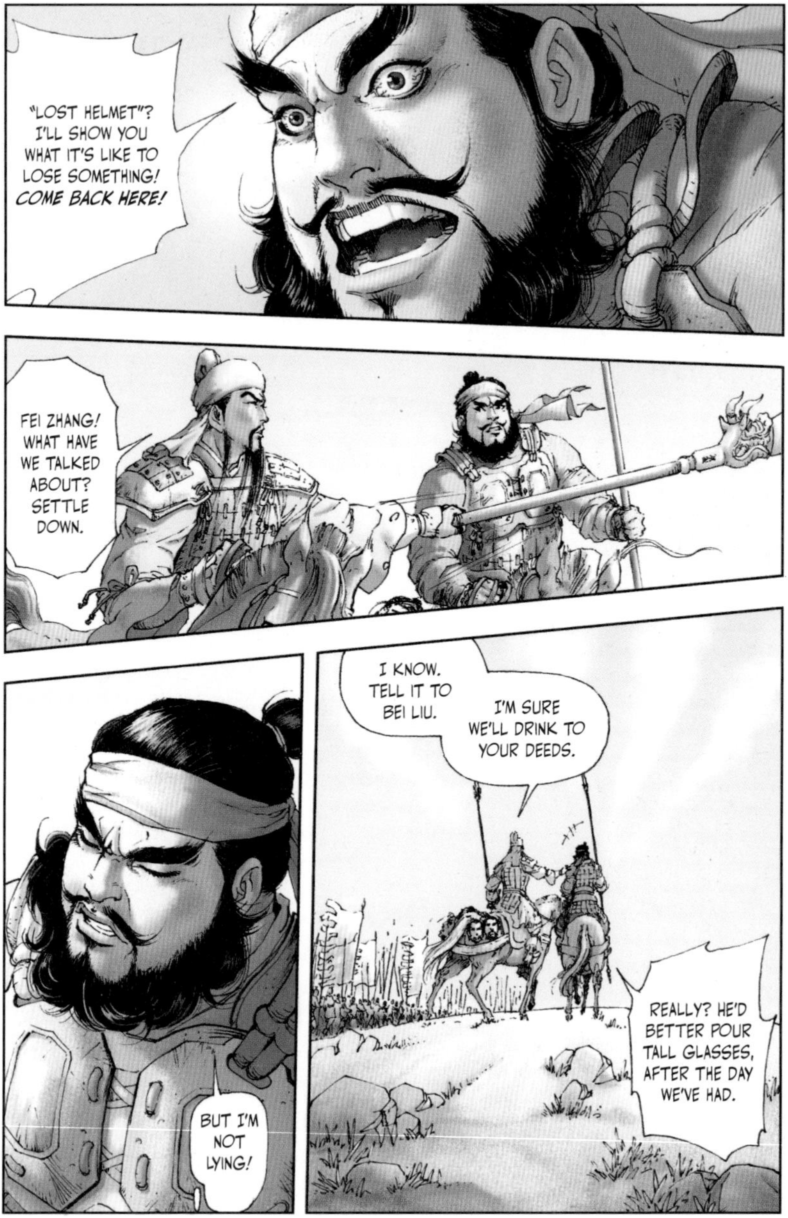
"LOST HELMET"? I'LL SHOW YOU WHAT IT'S LIKE TO LOSE SOMETHING! COME BACK HERE!
FEI ZHANG! WHAT HAVE WE TALKED ABOUT? SETTLE DOWN.
BUT I'M NOT LYING!
I KNOW. TELL IT TO BEI LIU.
I'M SURE WE'LL DRINK TO YOUR DEEDS.
REALLY? HE'D BETTER POUR TALL GLASSES, AFTER THE DAY WE'VE HAD.

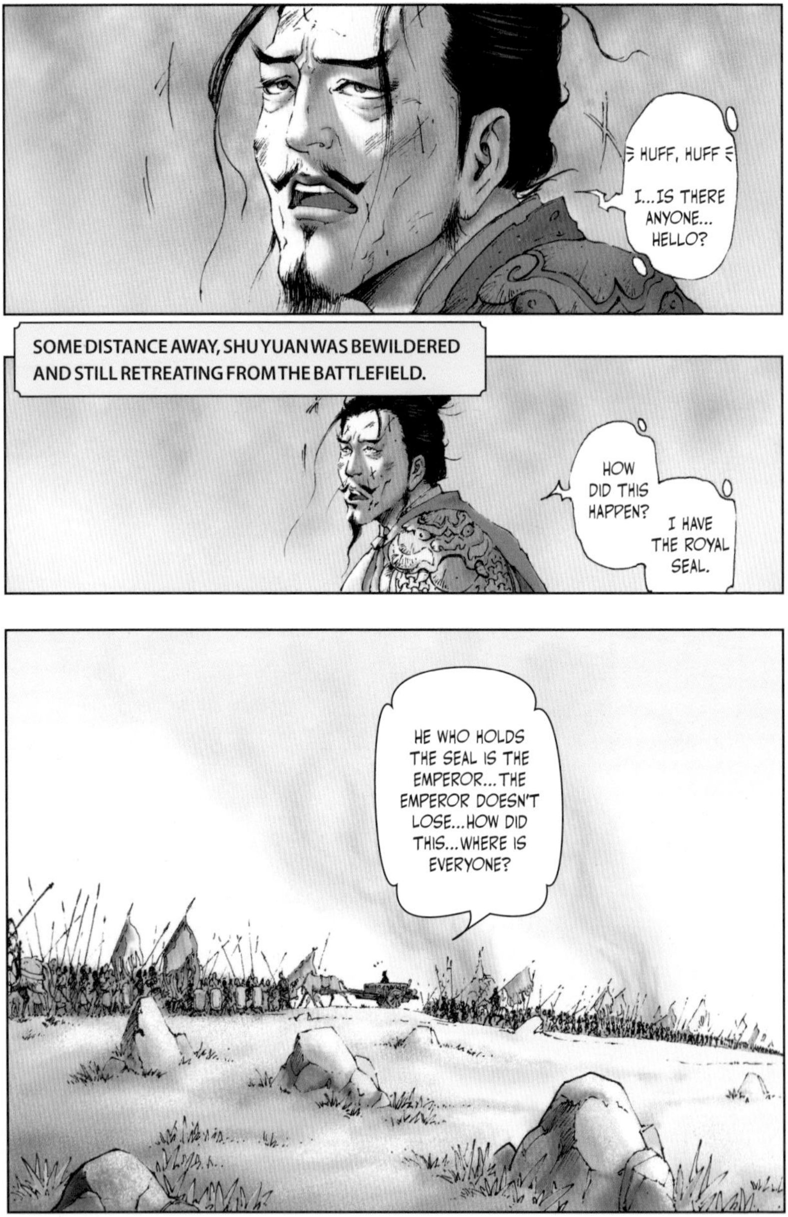
HUFF, HUFF
I...IS THERE ANYONE... HELLO?
SOME DISTANCE AWAY, SHU YUAN WAS BEWILDERED AND STILL RETREATING FROM THE BATTLEFIELD.
HOW DID THIS HAPPEN?
I HAVE THE ROYAL SEAL.
HE WHO HOLDS THE SEAL IS THE EMPEROR...THE EMPEROR DOESN'T LOSE...HOW DID THIS...WHERE IS EVERYONE?

Shu Yuan

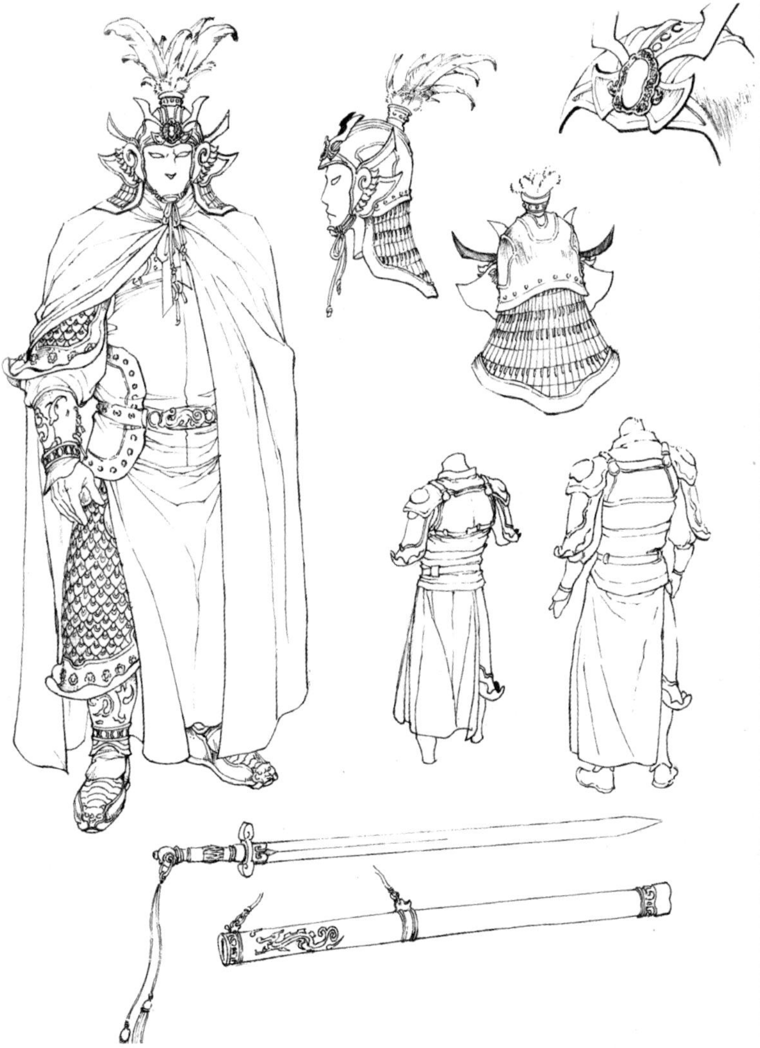

Chapter 4

Cao Cao, the Villainous Hero AD 198

Summary

With Shu Yuan out of the picture, only Shao Yuan and Bu Lu remained as Cao Cao's greatest adversaries. Cao Cao lacks the power to attack Shao Yuan directly, so he follows Jia Guo's advice and goes after Bu Lu first. Shao Yuan's greedy acceptance of the role of "High Commander of the Lower Guard" has taken him and his army to the northern lands, away from the XuZhou and the impending attack on Bu Lu.

With Shao Yuan out of the picture, Cao Cao attacks Bu Lu in XuZhou. Bu Lu flees to the city of XiaPi, where he is quickly trapped. Gong Chen, Bu Lu's chief advisor, tells him that all is lost, and that they are walking dead men. Bu Lu is enraged and orders his men to continue fighting. In his fury, Bu Lu falls asleep and imagines those who have died coming to claim him. When he wakes, he discovers that his own men have bound him and intend to hand him over to Cao Cao. Bu Lu is taken into custody as Bei Liu mourns the course of events and Cao Cao thinks ahead to ruling the kingdom.

Zhuo
A
ChangShan
BeiHai
PuYang
XiaoPei
HuLuo
B
XiaPi
GuanDu
LuoYang
XuZhou
XuChang
ChangAn
NanYang
ShouChun

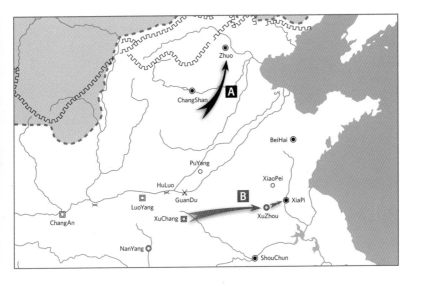

A Having accepted the title of High Commander of the Lower Guard, Shao Yuan leads his army away from Xu to occupy the northern territories.

B With Shao Yuan out of the way, Cao Cao attacks Bu Lu, driving him to XiaPi and eventually capturing him.

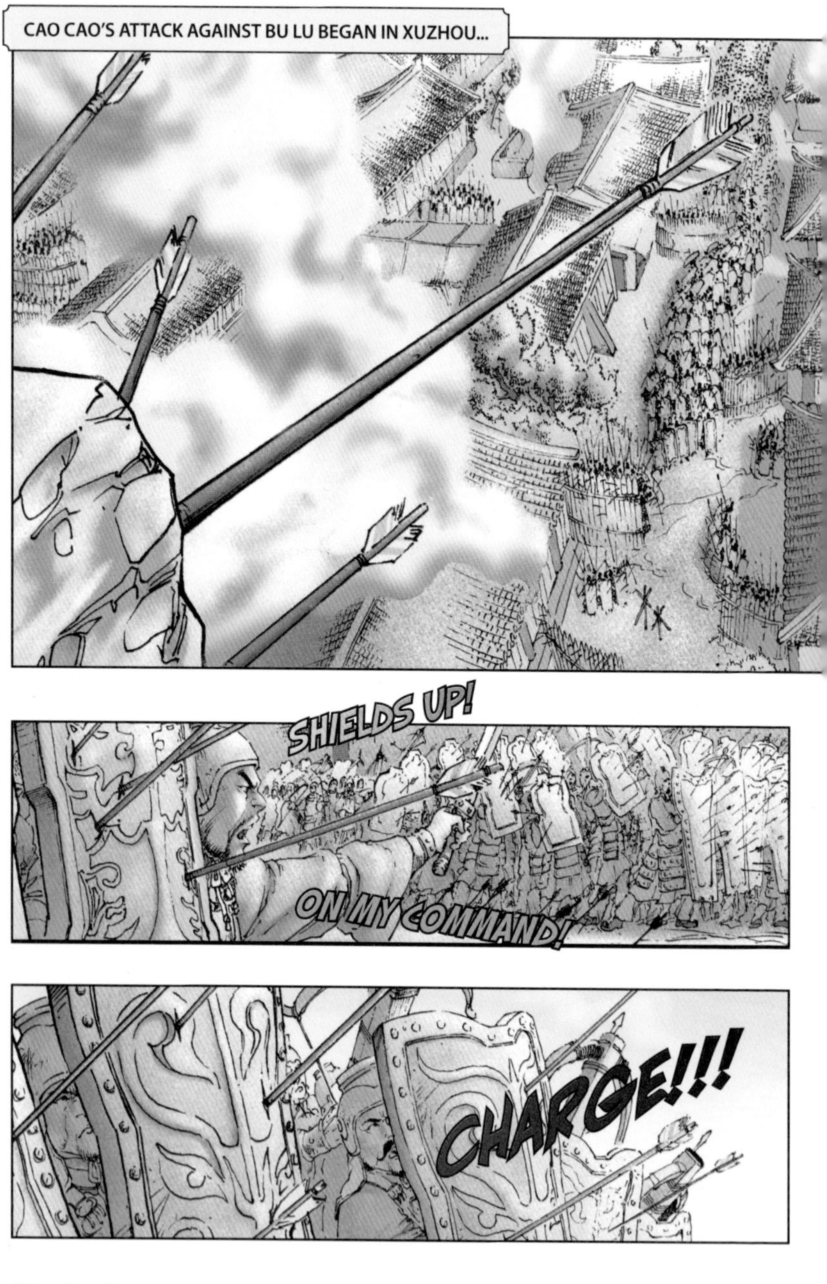
CAO CAO'S ATTACK AGAINST BU LU BEGAN IN XUZHOU...
SHIELDS UP!
ON MY COMMAND!
CHARGE!!!

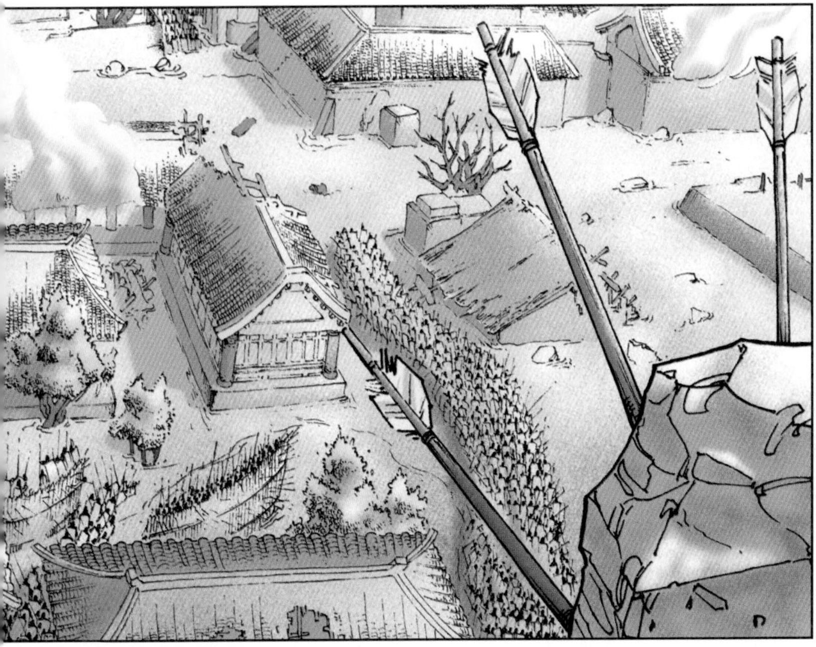

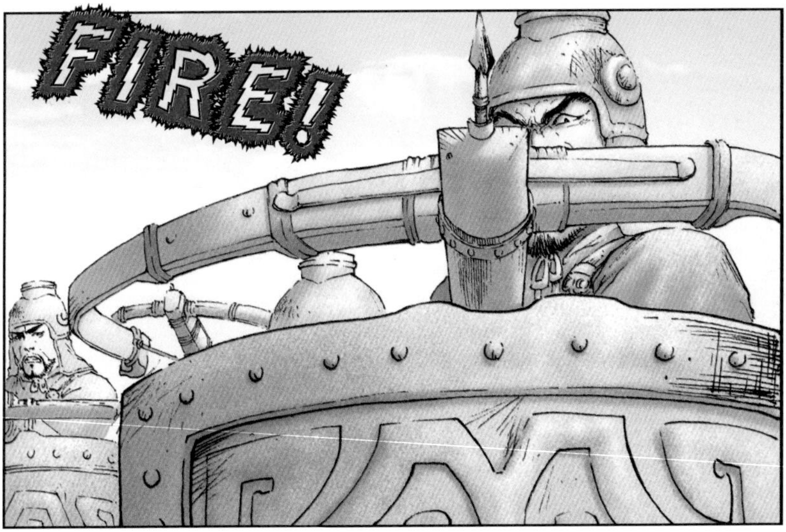
FIRE!

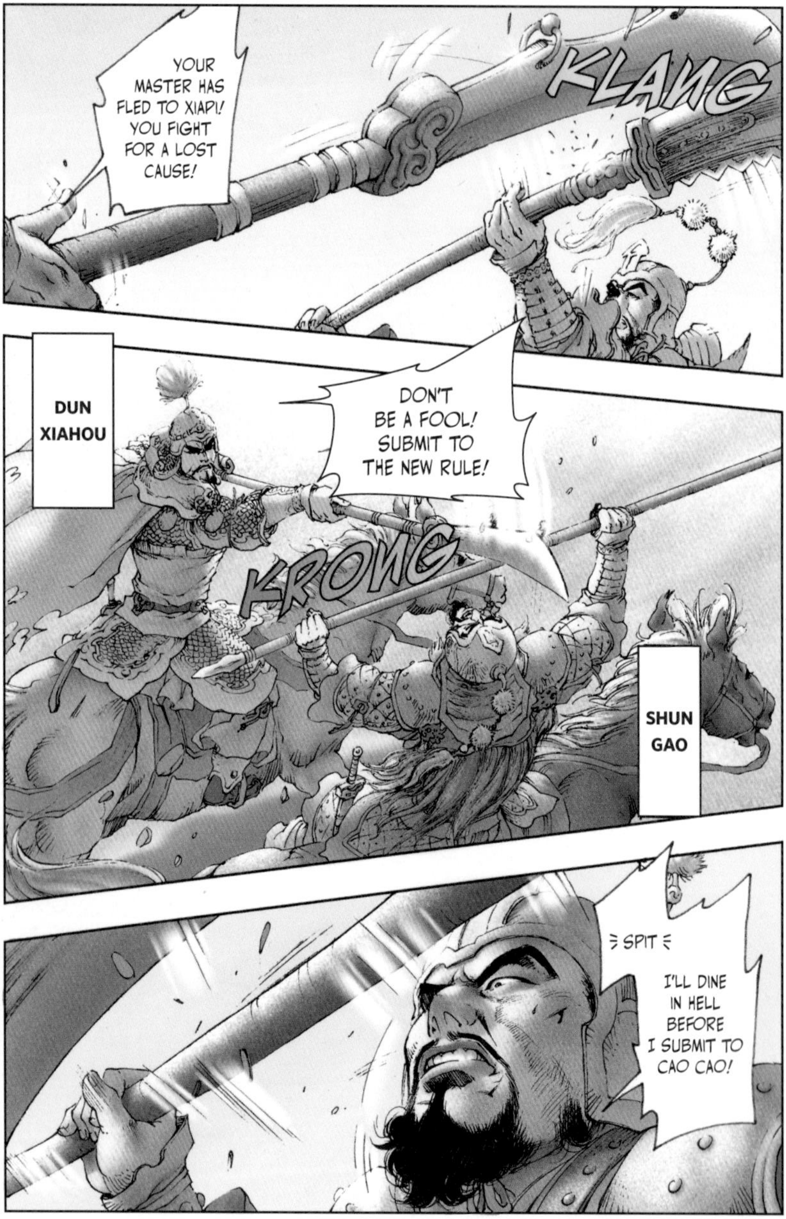
YOUR MASTER HAS FLED TO XIAPI! YOU FIGHT FOR A LOST CAUSE!
KLANG
DUN XIAHOU
DON'T BE A FOOL! SUBMIT TO THE NEW RULE!
KRONG
SHUN GAO
SPIT
I'LL DINE IN HELL BEFORE I SUBMIT TO CAO CAO!

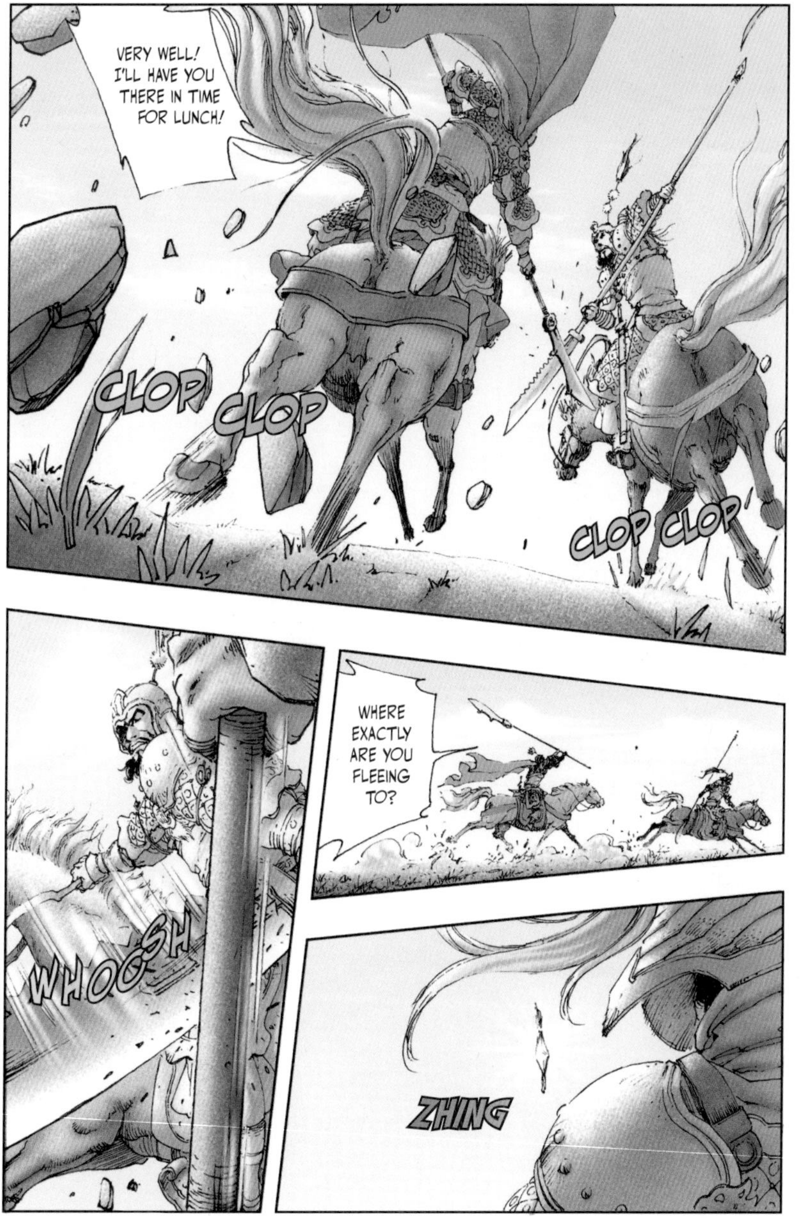
VERY WELL! I'LL HAVE YOU THERE IN TIME FOR LUNCH!
CLOP CLOP
CLOP CLOP
WHOOSH
WHERE EXACTLY ARE YOU FLEEING TO?
ZHING

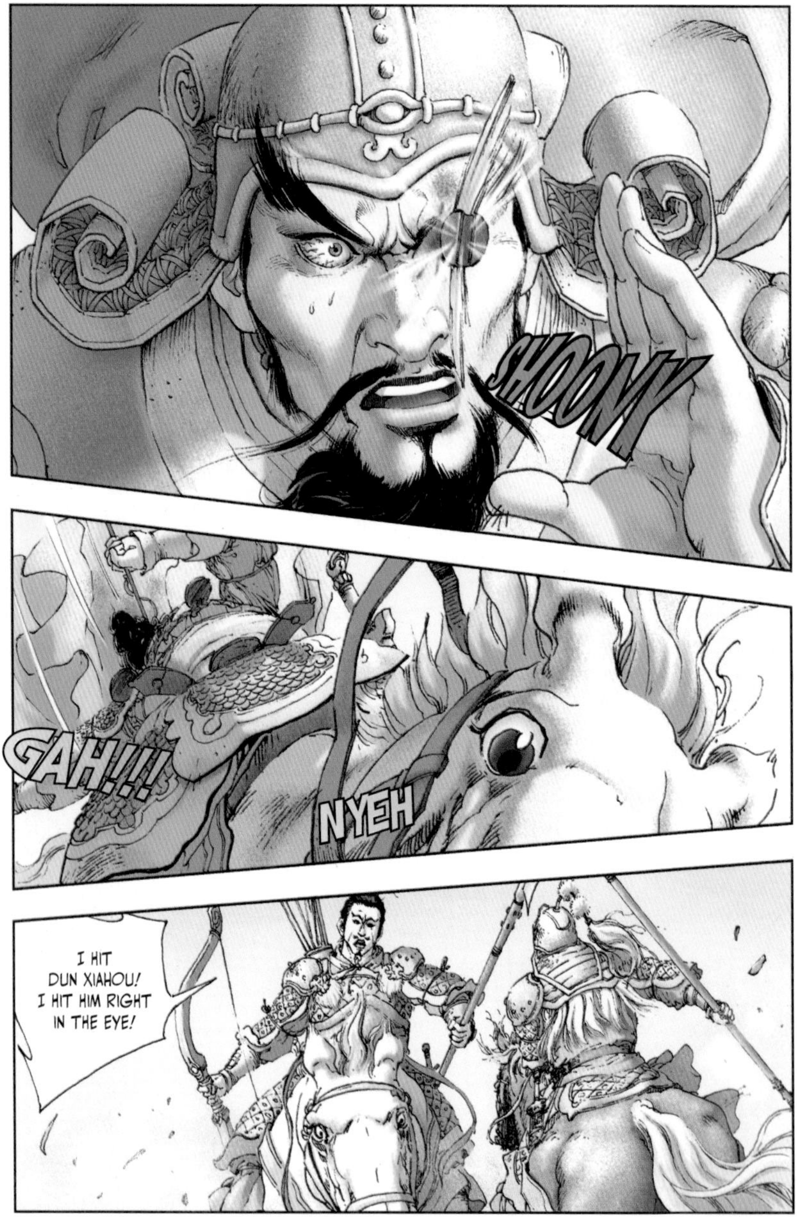
SHOOM
GAH!!!!
NYEH
I HIT DUN XIAHOU! I HIT HIM RIGHT IN THE EYE!

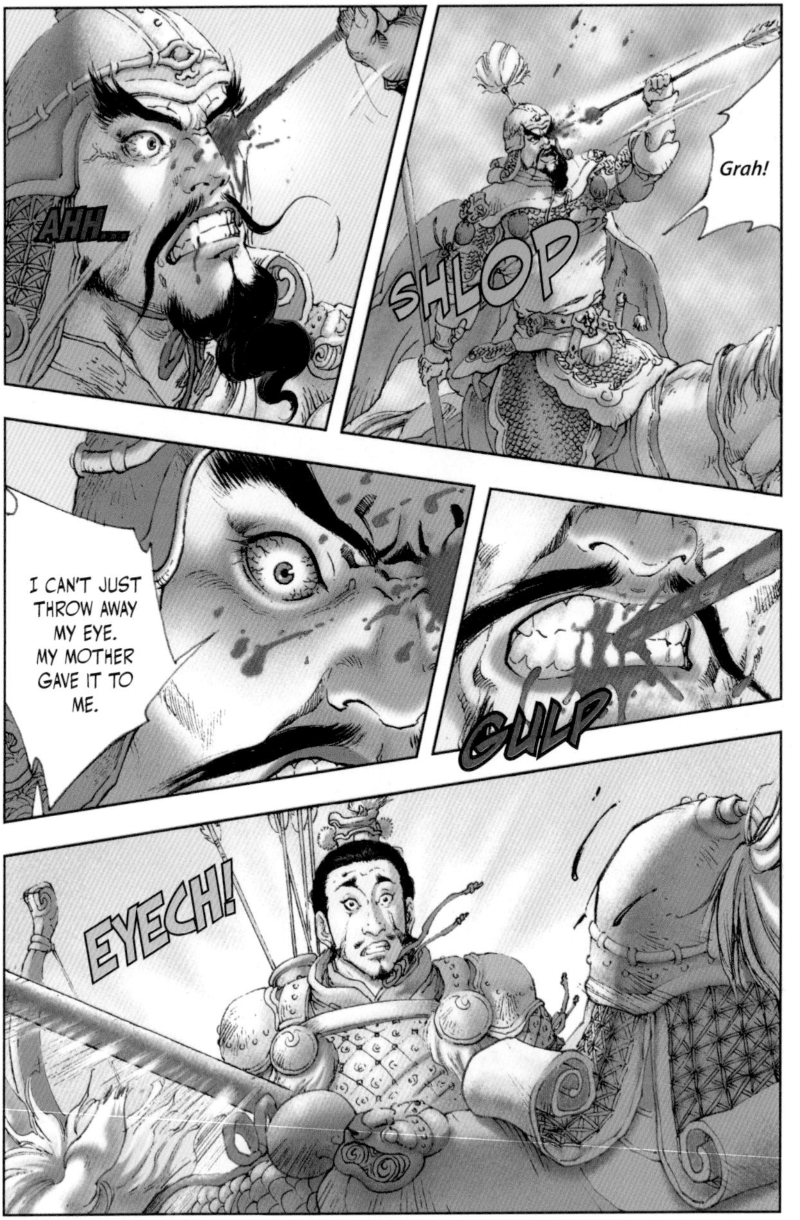
AHH...
Grah!
SHLOP
I CAN'T JUST THROW AWAY MY EYE. MY MOTHER GAVE IT TO ME.
GULP
EYECH!

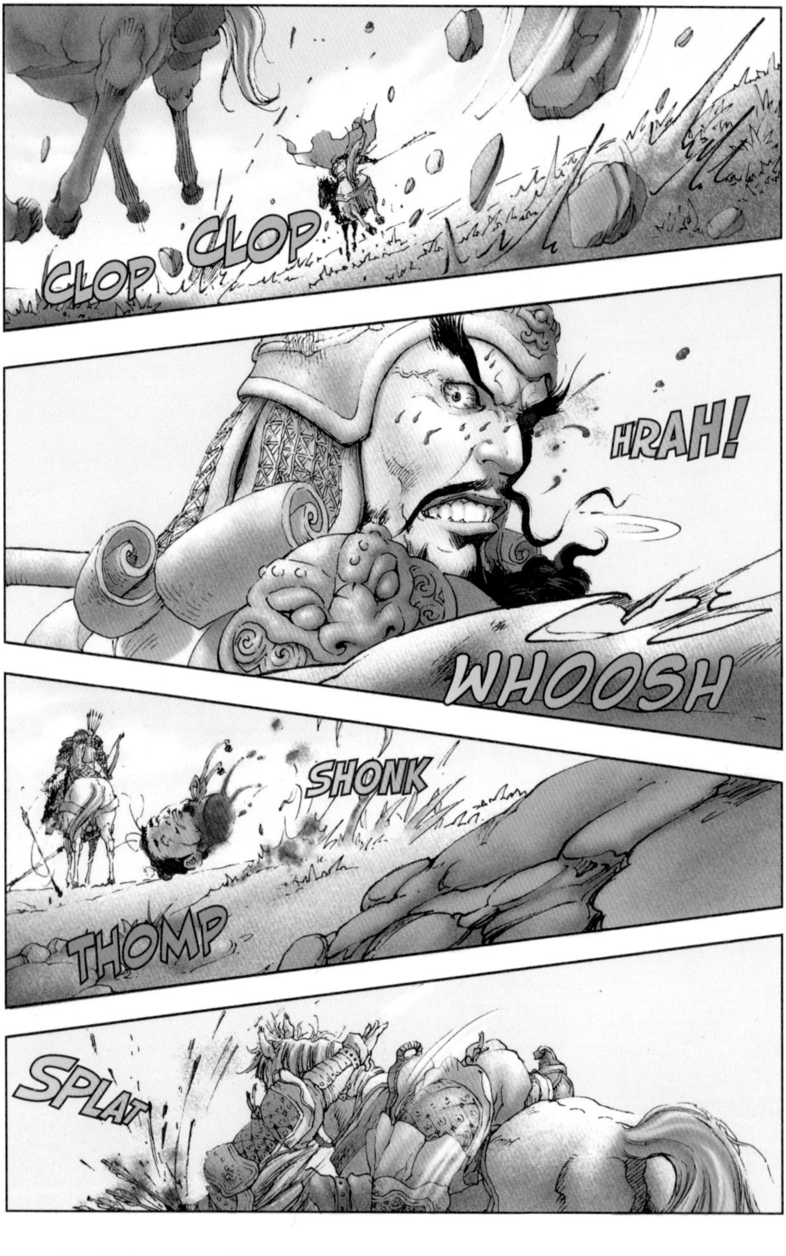
CLOP CLOP
HRAH!
WHOOSH
SHONK
THOMP
SPLAT

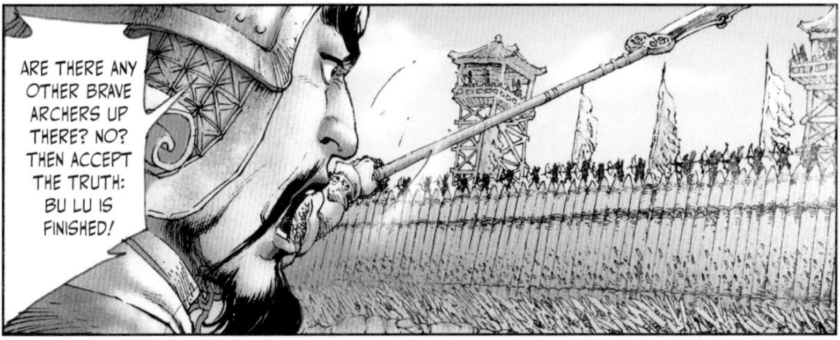
ARE THERE ANY OTHER BRAVE ARCHERS UP THERE? NO? THEN ACCEPT THE TRUTH: BU LU IS FINISHED!

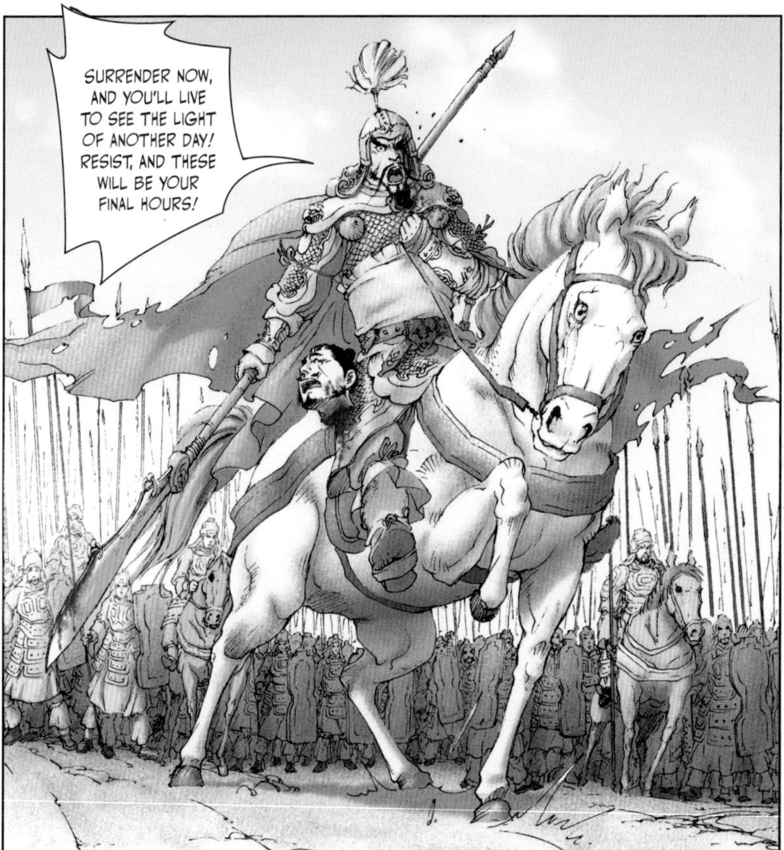
SURRENDER NOW, AND YOU'LL LIVE TO SEE THE LIGHT OF ANOTHER DAY! RESIST, AND THESE WILL BE YOUR FINAL HOURS!

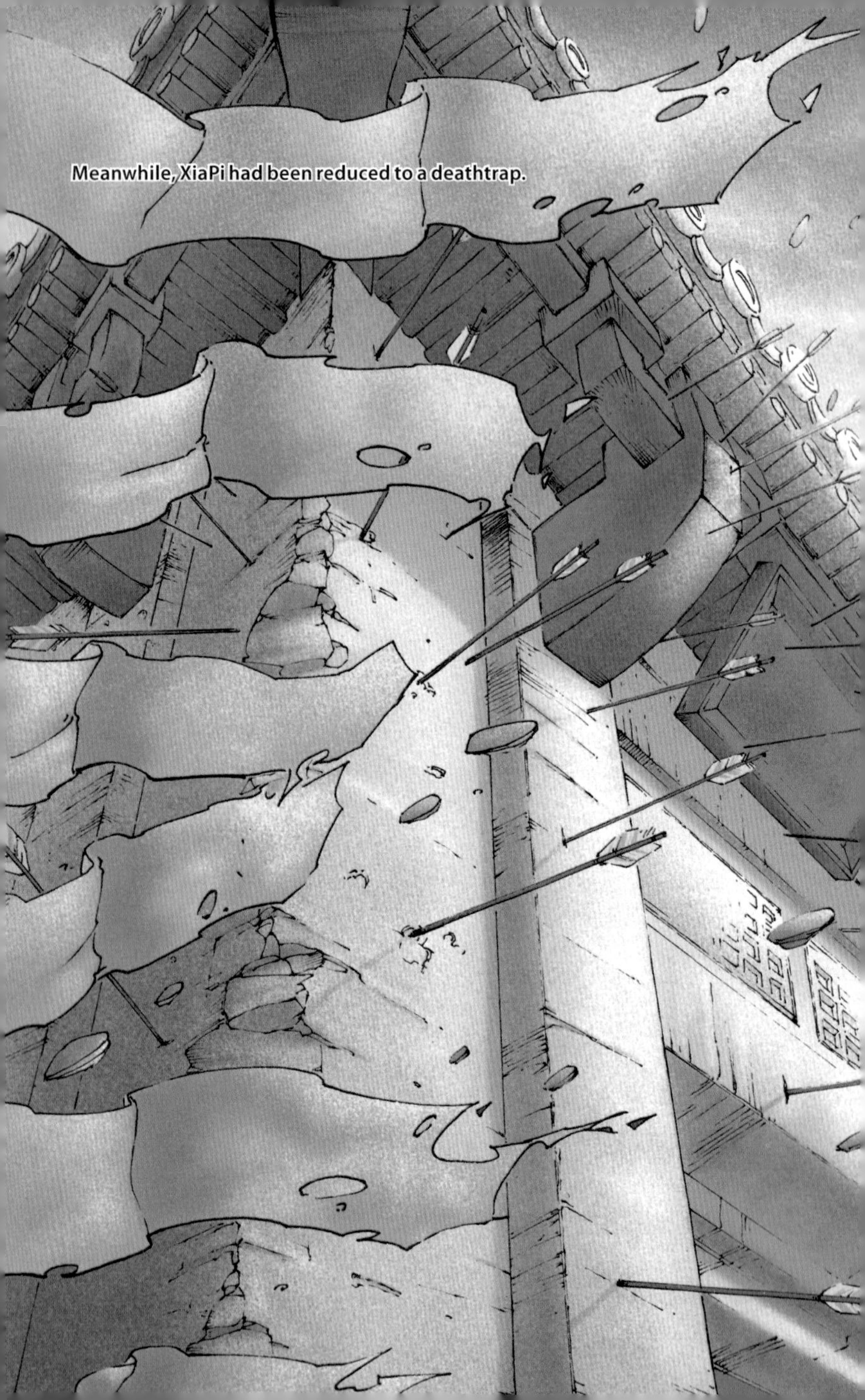
Meanwhile, XiaPi had been reduced to a deathtrap.

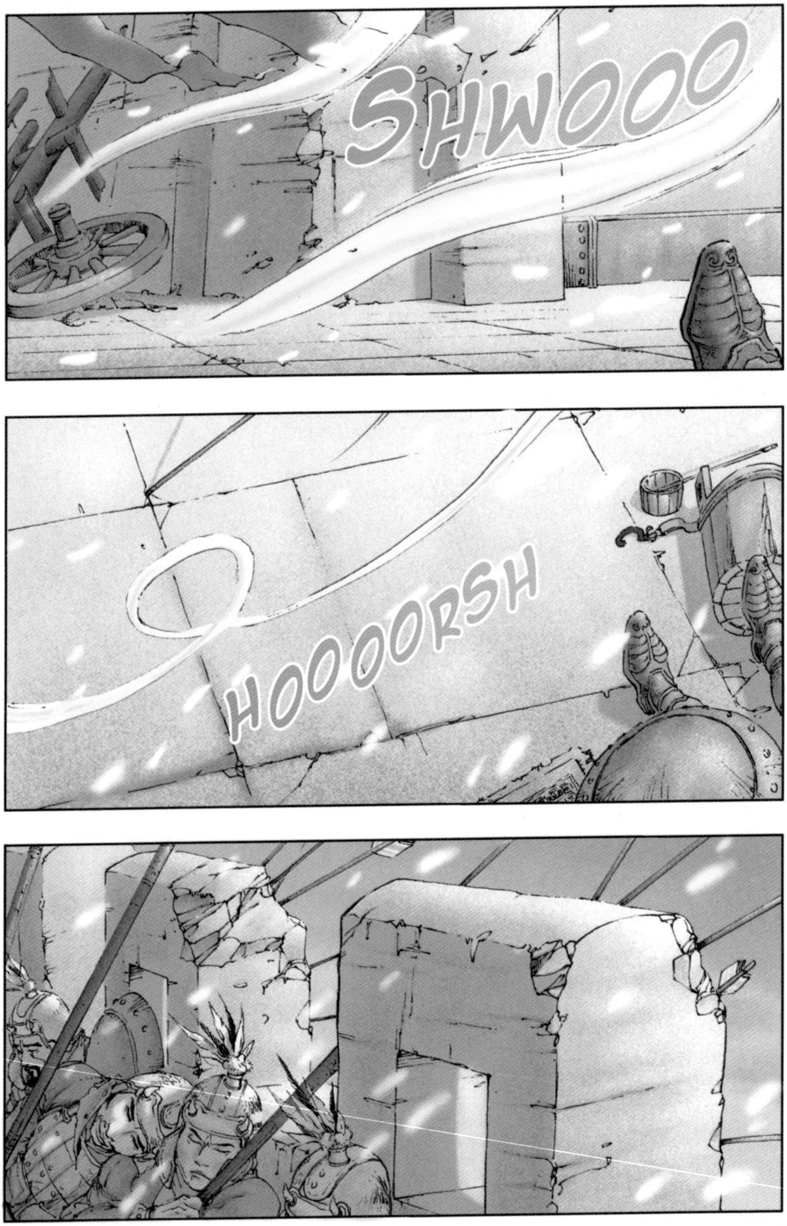
SHWOOO
HOOOORSH

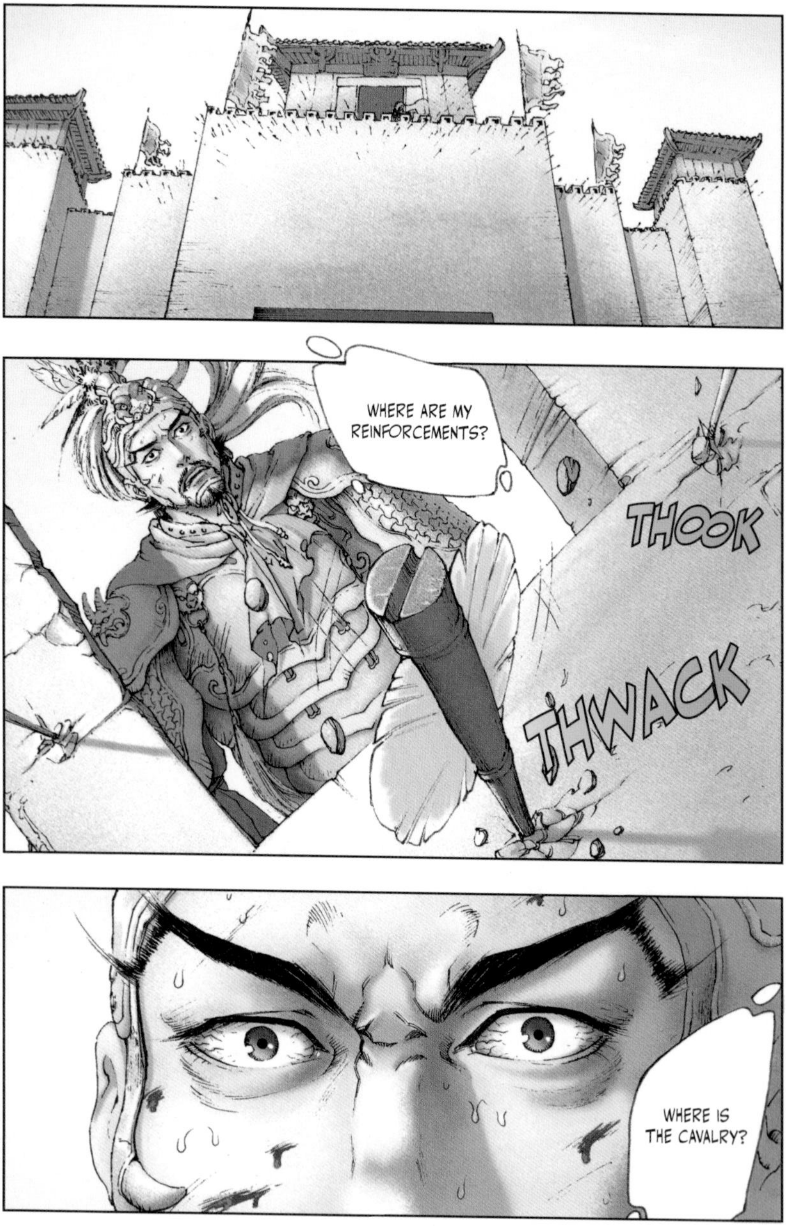
WHERE ARE MY REINFORCEMENTS?
THOOK
THWACK
WHERE IS THE CAVALRY?

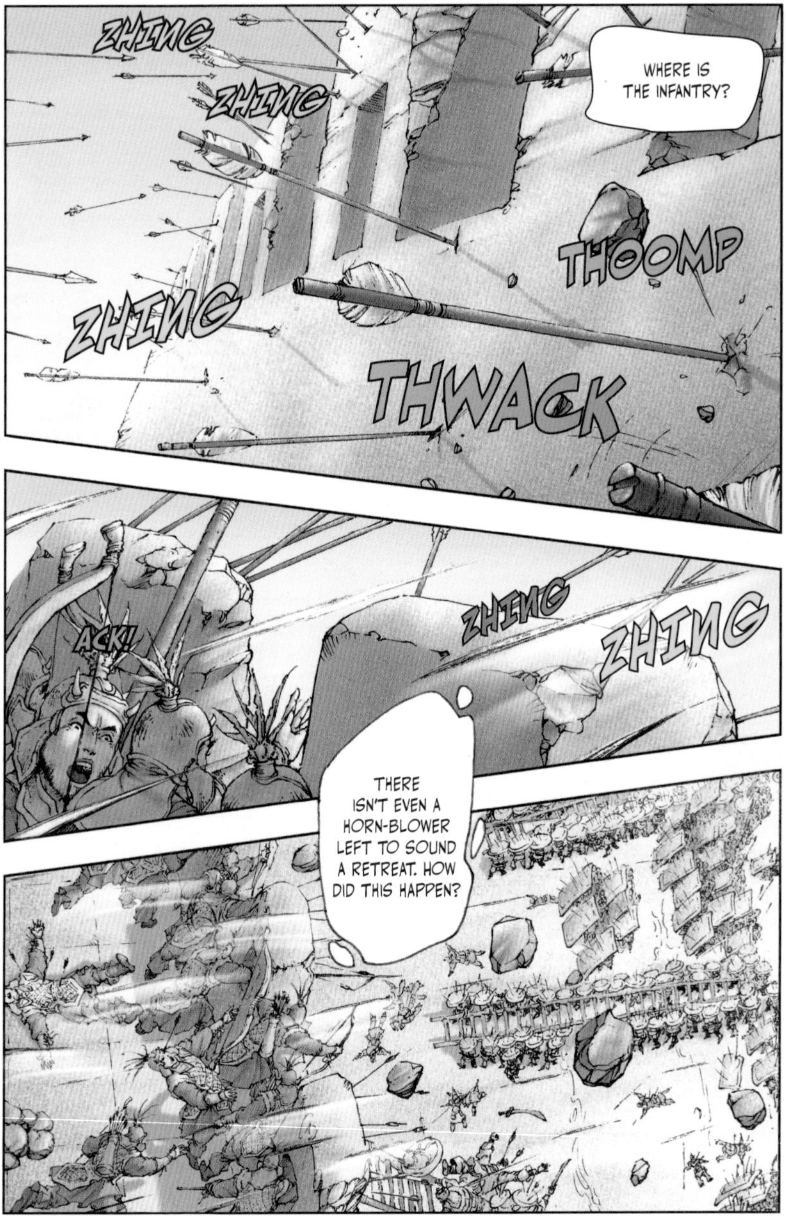
ZHING
ZHING
WHERE IS THE INFANTRY?
ZHING
THOOMP
THWACK
ACK!
ZHING
ZHING
THERE ISN'T EVEN A HORN-BLOWER LEFT TO SOUND A RETREAT. HOW DID THIS HAPPEN?

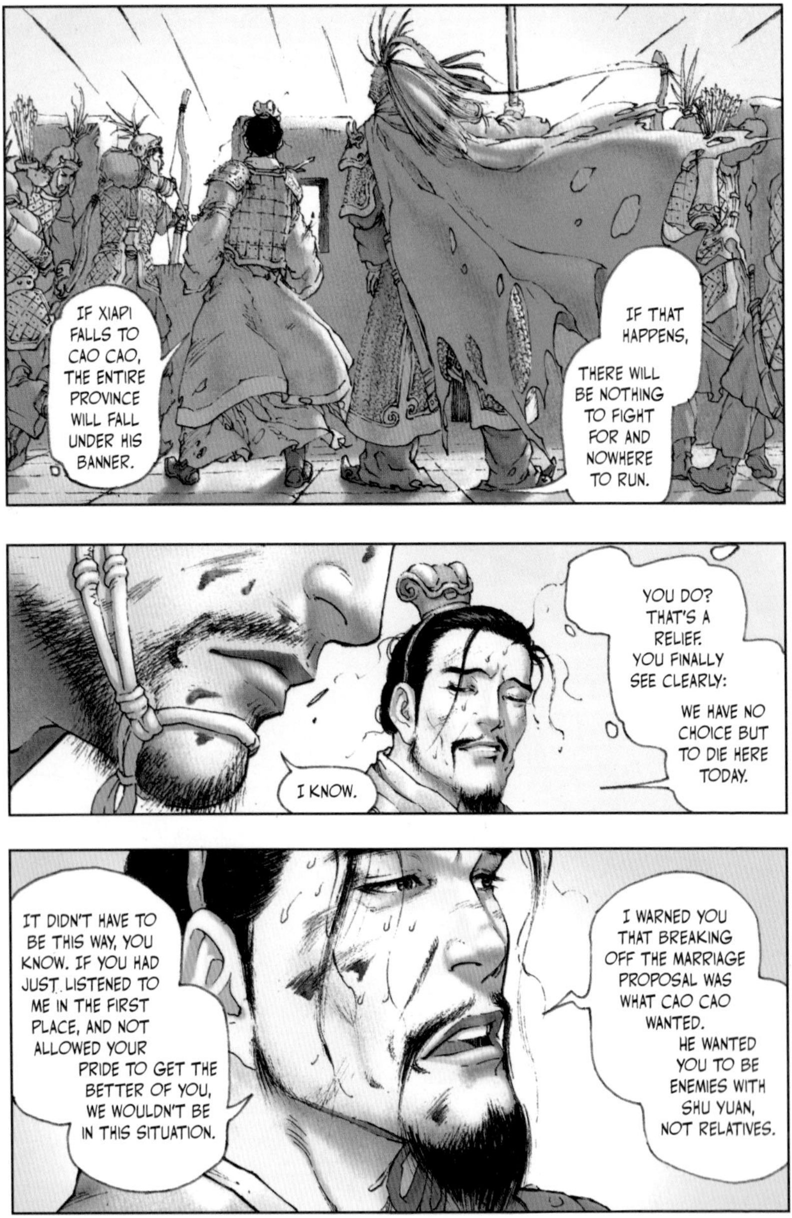
IF XIAPI FALLS TO CAO CAO, THE ENTIRE PROVINCE WILL FALL UNDER HIS BANNER.
IF THAT HAPPENS,
THERE WILL BE NOTHING TO FIGHT FOR AND NOWHERE TO RUN.
I KNOW.
YOU DO? THAT'S A RELIEF. YOU FINALLY SEE CLEARLY:
WE HAVE NO CHOICE BUT TO DIE HERE TODAY.
IT DIDN'T HAVE TO BE THIS WAY, YOU KNOW. IF YOU HAD JUST LISTENED TO ME IN THE FIRST PLACE, AND NOT ALLOWED YOUR
PRIDE TO GET THE BETTER OF YOU, WE WOULDN'T BE IN THIS SITUATION.
I WARNED YOU THAT BREAKING OFF THE MARRIAGE PROPOSAL WAS WHAT CAO CAO WANTED.
HE WANTED YOU TO BE ENEMIES WITH SHU YUAN, NOT RELATIVES.

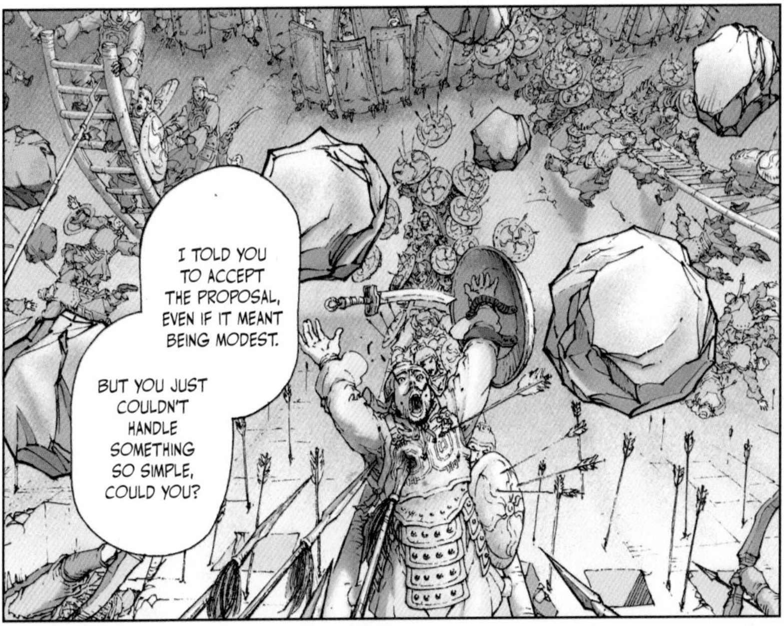
I TOLD YOU TO ACCEPT THE PROPOSAL, EVEN IF IT MEANT BEING MODEST.
BUT YOU JUST COULDN'T HANDLE SOMETHING SO SIMPLE, COULD YOU?

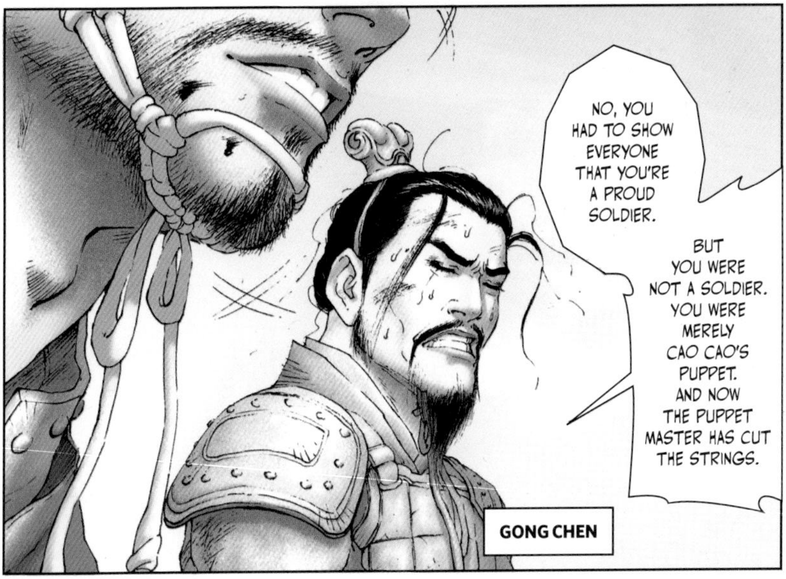
NO, YOU HAD TO SHOW EVERYONE THAT YOU'RE A PROUD SOLDIER.
BUT YOU WERE NOT A SOLDIER. YOU WERE MERELY CAO CAO'S PUPPET. AND NOW THE PUPPET MASTER HAS CUT THE STRINGS.
GONG CHEN

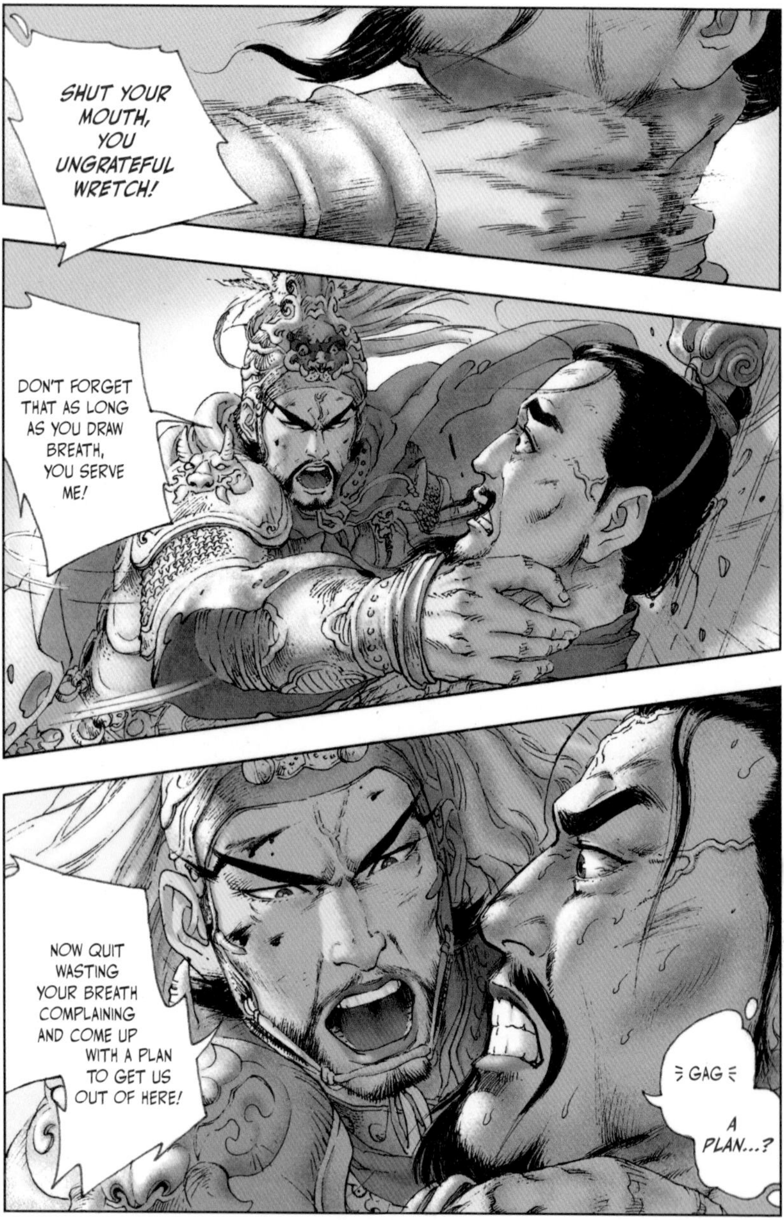
SHUT YOUR MOUTH, YOU UNGRATEFUL WRETCH!
DON'T FORGET THAT AS LONG AS YOU DRAW BREATH, YOU SERVE ME!
NOW QUIT WASTING YOUR BREATH COMPLAINING AND COME UP WITH A PLAN TO GET US OUT OF HERE!
GAG
A PLAN...?

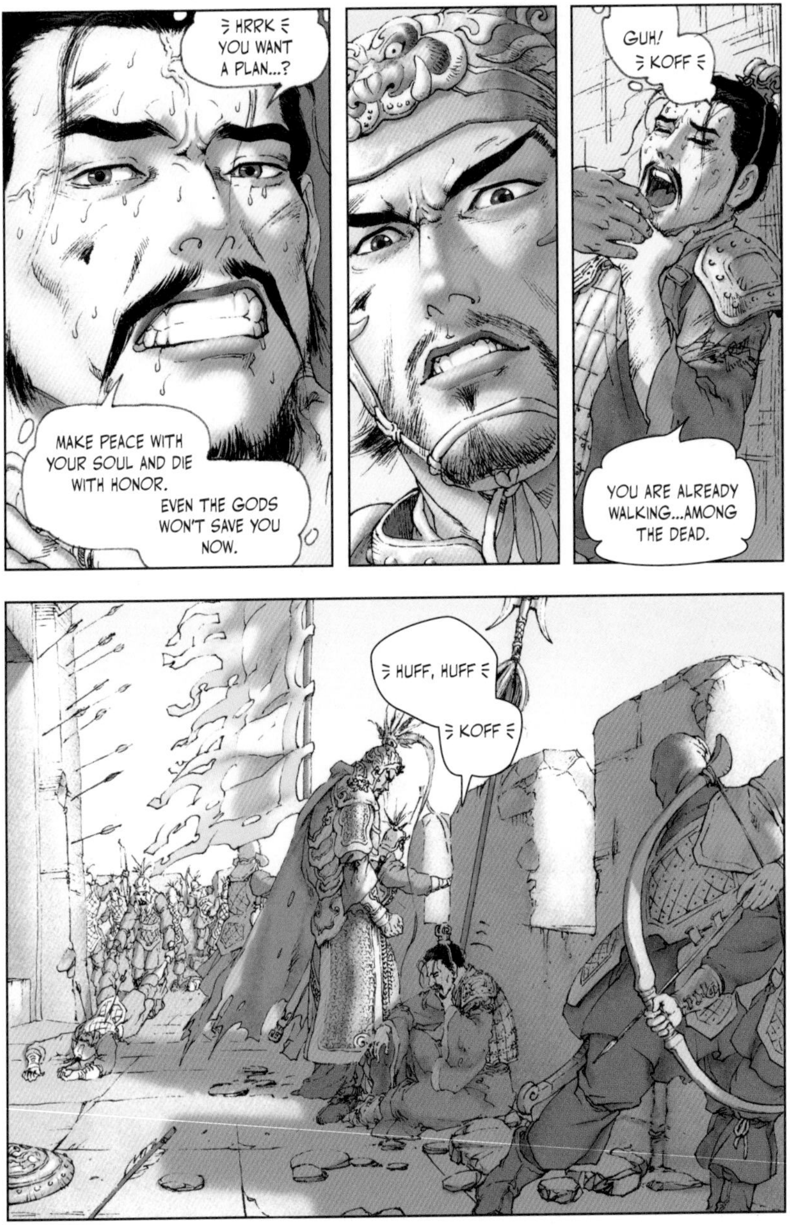
≡ HRRK ≡ YOU WANT A PLAN...?
MAKE PEACE WITH YOUR SOUL AND DIE WITH HONOR.
EVEN THE GODS WON'T SAVE YOU NOW.
GUH! ≡ KOFF ≡
YOU ARE ALREADY WALKING...AMONG THE DEAD.
≡ HUFF, HUFF ≡
≡ KOFF ≡

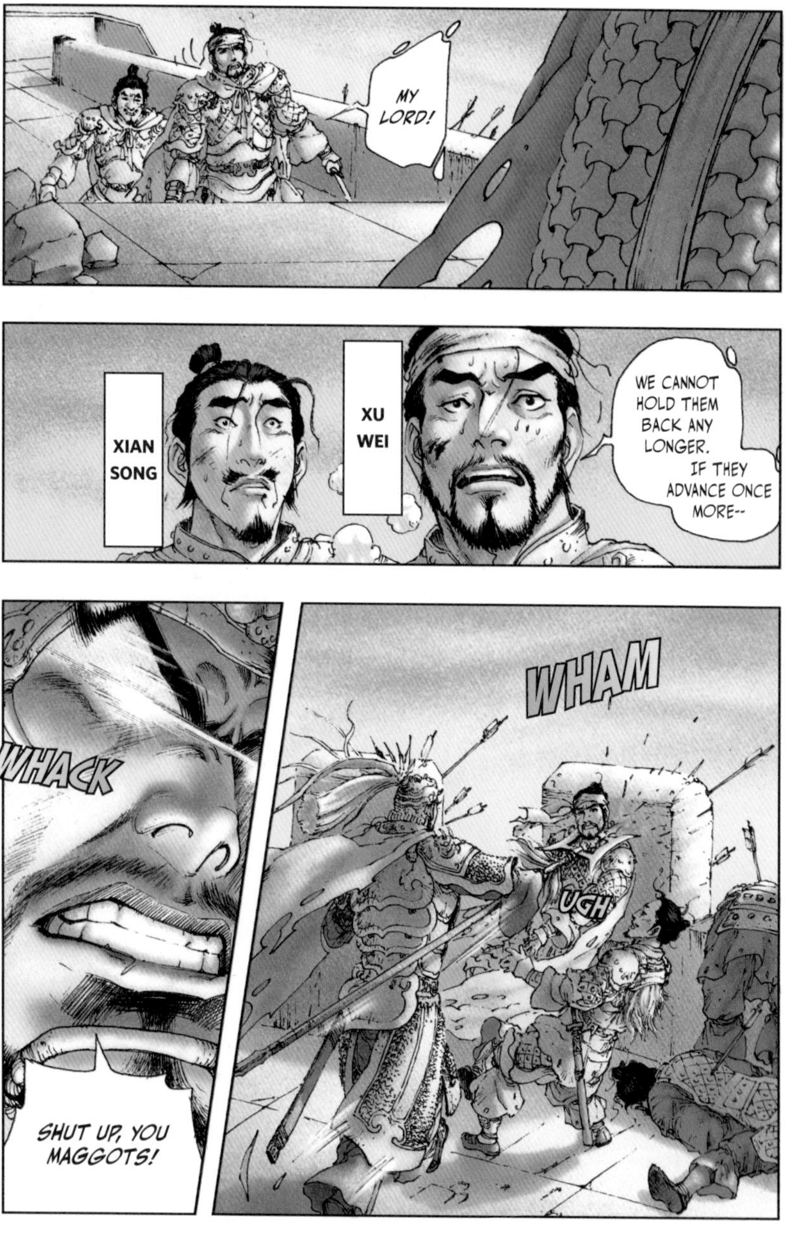
MY LORD!
XIAN SONG
XU WEI
WE CANNOT HOLD THEM BACK ANY LONGER.
IF THEY ADVANCE ONCE MORE--
WHACK
WHAM
UGH
SHUT UP, YOU MAGGOTS!

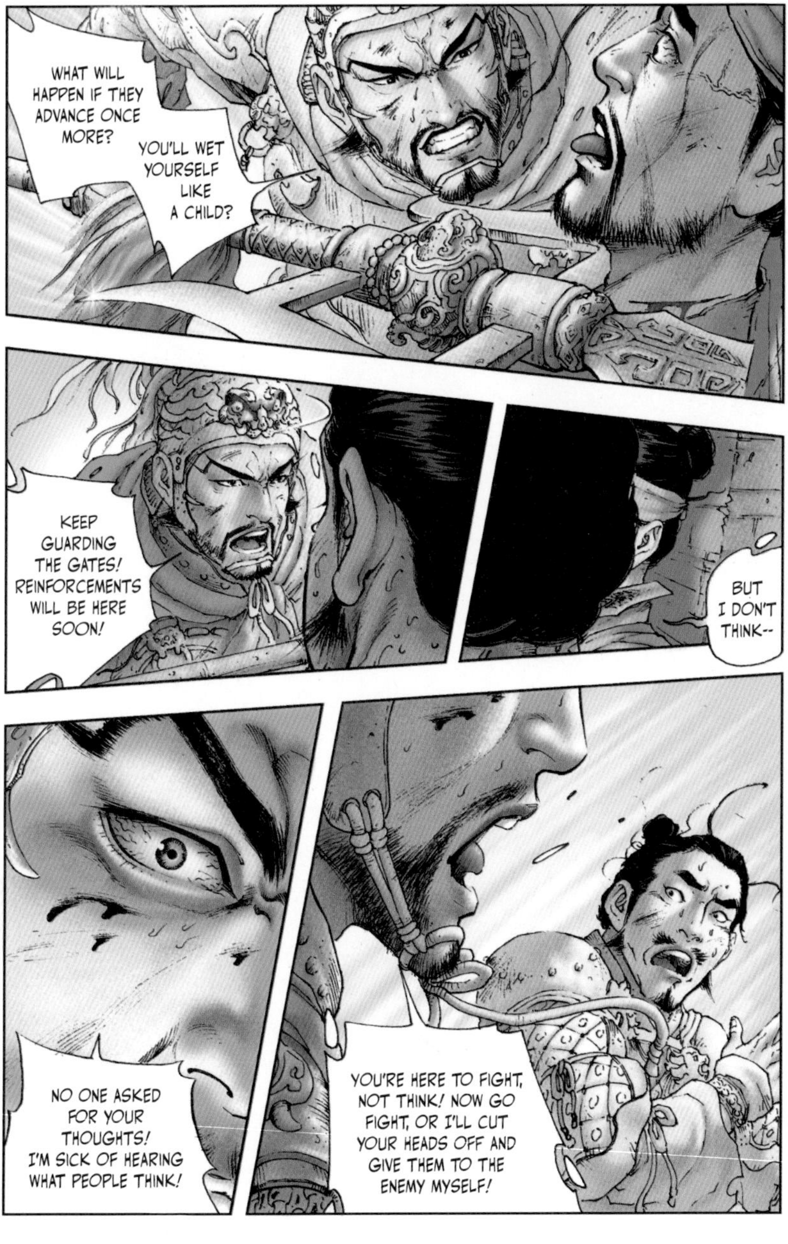
WHAT WILL HAPPEN IF THEY ADVANCE ONCE MORE?
YOU'LL WET YOURSELF LIKE A CHILD?
KEEP GUARDING THE GATES! REINFORCEMENTS WILL BE HERE SOON!
BUT I DON'T THINK--
NO ONE ASKED FOR YOUR THOUGHTS! I'M SICK OF HEARING WHAT PEOPLE THINK!
YOU'RE HERE TO FIGHT, NOT THINK! NOW GO FIGHT, OR I'LL CUT YOUR HEADS OFF AND GIVE THEM TO THE ENEMY MYSELF!

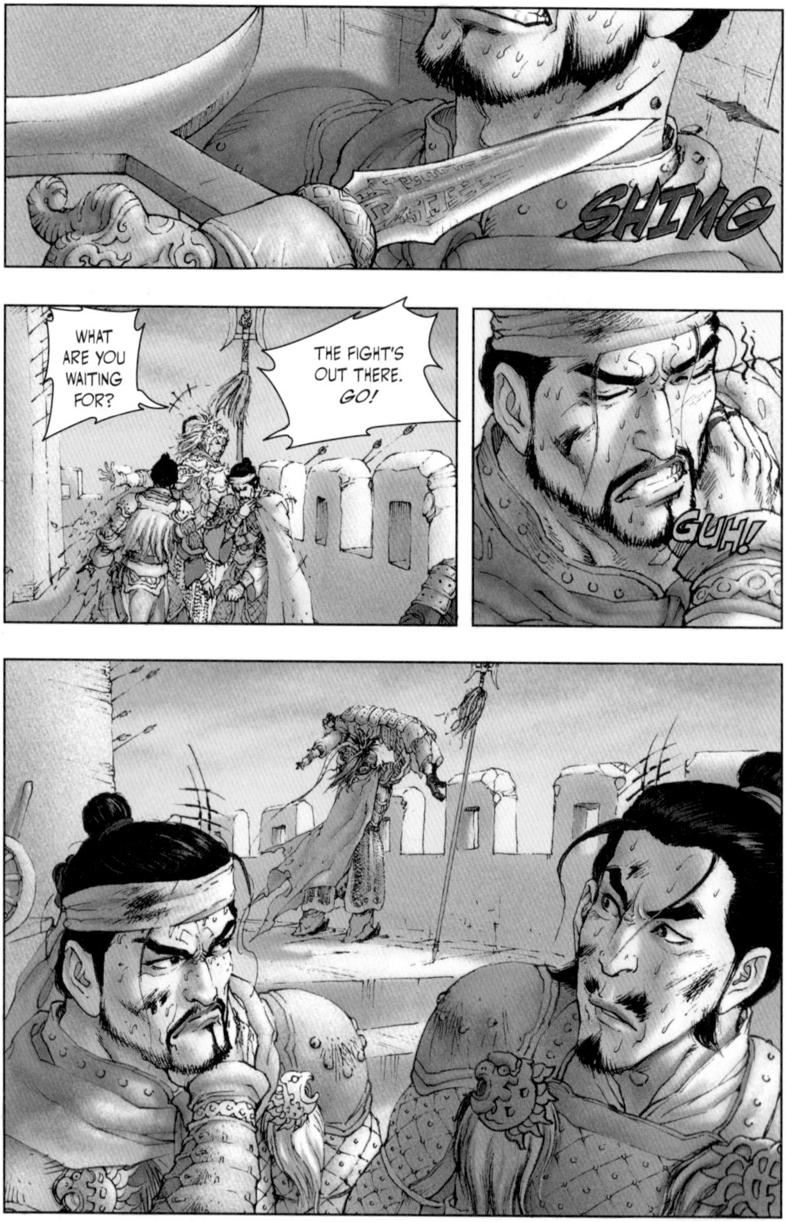
SHING
WHAT ARE YOU WAITING FOR?
THE FIGHT'S OUT THERE. *GO!*
GUH!

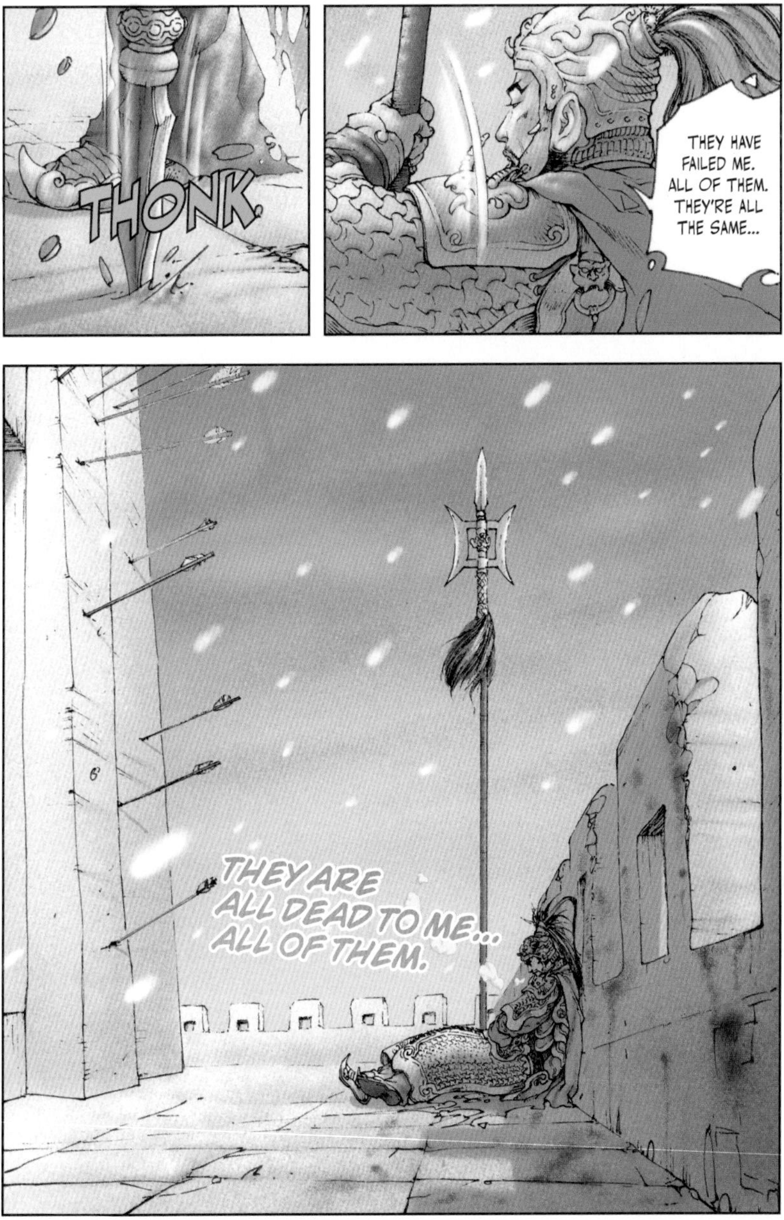
THONK
THEY HAVE FAILED ME. ALL OF THEM. THEY'RE ALL THE SAME...
THEY ARE ALL DEAD TO ME... ALL OF THEM.

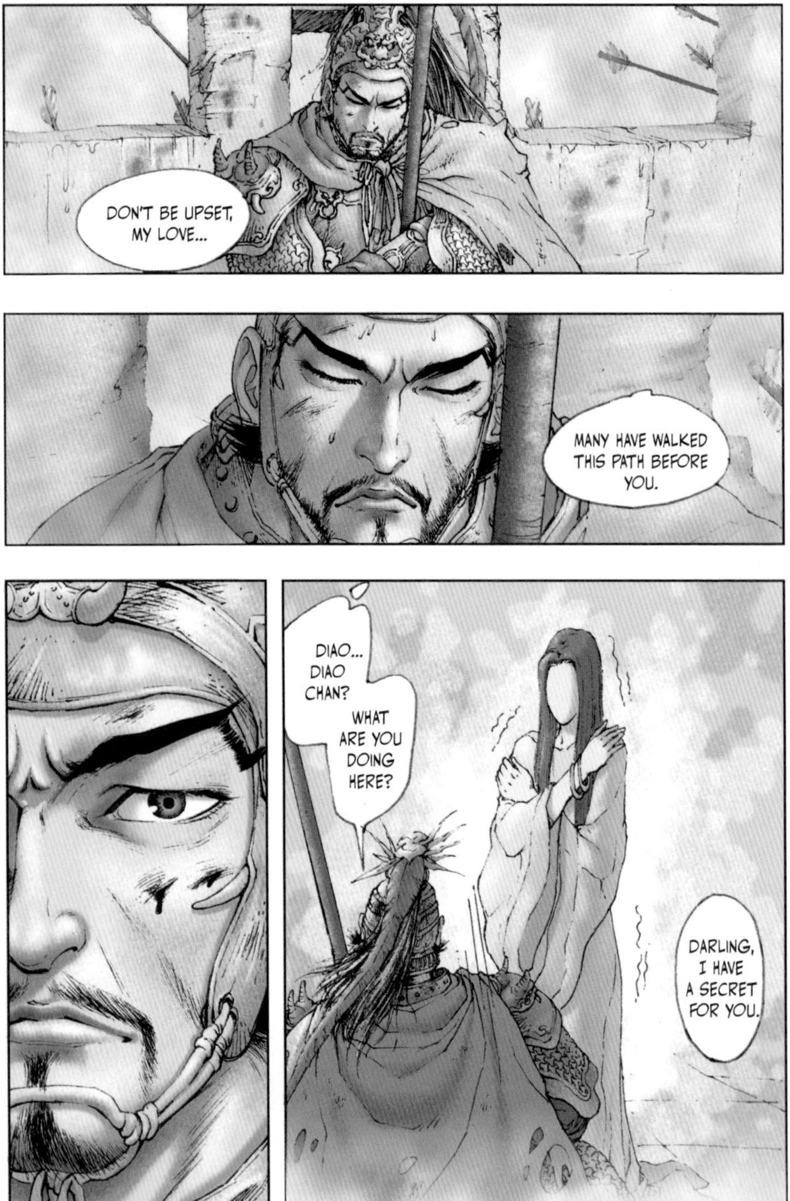
DON'T BE UPSET, MY LOVE...
MANY HAVE WALKED THIS PATH BEFORE YOU.
DIAO... DIAO CHAN?
WHAT ARE YOU DOING HERE?
DARLING, I HAVE A SECRET FOR YOU.

TELL ME, MY LOVE!

IT'S OVER.

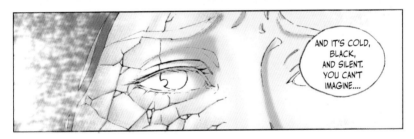

AND IT'S COLD, BLACK, AND SILENT. YOU CAN'T IMAGINE....

KRACK

KRACK

IMAGINE WHAT, MY LOVE? DIAO CHAN!

151

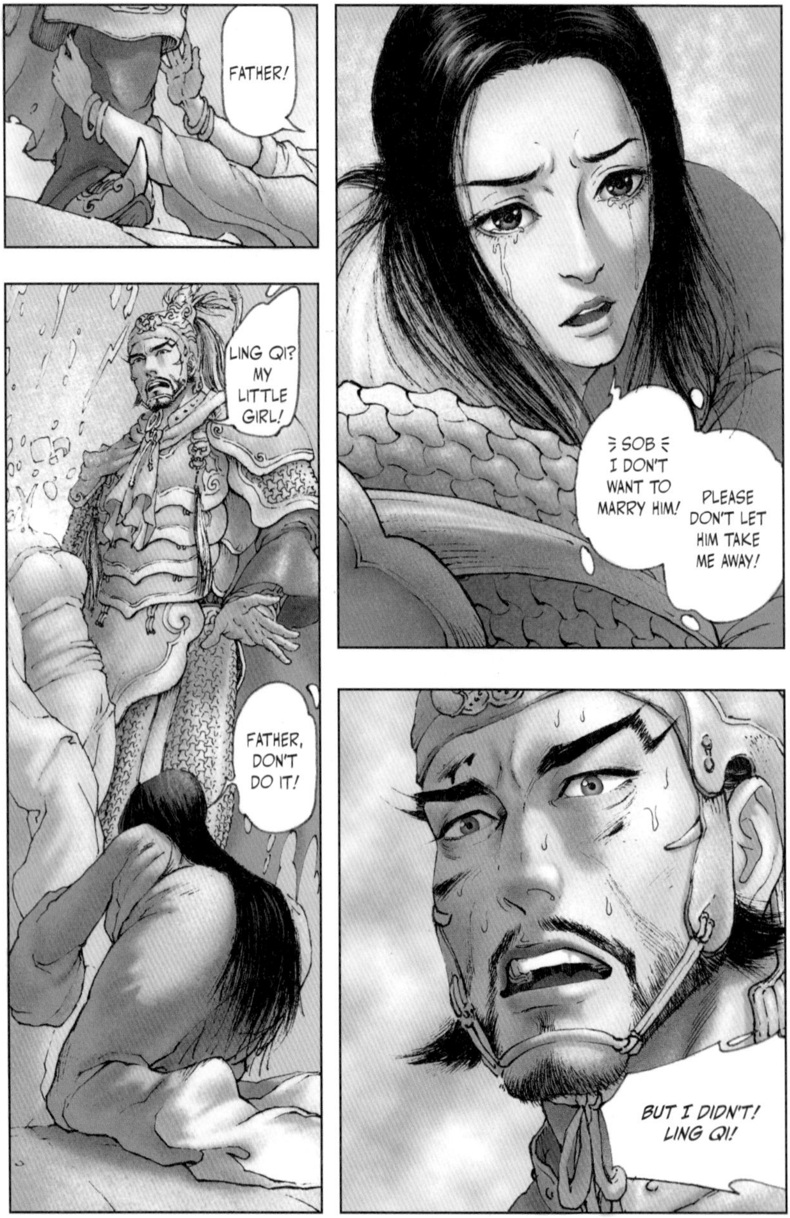
FATHER!
SOB I DON'T WANT TO MARRY HIM!
PLEASE DON'T LET HIM TAKE ME AWAY!
LING QI? MY LITTLE GIRL!
FATHER, DON'T DO IT!
BUT I DIDN'T! LING QI!

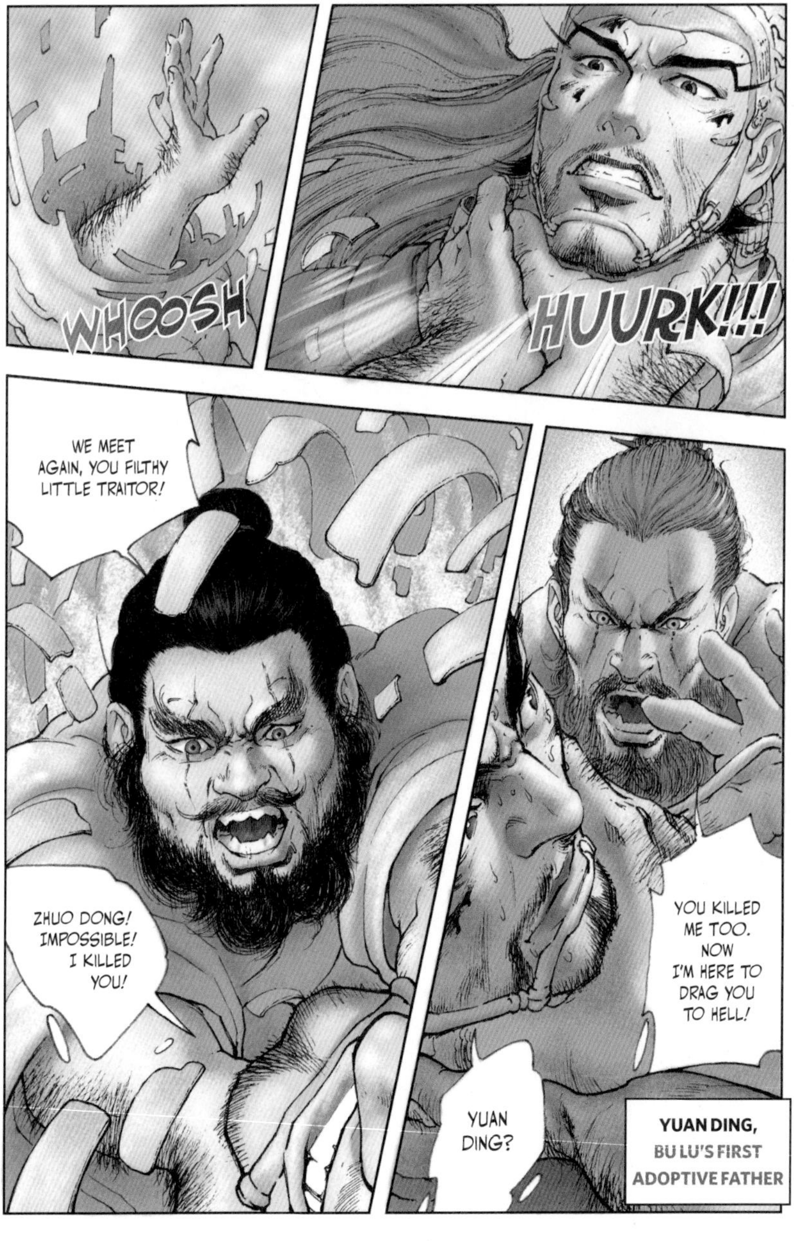
WHOOSH
HUURK!!!
WE MEET AGAIN, YOU FILTHY LITTLE TRAITOR!
ZHUO DONG! IMPOSSIBLE! I KILLED YOU!
YOU KILLED ME TOO. NOW I'M HERE TO DRAG YOU TO HELL!
YUAN DING?
YUAN DING, BU LU'S FIRST ADOPTIVE FATHER

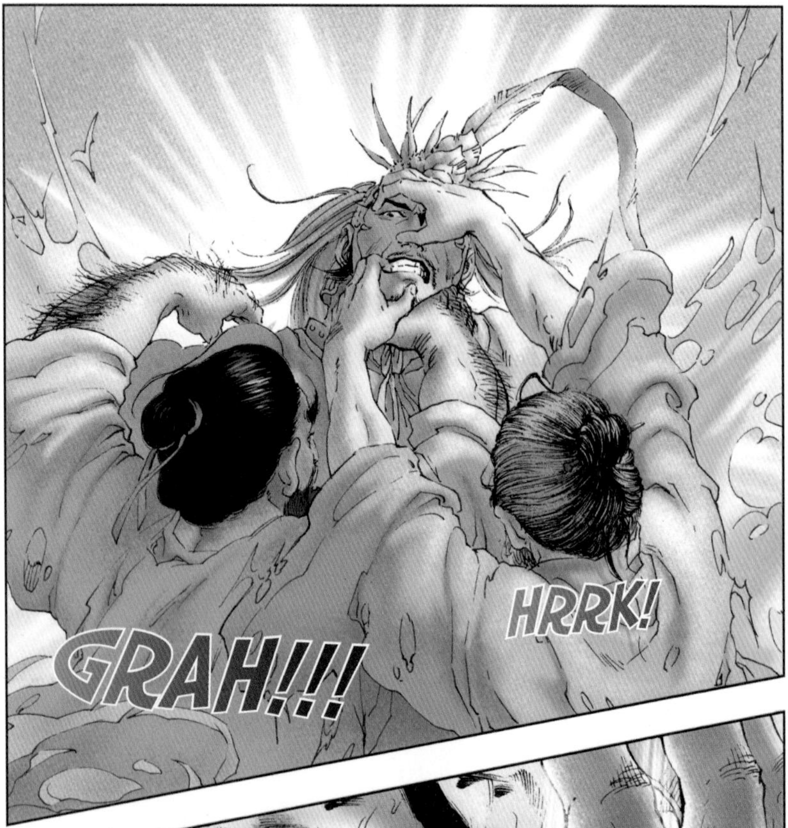
HRRK!
GRAH!!!

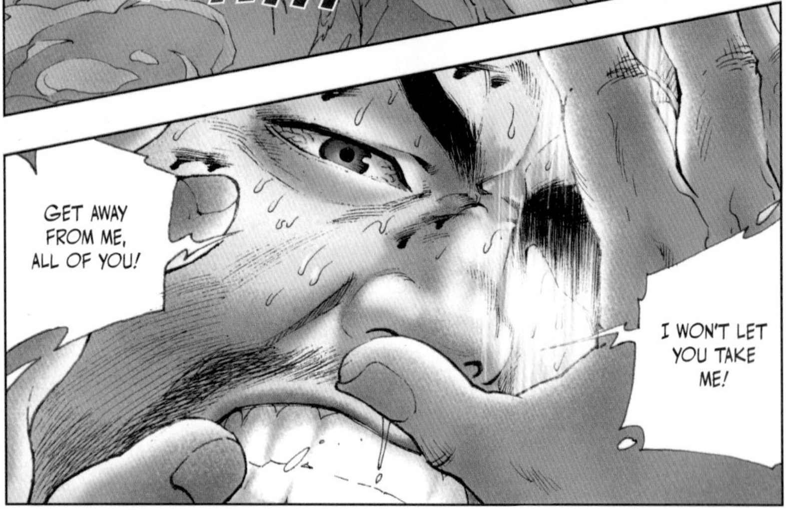
GET AWAY FROM ME, ALL OF YOU!
I WON'T LET YOU TAKE ME!

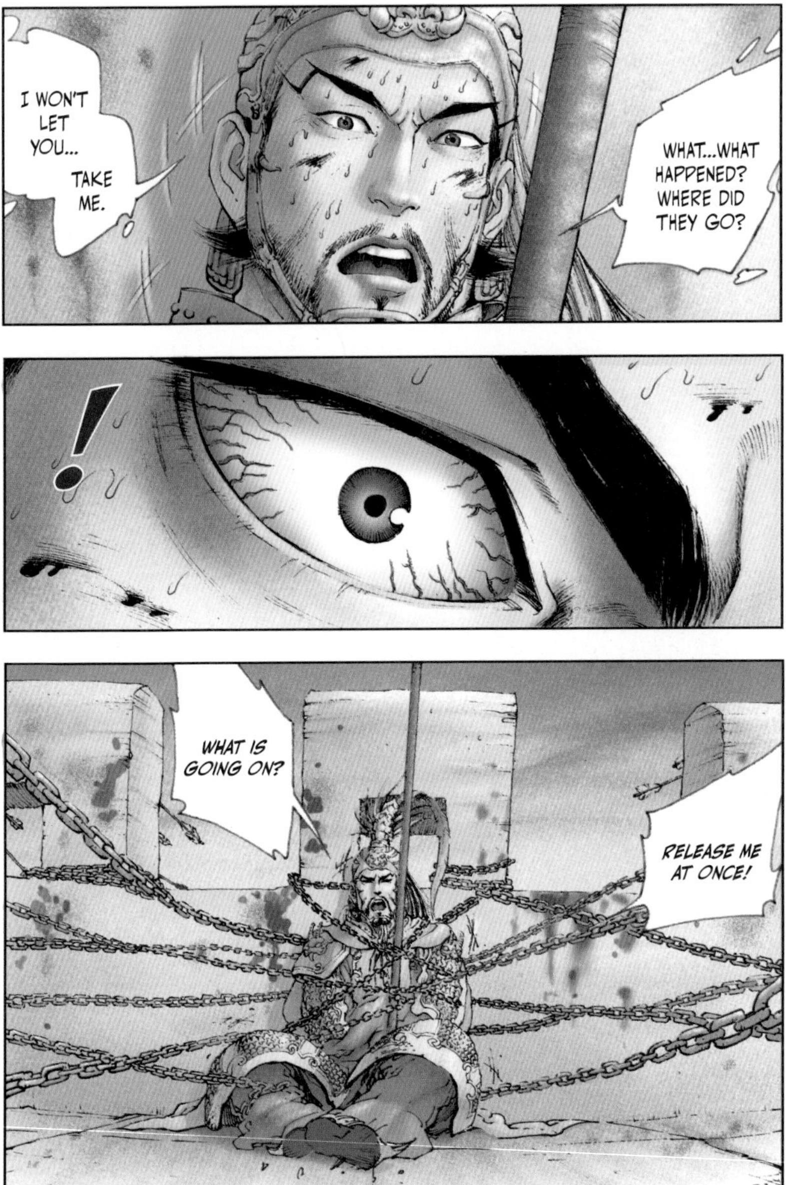
I WON'T LET YOU... TAKE ME.
WHAT...WHAT HAPPENED? WHERE DID THEY GO?
!
WHAT IS GOING ON?
RELEASE ME AT ONCE!

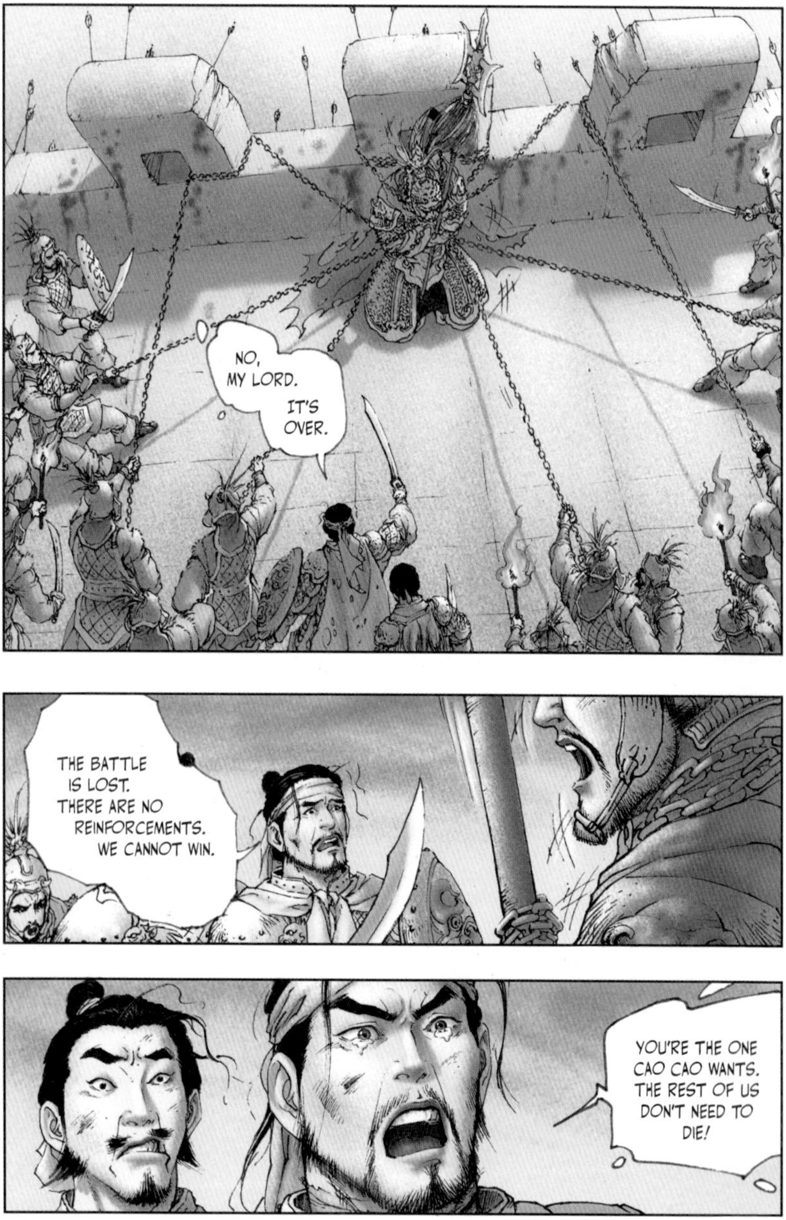
NO, MY LORD.
IT'S OVER.
THE BATTLE IS LOST. THERE ARE NO REINFORCEMENTS. WE CANNOT WIN.
YOU'RE THE ONE CAO CAO WANTS. THE REST OF US DON'T NEED TO DIE!

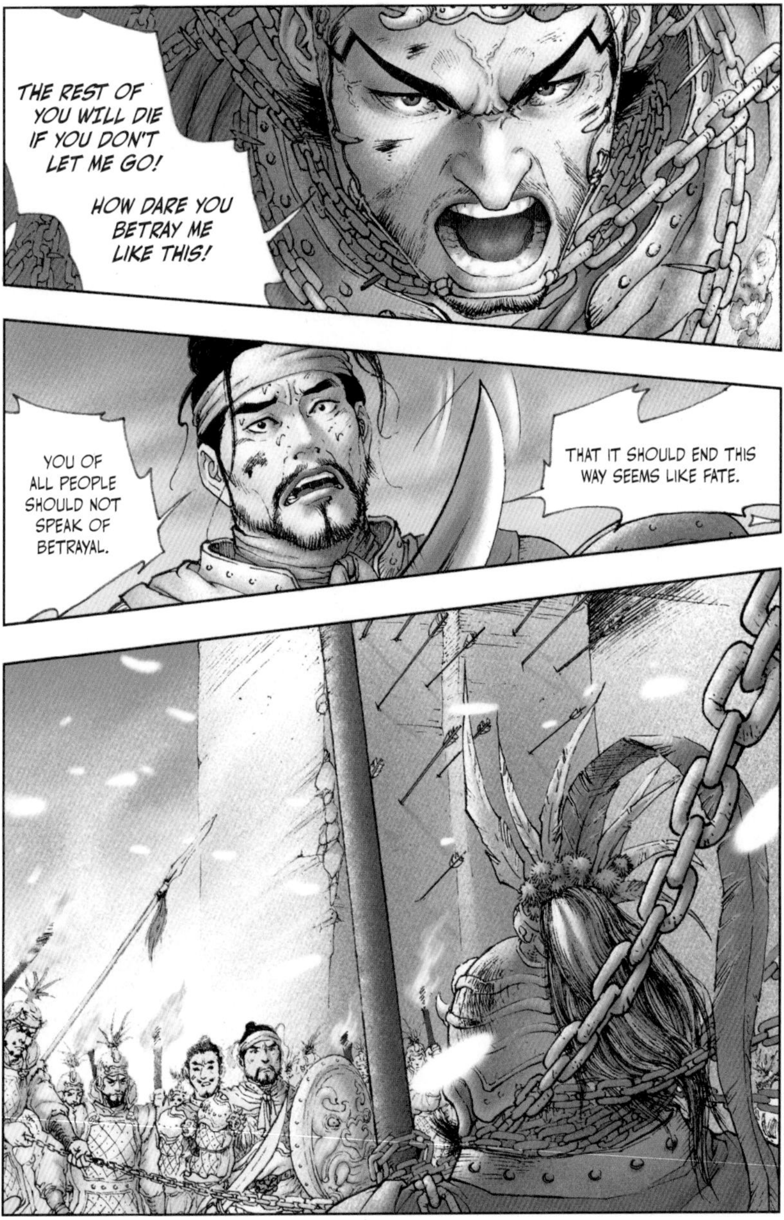
THE REST OF YOU WILL DIE IF YOU DON'T LET ME GO!
HOW DARE YOU BETRAY ME LIKE THIS!
YOU OF ALL PEOPLE SHOULD NOT SPEAK OF BETRAYAL.
THAT IT SHOULD END THIS WAY SEEMS LIKE FATE.

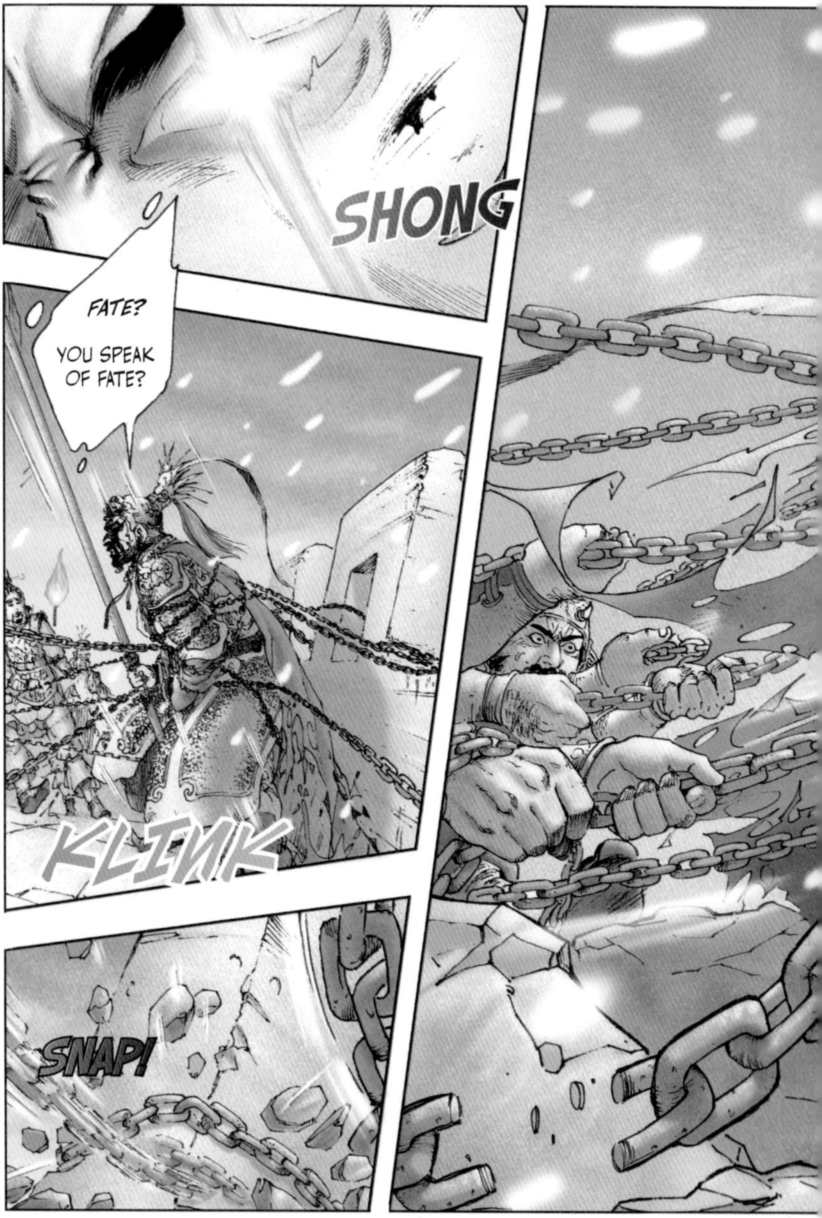
SHONG
FATE?
YOU SPEAK OF FATE?
KLINK
SNAP!

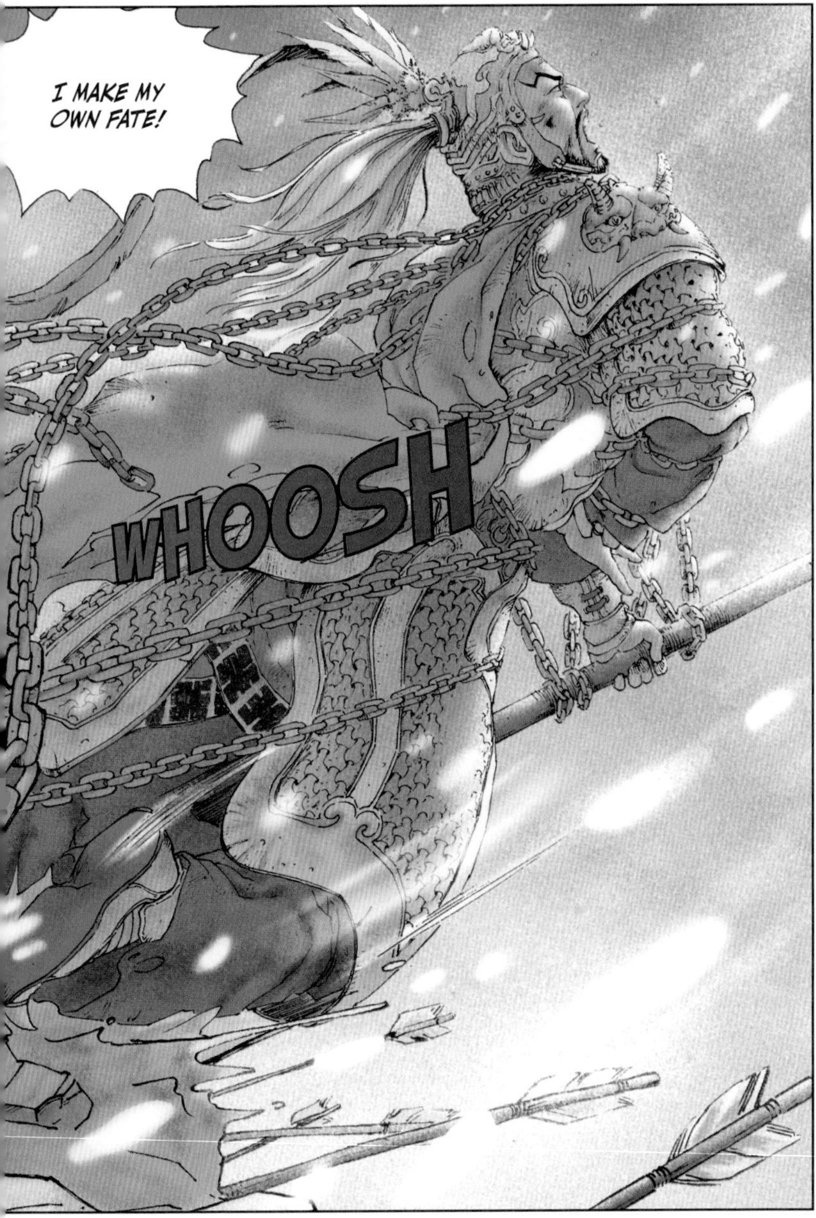
I MAKE MY OWN FATE!
WHOOSH

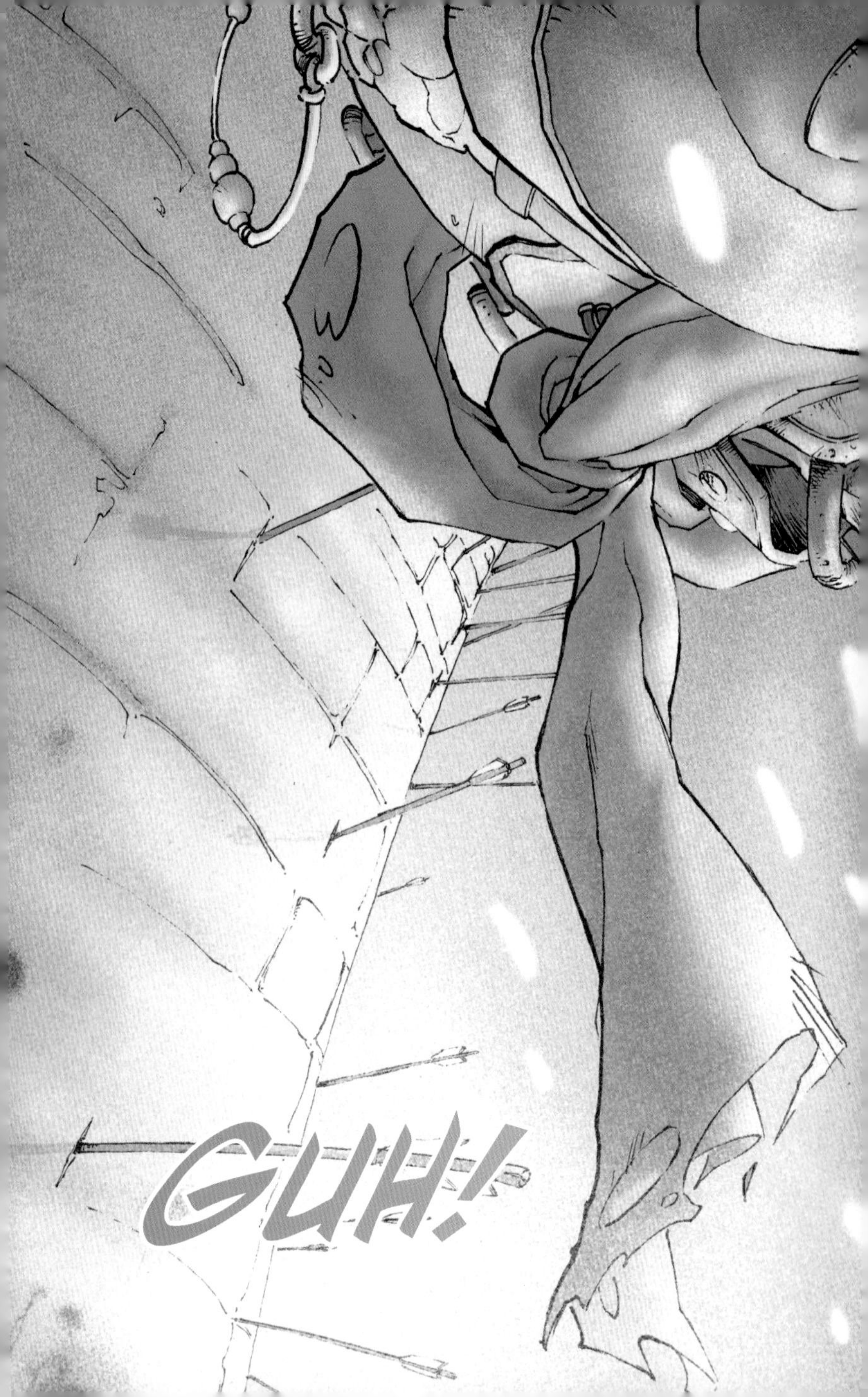
GUH!

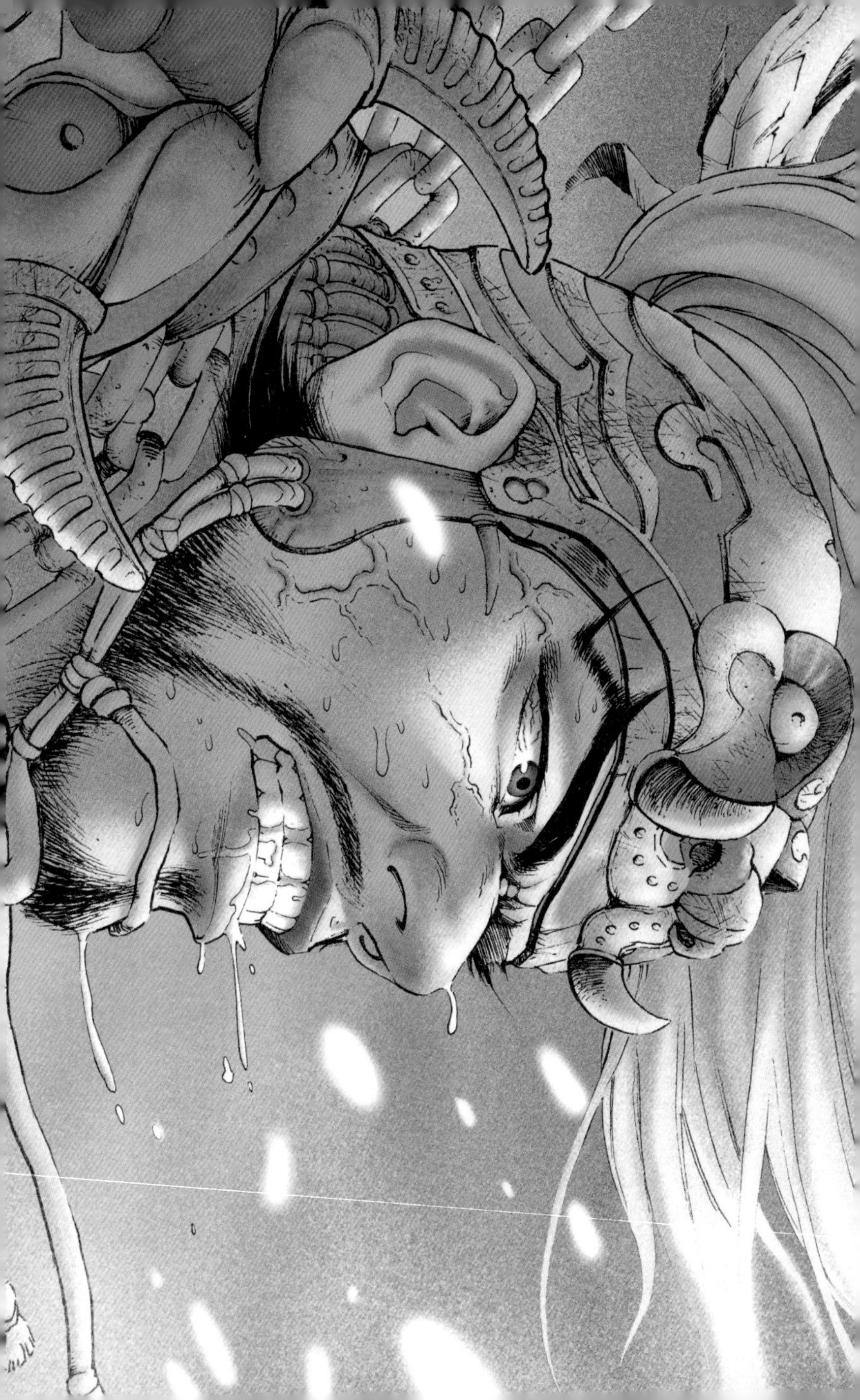

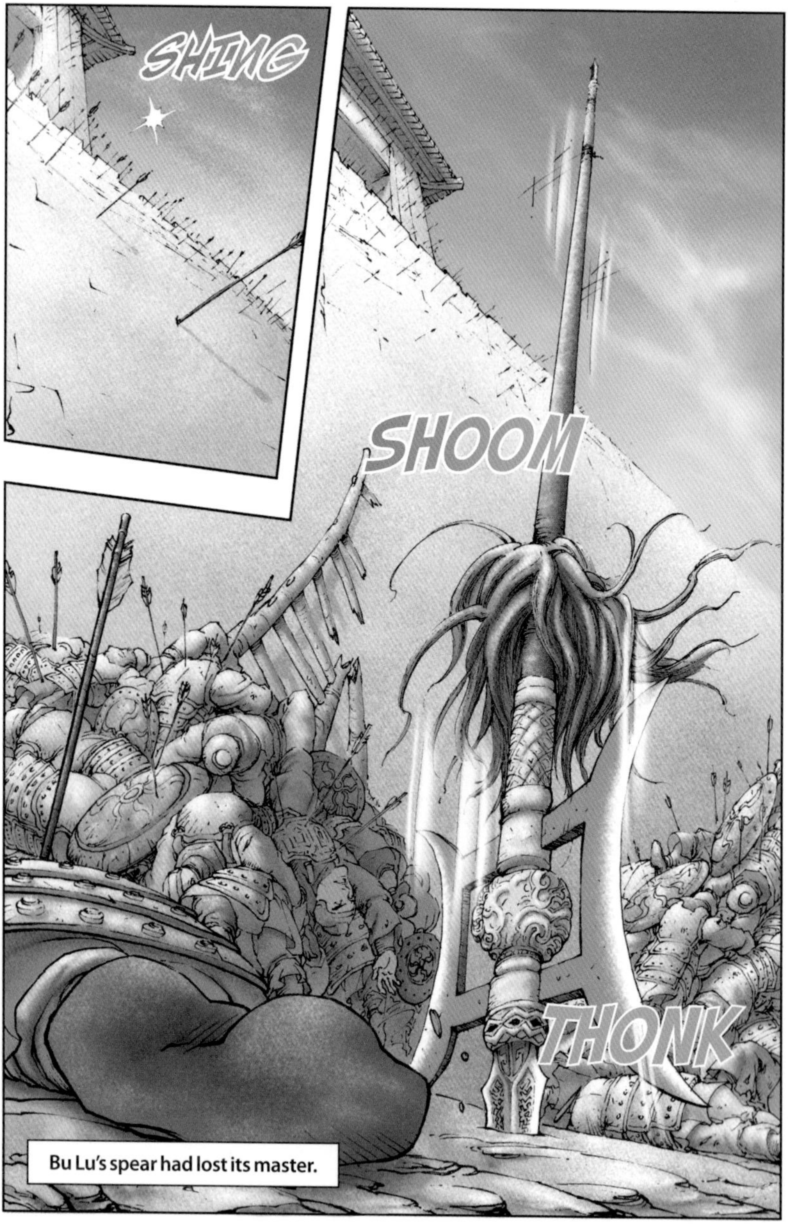
SHING
SHOOM
THONK
Bu Lu's spear had lost its master.

BU LU

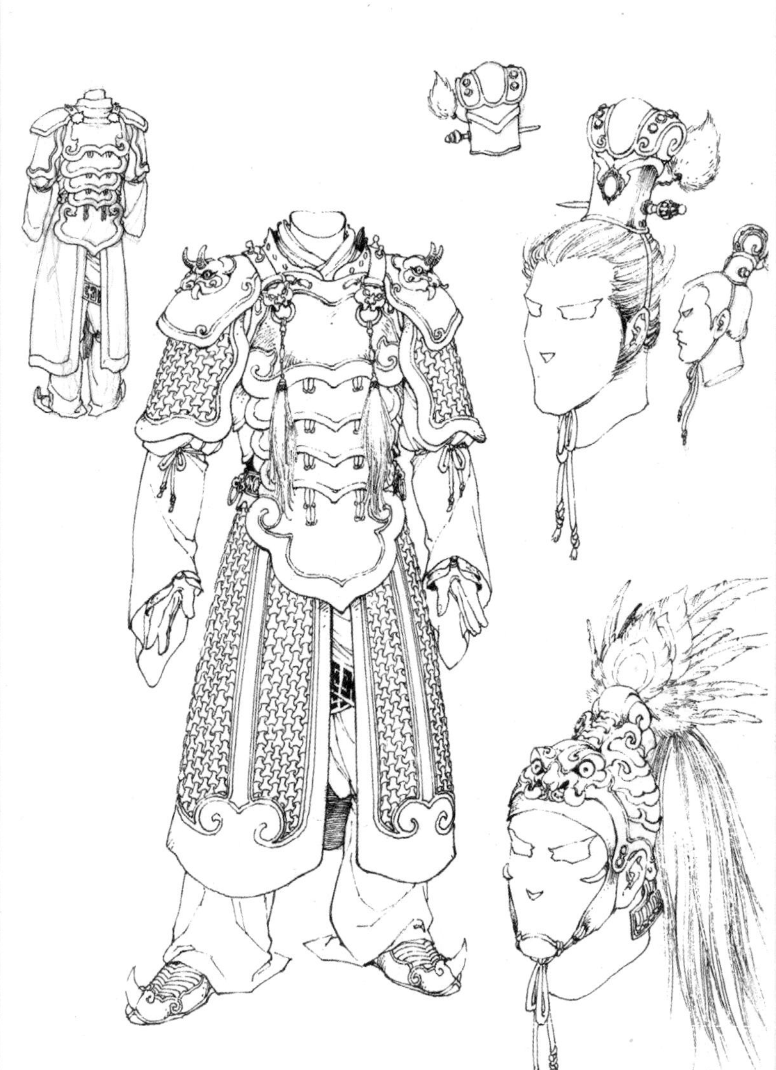

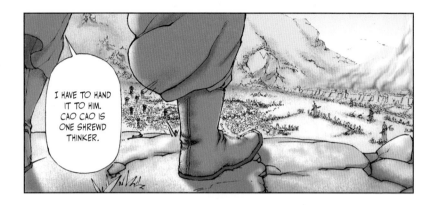

I HAVE TO HAND IT TO HIM. CAO CAO IS ONE SHREWD THINKER.

HE HAS MOVED THE PIECES AND RESET THE BOARD.

AND NOW BU LU IS CONFINED TO XIAPI.

HMPH.

TO THINK I ALMOST BROKE HIS NECK.

NOT BAD.

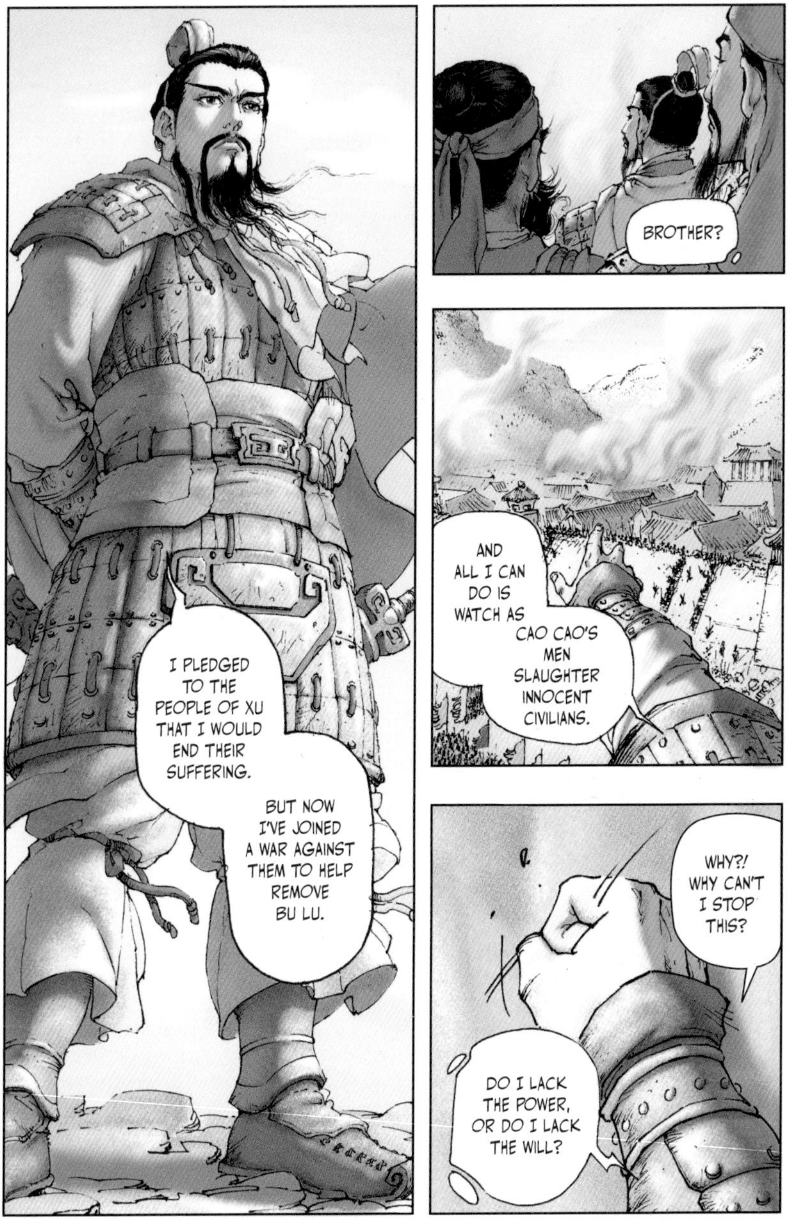
BROTHER?
I PLEDGED TO THE PEOPLE OF XU THAT I WOULD END THEIR SUFFERING.
BUT NOW I'VE JOINED A WAR AGAINST THEM TO HELP REMOVE BU LU.
AND ALL I CAN DO IS WATCH AS
CAO CAO'S MEN SLAUGHTER INNOCENT CIVILIANS.
WHY?! WHY CAN'T I STOP THIS?
DO I LACK THE POWER, OR DO I LACK THE WILL?

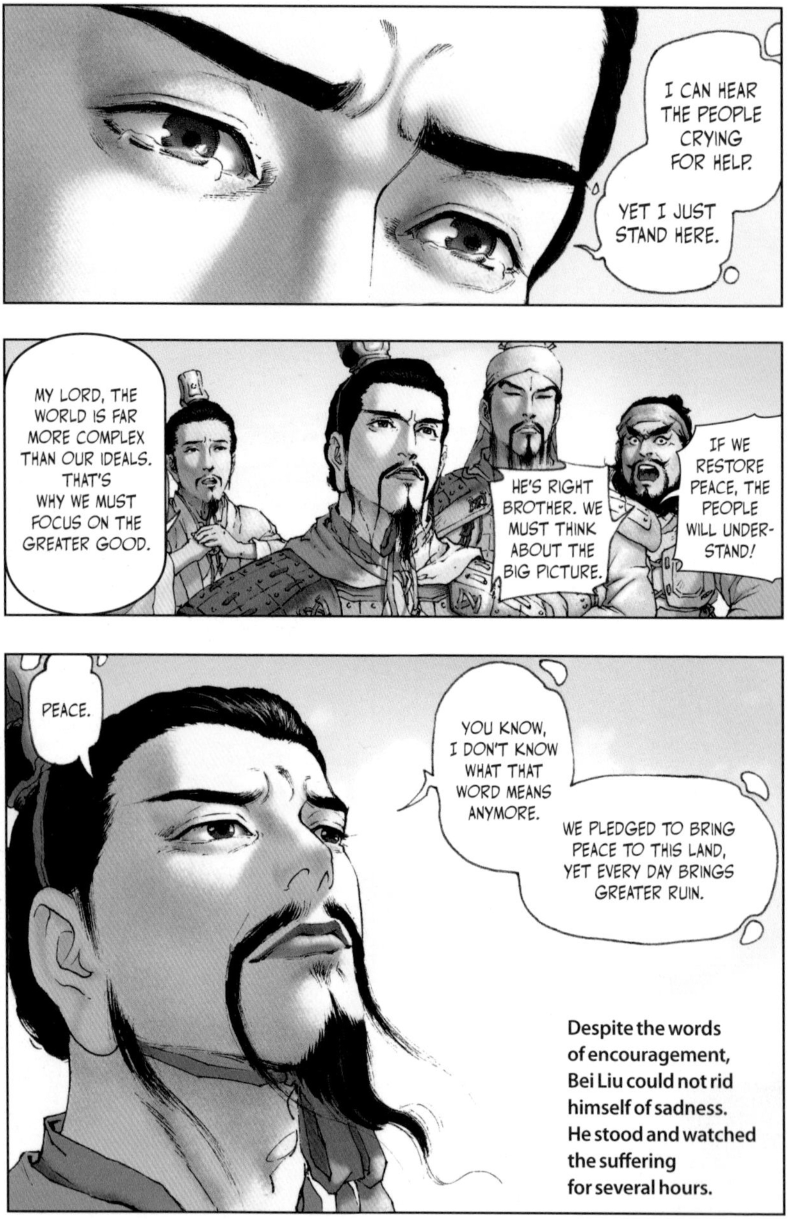
I CAN HEAR THE PEOPLE CRYING FOR HELP.
YET I JUST STAND HERE.
MY LORD, THE WORLD IS FAR MORE COMPLEX THAN OUR IDEALS. THAT'S WHY WE MUST FOCUS ON THE GREATER GOOD.
HE'S RIGHT BROTHER. WE MUST THINK ABOUT THE BIG PICTURE.
IF WE RESTORE PEACE, THE PEOPLE WILL UNDER-STAND!
PEACE.
YOU KNOW, I DON'T KNOW WHAT THAT WORD MEANS ANYMORE.
WE PLEDGED TO BRING PEACE TO THIS LAND, YET EVERY DAY BRINGS GREATER RUIN.
Despite the words of encouragement, Bei Liu could not rid himself of sadness. He stood and watched the suffering for several hours.

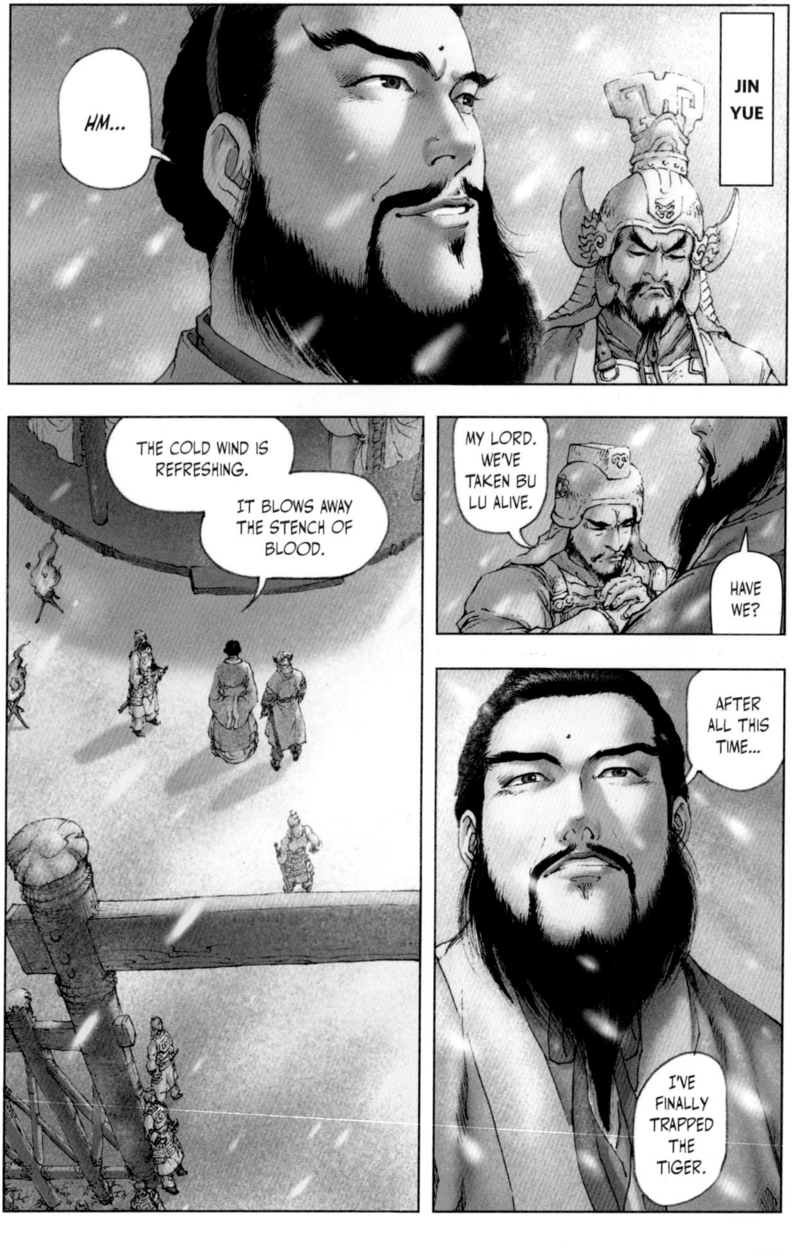
HM...
JIN YUE
THE COLD WIND IS REFRESHING.
IT BLOWS AWAY THE STENCH OF BLOOD.
MY LORD. WE'VE TAKEN BU LU ALIVE.
HAVE WE?
AFTER ALL THIS TIME...
I'VE FINALLY TRAPPED THE TIGER.

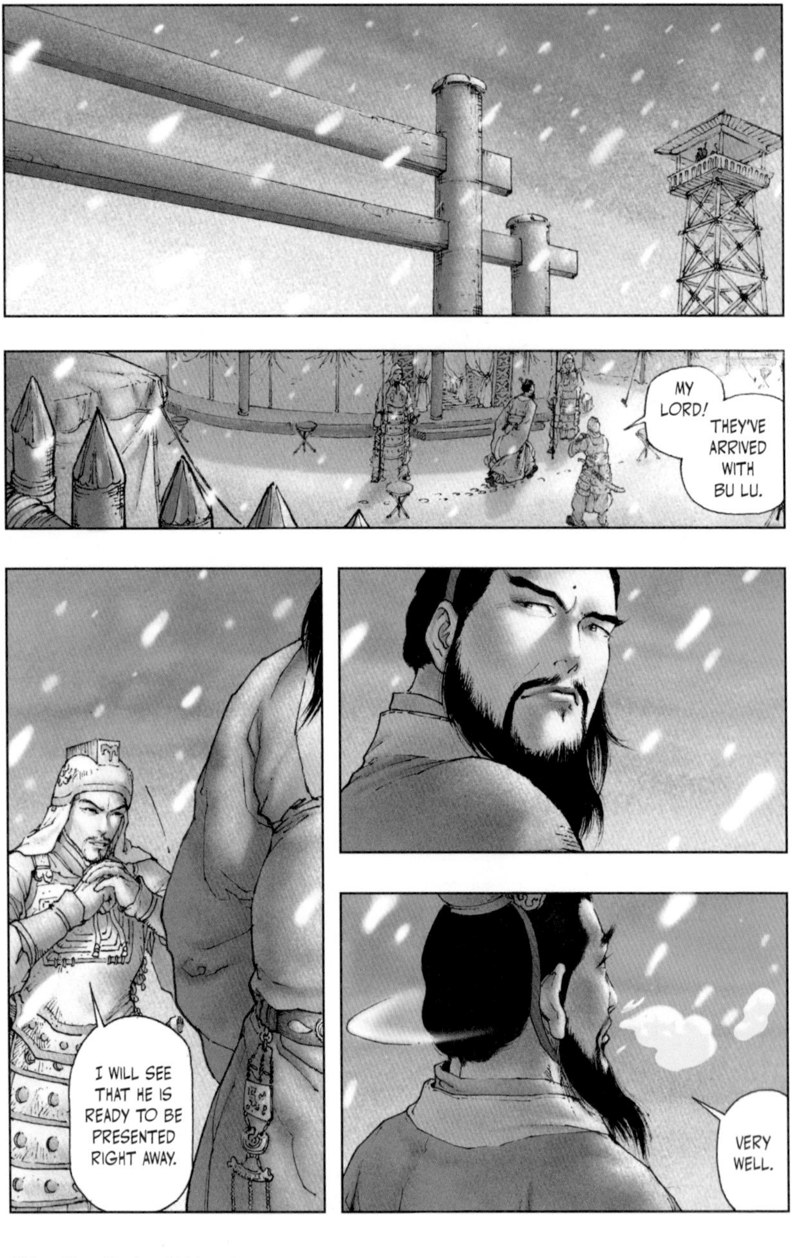
MY LORD!
THEY'VE ARRIVED WITH BU LU.
I WILL SEE THAT HE IS READY TO BE PRESENTED RIGHT AWAY.
VERY WELL.

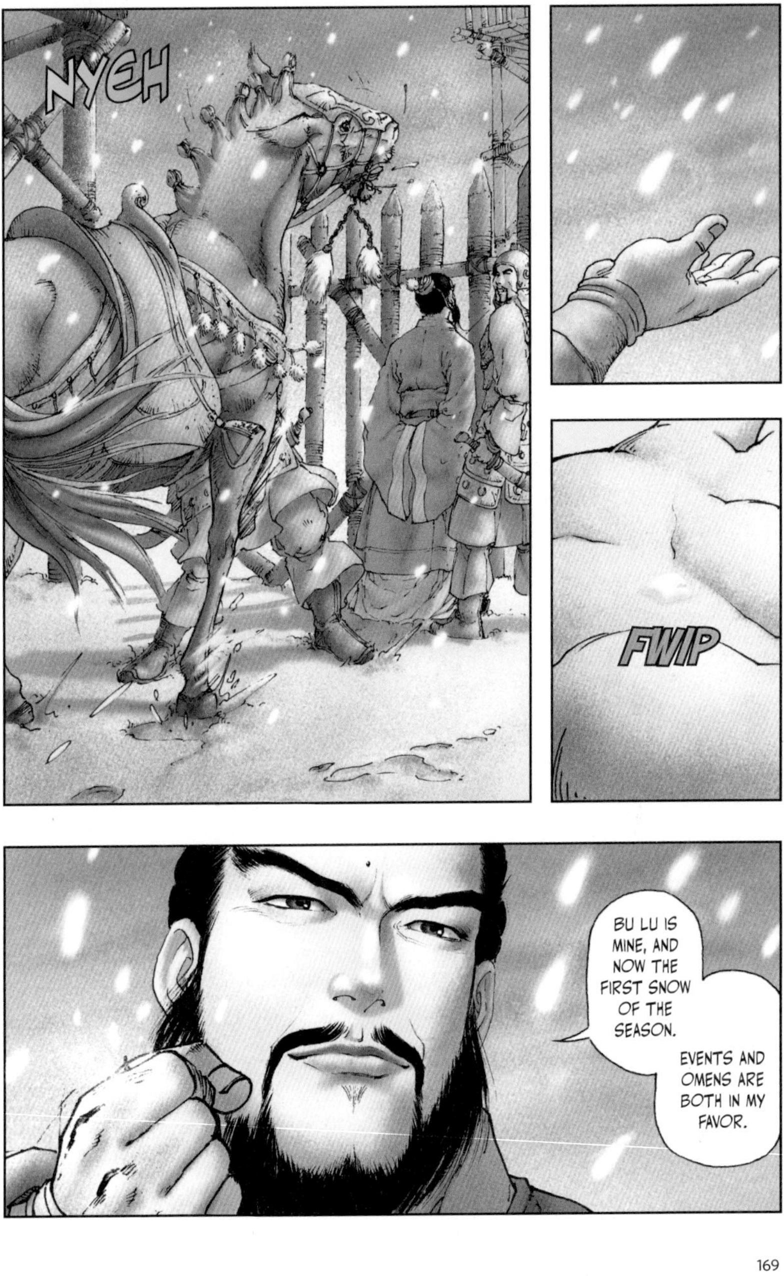
NYEH
FWIP
BU LU IS MINE, AND NOW THE FIRST SNOW OF THE SEASON.
EVENTS AND OMENS ARE BOTH IN MY FAVOR.

THE WALKING DEAD

Death is a constant presence in the story of the Age of the Three Kingdoms. From the moment the Han Dynasty begins to lose its grip on the nation, death is not merely the cost of revolution; it is also the measure of power, a tool of intimidation, and the inspiration behind numerous acts of betrayal and vengeance that wouldn't otherwise occur. The magnitude of death's influence on the struggle for power during the post-Han era cannot be understated, and it illuminates perhaps the central theme of the story: that the struggle for power does not take place only among those who are living, because each combatant carries with him the ghosts of those lost in prior struggles, and those ghosts alter the thinking and action of those who hold on to their memories.

Death is also the seed of betrayal throughout much of Three Kingdoms. Alliances fall apart with startling ease just as soon as one of the allies decides to act on behalf of a fallen friend or family member. When Ce Sun decides to emerge from Shu Yuan's shadow by reclaiming the eastern territories, he does it not only to establish himself in the eyes of other feudal lords; he does it to honor the memory of his dead father, who was a beloved and feared military commander, and a hard act to follow. But doing so sets off a chain reaction of events that result in the downfalls of both Shu Yuan and Bu Lu. Ce Sun's campaign to reclaim the eastern territories makes him a potential future threat to Shu Yuan, so the older lord seeks out an alliance with Bu Lu. When Bu Lu refuses the alliance, Shu Yuan foolishly attacks him. But Cao Cao and Bei Liu come to Bu Lu's aid, and Shu Yuan's army is almost completely wiped out. Cao Cao then attacks Bu Lu while his guard is down and takes him hostage. This is a course of events that Jian Sun would have been proud of. Indeed, it's something he probably would have tried had he still been alive. But even in death, he was the motivating factor behind what happened.

Death also weighs heavily on the mind of Bei Liu,

albeit in a more abstract way. He and his sworn brothers pledged an oath to deliver the people of China from war, famine, and cruelty, yet the actions they've taken since their oath, although necessary for their survival, have done nothing but make the situation worse. This weighs heavily on Bei Liu's conscience, which is almost paralyzed with guilt by the end of the battle against Bu Lu. Meanwhile, Cao Cao stands triumphant in the newly conquered province of Xu when the first snowfall of the season occurs. He sees this as an omen of continued good fortune, but as he is slowly enveloped in a white shroud of snow, it's worth remembering that white is the color of death and mourning. The suggestion is that death will follow Cao Cao for some time to come.

CI TAISHI

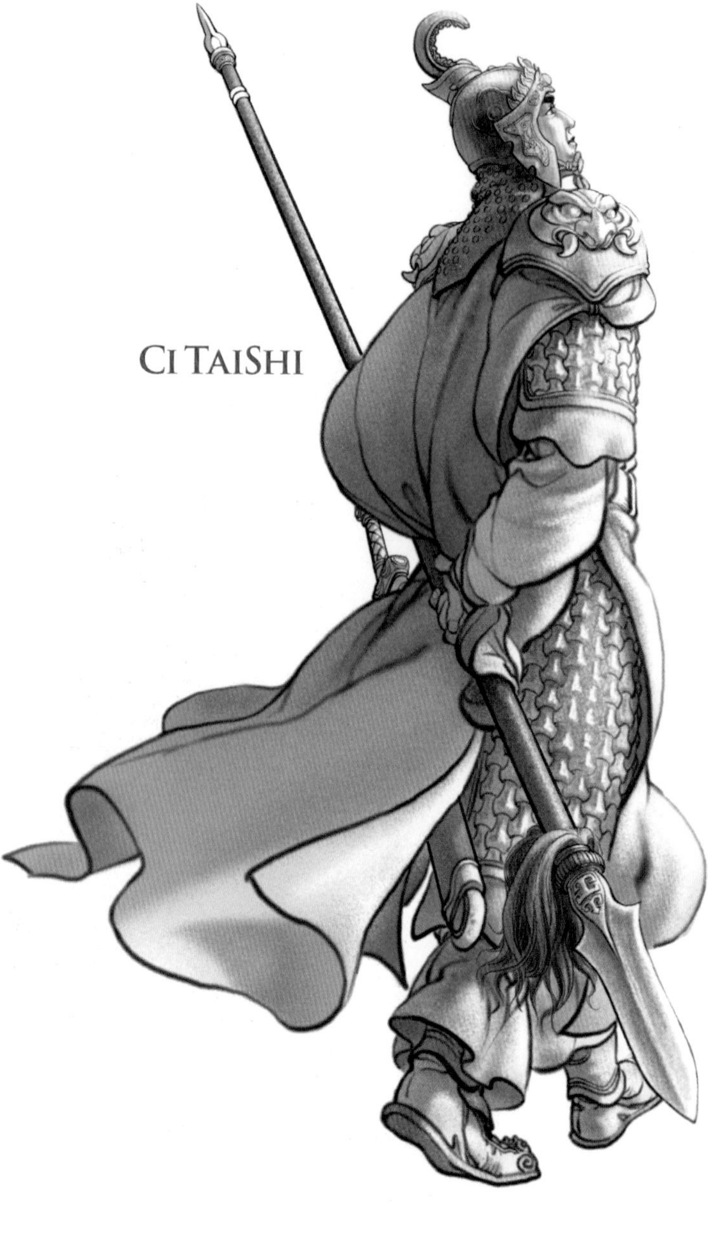

SHU YUAN

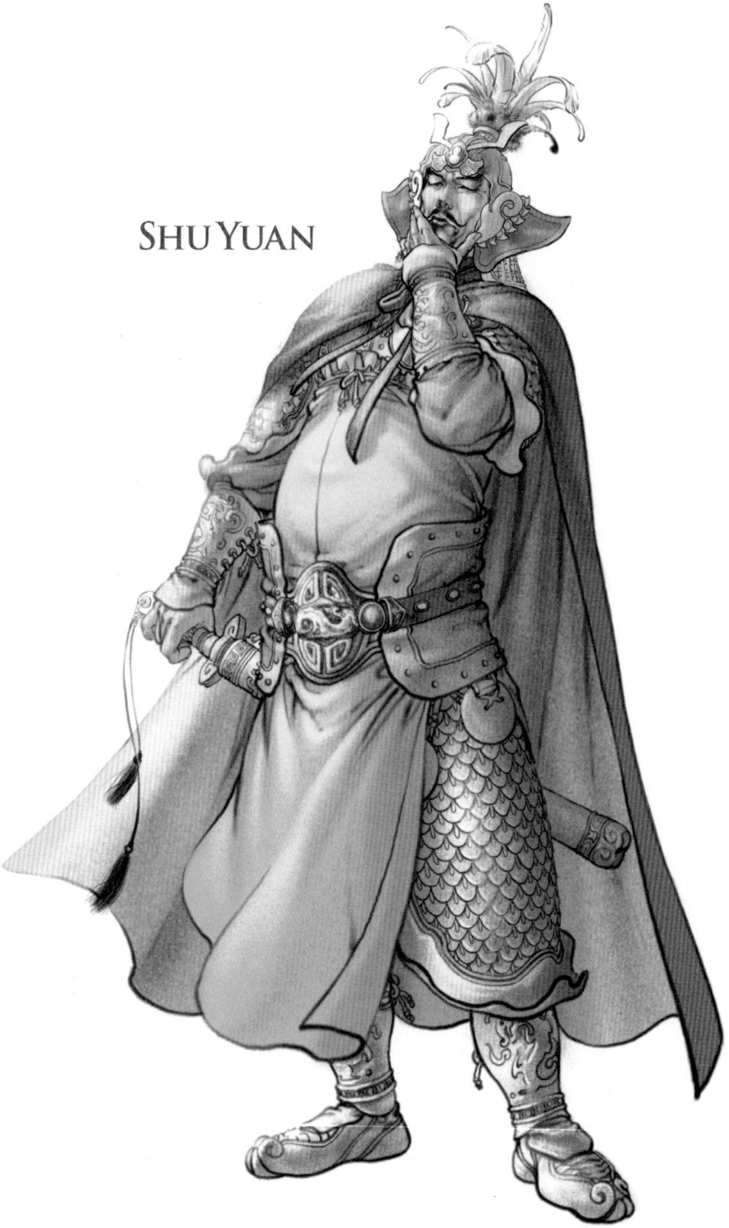

Legends from China THREE KINGDOMS

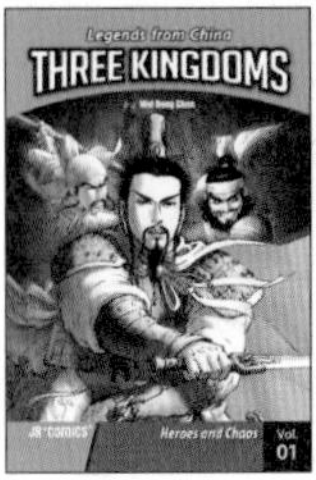
Legends from China
THREE KINGDOMS
Heroes and Chaos
Vol. 01
Vol.01

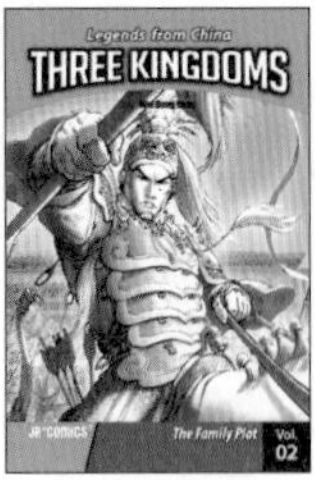
Legends from China
THREE KINGDOMS
The Family Plot
Vol. 02
Vol.02

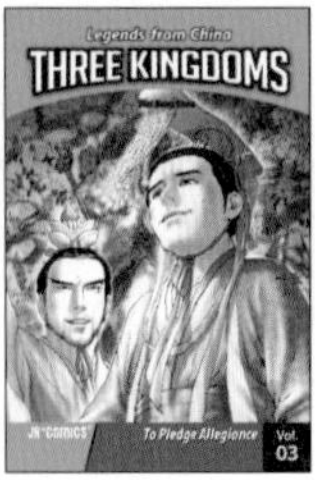
Legends from China
THREE KINGDOMS
To Pledge Allegiance
Vol. 03
Vol.03

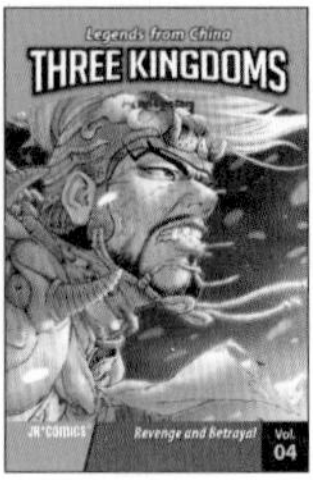
Legends from China
THREE KINGDOMS
Revenge and Betrayal
Vol. 04
Vol.04

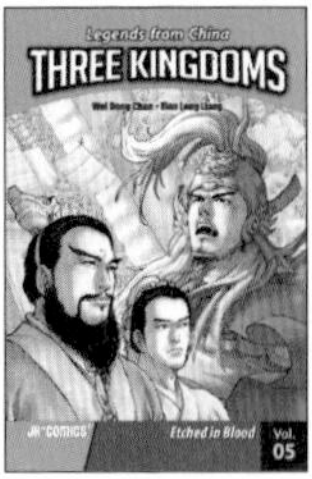
Legends from China
THREE KINGDOMS
Etched in Blood
Vol. 05
Vol.05

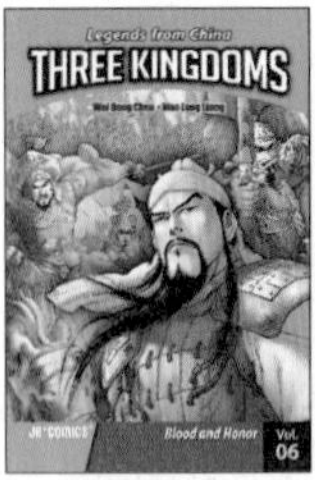
Legends from China
THREE KINGDOMS
Blood and Honor
Vol. 06
Vol.06

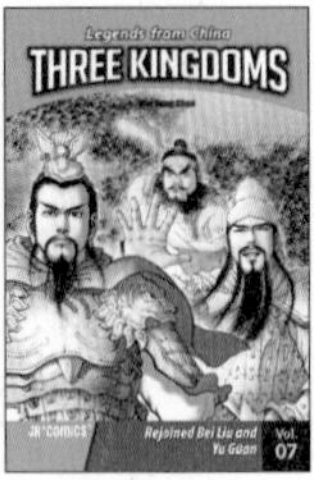
Legends from China
THREE KINGDOMS
Rejoined Bei Liu and Yu Guan
Vol. 07
Vol.07

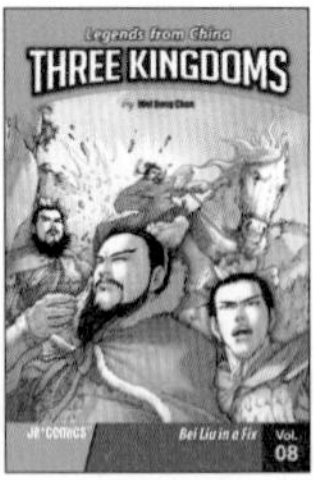
Legends from China
THREE KINGDOMS
Bei Liu in a Fix
Vol. 08
Vol.08

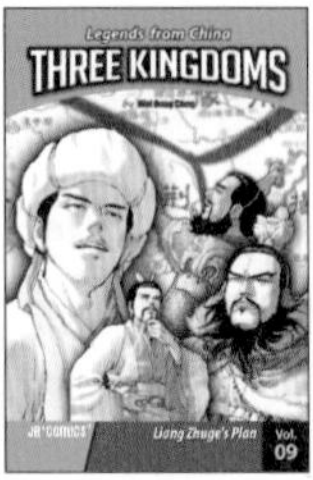
Legends from China
THREE KINGDOMS
Liang Zhuge's Plan
Vol. 09
Vol.09

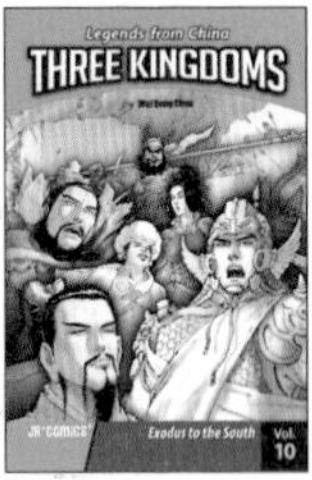
Legends from China
THREE KINGDOMS
Exodus to the South
Vol. 10
Vol.10

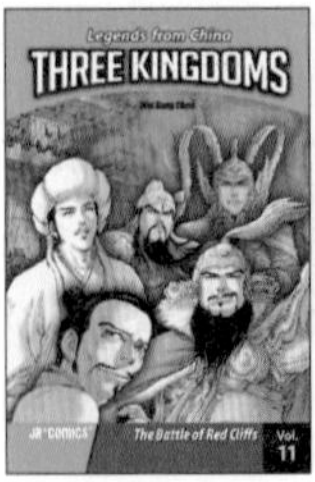
Legends from China
THREE KINGDOMS
The Battle of Red Cliffs
Vol. 11
Vol.11

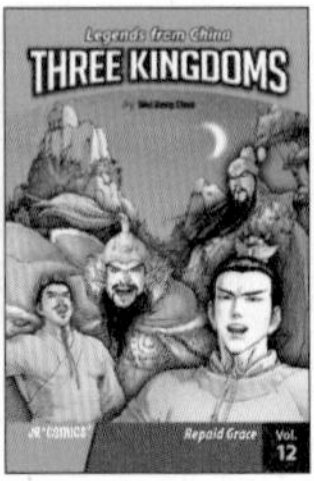
Legends from China
THREE KINGDOMS
Repaid Grace
Vol. 12
Vol.12

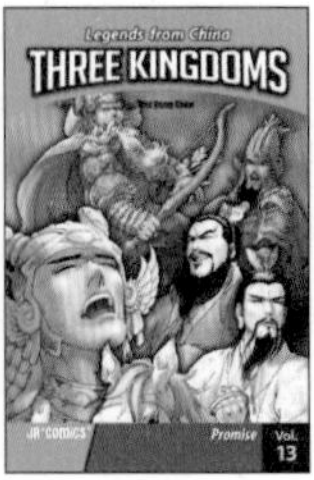
Legends from China
THREE KINGDOMS
Promise
Vol. 13
Vol.13

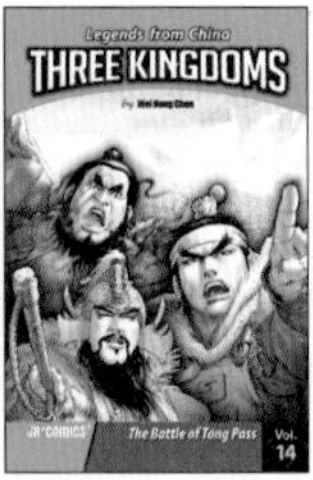
Legends from China
THREE KINGDOMS
The Battle of Tong Pass
Vol. 14
Vol.14

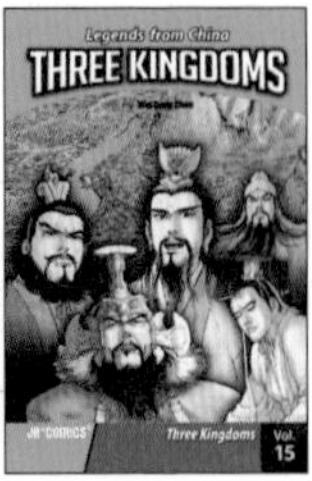
Legends from China
THREE KINGDOMS
Three Kingdoms
Vol. 15
Vol.15

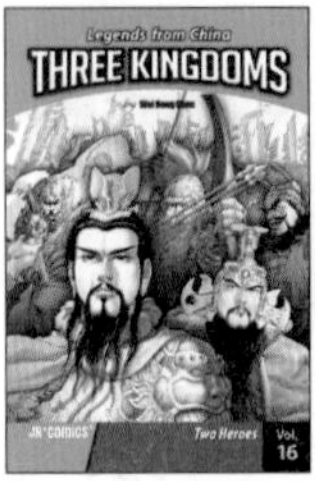
Legends from China
THREE KINGDOMS
Two Heroes
Vol. 16
Vol.16

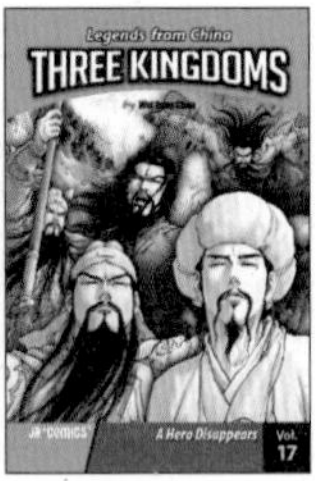
Legends from China
THREE KINGDOMS
A Hero Disappears
Vol. 17
Vol.17

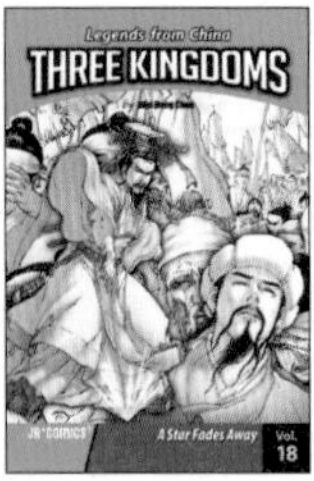
Legends from China
THREE KINGDOMS
A Star Fades Away
Vol. 18
Vol.18

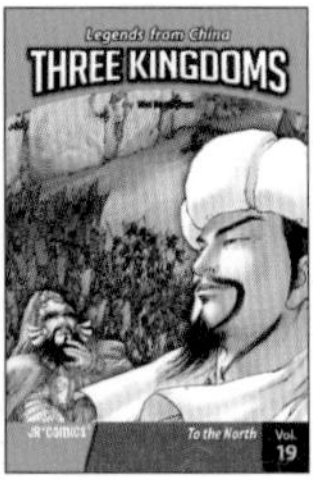
Legends from China
THREE KINGDOMS
To the North
Vol. 19
Vol.19

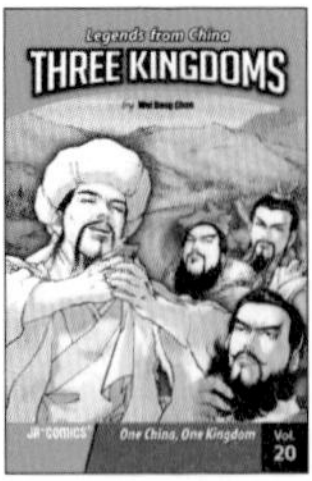
Legends from China
THREE KINGDOMS
One China, One Kingdom
Vol. 20
Vol.20